SLAVERS OF THE SAVAGE CATACOMBS

BOOK 2 OF THE SHADOW WARRIOR

BAEN BOOKS
BY JON F. MERZ

The Shadow Warrior
The Undead Hordes of Kan-Gul
Slavers of the Savage Catacombs
The Temple of Demons (forthcoming)

SLAVERS OF THE SAVAGE CATACOMBS

BOOK 2 OF
THE SHADOW WARRIOR

JON F. MERZ

SLAVERS OF THE SAVAGE CATACOMBS

A Baen Books Original

Baen Publishing Enterprises
P.O. Box 1403
Riverdale, NY 10471

www.baen.com

ISBN 13: 978-1-4767-3697-6

Cover art by Sam Kennedy

First printing, January 2015

Distributed by Simon & Schuster
1230 Avenue of the Americas
New York, NY 10020

Printed in the United States of America

10 9 8 7 6 5 4 3 2 1

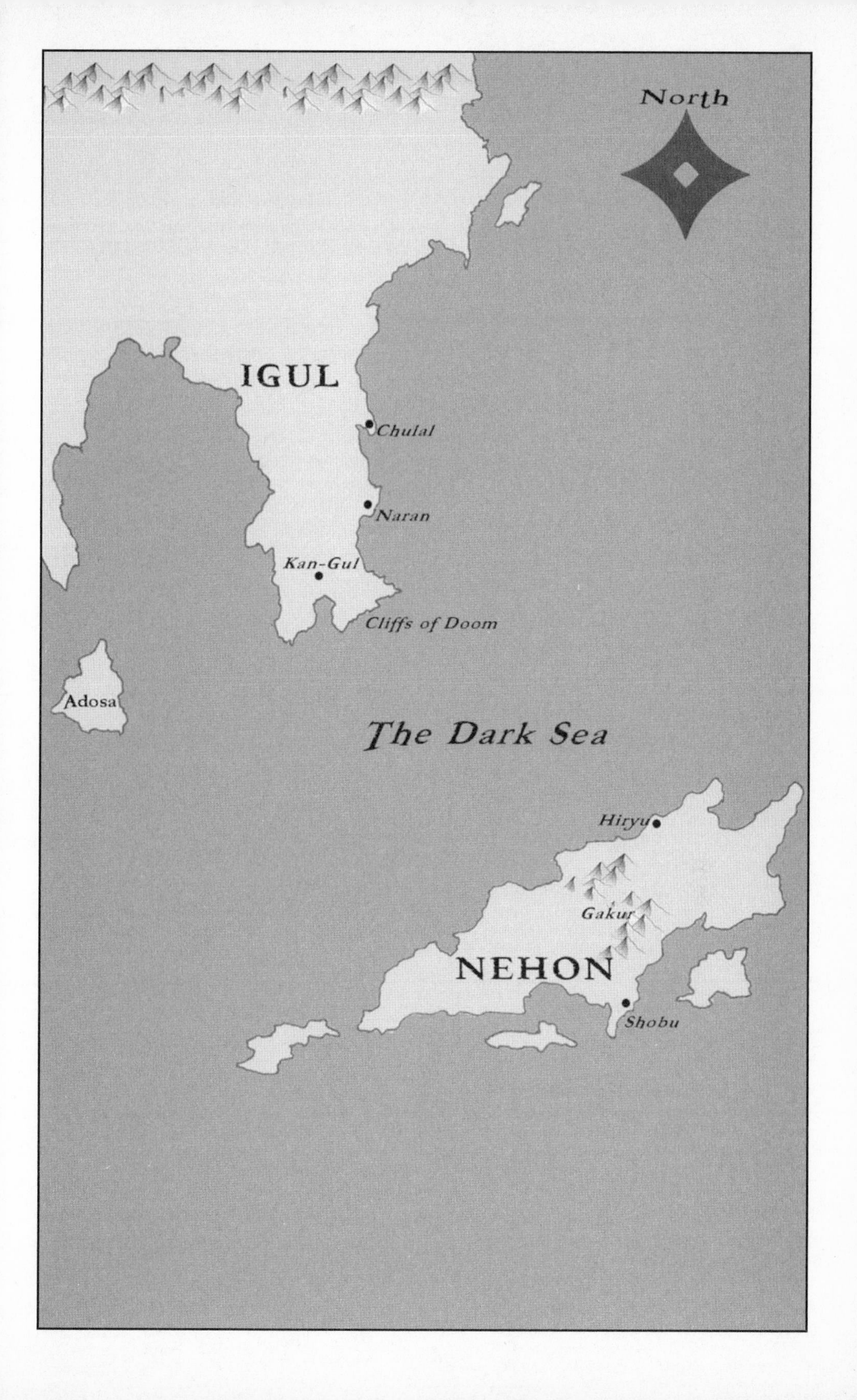

North
IGUL
Chulal
Naran
Kan-Gul
Cliffs of Doom
Adosa
The Dark Sea
Hiryu
Gakur
NEHON
Shobu

SLAVERS OF THE SAVAGE CATACOMBS

BOOK 2 OF
THE SHADOW WARRIOR

Chapter One

Ran watched the last rays of sunlight bleed over the top of the temple of Narah-Jah and said a silent farewell to Jysal, now safely ensconced behind the temple walls. The journey to bring her here had not been as easy as Ran had imagined it would be, but he'd managed. Now she was set to start her training as a sorceress; she needed much tutelage to bring her immense magical energy under control. And Ran, of the Nine Daggers shadow warrior clan, had other roads to travel.

He turned and regarded the way before him. The passage wasn't really much of a road, but more a dirt track twisting and winding through the cypress and oaks that hemmed it in on either side. The dense canopy meant that darkness had already fallen under the trees. To most travelers, darkness meant an end to their journey until the sun once again spit its light across the sky. But to Ran, the darkness was an ally far more useful than mere daylight.

As a shadow warrior, he was expected to be able to operate in any environment. To drive that point home, his instructors back at the school on the island nation of Nehon had forced their young recruits to go out in the woods alone at night. Ran remembered the first time he'd ventured out alone, sitting with his back to the massive sequoia tree until dawn started lightening the woods around him. He'd survived the night without being taken by any monsters. And once he knew that he could see things even in the complete darkness, Ran's confidence grew until the dark was never the same again. Over the years, he'd become so comfortable at moving through the shadows and deeper black of night that he truly considered it more of a friend.

That said, he kept his left hand on the scabbard of his long sword, ready to draw it free with his right if anything should threaten. He wasn't in Nehon, after all, but in northern Igul. He was unfamiliar with the land and its denizens. Already he'd battled an evil sorcerer and his minions of undead warriors, losing several comrades in the process. Ran frowned. It wouldn't have been fair to call them friends; he'd only known them a short while.

But still, he supposed they had become something like friends.

Ran moved down the trail easily, his feet rolling over roots and branches without making any sound. The long years he'd spent perfecting the skills to move silently had paid off in his ability to not even have to think about how to walk stealthily anymore. His body knew the techniques and he did it subconsciously, adjusting as need be if the environment changed.

The trees yawned and heaved as a breeze blew through their boughs. Shadows retreated in the pre-moonrise darkness, forcing Ran to keep his eyes soft and unfocused. His peripheral vision would guide him and alert him to anything that might threaten farther down the road.

The head of the temple of Narah-Jah had warned Ran that this road had seen its fair share of brigands and murderers. She'd even insisted that Ran stay in the safety of the temple overnight, but Ran had declined, preferring to be on his way. He had a destination in mind: the city of Chulal. He knew that major trade caravans left the city frequently. He hoped to fall in with one of them heading west.

West.

Somewhere far away lay the kingdom of Valrus. That was where he would find the Princess Cassandra.

He smiled, but kept his lips closed—instinctively aware that his teeth would reflect light for hundreds of yards. The thought of finally catching up with Cassandra added fuel to his spirit. He'd spent much of the last month fighting for his life and the lives of others. A bit of relaxation and romance in the arms of a beautiful princess would no doubt help restore him. He just had to find her first.

His eyes picked out the fork in the road, and Ran hesitated only a second to confirm his heading before opting for the right fork. He knew that a few miles away lay a town that serviced the temple and farmed the surrounding lands for rice and other staples. Ran felt sure he could find an inn there that would serve him a hearty meal and give him a bed for the night. He could cover the miles easily if he did so running, but he refused to do so out of fear that he would miss any threats until it was too late. He was tired and preferred the idea of stealing around any potential opponents, rather than being forced to cut them down. He'd done enough of that lately.

His senses prickled and his eyes scanned quickly. There. About a hundred meters away, the darkness lightened like a soft glow. Ran frowned. A fire in the middle of the woods. Was it a campsite? He had no idea and slowed to a stop, then melted just off of the road behind a stand of young firs, finally opening his jaw to better allow sound to reach his ears.

Three distinct but muffled voices reached him. From the sound of it, they were deep in conversation. Ran considered his options. The fire was close to the road, so he couldn't travel farther without them seeing him. He could probably bypass them, but that would add time and distance to his travel.

The sound of metal chinking on stone caught his attention. A sword.

Ran's curiosity was piqued. He stole through the woods, lifting his feet higher to avoid deadfall and roots. Taking his time, he moved ever closer to the dancing fire. As he drew nearer, he stopped behind a thick cypress trunk and used two strips of cloth to mask his face, being careful to bring one of the strips down over his right eye. When he got close to the fire, his ability to see in the dark would be compromised. But by keeping one of his eyes closed, he could restore his night vision faster than he would be able to otherwise.

After checking to make sure his sword wasn't positioned in such a way that would create noise and give away his position, Ran moved closer to the fire. The voices of the three men were now sharp and distinct.

"It's an easy gambit. Three of us can clean them out without any problems."

"Easy? Nothing's ever easy. What if there are guards or something?"

"There won't be guards around, you oaf. It's a bunch of farmers. Any that are still awake are most likely drunk."

The voices grew quieter as Ran crept forward. He paused behind a giant rhododendron bush and peered through the branches at the firelight. The three men were of varying heights, but each held a sword. As the flames licked at the wood on the fire, the crackle of excitement hung in the air. Ran wondered why they'd stopped at all instead of just progressing to the town. But then he caught a whiff of something cooking and looked closer. A decent sized hare sizzled over part of the fire, its juices running into the flames and sizzling on the rocks nearby. Ran felt his mouth go awash in saliva at the thought of eating the juicy flesh.

On cue, the heaviest man took the spit from the fire and broke off portions for each of them. He took the biggest share and then handed a smaller bit to the second man. The thinnest man got the least bit of hare.

"Don't complain, Magya. It's lucky you get any at all what with your bitching about the chance of guards."

The second man chuckled at this, but each soon set to the task at hand, sucking at the bits of meat and lapping up any juice they could gather from the bones.

Ran watched them in silence and wondered if he ought to head to the town ahead of the robbers and warn it. But by doing so, he'd be opening himself up to suspicion. How had he learned of their plan? Ran's foremost task was to maintain his anonymity for as long as possible. Under no circumstances were people to know that he was a shadow warrior. The legend of his kind was known far and wide, even in the most unlikely places. There would be no shortage of people all too eager to kill him and collect the bounty many warlords had placed on the heads of members of his clan.

No, better to wait and then follow the men into the town. That way, Ran could keep the element of surprise in his favor. By coming up behind them, he could cut them down all the faster. Hopefully no one would even notice.

His ears caught a new sound, though, and one that he hadn't heard in some time. The soft whinny of a horse. Then he heard two more. Each distinct as the men who would soon ride them into town. And that meant that Ran would have trouble keeping up with them if they left the campsite.

Just as he was about to form a plan for attacking them now, the heavyset man threw the bones of his meal into the fire. "Enough of this rest. The horses should be refreshed, and I grow tired of sitting around. It's time we were off. Ejul, make sure you ride close behind me."

He strode out of the firelight, and Ran heard him swing up into his saddle. The other two followed quickly, although Magya at least stomped on the fire to try to put it out. The attempt was in vain, though, and the flames came back quickly.

They vanished down the road.

Behind them, Ran could only approach the fire and kick dirt over it, before he too continued down the road. There was little chance he could catch up with them. Even if he ran, he was only going to tire himself out before having to fight. Ran preferred fighting with as much energy as he could have. Despite his desire to reach the village in time to stop the attack, he had to remain calm and force himself to a light jog.

He set a pace and stuck to it, reasoning that if he covered the distance well, he should reach the village within an hour. Shortly before the hour passed, he saw light through the trees and knew he was close.

Even at this distance, he could hear screaming. He smelled smoke. But he heard no metal-on-metal clangs that told him any of the villagers were fighting off the intruders. Most likely all the able-bodied men and boys had already been killed.

Ran felt his face grow hot. By his nature, he disliked anyone who chose to attack hardworking farmers. They weren't warriors; they had little means to defend themselves. And yet, brigands and scum like them picked weaker targets all the time.

Ran loosened the sword at his hip. It was time for them to meet another warrior.

He threaded his way through the trees that hemmed the path, and then the land before him opened up to reveal a tiny hamlet of perhaps a dozen houses all set close together. One of them at the far end of the land was already on fire; flames shot through the thatch roof. Ran knew unless the villagers managed to get it under control, the fire would consume the entire town.

Laughter greeted his ears, and he recognized the voice of the heavyset man some distance away. As he walked, Ran counted the slain bodies of six men and two boys. Their throats had been cut, their guts splayed open, staining the ground with grizzled entrails. Ran set his jaw firm and battled the taint of death in his nostrils. As many times as he'd had chance to smell it, he never got used to the stench.

"Come here, my pretty. . . . don't fight. . . ."

Ran pushed through a few weeping old women and toward the center of the village. At last, he broke into the town square.

There.

The heavyset brigand was holding court near the well in the center of town. In his arms, a young farm girl wrestled to free herself. His arms were too massive for her to break free.

Ran's left thumb eased his long sword an inch out of its scabbard, breaking the seal and making it easier for him to draw it when the time came to cut down these fools.

"Let her go."

The heavyset man stopped and eyed Ran. Ran had removed the mask that had covered his face earlier and stood with his long hair flowing over his face. He'd carefully cultivated the appearance of a wandering warrior-for-hire over the last month or so. No doubt the heavyset man would think him no threat.

The girl continued to fight, and the heavyset man backhanded her across the face. The girl went sprawling into the dirt and lay still.

Ran shook his head. "You shouldn't have come here tonight."

"I go where I please," said the man. "I am Kayo. Whoever opposes me dies."

Ran nodded. "No doubt because you pick your opponents from the weak. I have known others like you—too afraid to battle a real warrior. You have no honor."

Kayo shrugged. "I do have no honor. But neither do I care for it." He sighed. "Magya, kill this fool."

Ran sensed Magya's presence an instant before his sword came slashing in from the side. The smaller man had been hiding in the shadows. His attack cut through the air where Ran had been standing a moment earlier. But the shadow warrior dropped to the ground, rolled once, and came up on his feet, drawing his sword free and cutting down through Magya's head. Ran wrenched the blade free as the second brigand, Ejul, came stabbing straight in at his heart.

Ran pivoted and brought his blade down on the man's outstretched hands, cleaving them off at the wrist. Blood sprayed the air and Ejul went screaming down to the ground.

Kayo watched this with growing alarm. He came down off of the well and drew his own two-handed sword. Ran had seen similar swords before and knew they required a lot of brute strength just to wield properly. Kayo was definitely strong, but his mind was weak.

When he attacked, the blade screamed down at Ran's head. Kayo meant to cleave him in two.

Instead, though, Ran stepped under the arc of the cut and stabbed Kayo through the base of his throat, shoving the blade until it erupted out of the back of his neck, severing Kayo's spinal cord. Ran turned the blade and then cut to the left and right, cutting Kayo's head off.

The sudden spurt of violence ended as Ran flipped his blade over and struck the back of the blade with the heel of his left palm, flicking the majority of blood free. Ran slid his blade back into his scabbard and then stood there, aware of how fast his heart beat in his chest. He willed it to slow down and surveyed the scene.

The fire was spreading from the first home, but the remaining villagers were now dousing it with water. Their men were dead. And there was little else Ran could do here.

He sighed, spotted Kayo's horse drinking from the well and grabbed the reins. Swinging up into the saddle, Ran looked around. There was no one here who would remember him. As he rode off into the night, the only memory of the shadow warrior's presence were the three dead brigands and the sound of a horse at gallop.

CHAPTER TWO

Two days of hard riding on Kayo's horse brought Ran to the outskirts of Chulal. While the horse drank its fill from a bubbling brook scoring a meadow of clover, Ran eyed the scene before him. Farms dominated the outlying areas, and he could see pack mules and horses working the fields as the sun rose higher in the sky. The fields were filled with tall stalks of grain while other farms had stepped irrigation plateaus filled with rice paddies. A well-maintained road cut a swath through the farming domain and led farther on to larger buildings. Beyond them rose tall spires of the city itself. Traffic along the road had also increased, although few people paid any attention to Ran. A man wearing a sword was nothing unique, even if Ran's twin blades marked him as an outsider.

Once the horse had drunk its fill, Ran remounted it and swung toward the city, allowing the horse to relax its gait to a mere walk. As he passed farms, Ran noted the higher cheekbones of the people who inhabited northern Chugal. He smirked as he remembered one of his elders in the Nine Daggers clan. Old Bunzo, who had always had a reputation as a ladies' man, had remarked once about the women of northern Chugal, "They're either extraordinarily beautiful or extraordinarily ugly. There is no in-between. So take care that you don't make a decision after drinking your noggin silly." He had winked. "Trust me on this one. You do not want to make the same mistake I did."

Ran had seen no women as he walked the horse down the road. But soon enough, the farms disappeared and Ran saw more built-up areas ahead of him. Stately homes with high walls, like they were their own fortress. He frowned. It was unusual to see wealth like this situated outside the high walls of a city. Either the owners were wealthy enough to afford their own private armies or else not very much danger ever came to the city of Chulal.

Ran drew a hand across his brow to wipe the sweat away. The sun beating down on him from overhead was hot, and he felt a thirst come over him. Without thinking, he dropped one hand to the small water skin on his belt and took several slugs before replacing it. As he rounded a corner, a large stone wall came into view and several guards manning a gate immediately hailed him.

"Visitor to Chulal, stop!"

Ran leaned back on the reins, and the horse drew to a halt. Ran stayed where he sat as one of the guards came over, his eyes already fixated on the two swords Ran wore at his side.

"What is your name?"

"I am Ran. From the island nation of Nehon."

The guard's eyes opened a bit more. "You're a long way from home."

"It depends on what you call home, I suppose," said Ran. "I grew tired of my small country and have come here to search for work."

"What type of work?"

Ran smiled and nodded at his swords. "These aren't used for making wine."

"Indeed." The guard frowned. "If what you say is true and your intention is sincere, then we will have no quarrel with you. I would caution you, however, that Chulal is a peaceful city. We do not tolerate any sort of mischief here. Any transgressions are dealt with severely." He pointed to Ran's right. "As you can see . . ."

Ran followed the man's finger and saw several large Xs hammered into the ground roughly two hundred yards away. Upon one of them, a man hung with his arms and legs outstretched. He didn't move. But there was motion around him anyway, and Ran saw several large birds of prey busily feasting on the man's entrails.

Ran swung his gaze back to the guard. "I have no desire to end up like that."

The guard grunted. "Entry fee to the city is twenty goran. I trust you can pay that?"

Ran shook his head. "I don't have any goran on me."

"Then entry is denied—"

Ran held up his hand. "I do have these, however." He withdrew a small sack from inside his tunic and slid two large pieces of gold into his hands. "They're Nehonian agara, but I think they should suffice."

"They will indeed," said the guard.

Ran handed them over, and the guard took them. "Stay here while I prepare your entry papers." He walked back to the gate and to a small house that stood nearby. Ran sat in the sun waiting. After several minutes, the guard returned and handed Ran a single piece of paper.

"Keep that with you at all times. If you are stopped for any reason, this will serve as your permission to be in the city."

"Should I worry about being stopped?"

The guard shrugged. "Only if you aren't what you say you are." He waved Ran ahead through the gate. "Best of luck finding employment here."

Ran smiled. "I make my own luck. But thank you." He ducked his head under the portcullis and rode through the portal.

Once through the gate, Ran saw the main city directly ahead of him. Another, higher wall stood before him, but the guards manning it only took a cursory glance at his papers before waving him through. As Ran came through this checkpoint, the spires in front of him loomed even larger. They stood on par with the mountaintop fortress of the Nine Daggers shadow warrior clan back in Gakur, and Ran felt a twinge of homesickness as he looked at them. He quashed the sentiment down deep inside him and reminded himself that he was there with a purpose: find a trading caravan and get himself hired on as security. If he could make his way to the west, he would be that much closer to reuniting with Princess Cassandra.

The main city street led him directly to the sprawling marketplace. No doubt the leaders of the city had purposely routed travelers through this section as a way to boost the local economy and make the city attractive to merchants. Ran nudged the horse down a side street and found lodging for the steed before walking back up to the market on foot.

The sights and sounds that assailed his senses were too numerous for him to catalog. He caught a smattering of at least six languages; the merchants and patrons were an equally diverse mixture of races and species. As he walked through the labyrinth of stalls, Ran was hailed by traders in Nehonga, the language of his native land. The two swords he wore marked his nationality. But he passed them all by, his eyes still marveling at the dizzying array of silks and spices and goods from lands he had only heard and read about.

His heart beat faster. This was what he had hoped his wandering quest would expose him to: the vastness of the world stretched before him with nothing but the promise of adventure and excitement.

He passed a large tent, and the man standing before the curtained opening hailed him. "You, sir, are you interested in seeing the most exotic women ever to walk these lands?"

Ran smiled. "Thank you, no."

"I have women here with breasts the size of giant melons. They know how to treat a fine man such as yourself. Only ten goran for a night's entertainment the likes of which you won't find anywhere else in the city."

Along with some strange and exotic sickness, no doubt, thought Ran. He moved on, and soon he smelled the scents of a hundred different cuisines. His mouth watered as he realized he hadn't eaten in some time. He passed row after row of bubbling cauldrons, blazing hearths, and sizzling grills. Slabs of meat hung on hooks while being basted with huge mops. Portable ovens served up steaming hot loaves of bread.

And there, in the midst of it all, stood a noodle stand selling the thick buckwheat zabo noodles of Nehon in a swirling steaming broth of chicken and vegetables. Ran grinned and headed for the stall.

The chef stood stirring the broth and smiled as Ran approached. "It's not every day I see one of my countrymen here."

Ran settled himself on a chair in front of the stand and waited for the chef to place a cup of tea in front of him before sipping the green mixture. "Tastes just like home."

"It should," said the chef. "I have it imported." He gestured to the noodles. "What would you like with your zabo?"

"Chicken, scallions, seaweed, chilies," said Ran, glancing around the food stalls. "I'm surprised you're not busier."

The chef shrugged as he set to preparing Ran's dish. "Some days are like this. Others I'm far busier. I do quite well here, although most of the city dwellers like more cabbage in their soup than I can stomach."

"Glad to know there's someplace I can come for more home cooking."

The chef set the bowl of steaming soup before Ran. "What brings you to Chulal?"

Ran touched his swords briefly. "Looking for work."

The chef frowned. "Not enough killing in Nehon for your liking?"

Ran slurped some of the noodles into his mouth and sighed. It was like he'd just been transported back to Nehon. "I'm restless by nature. Nehon was beginning to feel a little restrictive, so I thought I'd come across the Dark Sea and see where my fortunes lay. I'm hoping to improve them considerably, possibly looking to get hired on as a guard for a trade caravan leaving the city and bound for the west."

"Plenty of those leaving every day," said the chef. "Dangerous work."

Ran swallowed another mouthful of the noodles and smiled. "I don't mind the danger."

"No disrespect, but you seem a little young. Are you certain you can handle those swords?"

Ran smiled. "I'm absolutely certain."

"Fair enough," said the chef. "The best place to fall in with the caravans is over near the harbor. When the ships come in bearing goods, the caravan managers are usually there planning their trips. Any of them that are looking for more security are likely to be there as well."

"I'll be sure to look into that," said Ran. "Thank you."

The chef nodded at the bowl of soup. "Three goran."

Ran fished a single gold agara from his tunic and slid it across the counter. "Will this do?"

The chef snatched the gold coin and then placed a handful of the Chulal currency on the table as change. Ran slid some back across and nodded at the chef. "My thanks for the fine meal."

"Harbor lies to the east. That way," said the chef. "But I wouldn't want to get caught down near the docks after dark. The place is as dangerous as the docks in any seaside city. Probably even more."

"I was under the impression that crime wasn't tolerated here in the city," said Ran.

The chef sniffed. "They tell that to everyone who comes here. But don't go around thinking this city is safe. It's not. You mind yourself out there, friend. I'm sure you've already attracted attention from the likes of people you'd rather not."

Ran let his gaze soften and his eyes wander, but he could detect no real interest from anyone else around him. If it was a general warning, then that was just one Nehonian looking out for another. But if there was something more to it, Ran would have to watch where he walked around here. The last thing he needed was trouble.

He left the noodle stall and wandered through the rest of the food stalls, but his hunger was sated for the time being. As he walked, he doubled back several times on his route, checking to see if anyone seemed to be following him. But the only person he saw more than once was a beggar dressed in rags holding a small tin bowl. Ran walked past him and heard the old man's plaintive wails for food and drink. Ran was tempted to throw a few of the goran he'd gotten from the noodle stall into the bowl, but thought better of it. If anyone else saw him throwing his money around, word would spread fast that he might be wealthy. Regardless of the two swords he wore at his side, greed could drive people to attack him for his money.

He turned down a side street lined with weapons shops. He heard the clang-clang of the blacksmiths working in their forges. Ran smiled at the thought of what they might turn out. He hadn't heard many good things about Chugal blades, believing that the blades that were produced in Nehon were the finest in the world.

At the end of the street, he saw another beggar huddled in the alcove of a small temple devoted to one of the Chugal gods. Ran stopped and pretended to be looking at the signs on the wall. He could smell the increased salt in the air and knew that the harbor was close.

But the harbor wasn't what concerned him. It was the presence of the beggar at the end of the street. Ran was certain it was the same beggar he'd passed back during his trip through the food stalls. How had he managed to get ahead of Ran so fast? To do so, he would have had to run the entire way. Yet the beggar looked as though he had been sitting there the entire day.

Ran couldn't turn around without tipping his hand, so he resumed walking down the street, letting his left hand fall to his scabbard ever so slightly. As he drew closer, the beggar started up his plaintive wails.

"Please, good sir, a moment of your time for a wretched soul. I beg of you for a small coin with which to eat and drink my fill."

Ran frowned. "I've nothing for you, old man. Leave me be."

In the blink of an eye, the old man's hand darted out and grabbed Ran's wrist. The action was so smooth and quick, Ran didn't even have time to react before he felt the crushing grip as the old man smiled at him with a toothless cackle. "Now, now, my friend, surely you can spare me some help? I only ask in the name of all the hidden gods."

The words hit him like a punch between his eyes. Ran nearly stumbled back in disbelief, but managed to keep his composure as the old man removed his hand and let it fall back into his lap.

The words the beggar had used marked him as a fellow shadow warrior.

Chapter Three

Before Ran could recover himself, the old man spoke quietly. "At the end of this street, you'll find an alley running west. Take it to the end and you'll see an alcove. Above the alcove is a chalk mark. Wait for me there." Then resuming the stature of a beggar, the old man hobbled away singing to himself and rattling some coins in his bowl.

Ran watched him go for a second and then resumed his travel down the street. At the end, he saw the alley and veered into it. The buildings on either side closed in and gave the alley a very tight feeling. It would be difficult to fight anyone in the tight confines of the alley, which made Ran more than a little apprehensive. While the old man had said the right words, could he truly be trusted? Ran had never run into anyone from his clan in the outside world. The novelty of the experience made him feel like an acolyte all over again.

He saw the alcove and the chalk mark above it. The interior of the alcove smelled like festering urine and excrement, and as the horrible stench assailed his nostrils, Ran wondered how long he would have to wait for the old man to arrive. He certainly didn't seem to be in very good physical condition.

Ran sighed and counted away the minutes. After a half an hour, Ran was almost ready to leave. Then he felt a tap behind him and nearly shouted in surprise.

In the dim light of the alcove, a toothless grin greeted him. "Sorry I'm late. Had to make sure we hadn't attracted any followers." He held up a finger. "Follow me and stay low and quiet as we go, all right?"

Ran nodded, still marveling that the wall at the back of the alcove wasn't a wall at all, but a hidden door. The old man waited until he had passed through it into the tunnel beyond before once again closing and locking it. He smiled in the darkness. "The smell usually keep most people away. But the lock ensures they don't discover my tunnel."

"Where are we going?"

"Someplace where we can talk without being overheard," said the old man. "Now, low and quiet, like I said."

With that, he took off down the tunnel. He didn't use a light, and Ran had no need of it anyway. During the training, all shadow warriors learned how to best see in the darkness. It was practiced so often, it became a natural instinct anytime lighting conditions were less than ideal. Since they operated frequently at night, the skill was essential.

The old man took a turn, and Ran could hear voices all around them. But they kept walking, careful of their footing. At times, the tunnel led up and then down again. It bent, twisted, and turned. Ran spotted several options going left and right as they went, but the old man kept them in the main tunnel the entire time. If he'd been down here by himself, Ran surely would have gotten lost in the maze of tunnels. He supposed that was the point. If anyone discovered the old man's secret, they'd have a hard time locating him in here.

Finally, after twenty minutes of travel, they drew up to a wall, and the old man pressed a brick near the top of it. Instantly, the wall slid back to reveal a modest apartment appointed with a bed, kitchen, and dining area. Bookshelves lined the wall, including the one they now stepped out of. The old man waited until Ran had cleared the entry and then pushed a brazier. The entry disappeared behind another bookcase. Looking at the wall he'd just come through, Ran wasn't even sure he could pick out the outline of the secret door.

"Impressive."

The old man shrugged. "We can talk here. No one lives around me. I've taken steps to make sure I don't have any pesky neighbors." He headed toward a basin of water and pulled off the nasty hair as he did so. As he bent over the bowl, Ran watched him splash his face repeatedly until all the grime disappeared. Wrinkles vanished as well. When he stood upright again, the face belonged to a much younger man than the beggar who had greeted Ran earlier.

"It's always so nice to get out of the disguise."

Ran pointed. "Your teeth."

"Ah, always forget them." He coughed and spat a set of fake teeth from his mouth and set them down on the table. "Nasty buggers, those." He smiled again at Ran. "I'm Tanka."

"Ran."

Tanka nodded. "Been expecting you."

Ran eyed him. "You have? No one at the clan knew where I was heading."

"Tozawa knew you were going west. There are only so many routes you could take. I was told to be on the lookout for you. Glad to see you've made it here safe and sound. That's always a promising start for newly minted Shinobujin."

Ran removed the swords from his belt and set them down on the table before sitting. "What news from home?"

Tanka shrugged. "Not much of interest. I don't get much in the way of gossip. Although I did hear you made quite an impression on the clan elders after you took care of that evil sorcerer to the south. What was his name?"

"Seiryu," said Ran. "I couldn't believe the clan had allowed him to stay in power as long as they had. The things he was doing in his tower couldn't be tolerated."

Tanka sat down opposite Ran and nodded. "You'll get no argument from me there. But you did just ruin the graduation exercise for the next class of operatives."

"Excuse me?"

Tanka grinned. "Seiryu. He was the graduation exercise. For years. I had to recover that damned sword ten years back." He chuckled. "Glad to know that someone finally gave that old coot the what for."

Ran shook his head. "That would mean that the clan elders were allied with Seiryu."

Tanka held up his hand. "Now, don't get crazy thoughts. They tolerated Seiryu as long as he agreed to play along. I don't think anyone expected you to actually go back and confront the man. You were just supposed to get the sword back and that was it. You would have graduated. But then you took it one step further. I don't think the clan elders really gave a damn about Seiryu as much as they'll now need to find a new test for aspiring graduates."

"I had no idea," said Ran.

Tanka smiled and slapped him on the back. "To be expected. You'd only just graduated, and the final test is as tough as they come. No doubt you were feeling all cocky. That's completely natural. We all feel that way after the final exam. Like we could go out and set the world on fire with our confidence. Am I right?"

Ran smirked as he remembered how he'd been feeling. At the time, it hadn't seemed like cockiness, but in retrospect, it certainly might have been. He'd fairly demanded his graduation certificates from Tozawa. That wasn't exactly a smart thing to do. But Tozawa had not only tolerated it, he'd spared him punishment when he'd returned from killing Seiryu.

"Tozawa is an extraordinarily patient man," said Ran finally.

"He's had plenty of experience watching his new graduates go off into the world. He's probably plenty used to the attitude he gets from the likes of us." Tanka poured them both some wine and set a cup before Ran. "Besides, it's not like the real world doesn't set us all straight sooner or later, right? And if we don't learn, we don't come home alive."

"There's that," said Ran, thinking about his recent experiences with Kan-Gul and transporting Jysal to the temple. If he'd remained stupid and cocky, he would have surely ended up dead many times over. "Still, it would be good to apologize to Tozawa when I return."

Tanka shrugged again as he downed the wine. "Tozawa and the clan elders will be more appreciative of any information you can provide as you make your way on your shugyo."

"You know about that, too?"

Tanka nodded. "Of course. And I can just tell you that I'm jealous as hell about the fact you got one. Me? As soon as I graduated, I got sent here to set up shop. I've been in that dirty old disguise so much I sometimes wonder if my bones are getting old."

"Why here?"

Tanka gestured around. "Big trading post like this? Tons of news comes through here. It's my job to stay on top of it. Scuttlebutt, gossip, trade secrets, who is angry at whom, that sort of thing. Apparently my aptitude for disguise is what won me this posting. Should have known when I got exemplary marks on that course. They knew exactly how to put me to best use." Tanka sighed and drank more wine. "In any event, it's a living and it helps the clan. I get bored often, but it's great to see you come along. How long are you staying?"

"Long enough to secure passage with a trading caravan heading west," said Ran. "I've got business in a kingdom along the trade routes."

"Which kingdom?"

"Valrus."

"Never heard of it." Tanka sighed. "Should have known you wouldn't be staying long. Ah well, can I help you with anything?"

Ran gestured to his swords. "Those are the only weapons I have left. Lost most of my traveling kit when my boat ran aground on a reef and we had to swim for it. Any chance of some replacements?"

"Do you still have your senban?"

Ran shook his head. He'd lost the precious flat throwing plates along with the length of chain he carried. "Just the two swords."

Tanka eyed the shorter blade. "Not the match of the long sword. How'd you come by it?"

"It used to have a different owner," said Ran as he sipped the last of his wine. "I've only recently adopted it."

Tanka smiled. "Fair enough. I can help with the resupply. I've got a cache of weapons here for just that reason. Imported direct from Gakur, by the way." He rose and walked to another bookcase. When he pulled a single bound volume from the shelf, the case turned on an unseen axis and revealed an alcove with a chest set inside. Tanka rummaged through it, and Ran could hear the sound of clinking metal.

"Here we are," said Tanka. He set down nine edged throwing plates, each about the size of Ran's palm.

Ran picked one up and turned it over, feeling the weight of it. Tanka wasn't lying; the senban had come straight from the forges in Gakur. Ran smiled. "Good to have some of these again." He gathered them up, folding them over each other in a length of cloth that would inhibit any noise from them as he moved.

Tanka let a length of chain nearly a meter long dribble onto the table top. "Your kusari."

Ran hefted the chain and studied the links. They had to be perfectly forged in order to stop a sword blade. Fortunately, these were. He slid that into his tunic and nodded at Tanka. "Much better. What do I owe you for them?"

"Owe me?" Tanka grinned. "The clan supplies its agents free of charge, you know that. Besides, sitting here out of that ridiculous get-up and having a bit of wine with a fellow graduate is worth more than what you could pay me, believe me."

Ran hoisted his glass. "In that case, here's to the clan."

Tanka nodded. "Indeed."

They both drank deep before Tanka put his glass back on the table. "So, have you anything of import for me to pass back to the clan?"

"You have the means to do so here?"

Tanka smiled. "Absolutely. I can get a message back to the clan within twenty-four hours. I use a group of trained falks for just that service. Have you ever seen one?"

"Once. Back in Gakur. One of the teachers showed us. They're vicious birds."

"Predatory," said Tanka. "But indisputably loyal. Once they have a message, they won't let anything stop them from delivering it. Probably why the clan goes to such lengths to ensure that we have them as our messengers."

Ran said, "The only bit of information I've come across so far is probably better attributed to the maniacal ravings of a madman."

"Who?"

"Kan-Gul."

Tanka sat back. "There's a name I don't often hear about. They say he uses the undead as his own private army."

"He did," said Ran. "He's no longer alive."

"You? You killed him?"

Ran shrugged. "I had some help."

"Incredible. And how long have you been out of Nehon for?"

"Nearly a month, I think."

Tanka hoisted his glass in Ran's direction. "You've already seen more action than me, my friend. Good of you to rid the countryside of that guy, too, let me tell you. I heard stories about him. No doubt you've sent him to a far better place."

"Kan-Gul said an army was coming over the mountains to the north. Looking to invade the lower lands."

Tanka set his glass down and leaned forward. "Did you see any evidence to back that up?"

Ran shrugged. "Inside his fortress he had room for plenty of soldiers. There was an armory. Billeting areas."

"Nothing else?"

"Just the promise of mayhem from Kan-Gul himself. Nothing else."

Tanka leaned back and rubbed his chin. "I will need to send this back to the clan. Even if it's nothing, they need to know about it. Ours isn't to make decisions about the information we get ahold of. We just send it back and let those wiser men make the decisions."

Ran frowned. "How long until you hear back from them?"

"A day. Perhaps two."

"I'd hoped to be leaving sooner than that," said Ran.

Tanka stood. "I'll send the message immediately, but you'll have to remain here until I hear back. If the clan wants you to follow up on that information, then your quest will have to wait until such time as they're satisfied that it poses no danger to our clan."

"Understood," said Ran. Although he was loathe to wait any longer than necessary in Chulal.

"Don't worry," said Tanka. "Trade caravans won't be leaving until the end of the week anyway. They all think it's bad luck to leave before the day of feasts. With any luck, you can hang around, find a caravan that wants you, and, when the time comes, you'll be ready to ride."

"I hope you're right," said Ran. "I hope you're right."

Chapter Four

Tanka left Ran alone while he went to send the message via falk. Ran found his way out of the apartment and wandered the streets of Chulal. The sun was beginning to set, but Ran figured he still had at least an hour of daylight left. Besides, he wanted to see the harbor area for himself.

Fortunately, Tanka had set himself up only a few blocks from the wharves, and as Ran drew ever closer to the sea, the scent of salty air grew stronger. Ran smirked as he remembered his most recent sailing adventure and how seasick he'd gotten enroute to Chugal. He had no desire to repeat the experience any time soon.

As he came around a block of buildings, he set eyes on the bustling harbor for the first time. At least a half-dozen merchant transport ships were in port, their sails all furled, and secured to the docks. Ran cast his eyes over the men working to load and unload them. He heard snippets of the guttural sailing language they used and decided he couldn't think of a harsher-sounding language. He had no idea what they were saying, but the underlying tonality seemed to say that if things weren't done as ordered then there would be severe repercussions.

As he walked, he was careful to stay away from the stacks of crates and piles of sacks containing goods for sale. These were also guarded by any number of private soldiers that the merchants hired on to oversee their goods. No doubt stealing was rampant down here, and the merchants needed to protect their wares.

Ahead of him, Ran saw a gathering of men who looked different from the sailors. They were well-dressed and plump, which meant they didn't engage in manual labor as far as Ran could tell. He approached them. As he did so, they looked up in surprise. One of them, larger than the others, hailed him.

"What can we do for you?"

Ran smiled. "I'm wondering where a warrior like myself can inquire about hiring on with a trade caravan. Do you know?"

The man grinned. "What job did you have in mind exactly?"

"Security."

He laughed. "You're awfully young to be traipsing about with those swords. What do you know about security anyway?"

Ran's smile dissolved into a serious expression. "I'm not as young as I might appear. And as for my swords, they've seen plenty of action. I can assure you of that."

"Can you now?" The older man rubbed his chin. "Well, unfortunately for you, son, I don't take people's word for it. I need to see for myself what you're capable of doing. Surely you wouldn't object to a little demonstration?"

Ran shrugged. "If that's what you require, mister . . . ?"

"You can call me Yasseh. If you do well on the demonstration, you might even call me boss at some point."

"What did you have in mind?" Ran shifted his two swords.

Yasseh shook his head. "Nothing with those blades. The last thing we need is the authorities coming down here and making trouble for all of us. But you must possess some degree of unarmed combat skill?"

"I do," said Ran.

Yasseh smiled. "Excellent." He clapped his hands and a smaller man appeared out of nowhere. Yasseh didn't even look at him. "Tell Gunj to come here."

"Gunj?" Ran almost smiled. The name alone conjured up images of a giant bear with lots of hair sticking out of odd places. Ran removed his swords and handed them to one of the other men in the circle. "Be careful with those."

When Gunj showed up, he looked nothing like a bear. He looked more like a wisp of a man, but his forearms stretched taut over ribbons of muscle. His face showed a lot of hard living, and the way he moved told Ran that he was exceptionally dangerous. He came up to Ran's chest and no more. Ran nodded at him, but got no response.

Yasseh smiled. "This is Gunj. He's been with me for years. I will ask him to test you out. If he thinks you do indeed know how to handle yourself, then perhaps I'll have a spot for you on my team. If not, well, I'm sure you'll heal quickly enough."

"Rules?" asked Ran as he separated from Gunj and the circle around him widened.

Yasseh shrugged. "I wouldn't worry about rules. Do what you have to do to survive. Just don't do anything that'll make Gunj angry."

Ran frowned again. Gunj stood about ten yards away from him with his arms folded across his chest. He yawned and then removed his shirt. A blazing red dragon snaked its way down across his pectoral muscles, blowing fire toward his belly.

Ran pointed at the tattoo. "Nice work."

Yasseh chuckled. "All the members of Gunj's school have those emblazoned on them. It's not by choice."

"Which school?" asked Ran.

Gunj spat a wad of something at the ground and started moving around Ran. Ran brought his hands up in front of his chest. He had no idea what school of martial arts Gunj might have been from, so until he had some sense of what his fighting style was like, he would play it defensively.

Gunj feinted with a punch and then launched a side kick directly at Ran's ribs. But Ran didn't fall for the feint and sidestepped the kick before dropping an elbow onto the side of Gunj's leg above the knee. Gunj went with the blow and ducked down, trying to sweep Ran's legs out from under him. Ran leapt high and away, regaining some of the distance that had been lost when Gunj closed the gap.

Gunj came back up on his feet and looked at Ran with a bit more interest now. Ran couldn't call it respect. Not yet. But Gunj clearly recognized that Ran wasn't some idiot who thought himself a badass without any skill to back it up. He moved a bit more carefully, feinting and seeing if he could get Ran to commit to a defensive move.

Ran didn't take any of the bait, which forced Gunj to commit to an attack himself. The wiry man launched a series of punches aimed at Ran's head. Ran backpedaled, knocking the arms away with hard strikes to the underside of Gunj's arms. Gunj grunted loudly and redoubled his efforts, but Ran was ready for his next attack and countered before he could launch it. Ran snaked one arm over Gunj's left arm and dipped down and then back up, acquiring a steep shoulder lock.

Gunj went with the lock and threw himself into a back flip that brought him back onto his feet.

But not before Ran sank a heavy kick into his midsection. Gunj stumbled back, clutching his gut.

He held one hand up, and Ran halted his attack.

As Gunj got back up and sorted himself out, he glanced at Yasseh. "He is very skilled."

Yasseh nodded with a bit of a surprised look crossing his face. He glanced at Ran. "You realize that's the first time Gunj has ever been bested. Usually he mops the floor with aspiring security guards. Not you, though. You must be something special indeed."

Ran took his swords back from the man who had been holding them and shrugged. "Experience is paid for in other ways. I don't necessarily think I'm special given all the horrors I've seen in my short life."

Yasseh clapped him on the back. "Regardless, what will it cost me to have you come with us?"

Ran eyed him. "What are you transporting?"

Yasseh laughed. "A wise warrior at that." He shook his head. "We have a shipment of spices and fabrics that are feverishly sought after in the west. Expensive silks and robes that the rich in other kingdoms long to wear to impress their naive friends. We are one of the largest caravans leaving Chulal the day after next."

Ran wondered if he would have enough time to hear back from Gakur before heading out. He nodded at Yasseh. "What coin do you pay in?"

"I pay in gold," said Yasseh. "It's accepted everywhere without these annoying currency exchanges to worry about. One kingdom's gold is as good as another, I've found."

"I want a sign-on bonus. Three gold pieces."

Yasseh's eyebrows shot up. "That's a steep price. I'll give you two and another ten if we reach the safety of Durfun. From there, you can decide if you wish to continue with us on our way west or go off on your own. There are, after all, many ways for a young man to get distracted along the route."

"We'll see," said Ran. Asking if they intended to stop at Valrus wouldn't have been wise. Ran's appearance marked him as a wandering warrior and nothing more. He had no wish for anyone to suddenly become interested in his business. It would be easy enough to find out if Valrus was on their list of stops once the caravan was underway.

Yasseh reached into his tunic and brought out a silken purse with gold-threaded strings. He doled out two gold coins into Ran's hand. "Half now. I trust that you won't take these and leave me wondering where you are when we leave the morning after next?"

"Not all who wander are without honor," said Ran. "You got yourself a security guard."

Yasseh nodded. "You'll meet the other members of the security contingent when we depart. Gunj is also along for the ride, but not as an overt security man. He'll stay in the background unless things get out of hand somewhere. He prefers to leave the fighting to those he considers disposable."

Ran smirked. "Refreshingly honest."

"Gunj has had a lifetime of fighting, and he usually shies away from it unless he's helping me screen prospects."

"I thought you said he was never bested."

"He hasn't been, but just because he's better than just about everyone but you, we still need to hire people on to fight for us if bandits attack. Gunj just doesn't think very much of them is all."

"Fair enough," said Ran. "I have a horse. Shall I bring him?"

Yasseh waved his hand. "Not unless your horse has made it through the Kurzjak Desert. You'll have one of my steeds to take his place. Go and sell him off here in the city."

"Very well." Ran turned to leave, but Yasseh called him back.

"You still haven't given me your name."

Ran smiled. "I am Ran."

Yasseh nodded. "Get yourself a meal, drink, and a woman with those gold pieces, my friend. Once we start down the highway, it will be only time for working. Understand?"

"Perfectly," said Ran. He turned and walked down the street until he came back to a turn where he could be assured that no one from the wharves could see him. He doubled back several times to make sure Gunj or another of Yasseh's people wasn't tailing him. He doubted they were, but Gunj was an interesting sort. No doubt the little man was dangerous and had seen a lot of fighting in his time.

Ran would need to be careful around him during the length of the journey west.

It was possible, he supposed, that the elders back in Gakur would discount the supposed invasion from his reports. No doubt they must hear all sorts of crazy gossip. If they had to check out every rumor, it would require far too much manpower and resources to explore. Ran fully expected to return to Tanka's apartments and have his fellow shadow warrior tell him that he was free to go.

He hoped.

Ahead of him, the street narrowed and Ran realized that conducting business down at the harbor had used up the last bits of remaining sunlight. Already, the glow of candles could be seen in the pubs frequented by the sailors in this part of town. He heard raucous laughter and the sounds of breaking glass. Things were likely to get out of hand as the night crept in. Ran didn't want to get caught up in anything he couldn't get himself out of. He needed to be on that caravan when it left the day after tomorrow. Getting into a fight with drunks wasn't a wise move.

He steered down a side alley and avoided a group of sailors already scuffling with each other. As they went sprawling off to one side of him, Ran sidestepped and vanished into the shadows past another tavern. He smelled mutton and ale, and his mouth watered. He was ravenous, he realized, but judging by the look of things, the tavern was no safer than the other bars in this area.

Then he spotted something that vanished out of the corner of his eye as soon as he saw it.

Ran stopped short in the alley. He'd just passed a window looking into the tavern. His peripheral vision, which was sometimes more acute than his normal eyesight, had seen something. As it registered in his mind, Ran shook his head.

It couldn't be.

He turned and snuck back toward the window, using the edge of the building as cover so his entire head didn't appear in the window. He peered into the murky interior of the tavern and let his eyes scan the entire place.

At first, he thought he might have been mistaken. But on his second pass, he spotted him.

In the corner of a tavern, holding court with a group of equally surly thugs, sat someone who shouldn't be alive. Ran thought through the encounter again in his head. He frowned. It was possible, he supposed, but very unlikely.

Still, he couldn't argue with reality. And he couldn't discount the presence of the man sitting at the table in the corner of the tavern—without his two hands.

Ejul, the bandit Ran thought he had killed, was seemingly alive and well.

The question was: what was he doing in Chulal?

Chapter Five

The last time Ran had seen Ejul, the bandit had just had both his hands lopped off at the wrist and was apparently lying close to death on the ground. At least, that was how Ran had left him. Surely the blood loss from the arterial cuts should have finished him off, and yet here he was, holding court in the corner of a tavern down by the docks in Chulal. Aside from the fact that both of his arms ended in bandaged stumps, he didn't seem too badly off.

Should have followed up with a cut to his neck, thought Ran with a frown. That way he'd definitely be dead.

Ran kept his eyes on Ejul as he talked. Twice, the bandit brought his bandaged arms down on the table with a bang and an obvious wince, but the men he was with seemed to respect him. Had Ejul already found a new group of bandits to take command of since his former boss was dead? Or was this something else entirely?

Ran had no idea, but he knew he wanted to get closer to hear what was being said. The question was how could he do that without Ejul seeing him? True, it had been dark at the time they'd engaged in combat, but Ran couldn't take a chance that Ejul would recognize him. If he did, he could easily sic his new buddies on him. Worse, Ejul might have pull with the city officials and arrange for Ran to be delayed even more than a potential mission from Gakur would waylay him.

Fortunately, Ran had worn his hair loose that night. From his waistband, he pulled out a simple length of leather and tied his hair back behind his head, pulling it hard to stretch his face a bit. His beard had also grown in a bit more. He hoped it would conceal him enough.

It would be safer to wait for Ejul outside, but that would mean not learning what the bandit had up his sleeve. Ran wanted to know for sure. That meant taking a risk, but the shadow warrior was comfortable enough with it.

He entered the tavern.

Dozens of heads turned his way as he entered. Ran knew the instinct for most people would be to tuck their head down and try to disappear. He did the opposite. He stared down as many eyes as he could and wore such a grim expression that everyone in the tavern immediately assumed he belonged there. The customers all went back to minding their own business.

Ejul himself hadn't looked up, which Ran was thankful for. He was still having an animated conversation in the corner.

Ran drew himself up to the bar and ordered a pint of ale. He carried it to a table close to Ejul but not directly next to it. Sitting with his back to the wall, he sipped the ale and listened in as much as he could without appearing to.

"They're just sitting there plump for the taking," said Ejul. "This is an incredible opportunity for all of us."

"It's not like they're unguarded," said one of the men at the table. "It won't be as easy as you make it out to be. We'll have to fight for sure."

"So what," countered Ejul. "Since when are you lot afraid of fighting? I thought I'd gathered some of the toughest brutes in the land for this little venture. And now with the prospect of fighting, you all get cold feet? Hardly seems that you're living up to your reputation, if you ask me."

"And what about you, Ejul? Just how much fighting will you be doing? Seems to me it won't be much considering you haven't even got any hands to hold a weapon."

Ran nearly smirked. Ejul grumbled into his drink. "If I ever find the sorry bastard who did this to me, I will make sure that I cut his head off, scoop out his brains, and use the skull as a chamber pot. I'll shit myself silly every night."

"Still need hands for that," laughed another man. "Unless of course, you've found yourself a woman who doesn't mind wiping your arse."

Ejul sighed. "Look, the trade caravans will be leaving the day after tomorrow. All we need to do is ride out of the city ahead of them. We've got the perfect spot to lay an ambush. Once we have their goods, we can either take them for ourselves or ransom them back. It's easy and quick money."

Ran coughed into his empty tankard and called out for the barman to bring him another ale. The barman came and took his first empty back.

The conversation at Ejul's table continued. "Easy and quick for you because you won't be taking part in the fighting. As for the rest of us, we have to weigh the risks of attacking a caravan. It's not quite as simple a thing as you make it out to be. For instance, where is this ambush supposed to happen?"

Ejul cleared his throat. "There's a spot about ten miles outside of the city. It's on a lonely stretch of road and behind a hill. We can stage there, and, once the caravan has passed by, we can sweep in and attack."

Another man downed his ale and slammed the glass back down with a thud. "It's all well and good for you, Ejul. But like Jaeger says, you won't be doing any of the fighting. Hell, I don't even know how you're going to ride a horse, for that matter."

"I rode here, didn't I?"

"Aye, and what about those stumps of yours? What if they're infected?"

"They won't be," said Ejul. "I stuck them into the pit of a fire and let the flames kill the ends of my arms. I can barely feel a thing down there anymore."

"One thing's for sure," said the man called Jaeger. "You won't be playing with yourself anymore in this lifetime."

Jaeger's comment produced peals of laughter.

Ran gestured for another tankard of ale and slapped his second empty glass down a little less hard than the first.

Ejul pounded his stumps down on the table again. "Maybe I was wrong about you lot. Maybe you're just a bunch of big talkers. Where I'm sitting, none of you is man enough to take this seriously. I'm offering you a chance to make a good score, and all you can is take the piss out of me for having gotten my hands cut off, through no fault of my own, I might add."

"No fault of your own?" Jaeger let a belly laugh erupt form his mouth. "I'd say you definitely picked the wrong person to fight that night, my friend. No fault of your own. Oh my . . ." His voice trailed off, and Ejul said nothing for a long minute.

Finally, he cleared his throat again. "So that's it then. You lot aren't interested. I would have thought you'd be pounding down the door to get at this goodness. And yet here you sit, drinking away the night." He sighed. "Well, I'll have to find some other men to handle it then."

Jaeger held up his hand. "Now, now, don't get so glum, Ejul. Honestly, you look like a little boy who just got his heart broke by his first lay. We didn't say we wouldn't do it, we just don't think you're exactly sharing in the risk to the same extent that we are."

"I'm the one who came up with the plan. I've been thinking it through for weeks now."

"And then you went off on the fool errand that Kayo put you up to. Look where that got you."

"I needed the money."

Another of the men sniffed. "No sense having money if you can't live to spend it. You damn near died doing that village."

"That's true," said Ejul. "But I didn't, and now I'm back here trying to get this score launched." He paused. "Will you do it?"

"We want a bigger share," said Jaeger. "We're the ones riding into battle, not you. If you don't fight, you don't get a big cut. Those are our terms. It's up to you if you want to accept them or not, although I doubt you'll find a crew who will do it any other way. If anything, they'll probably just cut your throat and then do it themselves."

Ejul sighed. "All right then. I'll take a smaller share."

Jaeger slapped him on the back. "We won't be greedy, Ejul. You'll make enough to hire some pretty wench to look after you for the rest of your days. I'm sure you'll have all sorts of prospects for the job, and won't it be fun testing out the aspiring ones? Now drink up and let us get on with the planning of this raid. Have you figured out which caravan you want to attack?"

"Yasseh is the wealthiest merchant in the city," said Ejul. "I'd like to take him down."

"He's also got the most security."

"Big risk, big reward," said one of the men. "I say we go for it."

Ran frowned into his drink. If they were planning to hit Yasseh's caravan, that meant they would need to be prepared for it. Ran needed to get out of there and get word back to Yasseh about what he'd overheard. He finished his third drink, belched loudly, and then slumped forward, smacking his forehead on the table.

The action produced the desired result. Rough hands shook Ran, and he looked up with sleepy eyes. "Huh? Wha—?"

The tavern owner stood over him. "All right, you, that's enough. You can't stay here if you're not drinking or eating. Sleeping ain't allowed. Go home." He muscled Ran out of his chair and steered him toward the door. Ran kept his head down as he passed Ejul's table. The men sitting there gave Ran only a cursory glance. But Ran heard Ejul mumble something. He hoped he hadn't been recognized. All he could do was allow the scene to play out and hope for the best.

The tavern owner got Ran outside, whereupon Ran stumbled away down an alley. He passed the window he'd peered in earlier, but no one at Ejul's table had risen. Ran took that to indicate he'd pulled the ruse off without a hitch. It was time to get back to Tanka's apartments, and then tomorrow he would talk to Yasseh. Since the caravan wasn't leaving until the day after tomorrow, it wasn't an urgent matter. And given time to prepare, Ran felt they could easily thwart whatever attack Ejul had planned.

Ran navigated the streets of Chulal easily enough, thanking his instructors back at the Nine Daggers clan for instilling their students with such a good sense of direction. He ducked inside Tanka's apartment only after completing a loop several times to make sure he hadn't been followed. The last thing he wanted to do was lead anyone curious back to the resident shadow warrior lair.

Tanka was asleep but rose as soon as Ran entered. "How'd the walk go?"

Ran removed his swords and other weapons and set them on the table. "As well as could be expected."

"You smell like ale."

Ran nodded. "I had to down three tankards of the stuff to find out what was going on at a nearby table."

"Something good?"

"A group of bandits planning to hit the caravans when they leave the protection of the city."

Tanka sat up and rubbed his eyes. "How in the world did you happen to stumble on to that?"

"I broke up an attack on a village the other night. Three bandits set fire to the place. I thought I killed all three of them, but apparently I only wounded one of them. I passed a tavern and saw him inside holding court. Imagine my surprise. The last time I saw him, he was lying facedown in the dirt with no hands."

Tanka chuckled. "I'll bet."

"Anyway, I wanted to find out what was going on, so I sat and listened."

"Lucky the wounded guy didn't recognize you."

Ran stretched out on a bed nearby. "It was dark the other night. Plus, the way I wore my hair was different. I felt confident he wouldn't know it was me. I took precautions anyway, like having three drinks and pretending to be drunk."

"Are you?"

Ran eyed him and smiled. "You know that we can handle our drink easily enough. Just a matter of proper conditioning is all."

Tanka lay back down. "I have to admit, I always did enjoy those conditioning sessions."

"I might have overdone it once or twice," laughed Ran. "But that's the price we had to pay."

Tanka yawned. "So, what else did you do while you were out?"

"I got a job," said Ran.

"Doing what?"

"Like we discussed: security for the caravans."

"Lucky you heard about the attack then, huh? At least this way you can warn the owners what's being planned, and they can take steps to handle it appropriately."

Ran yawned himself. "I'll be talking to the caravan leader tomorrow morning about it. I figure since we've got this advance warning, we can disrupt it as we see fit." He turned over. "How was your evening?"

"Sent the falks off to Gakur. Now it's just a matter of waiting. I'm sure we'll hear back pretty fast. The journey isn't too long for the birds, and the elders at the clan will want to make a fast decision while you're still here in town. As soon as they do, they'll send word back. Probably hear sometime tomorrow if I had to wager a guess."

"It's probably nothing," said Ran. "Kan-Gul was a crazy bastard. He could have been making it all up for all we know."

Tanka eyed him in the darkness. "Maybe, but you know how things like this go. We have to run it past the clan. And if they decide that you need to do a scouting mission farther north, then that's exactly where you have to go."

Ran sighed. "I know. I'm hopeful they won't, though."

"Understandable," said Tanka. "But what the clan needs done comes first. What we want doesn't matter when the safety of our people is threatened. Regardless of what you want, if the clan commands it, you have to do what they say."

"We'll see what they say," said Ran. "No sense thinking it over right now."

"Nothing to think over," said Tanka. "We don't disobey the clan." And with that, Tanka turned over and promptly fell back to sleep.

Chapter Six

Dawn broke with brilliant sunshine and a cool breeze sweeping in off the ocean. Ran woke and found Tanka already dressed.

"Going to check the falks and see if they've brought word back yet."

Ran swung his legs out of the bed. "I'll head down to the harbor and see about talking to the caravan master."

Tanka pointed to the dining area. "Left you some food there for your meal. Tea should still be nice and hot."

"Thanks."

Tanka left and Ran quickly downed the food. He was eager to see what Yasseh would say when he informed him of the plot to attack the caravan and rob them of their possessions. He took his time belting on his weapons, making sure the senban were properly positioned along with the length of kusari. When he stuck his two swords into his belt, he headed out of the apartment and into the streets of Chulal.

Crowds already bustled along the main thoroughfares. Pushcarts filled with exotic fruits and baked goods clambered along, stopping frequently as patrons came to buy. Ran sidestepped a number of them on his way toward the harbor. Ahead of him, he spotted a contingent of the city guard on patrol. Ran waited as they marched by and then resumed his journey to the waterfront. He inhaled deeply, feeling invigorated after a good night's sleep. The salt air tasted good, and while he might not like traveling on boats, Ran had always enjoyed being near the ocean.

Around the corner, he caught a glimpse of one of the merchant vessels under oars rowing out of the harbor. As she passed around the jetty of stones and the pair of watchtowers guarding the harbor entrance, her sails unfurled and immediately blossomed as they caught the wind. Off on another adventure, thought Ran. He hoped he'd be off soon for one as well.

He found his way to the same location where he'd met Yasseh the evening before and found Gunj busy loading several pack mules. Gunj nodded at him as he approached and came over.

"You need something?"

Ran smiled. "I was hoping to talk to Yasseh. I have some information he needs to hear about."

"What sort of information?"

"I'd prefer to tell him directly, if it's all the same to you." Ran said this with a smile still on his face so Gunj didn't take it the wrong way.

But the smaller man merely shrugged. "He's out right now, but he should be back in an hour or so." Gunj walked back toward the pack mules.

"I'll wait then," said Ran.

Again Gunj only shrugged. "Doesn't matter to me. You're part of the company now. You can do what you wish."

Ran watched him lace up straps on another mule. "How go preparations for tomorrow's departure?"

"We'll be ready to leave as soon as dawn breaks. That's about how you know things are prepared." Gunj eyed him. "Have you ever ridden with a caravan before?"

Ran shook his head. "Nope. I'm afraid I'm brand new to the experience."

"But you've done a lot of fighting in the past. That much is obvious." Gunj turned back to the mules. "And someone trained you very well."

"My father was Murai. Do you know of them?"

Gunj grunted. "I know what the Murai are. They are exceptional warriors." He glanced at Ran. "But you do not fight like a Murai warrior."

Ran tried to laugh it off. "That's very true. Much to the consternation of my father. He always wanted me to be like him, and I guess I failed at it. Never had a head for memorizing complicated technical movements and the like. I guess I just preferred to think about fighting in another way."

Gunj cocked an eyebrow. "Is that so?"

Something about how the little man asked unnerved Ran a bit. Gunj was a worldly guy. He had no doubt seen his share of fighters over the years. Was it possible that he also knew about the shadow warriors? Ran guessed that it was entirely possible. Maybe even likely. But the question was, did he suspect Ran of being one? Or had his fighting style simply confused the smaller man? Either way, Ran would have to be sure to disguise himself as much as possible in his mannerisms and actions.

Ran wandered around the warehouse and looked inside, spotting huge pallets of merchandise. He found Gunj again. "Are we taking all of that with us?"

Gunj nodded. "Not to worry, we have the transportation to handle it."

"And the security to protect it?"

Gunj laughed. "Well, that's what you're here for, isn't it?" He moved off, humming a song to himself.

Yasseh showed up a few minutes later with several workers in tow and hailed Ran when he saw him. "What brings you down here so early? We're not due to leave until dawn tomorrow."

Ran tugged on his sleeve. "Is there somewhere we can talk? Privately?"

Yasseh glanced at the men around him. "Leave us." He waited until the men vanished and then smiled at Ran. "What's this about? I hope you're not reconsidering our employment arrangement?"

"Not at all," said Ran. "However, something has come to my attention, and I felt you should know about it so we can take the appropriate steps to counter it."

"And what would that be?"

Ran eyed him. "There's a plan afoot to rob your caravan."

If he'd expected Yasseh to look alarmed, Ran was sorely disappointed when the elder merchant merely let loose a hearty laugh. "Rob my caravan, is it? Is that what's got you so worried?" Yasseh pulled out a long-stemmed pipe and started filling it with tobacco. "Let me tell you something, Ran. The nature of my business is that we are always under threat of attack. When you get as successful as I have become, the threat of robbers and brigands and the like is always with you. And we have seen more than our fair share of such things over the life of my company. It's one reason why I take security as seriously as I do."

"I just thought you would want to know," said Ran.

"Indeed I do," said Yasseh. "How did you come by this information?"

"I overheard it in a tavern." Suddenly, it didn't sound as reputable as it had when Ran had played this scene out in his head beforehand.

Yasseh clapped him on the back. "Listen, son, if everything that was spoken by drunks around a table in a tavern was to be believed, the world as we know it wouldn't last a day. So many schemes and machinations have been born amid the tankards and liquid bravado that inhabits such places, yet have never seen the light of day. I've heard fairy tales of demons and dragons and dungeons filled with magical weapons and more gold than can be yanked from the earth itself. To this day I have never seen a demon. Nor a dragon." He chuckled. "I may have seen a dungeon or two, but never one filled with gold or magic weapons. Pity, that."

Ran smiled. "I guess you're right. After all, if you weren't, then you wouldn't be as prosperous as you are."

Yasseh blew out a smoke ring and sighed. "Danger comes with the territory. At my age, I don't have to keep going out on the caravans, you know. I could easily hire someone else to oversee them. But you know why I still do it?"

"You enjoy the uncertainty," said Ran. "The risk attracts you."

"Aye," said Yasseh. "What else is there in life that lets you know you're truly alive if not for the risk of death? Only when we are close to the edge of oblivion do we fully appreciate what it is to draw a breath, see a sunrise, or lay with a woman. I'm never as happy sitting around a city some place as I am when I'm out on the roads that connect civilizations. I get to meet new people. I get to see places most never do. Even with the risk of attack, this is a fine life."

Ran eyed him. "And if the attack is legitimate and you die in the process?"

Yasseh shrugged. "Then it is Argul's will that such a thing happen to me."

"Argul? Is that your god?"

Yasseh blew out another smoke ring. This one failed to float high. He frowned at it and then shook his head. "Argul was my second wife. And never has a more bitter, hate-filled woman walked the grass of this world. She cursed me to die when my proclivity for chasing skirts got the better of me. So far, I've kept that curse at bay." He smiled. "But I suppose one day it will catch up with me. You can't put that much hatred out into the universe and not expect it to manifest somehow."

They were distracted by the sound of an approaching horse. Yasseh turned, and Ran saw a broad smile spread across his face. "Ah, my son is here at long last."

Ran turned and nearly forgot to control himself. The man on the approaching horse was none other than Ejul the bandit. But Ran managed to keep the shock from registering with a quick series of shallow breaths.

Ejul paid him no mind anyway and smiled at Yasseh before sliding down out of the saddle. Ran could see that Ejul's two stumps had been fitted with two metallic hooks that enabled him to ride the horse.

Yasseh embraced his son and then pulled away. "Better now?"

Ejul held up his hooks and shrugged. "Thank you for the gift, Father. They will enable me to perform many tasks. Not as much as I would like, however."

Yasseh turned to Ran. "You see the sort of danger that exists. My son, Ejul, here was out of town for a few days. He was attacked in a village by a crazed swordsman who hacked off both of his hands. Can you imagine such a thing?"

"The world can be a terrible place," said Ran.

"And a wonderful one for sparing my only son," said Yasseh. He turned to Ejul. "This is Ran. I've hired him on as security for the upcoming trip."

Ejul eyed Ran for the first time, and the shadow warrior felt the man's gaze rove over him, quietly appraising him. After a moment, Ejul frowned. "You look familiar. Have we met before?"

Ran wished for nothing more than a convenient disguise at that moment. But to shrink and become shy would only confirm any suspicions Ejul might have. So instead, Ran did the opposite and opened up with a hearty laugh. "I shouldn't think so. I've only recently arrived in the city. But perhaps we passed in the streets."

"I've only just returned myself," said Ejul. "Where did you come from before this?"

"Naran."

Ejul smirked. "That place. It's a wonder you made it out of there alive."

"Not really a wonder," said Yasseh. "Ran is a skilled warrior. Even Gunj says so."

Ejul's eyebrows creased his forehead. "Is that so? Well, you must be very special, indeed. You're lucky to be able to wield those swords. I no longer have such luck, myself."

"And yet you are handling this adversity as well as any man could," said Yasseh. "I am extremely proud of you for that."

"Most noble," said Ran. He turned toward Yasseh. "I have a few remaining items to handle before I join you at dawn tomorrow, so I'll take my leave now." He nodded to Ejul. "Good to meet you. Will you be accompanying us on the caravan?"

"Me? No, I'm afraid I'd be more of a liability than an asset. If we were attacked, I'd scarcely be able to do anything, I fear. I will remain here in Chulal and see after the business. Someone has to balance the books and make sure we don't run out of money."

Yasseh laughed. "Ejul has a great mind for business. Once I'm tucked away in the ground somewhere, I expect he will have no trouble assuming leadership and continuing the family's success."

Ran bowed. "I will leave you to that, then. Good day." He moved back down the quay toward the busier streets of Chulal, fully aware that Ejul's eyes were still on him as he did so. What were the chances that the man he'd nearly killed a few nights ago would turn out to be the son of the man Ran now worked for? He almost grinned. He'd been told many times by the elders at the clan that the universe worked in mysterious ways. It wasn't worth the effort trying to figure out what sort of bizarre conditions must have come into alignment to make this connection, but they had. And now Ran would be forced to deal with it. The good news, he supposed, was that Ejul was staying back here in Chulal. Of course, Ran suspected that was a convenient lie to facilitate the actual ambush.

The real question was why? Ejul seemed to have a privileged life of wealth and opportunity. How was it that he had fallen in with the likes of thugs and bandits? He only had to wait out his father's death before he would inherit a large company that would guarantee him financial security for the rest of his life. Why would he attack his own family's business?

It made no sense, Ran decided. But then again, so often the workings of the minds of men failed to make sense. Perhaps Ejul was impatient. Perhaps he owed large sums of money to people. Whatever the case, Ran would need to keep his wits about him during the trip. If Ejul suspected Ran was the man who had cut off his hands, then Ran's life would be in serious jeopardy.

As a precaution, he took the long route back to Tanka's apartments, tripling back upon his long and winding trail several times to throw off any interested pursuers. Each time he did so, he detected nothing amiss, and it was finally nearing late afternoon when he opened the door to the apartment and walked inside.

Tanka was already there. As Ran came in, he waved him over to the small table and the oil lamp that burned on it.

"The falks have returned from Gakur."

Ran's heart ticked over. "What is the word?"

"I'm decoding it now," said Tanka. "Pull up a chair and help me."

Chapter Seven

The technique for decoding messages from Gakur changed depending on the time of year. But since Ran wasn't assigned to an outpost, he didn't have access to the various codes employed by the Nine Daggers clan to keep its messages secure. So as Ran watched, Tanka took the lead and began writing two lines of script beneath the coded message.

"We're using a special key that Ginjo developed," said Tanka. "How he comes up with these things is beyond me. I can't imagine anyone ever being able to break our codes, but he certainly tries to ensure that even we have a tough time of it."

Ran grinned. "I remember Ginjo's class on secret inks and how to use them. Who would have thought that urine had so many uses?"

Tanka chuckled. "That was a smelly session, if I recall correctly."

"You were years ahead of me, but it was pungent to say the least when we used it." Ran watched Tanka copy down another line of code. "Four lines?"

Tanka nodded. "Ginjo is never complacent. So he builds a false message into the coded transcripts. If someone intercepts this and they're able to break the code to a certain point, they'll get a whole lot of misinformation."

"So once you get something that looks like a real message, it's not?"

"Exactly. The real message is a further two lines down. You have to keep decoding it. Ginjo thinks that most people are inherently lazy and won't commit to continuing to decode when it appears they've got a legitimate message staring them in the face."

"It must take real talent to embed a false message within the code."

Tanka sighed. "Talent? I guess so. But most of us think that old Ginjo might be getting a bit touched in the head in his old age. And frankly, it's a pain in the backside to have to handle such a decoding. It would be far easier to not make it this complex."

"But less secure, too," said Ran. "Seems like Ginjo might know best in this case."

"I suppose. I'd just like to see him have to decode one of his own messages sometime and let him feel what a delight it is to sit here for the better part of an hour." Tanka refreshed the ink in his quill and began writing again.

Ran watched as the script continued to flow, recognizing certain characters and not knowing others. As Tanka worked, tiny beads of sweat pooled on his brow. Ran poured him a cup of water and brought it over. Tanka took it with a grin.

"Thanks."

"You look like you need it." Ran pulled a chair up again. "Almost done?"

"Not just yet. One more series to go through and I should have it complete." Tanka nodded at the candle above them, which had burned down low. "It's already taken far too long as it is. If this was some sort of emergency, imagine trying to decode it. Sometimes the precautions get to be a bit overkill. We need a quicker alternative."

"Do you have to encode them the same way?"

Tanka sighed. "Thankfully not. We use a simpler method, which helps in the event of a crisis or something urgent. I wonder if Ginjo simply does this to keep all of his former students up to the task of dealing with his codes." He set the quill down. "There. Finally."

Ran peered over his shoulder. "Well?"

Tanka read the message and then handed it over. "I'm sorry, Ran. I know how much you wanted to leave with the caravan."

Ran looked down and read:

> *Agent hereby ordered to proceed north and fully investigate claims of forthcoming invasion.*

Ran frowned and handed the message back. Tanka took it and held the parchment to the candle flame. The fire licked its way up and over the edges, curling the paper up as it did so. Ran watched the ink bubble again and then dissolve into dark ash. Tanka held it until the last possible second before dropping it onto the table, where it burned itself out. Tanka dutifully gathered the ashes, carried them to the window, and sprinkled them upon the breeze.

"Well, so much for that." He turned away from the window and nodded at Ran. "When will you leave?"

Ran shrugged. "Tomorrow is as good a day as any, I'd expect. Can you set me up with some supplies?"

Tanka nodded. "I've got a store of dried-food provisions. You'll have to acquire any cold-weather gear on the way. It would look a bit suspicious to send you out of town wearing heavy garb and boots."

"Good point. I'm sure there are towns along the way north I can stop at."

Tanka went to his shelf and drew out a map of northern Igul. "There's Kalang-yao, which is about the last outpost of civilization before the Shard Mountains. No doubt you can find what you need there. If I were you, I'd make my trip north as quick as possible. From what I've heard, Kalang-yao is not the most hospitable place. The locals are wary and a hard folk to get along with."

"Why so?"

"The proximity of the mountains makes them hard. Living up there is nothing short of a struggle year round."

"So why stay?"

"The locals hunt the ice tigers that live in the snowy mountains. Ice tiger pelts are prized by people to the west, and they're willing to pay a hefty price indeed for the luxury of the skins. As far as I know, the people who live in Kalang-yao are the only ones who have the skill to hunt the big cats without getting killed by them. Definitely a tough way to live life."

"No doubt they'll be even more suspicious when I show up. What are the odds someone from Nehon has ever been to the town before?"

"I don't know," said Tanka. "It hasn't really been of interest to the clan, so I know none of our kind have ever there. But a merchant or two from Nehon may have made it that far north. They do trade, after all."

Ran nodded. "Then that would be my way in, I suppose. A young trader from Nehon looking to import exotic items from the frozen north. It could work."

"Better than going as a sword-for-hire," said Tanka. "There'd be no need for that up there."

"All right then. I'll have that store of dried food, if you can manage it. Also, a map of the area would be good. I'll need to study it before I head up there. Try to find the most logical point for an invading army to come through."

"I've heard rumors of a hidden pass so remote and harsh that most don't even try to travel through it. But I have no idea where it might be. Something tells me that you'll have to figure that out once you're there."

"No doubt," said Ran. "If I can get the locals to take a liking to me, perhaps they will be kind enough to show me the pass. After all, if they're hunting tigers in the snow and ice, they ought to know the area well enough."

Tanka eyed him. "And what will you do when the locals figure out you're not a trader?"

"Disappear," said Ran with a grin. "Isn't that what we're best at?"

Ran lay awake for a long time that night. The coded message from the clan back in the misty peaks of Gakur had left nothing to question. Ran's orders were clear: go north, figure out if there was any truth to what Kan-Gul had boasted about. He was being sent away from his planned excursion west and redirected north to investigate what would probably turn out to be nothing but the ravings of a madman he'd already killed.

And what if the rumors did indeed turn out to be true? What then? Ran would no doubt be used in some fashion to try to thwart the invasion. That meant even more time away from his quest and more time away from the promises of a beautiful princess. Ran sighed. This was not shaping up the way he had envisioned things in his mind when Tozawa had first given him the wandering-quest directive.

Not at all.

Still, Ran couldn't complain that he wasn't acquiring experience. Nor could he say that things had been dull. He had already surpassed his expectations in that regard. His training had kept him alive, and what his training hadn't prepared him for, real-world experience had quickly taught him to handle.

But the thought of traveling west on the caravan held such allure.

Ran wanted nothing more than to disappear in the night and go with Yasseh's band of merchants at dawn. Once they left Chulal, there would be no one who would know if Ran had done as the clan directed. He frowned, knowing that was not entirely true. The Nine Daggers clan had eyes everywhere—even in the most unlikely of places. Ran might think that his actions could go unnoticed, but he knew that there were other shadow warriors out there. They had been stationed everywhere across the known lands. Each of them would have a communication link back to Gakur. If Ran went rogue and refused to follow the wishes of the clan, then they would presumably start hunting him down. He might get away with it for a while. Years, even. But eventually, the clan would reach out and get its claws back on him. He would either be taken back or simply killed.

He turned over in the bed and tried to find a more comfortable position. Nothing seemed to give him the rest he craved. He couldn't still his mind, despite the years of training. It was something he was completely unprepared for. This wasn't bending some stodgy old rule; this was putting his own desires before the needs of his clan.

When the last bits of night started to dissolve into daybreak, Ran rolled out of bed and prepared himself. Tanka rose soon after and made them a light breakfast of tea, rice, and dried beef. Ran ate without talking.

"You didn't sleep well last night," said Tanka.

"Terribly, in fact," said Ran.

Tanka nodded. "I know what you're going through."

Ran looked up. "And what is that?"

Tanka smiled. "You're thinking that you could go west and no one would know. And if they did find out, you'd be long gone and out of the clan's grasp."

Ran said nothing. What was the point?

Tanka held up his hand. "I'm not trying to get you to admit anything. I'm only telling you that I understand how you feel. Imagine graduating and immediately being told to go to this city. I've been here since I left Gakur. I'm so homesick, it drives me crazy. There's nothing I'd like better than to leave this horrible place and go home."

"Have you asked for reassignment?"

"Three times," said Tanka. "But the clan's needs come first. I've been told I'll be replaced at some point. But when that day might come,

I have no idea." He sighed. "So while it's not the same thing, trust me—I've thought about running away. Several times, in fact."

"What stops you?"

Tanka shrugged. "Maybe I'm not brave enough. There's a funny thing for one of us to say, huh? A shadow warrior not brave enough to go off on his own. I don't know. Maybe it's the thought that the clan would find me some day. Maybe it's the idea of being loyal to the clan no matter what the cost."

"And so here you stay."

"I'm optimistic, though," said Tanka. "Surely one day they will realize I've been here too long, and they'll bring me home. Perhaps as an instructor."

"For disguises," said Ran with a grin. "You'd be marvelous at it."

"I would," said Tanka. He stood up then. "Well, enough of that. You've got a reconnaissance mission to get on with, and I've got things to do." He paused. "I hope that last bit of conversation will remain strictly between us."

Ran nodded. "Have no fear. Just two clan members discussing the state of things. Nothing to it."

Tanka nodded once. "Thank you, Ran. I can't tell you how nice it's been to have someone else here from Gakur. It's going to be tough when you leave, my friend."

"You never know," said Ran. "I might need some help up north. I can't think of anyone I'd rather have beside me than you, so be ready." He belted on his swords and hefted his pack onto his shoulders.

Tanka clapped his hands. "That reminds me. You need a means of getting in touch with me if things are indeed dire." He vanished into a back room and came back with a falk on his arm. The bird sat still, its eyes roving around the room before settling on Ran.

Ran could see the sharp talons and the knife edge of its hooked beak. Brown and black feathers covered its body. Tanka held it up, and the falk took flight once around the room before coming back to rest on the edge of the table.

"It's easy enough," said Tanka. "These have all been trained back in Gakur. This one is trained to return here. All you need to do is put the message in the compartment at the base of its leg and release it with a simple command of 'ichi.'"

"'Ichi.'"

Tanka nodded. "The falk will return here as fast as possible. They don't get excited unless there's danger nearby, so you don't need a hood for it." Tanka clapped his hands once, and the falk took flight again.

"Hold out your arm."

Ran did so without thinking, and an instant later the falk settled its weight on to his left arm. Ran winced, expecting to feel the sharp talons bite into his skin, but the falk only tightened its grip without piercing Ran's skin.

"They're something, aren't they?" Tanka smiled. "This one is called Ryu."

Ran smiled. "I'm sure we'll make quite a team."

"They look after themselves. Once a day, let him hunt in the early evening. Otherwise, he will follow you everywhere, even when he's not resting on your arm."

Ran looked down at the falk, and the bird stared back with unblinking eyes. "I guess I'm as ready as I ever will be."

Tanka clasped his right hand. "Be careful out there. The way north is a dangerous one. And there's no guarantee the people in Kalang-yao will be receptive."

"I'll just have to win them over with my charm," said Ran. "Take care of yourself, Tanka. And thank you for the hospitality."

Tanka showed him to the door. "Good luck."

Chapter Eight

"Where in the world did you get that?"

Ran climbed up in the saddle of the horse and waited for Ryu to perch on his arm again before answering. "I bought him in town. I used to have one when I was a boy. They're excellent scouts."

Yasseh shrugged from his own steed. "As long as he doesn't become troublesome I see nothing wrong with it. Make sure he doesn't spook your horse, though."

Ran glanced down at Ryu, but the falk sat unmoving on his arm. His eyes continued to rove over the vast convoy of horses and wagons, however. Ran looked back at Yasseh who was busy calling out commands, and wondered what he'd just gotten himself into. His orders were to go north and perform reconnaissance in the event of an invasion. Instead, he had disregarded those orders and was heading out of the city of Chulal with a trade caravan heading east.

What would the clan do to him if they found out? Would they track him down and kill him? Would he simply be punished? Ran sighed as his horse shifted its feet. He wasn't sure why he'd done what he'd done. The lure of Cassandra was certainly strong. But Ran sensed there was something else inside of him that was now directing him. All of his life had been spent following the orders of the clan. They'd taken him in after he'd wandered for months. They had trained him to become a formidable warrior and spy. And then they had loosed him upon the world with only the stipulation that he be there for the clan if they needed him.

The first time they came to him, Ran had turned his back on them.

So much for loyalty, he thought with a wry grin. He was thankful to the clan, obviously. Indebted to them, even. Yet something else drove him now. Deep down his instincts told him that journeying west with the caravan was the right thing to do instead of heading north. Ran had no way of verbalizing what the instinct felt like, only that it was stronger than anything he'd known before.

But it was an uncomfortable position to be in. Ran kept turning in his saddle, wondering if Tanka had come down to see him off and even then was watching Ran from the shadows or some disguise. Would he send word back to Gakur immediately, informing them of Ran's betrayal? Or would he remember their talk and keep quiet about it?

Was Tanka even there at all? Ran had lied to him, of course, but if Tanka thought he'd already left town for the Shard Mountains, there was no reason to see if Ran had truly gone off that way.

Yasseh finally lifted his hand, and then entire caravan started off down the quay toward the rear gate of Chulal. Gunj rode one of the wagons, steering the horse team that pulled it. Ran spotted other members of the security detachment riding back and forth among the other merchants and pack mules. The caravan was comprised of ten wagons, numerous other pack mule teams, and roughly twenty riders of lesser stature. Two of the wagons held supplies for the long trip, but the remaining eight all held expensive goods for trading along the route west.

Yasseh led the caravan down the widest street in Chulal and brought the entire convoy to a slow trot before exiting the main gate. Ran watched as he turned in his saddle, took a long look at the caravan, and then waved to someone. Ran turned and saw Ejul sitting astride a horse of his own. He raised one hook in his father's direction then turned his steed and rode off back into Chulal.

Ryu gave a single squawk and shook its head so a few feathers fluttered off its nape. Ran nodded once. "I know."

Yasseh clapped once, and the entire caravan started up again. The city guards held back and opened the rear gate. Yasseh sat at the head of the procession and led the way through the huge stone portal and outside the main gates of Chulal. Ran glanced back over his shoulder but saw nothing to indicate that Tanka was anywhere about. Of course, Tanka was a seasoned shadow warrior. Spotting him would be next to impossible.

Ryu fluttered its wings once, and Ran took that as a sign the falk wanted to fly for a bit. "Go ahead."

Ran raised his arms, and Ryu took flight. Ran watched it circle high overhead before darting off over the nearby hillside.

"Where is he going?"

Ran glanced to his right and saw one of the other security warriors riding nearby. Ran shrugged. "To hunt, I'd imagine. He's quite good at it."

The warrior nodded. "I'm Kuva. I heard you were Ran."

"That's right."

Kuva was broad across the shoulders, and his arms hung like meathooks as he gripped the reins on his horse. "Heard you were the only one of us to get the okay from Gunj. How'd you manage that?"

Ran smiled. "I didn't let him win."

Kuva grunted. "I'd say you're surprising, because your build isn't all that muscular. But then again, neither is Gunj. And that little twerp beat the stuffing out of me. I'm still nursing a sore shoulder thanks to him."

"Appearances can be deceiving, I guess," said Ran. "Isn't that the old saying?"

Kuva rubbed his shoulder. "Yeah. But before Gunj, I'd never lost to anyone."

"There's definitely more to him than meets the eye," said Ran as he watched Gunj steer the wagon he drove. "I don't know where Yasseh found him, but it's clear the man knows how to fight."

"And fight well," said Kuva. "I'm just glad he's on our side." He chuckled. "For that matter, I'm glad you're on our team as well."

"Thanks," said Ran. "Do you know the others that are working with us on this journey?"

Kuva shook his head. "Nope. I only just hired on a few days back."

"What were you doing before that?"

Kuva shrugged. "Nothing good. I think the city authorities were getting ready to chuck me out for being a beggar. I'd nearly lost everything I owned in a card game. Plus, the drink held me fast in her grip, and I indulged far too much. I finally got my stuff together, grabbed my sword, and approached Yasseh. After Gunj put me through the wringer, I was hired on." He nodded toward the front of the caravan. "I owe that man a lot. He could see I was a mess, and he gave me a break anyway. I think that speaks volumes about the type of man he is. You know?"

Ran nodded. "Absolutely. He strikes me as a good man. It would be terrible if anything happened to him while we're on his team."

Kuva patted the heavy two-handed sword strapped to his side. "I'll be damned if I'll let that happen. Not on my watch."

Ran watched him move off to resume his place on the right flank of the convoy. The caravan slowly wound its way up into the low hills that surrounded Chulal. The road was wide and well-traveled, but Ran suspected it would not stay that way for long. The way west was a dangerous one, and larger roads gradually gave way to smaller tracks and trails. Here and there, he could see where locals had attempted to build a better highway, but in other places, the forest loomed in, trying to reclaim the ground for itself.

Ryu returned close to dinner time. Ran sniffed the scent of blood on its talons and knew that the falk had found itself a meal with little problem. As Ryu sat perched on his wrist, Ran considered the bird. Its eyes never ceased movement, even though the rest of its body stayed dead still.

The forests yielded to open fields and meadows. Ran was about to wonder aloud when the caravan would halt for the evening, when Yasseh led them off the road and into the short grass off to the left side. He circled around and rode back.

"We'll set camp here for the night."

Ran looked at Kuva, who only shrugged. A moment later, Ran heard Gunj's voice.

"Ran."

"Yes?"

"Set the order of watch for tonight."

Ran nodded, and Gunj turned back around to steer his own wagon into the grass. Ran rode over to Kuva. "You want first watch? I'll see to it you get your supper."

"Fine with me," said Kuva. He pointed to a nearby hillock. "I'll position myself up there. That should give me a good vantage point for miles around us."

"Good," said Ran. "I'll keep two others on guard per shift, and we'll break it up into two-hour segments. I'm sure we can all use some good sleep tonight. My rear is sore."

Kuva laughed. "That is the truth." He rode off, and Ran watched him for a second before turning his attention back to the caravan.

Gunj was directing several merchants on where to set up their camp. Clearly, Ran thought, Yasseh trusted the smaller man as his primary manager. Gunj never raised his voice, but when he spoke it was with an air of authority that no one questioned. It made Ran all the more curious as to what his background was.

Yasseh came walking over as Ran dismounted and tied his horse to a small tree nearby. "So, are you glad you hired on?"

Ran smirked. "I haven't tried the cooking yet. I'll refrain from judgment until after I eat."

Yasseh watched him for a moment. "You know, my son is convinced he's met you somewhere before."

Ran placed Ryu on one of the branches of the tree and shook his head slowly, as if he was thinking about what Yasseh had said. "I can't recall ever meeting him. Did he say where? I've only been in Igul for about a month. Not much chance of meeting him unless he was in Nehon before that."

Yasseh laughed. "Nehon? No, there's no chance of that. He's probably mistaken, but he seemed so convinced. Strange." The older man shrugged. "Anyway, Gunj tells me he told you to set the watch. Are you getting some food?"

"As soon as it's ready. I'll make sure the rest of the team gets fed as well."

"Good." Yasseh turned to leave.

"Where did you find Gunj, by the way?" It was a simple enough question, but Ran wanted to catch Yasseh as unaware as possible and hopefully get an unguarded answer out of him.

Yasseh stopped and turned halfway back around. "I think it's probably a better idea if Gunj tells you about himself. Give him time and he will. But don't pester him about it. He gets . . . ornery if he thinks you're digging for information. He's a very guarded man."

"Dangerous, too," said Ran.

"Dangerous is probably an understatement," said Yasseh. "Although he seems to have taken a liking to you. I wouldn't do anything to get on his bad side. Once you're there, I'd imagine it would be hard to get in his good graces again."

"Understood."

"And Ran?"

"Yes?"

"Gunj is exceptionally talented at certain aspects of combat. You may have bested him in an open fight, but he has certain . . . skills, in other areas. Do your job and he'll get along with you just fine. If he thinks you're a threat, however . . ." Yasseh's voice trailed off.

Ran nodded then moved off in the direction of the cooking he could smell nearby.

Ran hadn't gotten a great deal of information, but he'd gotten some. And it just made Gunj all the more interesting.

Ran wandered over to the cook tent and smelled deeply the evening meal. A fire already blazed nearby, and big cauldrons of soup were being prepared. Ran's mouth watered at the scent, and then he saw the cook slicing up a great side of beef into thin slices that he paired with cooked potatoes and bread. The cook looked up as Ran entered.

"It's not ready yet."

"Smells incredible," said Ran. "Not exactly what I'd expect on a caravan like this."

The cook smirked. "The master likes to eat, in case you hadn't noticed. He demands the best even on his journeys, so it falls to me to make sure that the entire company eats well. Yasseh says that when men are well fed, they are better able to handle the challenges of an overland crossing like this."

"I like that philosophy," said Ran. "A good meal can do wonders."

"You're the new one that Yasseh hired after you beat Gunj, right?"

Ran glanced around. He didn't like the fact that the cook had phrased it quite that way. He felt certain that Gunj wouldn't like that sort of talk. He shushed the cook and nodded. "I was hired after Gunj put me through that test."

The cook smiled again. "That's not how we heard it. Some of the people who saw it said you took care of him handily. That's no easy feat. Gunj is reputed to be one of the best fighters in Igul. How'd you manage to take him down?"

"I didn't really take him down," said Ran. "We were going at it, and then he simply stopped and told Yasseh that I had some measure of skill in fighting. That's all there was to it. It wasn't some incredible beating one way or the other. Just two warriors going at it. He underestimated me, probably because I look so young."

"Call it whatever you want," said the cook. "It's impressive just the same." He gestured to the beef. "I can get you a serving of this right now if you'd like."

"Before anyone else?"

The cook shrugged. "You're here, they're not. Besides, it's the least I can do. I've got no love for Gunj, and anyone who can hold their own against him is well-deserving of a good meal in my book. Besides, once you get done eating you can let the other guards come and eat."

"Fair enough," said Ran. He grabbed a plate and watched as the cook began shoveling potatoes onto it. A thick slab of beef followed, and Ran took a container of the piping-hot soup as well. "Thank you for this."

"Enjoy," said the cook. He went back to preparing the meal, and Ran turned to leave the tent. As he approached the flap, he sensed someone just beyond it.

Gunj.

As Ran let the flap fall back into place, the smaller man eyed him with a grin. "There's a lot more to you than meets the eye, isn't there, Ran?"

Ran held his gaze. "I suppose the same could be said for you."

Gunj nodded. "I respect the fact that you didn't let the cook hold on to his version of our match the other day."

"It was the right thing to do."

"And yet a lot of these people wouldn't have corrected him. They would have basked in the glow of his praise. Not you, though."

"The truth speaks for itself. You did think I was inexperienced and I used that to my advantage. I doubt I could ever land that kick on you again."

Gunj eyed him for another moment and then nodded once more before passing into the cook tent. Ran stood there a second longer and then left to eat, unsure of how to take the exchange that had just happened.

Chapter Nine

Ran felt full and content as he settled in for his first shift of sentry duty. He'd already relieved Kuva and sent the burly warrior to get some sleep. As Ran shifted in the deep shadows on the hill overlooking the caravan's camp, he felt a cool breeze wash over him, and he shivered in the night. He looked away from the camp and off into the wilderness that extended in all directions. Fortunately, Yasseh had picked an excellent spot to make camp. There were meadows on all sides for at least half a mile. The hill Ran stood on gave him a perfect vantage point, and he would be able to spot anyone trying to creep up on the camp.

If Ejul and his band of thugs really did intend to attack the caravan, this would be a foolish place to attempt it. Ran or any of the other warriors would be able to spot them long before they got close and could take appropriate steps to counter their attack. The question was, would Ejul really do what he'd said he would do to his group?

Ran felt fairly confident that he would. If Ejul had thought nothing of throwing his lot in with Kayo and Magya, then he would certainly have little problem attacking his own father's caravan. Again Ran wondered what would make Ejul betray his father. He couldn't fathom doing such a thing, but then again, Ran had only the foggiest memories of his own father before their farm had been attacked and his family killed. That he could even remember his father at all was something of a miracle, Ran decided.

His eyes scanned the dark, but Ran was careful to not focus on anything directly in his line of sight. He'd long since been taught to look out of the corner of his eyes to see better in the dark. Movements registered better that way. At this time of night, anything that moved meant it was either an animal or a man. Ran's hand stayed on the scabbard of his sword in case he sensed something moving out there in the night.

He shivered again and thought about Cassandra. This journey west would bring him to Valrus eventually. What would her reaction be when they saw each other again? He shook the image of her out of his head and tried to concentrate on watching the evolution of the night. There would be time enough to think about Cassandra later.

There was also the fact that Ran had disobeyed an order from the Nine Daggers clan that he had to worry about at some point. Even now, the elders in Gakur might be deciding whether or not to have Ran killed for his betrayal. But did they know yet? If Tanka had seen him leave with the caravan and informed Gakur, that would be the only way for them to find out. If Tanka had not seen Ran or decided not to tell the clan, then Ran was safe.

He smirked. Safe was a relative term, of course. He was heading west on a highway where travelers were frequently ambushed by brigands. Ran felt fairly certain that the caravan had enough guards with it, but if they were attacked by an overwhelming opposing force, then things would get bad pretty fast. He couldn't worry about the what-ifs, however. At least not right then. Sentry duty was boring enough, and Ran had to force himself to maintain a disciplined mind so he would be alert in case anything happened.

His shift passed without incident, and Ran found his way back to his bedroll a few hours later. With his hand on his long sword and Ryu perched nearby, Ran dropped into a deep sleep by laying on his back and rolling his eyes back under their lids.

At dawn, Ran woke and glanced around. The rest of the camp was still fairly quiet, but Ran was used to waking earlier than most thanks to the years of intense training back at the shadow warrior school in Gakur. Ryu eyeballed him as he rose. He grinned at the bird and then watched as it took off to do some flying about. Ran walked to the water basins and threw some of the cold liquid on his face to help reinvigorate him for the long day ahead. Within the hour, the entire camp had eaten a quick breakfast and the wagons started rolling out of the meadow. Yasseh once again assumed the lead position and waved them all forward.

Kuva found his way to Ran again. "How'd you sleep?"

Ran shrugged. "No complaints. I went to bed and woke up alive. There's something to be said for that."

Kuva grinned. "An interesting perspective. I heard you were from Nehon."

The question was far more direct than Kuva should have been, but Ran nodded anyway. "That's right. I came over to Igul from Hiryu. Do you know it?"

"Never been there," said Kuva. "I hail from Adosa. The journey to Nehon was always deemed far too unsafe for any of us to attempt. The Dark Sea claims many. I didn't want to be another of her victims."

"I was shipwrecked in southern Igul only a few weeks ago thanks to a terrific storm that blew us off course. The fact that I survived was pure luck."

Kuva grunted. "That and your ability to fight. They kept you alive. A warrior spirit is so often misunderstood, confused with only seeking violence. But the real truth is that the spirit of a warrior allows one to endure under the harshest environs. As you certainly found out."

"A philosopher, too?" Ran smiled.

"Probably a better philosopher than a warrior, if truth be told," said Kuva. "But don't tell old Yasseh that. I need the money, and this journey should go a long way toward helping me pay off some debts back in Adosa. I hope to go back there some day and grow old while I make wine."

"Well, I happen to agree with your assessment about the warrior spirit. Most don't understand. And those that claim to are sometimes far worse than those who are simply dumb to it."

"Indeed," said Kuva. "Gunj would understand it probably. If you could get him to talk to you."

Ran cast a glance over at Gunj, who sat astride a horse today instead of a wagon. The horse seemed miles too large for the small man, but Gunj rode it with a sense of authority and the animal obeyed him without question. Ran frowned. What was it about the little man that intrigued him so much? If Gunj had been from Nehon, Ran might even have suspected him of being a fellow shadow warrior. But Gunj hailed from Igul. And northern Igul at that. The Nine Daggers clan would never have allowed him entrance to the training program. But Gunj clearly had a warrior background.

"I think Gunj talks to whomever he wants, whenever he wants," said Ran finally. "If you happen to catch him at the right time, then maybe he'd tell you something interesting. Otherwise, it's probably just wasting your breath."

Kuva nodded. "Agreed. I can't help but think he doesn't feel too inclined toward me. When Yasseh had him test me, I threw a single punch, and then it was all over." He smirked. "As I said, probably a better philosopher than warrior, but there you go."

Ran smiled. "Kuva, your appearance might be one of your best assets. You look utterly intimidating. Those arms are huge, and you look like you could easily kill anyone you happened to look at."

"Thank you," said Kuva. "Hopefully my dreadful appearance won't scare off the women. I'd like to meet a nice girl in the west and bring her back home to Adosa."

"There aren't enough nice girls in Adosa for you to marry?"

Kuva sighed. "I'm bored with them. They all look rather the same, and I want someone different. I've heard tell of a kingdom far west of here where the women are more like warriors in their own right. Adosian women are more content to raise children and do little else. I want someone I can appreciate as a fighter. Strength attracts me, you know?"

Ran thought about Cassandra and how adept he'd seen her in combat. "I think I can appreciate that."

"Anyway," said Kuva with a sigh. "It's still a ways off. But a man can dream, can't he?"

"Sometimes that's all we have," said Ran.

Ryu suddenly swooped down and perched on Ran's wrist. Unlike most times, Ryu gripped him harder this time, and Ran felt the power of the falk's talons coming close to breaking his skin. Ryu also seemed agitated and kept fluttering its wings.

Kuva pointed. "Something's got your friend there upset."

Ran remembered Tanka telling him that the falk would only get upset during times of danger. Ran frowned. "Something's not right. Get to your station."

Kuva wheeled himself around and rode off to the right flank again. Ran kicked his horse in its side and urged it toward the front of the caravan. Ryu squawked as they rode. The bird had obviously seen something on the road ahead. As he rode up, Ran glanced around and noticed that they had come into steeper terrain now. Steeper terrain meant better opportunities for ambush.

Yasseh glanced back when he heard Ran approach. "Everything okay?"

Ran shook his head. "The bird is upset."

Yasseh guffawed. "Maybe it's just hungry. Did you feed it earlier?"

"It feeds itself," said Ran. "Falks don't get agitated unless there's danger nearby. And Ryu is quite obviously agitated now." Ryu squawked once as if to underscore this point.

Yasseh frowned. "What would you have me do?"

Gunj rode up a moment later. "Is there a problem?"

Yasseh pointed at Ryu. "Ran says his bird here only gets upset when there is danger. Do you know anything about those birds?"

Gunj shrugged. "I do not, but I have heard that they are remarkable creatures. Perhaps it would be wise to listen to this one."

Yasseh shook his head. "I've got a convoy of wagons to keep on schedule. I can't simply stop here because a bird, of all things, thinks there might be trouble ahead."

Ryu squawked again and then took flight. Ran watched as it circled high overhead. "That's perhaps a mile away."

"Then we'll soon find out if there's any truth to what the bird claims," said Yasseh. "Keep your men ready, but we're moving on." He rode off, leaving Ran and Gunj behind.

Gunj eyed Ran. "Yasseh is sometimes more a businessman than a worldly traveler." He shrugged. "This is his way."

"And do you agree with him?"

"I'm not paid to agree or disagree," said Gunj. "But I do think he's right. Keep your men ready for an attack. If one comes, it will be quick. These hills have caves aplenty in which to hide." Gunj urged his steed on to catch up with Yasseh.

"My men?" Ran frowned. Since when had he been promoted to captain of security? He turned and waved Kuva over. "Pass the word that there may be trouble. If it happens, Gunj says it will be quick. I'll take the front, and you cover the flanks with the other men."

"Understood." Kuva rode off to relay directions. Ran kicked his horse again and drove to catch up with Gunj and Yasseh. As he did so, he noticed that Gunj had a curved saber, the likes of which Ran had never seen, in his hand. It would be interesting to see him use that in battle, he thought.

Ahead, the road curved around behind a hill. Ran glanced up and saw Ryu circling just beyond it. He shook his head. The location was the perfect spot for an ambush.

Yasseh had slowed to a trot now, and Gunj had as well. They were about half a mile away from the bend in the road. Yasseh held up his hand and signaled for the caravan to stop. Ran heard the snort of horses and pack mules as they ceased their forward momentum.

Ran drew alongside his employer. "That bend in the road concerns me."

Yasseh nodded. "Agreed. The positioning would be a perfect one for an attack. And your bird seems to be circling overhead as well."

"If there was an ambush party waiting, they would no doubt try to shoot the bird out of the sky," said Gunj. "It is, after all, acting a bit like a marker."

Ran eyed him. "You don't think there's anyone there?"

"I don't know," said Gunj. "But it seems a bit ridiculous to imagine a bunch of thieves lying in wait while a falk circles overhead. Don't you think?"

"A lot of people never look up," said Ran. "It's possible they don't know he's there."

Ryu let loose a loud squawk at that point. Ran sighed. "They'd certainly know he's there now." He waited for an arrow to pierce Ryu's side, but none came. Ran shrugged. "You might be right, Gunj. Maybe there's nothing there."

"Excellent," said Yasseh. "Then we can continue."

Gunj put a hand on his arm. "No. Not yet." He looked at Ran. "Ride ahead. See what the bird is upset about."

"All right." Ran eased his horse forward. As the horse sauntered down the road, Ran kept his eyes peeled to either side of him. Spindly shrubs that offered little concealment lined the road. Beyond them, linden trees and tall grass obscured his view. *Someone could hide an army in there,* thought Ran. *And you wouldn't know it until it was too late.*

He approached the bend in the road. Ryu squawked again and then flew down to perch on Ran's shoulder. Ran slid out of his saddle and eased his long sword two inches out of its scabbard. As he walked, he kept his right hand on the hilt, ready to draw and cut in a single motion if he was attacked.

The road curved, and Ran craned his neck to look around it, aware that every eye in the caravan was on him at that moment. If he'd been alone, Ran would have approached this location in a far different manner. But no one knew that he was a shadow warrior. He had to act like a normal warrior, not one trained to infiltrate and conduct reconnaissance.

There.

He smelled it before he saw it. The scent was one he knew all too well, but Ran kept his hand on the hilt of his sword.

The stench of death hung in the air as he rounded the corner. Ran's eyes roved all over, but he saw nothing moving in the brush. Nothing stirred at all.

Certainly not the body in the middle of the road.

Chapter Ten

Ran eyed the body for a few seconds. While he'd never personally seen this, he had heard accounts of robbers using a corpse to conceal some type of booby trap—usually snakes or dangerous spiders. When someone came around and rolled the body over, the snake or spider would bite them. Ran frowned. He had no desire to be bitten by some poisonous beast. The convoy was only a day old; getting injured now would be the worst.

Ran knelt in the dirt track and studied the clothing. Something seemed familiar about the clothes. Ran recognized the pattern; he'd seen it somewhere recently but couldn't quite place it. He moved around and tried to examine the corpse from every angle. As he got closer to the face, his heartbeat quickened. He glanced down toward the arms, but the hands were tucked under the corpse.

Ran used the scabbard to pry it under the corpse and heave it over.

He exhaled as he did so, almost surprised that there were no snakes underneath. But what he saw confirmed for him what he had suspected only moments earlier. He walked back around the corner and waved the caravan forward. As he waited, Ran kept eyeballing the surrounding landscape. It was possible that even now they were being watched. He tried to pick out which of the high hills that encircled them would provide the best cover. There was one he thought a likely candidate a half mile away.

His concentration was broken by Yasseh riding up. "What have you found?"

"You'll need to see it," said Ran. "Come down off of your horse, though."

Yasseh frowned but slid down from the saddle. Behind him, Gunj reined in his horse and slid down as well. As his feet touched the ground, Ran noted that he had one of his hands on his sword scabbard.

Yasseh rounded the corner with Ran and then stopped short. "Is it . . . ?"

Ran nodded. "I'm sorry."

Yasseh fell beside the corpse of Ejul and took one of his son's lifeless hooked hands in his own. Ran heard a smattering of some obscure language, and then turned away to give Yasseh time to grieve. He met Gunj's stare.

"You found him like this?"

"No. He was on his stomach. I turned him over in the event that his murderers chose to leave something nasty behind."

Gunj only nodded. "Good thinking."

Yasseh had recovered himself, and, as he stood, he dusted his pants clean of dirt and dust. "Who did this to him?"

Ran looked at the gaping wound in Ejul's neck. They'd slit his throat and bled him dry before leaving his body in the middle of the road. The only candidates that Ran could imagine were the band of robbers Ejul had been convincing to attack the caravan the other night. But could he tell Yasseh that? Ran didn't think he could without bringing undue suspicion down on himself.

"If I had to guess," he said finally, "I might think that a band of robbers kidnapped and tortured Ejul into revealing the direction of our travel." Ran pointed at Ejul's corpse. "This is a warning that they're out there. Watching us. Even now, perhaps."

Yasseh drew close to Ran, rage on his face. "That . . . is my son."

Ran held his gaze and didn't blink. "I know it. I mean no disrespect to him. But they clearly wanted us to find him here. They wanted us to know what they did and what they know."

Gunj steered Yasseh away from Ran. "He is right, master."

Yasseh let a big gulp of air slide from his lungs. "I know it. Damn it all to the gods. I know it. My poor son . . . my poor son . . ." His voice trailed off, and Gunj nodded toward Ran as he steered him back toward the horses.

The remainder of the caravan trundled up and slowed down some distance once they spotted the figure in the middle of the road. Ran waved Kuva over, and the big man jumped down from his horse.

"What is it?"

Ran thumbed over his shoulder. "Yasseh's son. They murdered him and left him here."

"Why would they do such a thing?"

"I don't know," said Ran. "But what matters now is that we keep our guard up. There's every likelihood that they're watching us even now."

"You think?"

"It's what I would do," said Ran. "They're probably trying to judge our strength and the best time to attack us."

Kuva shielded his eyes and looked off into the landscape. "Where would they hide?"

"Pick any of the hills that are encircling us right now. Any one of them could provide enough cover for an attacking force." Ran wondered if the men he had seen talking to Ejul the other night had recruited others to help them or if they were still the same number. He'd have to assume the force would be large enough to overwhelm the caravan. That meant at least a dozen heavily armed men against Ran, Gunj, Kuva, and the three other guards. Probably some of the merchants and their employees would fight, but not all of them. They were merchants, after all. Not warriors.

"You think the attack will come soon?" asked Kuva, lowering his hand.

Ran nodded. "They will wait for what they think is inevitable."

"Which is what?"

Ran held up his hand. "Wait a moment."

Gunj walked over. "Yasseh says that we are to bury Ejul now."

Ran eyed Kuva. "You see?" He looked back at Ejul. "If we bury Ejul now, we will be attacked either before or during the funeral proceedings."

Gunj sighed. "I tried explaining that to Yasseh. He is insisting that his native traditions be followed, however."

"Is he willing to risk the entire caravan for that?" asked Ran. "Because if we stop to do this, we are handing it over to whoever killed his son. That doesn't strike me as being very smart. And I would think Yasseh would understand that."

"He's just lost his son, Ran," said Gunj. "Perhaps we can all use a bit more latitude in our thinking? Empathy, perhaps?"

"I was hired to help guard this caravan," said Ran. "I'm not trying to be heartless. Or cruel. But I am trying to make sure that we consider all of the eventualities of our decisions. And deciding to hold a funeral right now while we're sitting here surrounded by hills that could easily conceal an overwhelming attacking force is a foolish thing to do. If you don't want to tell Yasseh that, then I will. I didn't sign on for a suicide mission here."

"You are right."

Ran turned and saw Yasseh standing there. The merchant's face looked pale and haggard. But Ran saw enough anger still lurking in the man's eyes that Ran hoped he'd be a decent fighter when the attack came.

Yasseh walked over to Gunj. "He is right. Wrap Ejul's body in the funeral shroud and place him in the back of one of my wagons. We will bury him later, after we are free of these accursed hills. Hopefully, the gods won't be too angered by my actions." He walked away and remounted his horse.

Gunj eyed Ran. "That was fortunate."

"Shall I detail the men to wrap the body?"

Gunj held up his hand. "I'm more familiar with the customs of Yasseh's people. I will take care of it."

"How long?"

Gunj shrugged. "A few more minutes shouldn't matter."

Ran eyed the hills. "I hope they believe that."

"Let them come," said Gunj. "I've seen Yasseh fight when he's angry. It's not a pretty sight. But it is effective. He'll hold his own when we're hit."

"Good to know," said Ran. "We're pressing on though, right?"

"Yasseh appears to be taking your advice, so yes, we are. Let me get Ejul's body taken care of and then we'll keep moving. Make sure your men have their wits about them as we continue. This is going to get tricky now."

As if it wasn't already, thought Ran. He glanced at Kuva. "All right, pass the word to the other men. I'm going to scout ahead of the main caravan. See if I can find any tracks or sign of what we're dealing with here."

Kuva's eyebrows knotted. "You sure that's a good idea, boss? Being out there alone . . . I don't know."

Ran smirked. "Don't call me boss. And I'll be fine. Hopefully, they left some sort of sign when they ditched Ejul's body in the middle of the road. If I can use that to locate them or at least get an idea of how many we'll be facing, it's worth the risk to me."

"Fair enough. Give a yell if you need backup."

"I will." Ran eased through the throng of the caravan and slid up into his saddle again. It had been years since he'd tracked from atop a horse. Ordinarily, he would have preferred being down on the ground, where he could read the sign better. But his reasons for staying on his horse were twofold. First, if he got into trouble, he could hopefully outrun his attackers and at least get back to the relative safety of the convoy. Second, if they were being watched, and the attackers suspected someone was tracking them, it might compel them to attack early. Ran wanted to know what he was facing without giving them any indication of what he was doing.

At least that's what he hoped to accomplish.

From his saddle, Ran looked at the edges of the road. In particular, the scrub brush that framed the dirt highway. He recognized a few species of scrub pine and juniper, but otherwise the flora was foreign to him. Regardless, Ran knew what he was looking for and roughly two hundred feet down the road, he found it.

The broken branch might have been the result of a bird landing on it. Or it might have been due to a large animal passing through the underbrush. As Ran drew closer, however, he saw the impact of a boot heel in the soft earth near the branch. Judging from the lack of wear on the track, it was recent. Ran estimated it was perhaps an hour old. He eased his horse over to a nearby bush and let it munch on some of the branches while he studied the ground. From where he spotted the track, the ground sloped up and away into the hills. A few feet farther up he saw more tracks and counted at least three distinct sets.

Ryu squawked overhead and landed on Ran's arm. The bird perched there quietly. Ran eyed it. "You're not fidgeting."

Ryu's eyes swung and met his. The bird blinked once and then took off again. Ran watched it spiral around the sky overhead, gradually extending its circles as it did so. At the outer edge of its circle, perhaps two miles off in a northwesterly direction, the falk squawked again.

Ran grinned. He'd have to remember to thank Tanka when he saw him again. The falk was proving to be a very useful companion. Ran watched as it came zooming back and then lighted on his arm again.

"Thanks."

Ryu cooed and then settled down on Ran's arm. Ran turned his horse back toward the caravan and trotted back to meet them as they approached. Kuva's face lightened as Ran drew in alongside him.

"Find anything?"

"Tracks," said Ran. "They lead up into the hills. At least three men, but I'm guessing there are many more. They probably just used three to get the body down and then to erase the signs as they retreated."

"Which hill?"

"According to this fellow," said Ran, pointing at Ryu, "there's a hill to the northwest of our current position. That's where they are."

Kuva raised an eyebrow. "We're going to trust a bird now?"

Ryu's head swung toward Kuva, and the falk squawked once at him. Kuva drew back. "What in tarnation is that thing anyway?"

"Falk," said Ran. "They're very special birds, apparently."

"Bred and raised in Nehon," said Gunj as he rode up. "Most people have never seen them outside of that island nation. But they are excellent trackers. Their eyesight is rumored to be extraordinary. If Ran thinks the bird was able to locate the raiding party, then I think it's wise that we trust it. The bird, after all, can see things we cannot."

"You heard?" asked Ran. "About the hill?"

Gunj nodded. "What do you think?"

Ran smiled. "If it was up to me, I'd pitch camp. Make a show out of preparing a funeral. Once the sun sets, we lead a small party out to that hill and ambush them before they can mount their attack."

"Risky," said Gunj. "What if we stumble into them on the way to the hill?"

Ran shrugged. "We'll hear them coming, and we can put an improvised attack in on them still. They'll think that they have the element of surprise when it's us that has it. Even if they have superior numbers, our offensive move can disrupt them. If they haven't planned for it, they won't know what to do."

"Most of these raiding parties are comprised of thugs, not warriors," said Gunj. "There's a chance your idea might work."

"The other option is to sit here and let them work their way into a superior position and attack us. We'll be purely defensive. I don't like waiting to be attacked."

"Nor I," said Kuva. "I say we bring the fight to the bastards and get vengeance for Ejul."

"Don't let vengeance cloud your judgment," said Gunj. "I happen to agree with you both, but I'll have to talk it over with Yasseh." He wheeled away and worked back toward where Yasseh sat. Ran watched the smaller man talk to Yasseh and then glanced at Kuva.

"Here's hoping."

Kuva grunted. "Your plan makes the most sense. Yasseh is a reasonable enough man. He listened to you back at the kill site. He should listen to you again."

"Or at least listen to Gunj. Either way is fine."

"How many of us in the raiding party?" Kuva eyed Ran. "Because I don't want to be left behind and miss out on the fun."

"All of us," said Ran. "It's a risk, but it's a bigger risk to leave any capable fighters behind. Especially if we blunder into a huge force. We'll need everyone there. If we lose, it won't matter anyway. Will it?"

Kuva grinned. "I like the way you think. Big risk, big reward."

"I'm young," said Ran. "Some would say I'm impulsive."

Kuva shrugged. "If it works, who's going to argue?"

Gunj rode back over to them. "All right. Yasseh agrees to the plan. We will pitch camp at the next suitable location and wait." He eyed Ran. "There's just one thing."

"What's that?"

"Yasseh wants to come along on the raid."

Chapter Eleven

A mile farther down the dirt highway, the convoy found shelter under a copse of small fig trees that blanketed a field. Yasseh led them under the canopy and then pulled around before sliding down from his saddle. Ran rode over and dismounted.

"Couldn't have asked for a better location."

Yasseh grunted. "The trees will obscure what they can see. If we light several fires, they may well decide to attack."

"They will," said Ran. "But not until they're sure it's the right time. By that point, we should already be in position to attack them."

Yasseh regarded him. "You're awfully confident this is going to work."

"I am," said Ran. "But it's not mere bravado; it's human psychology. There's no way they would ever expect us to do what we're about to do. They left us a warning, and they probably think that they've got us scared now. Presumably, we will do what any other convoy would do in our situation: pull up and form a defensive position as best as we're able to. They think we'll rally and try to hold them off when they attack. It's what most people would do."

"Not you."

"Not me," said Ran. "Of course, it's not my caravan, but since you've agreed to the idea, then it's important that we do this as quietly as we are able. Surprise is the one thing that will tip the odds in our favor if we find that we are indeed confronting an overwhelming force."

"I still have a hard time thinking it wise that we shouldn't leave any sort of security behind."

Ran nodded. "Let's put it this way: we need all of our seasoned warriors out there with us. And if you leave some of them behind, not only does it hamstring our efforts, but it makes the other merchants in this convoy lazy. They'll leave the fighting to the security and never lift a sword to help. If they know they're out here alone, however, then their survival instincts will kick in and make them fight. That's another win for us."

Yasseh patted his horse and secured a feed bag to it. "You certainly seem to know a lot about how humans think."

"I've done a lot of careful observing in my short time alive. Sometimes the simplest things are the hardest to see. What we're about to do is one of them." Ran cleared his throat. "Now, I do have one question to ask you."

"Yes?"

"Are you so certain that coming along is a good idea?"

Yasseh turned to face him. "As you said, this is my caravan."

"No disrespect intended," said Ran. "But we are going to have to crawl around in the mountains. Forgive me for saying so, but it doesn't look like you've done much hard scrambling in a long time."

Yasseh grinned and patted his girth. "I haven't. Good living makes lazy fools of us all. But I haven't forgotten my upbringing. Long before I was a wealthy man, I used to have to work like everyone else to find food, and I once survived on my own for several weeks when I got lost in my native land. I can wield a sword as well as any man, too. So while I understand your hesitation, there is no need to worry about me. I will be able to hold my own."

"I hope so," said Ran. "Our survival may well depend on it." He moved off and watched as Gunj directed several of the guards to light up fires. He dispatched more of the merchants to gather wood and place it in piles next to the fires. Their job would be to keep the flames stoked throughout the night.

Ran walked to the edge of the canopy and looked to the sky. The sun was fading quickly in the west. Ran estimated they had perhaps twenty minutes before the twilight would consume them. Perfect, he thought.

Kuva appeared next to him. "We've lit the fires. Anyone watching from the northwest won't be able to see much beyond the glow of the flames."

"Exactly what we want," said Ran. "Have the men ready to move out within twenty minutes. As soon as we can use the deepening night to our advantage and steal away unobserved, we'll be on our way. And make certain that anyone staying in camp moves about, to make it seem like there are still plenty of men in camp."

Kuva left, and Ran adjusted his swords. He felt for the package of senban concealed inside of his tunic. The flat throwing blades had been wrapped securely so as not to clink against each other. But Ran checked anyway. Better to check and be sure than risk a noise in the night air. Sound could travel for miles given the right conditions. And with the cool bite to the air, Ran had no doubt that any noise could compromise their element of surprise.

He turned back into the dense trees and saw Gunj squatting near one of the fires. The flames lit up his face and cast shadows into the deep crevices that pockmarked Gunj's skin. The smaller man looked up as Ran approached.

"Yasseh tells me he had a talk with you."

Ran sank to the ground and found a charred piece of wood that he plucked out of the fire. "We talked. I wanted to be sure he knew what he was getting himself into. This isn't the sort of thing just anyone can attempt."

"Indeed. But Yasseh has better claim to come along than others. They did murder his son, after all."

Ran used his thumb and forefinger to pluck off burned bits from the end of the charred stick. He spat into his hand and rubbed the charred ash into the mixture before applying it around his face.

Gunj grinned. "The moon won't be up for hours yet."

Ran smirked. "I'm not as worried about the moonlight as I am other things. Plants and fires from a distance can reflect off of my skin. I'd rather daub it as much as possible than risk giving us away."

"You've done this before?"

Ran shrugged as he applied more of the charcoal camouflage to his face. "I've been out in the night before, yes. No big deal."

Gunj spat into his own hand and started rubbing char on his face as well. "The night is both a hider and revealer of people. It will be interesting to see how your plan works. If it actually does."

"The only danger," said Ran, "is if they have scouts out ahead of the main attacking force. They'll be disciplined and quiet. Trained for exactly the type of thing that we're going to be attempting. If we blunder into them and they raise the alarm, then our gambit is over before it gets a chance to begin."

"I'm comfortable working at night," said Gunj. "The dark hasn't affected me in quite some time. Not since I was a child and my father made me spend a night out in the woods by myself."

Ran smiled. They'd done much the same thing at the shadow warrior school back in Gakur. "How long did it take you to get comfortable?"

"You mean once I stopped screaming?" Gunj chuckled. "A few hours. But once I was able to see better, the shadows didn't look so dangerous. And when I started exploring and seeing how much life there is in the night, I actually grew more and more curious about the nocturnal hours. So much so, I kept going out at night. My father realized his plan had somewhat not produced the results he was looking for. Or rather, it did, but then it went far beyond."

"And here we are."

"Indeed," said Gunj. He stood and glanced around. The twilight was drawing down upon the encampment. "We should get ready to leave as soon as possible."

Ran nodded. He made sure the other members of their small raiding force blacked out their faces. Yasseh saw what they were doing and immediately helped himself to some of the charcoal mixture, streaking his face with it. He turned to Ran.

"How does it look?"

"Fine," said Ran. "You don't have to make any sort of pattern, just be sure that the charcoal breaks up the lines of your face. The darker and less reflective your skin is, the better."

Yasseh took another few minutes to go over his face once more before nodding to himself that all was well. Ran watched him jam a curved saber into his belt along with three smaller daggers, each complete with jeweled hilts.

"Wait."

Yasseh turned. "Is there a problem?"

Ran pointed at the daggers. "Their handles. Those jewels will reflect any sort of light and twinkle as we make our approach. I'm sorry, but you can't wear them."

"These knives have been in my family for generations. Seven, in fact. They are as old as they are priceless."

"I'm sure they are fine weapons," said Ran. "But you can't bring them with you. If you do, you risk all of our lives."

Yasseh frowned. "The problem is with the jewels?"

"That's right."

"Very well," Yasseh pulled out one of the daggers and used its blade to pry the jewels from the handle of the other blade. When he was finished, he used that dagger to pry the jewels from the first.

As Ran watched, the tiny rocks spilled to the ground and laid there until Yasseh scooped them all up and placed them in a small drawstring bag that he tossed to an assistant. "Put those in my wagon." He looked at Ran. "Will that be satisfactory?"

"You didn't need to do that," said Ran. "You could have simply chosen another set of knives."

But Yasseh held up his hand. "No. These daggers go into battle with me. They have served the men of my family for almost a thousand years. I'm not about to go off into the night without the skill of my ancestors to help me should I require it." He tucked the blades away again and turned.

Gunj slid up next to Ran. "He is a proud man."

"I hadn't noticed," said Ran with a grin. "In any event, at least he got rid of the jewels."

"When should we depart?"

Ran looked around. The entire encampment was already swathed in darkness, save for the glow of the fires burning around them. "Now is as good a time as any." He waved Kuva over. "We're moving out. Be ready."

Kuva moved off. Gunj looked at Ran. "He's big. Possibly too big to move quietly."

"Agreed," said Ran. "But what he lacks in finesse he more than makes up for in sheer strength and his ability to instill fear in anyone we come across. Chances are good we're going to need him when we make contact."

"I'd rather it was just you and me on this venture," said Gunj. "We could be there and back within a matter of hours."

"And what if we ran into a force that outnumbered us significantly?" asked Ran.

Gunj shrugged. "It would be a good death, at least."

"I'm not anxious to die yet," said Ran. "I have places to go and a woman to visit in a faraway land. That alone makes me think that dying prematurely would truly be a crime I could never commit."

Gunj clapped him on the shoulder. "The love of a woman will do that to you. Not a bad thing at all."

"But you?" asked Ran. "You're ready to die?"

"Any warrior worth their weight is always ready to die." He eyed Ran. "Even you. You might say that you don't want to. You might talk about this woman. But the truth is, you're prepared to die. We all are. If we weren't, the gods would have chosen another life for us to lead. We are here for a reason. And if we die in the course of that, so be it. There can be no arguing with one's destiny."

"I choose my own destiny," said Ran. "If the gods don't like it, I don't really care."

"You might anger them," said Gunj.

"Maybe," said Ran. "I'd rather take the chance that they get angry with me than live like a sheep being led about by the whims of supposedly divine beings. At least this way, I'm in full control of my life. If that means I die in the process, then I'll take that chance."

"You often take chances, Ran?"

Ran smirked in the shadows. "More often than I probably should. But what's life without risk?"

"No life at all, I suppose," said Gunj. He rested a hand on his sword. "Shall we?"

They moved to the edge of the canopy again, and Ran saw Kuva, the other guards, and Yasseh already waiting for them. Ran checked the position of his swords again, and then looked at the others, checking them over to see if they wore anything that would glint or otherwise reflect light. Each man's face had been darkened, and they had also done the same to their hands. Any other bits of exposed skin were also coated with soot to help them blend in to their surroundings.

"All right," said Ran. "We'll head out on a northwesterly track. If we're right, we should come across the bandits before they have any idea that we're bringing the fight to them."

"If we're not lucky?" asked Kuva.

Ran shrugged. "Then we'll be fighting for our lives before we want to. But I don't think that will happen. My guess is they'll schedule their attack for just before daybreak. Bandits are mostly a lazy lot. They'll want their sleep tonight. And when they go to bed, that's when we'll catch them unaware. There will be sentries to deal with, possibly a scout or two out to report on our camp. Let me deal with them. I can make sure to do it quietly. I'll be at the lead of our column, anyway, so if you see my fist go into the air, that's signal to freeze and not move."

Gunj spoke up. "I can spell you as scout if you get tired. I'm fairly adept at night travel myself."

Ran nodded. "Good, I may need a break. I'll let you know if I do, and we can switch places."

"Fair enough," said Gunj.

"Any other questions or comments?" asked Ran.

There were none, so Ran grinned. "All right then. Let's get going. Remember, our goal is to get to them before they get to us. These are the bastards who killed Yasseh's son, Ejul. When the time comes, strike hard and fast. Surprise is our best weapon right now, so don't do anything to compromise us. It's better to move slow and quiet than fast and noisy."

Gunj added, "If Ran or I call for retreat, get out as quickly as you can. We'll destroy them all if we can, but better to use the element of surprise to our advantage for as long as possible, then escape with our skin intact. We do enough damage without sustaining any, they'll think twice about moving against us."

"For Ejul," said Yasseh quietly.

The other men repeated Yasseh's declaration. Ran took a final look at them and then they moved out into the night.

Chapter Twelve

Ran led them out of the canopy of fig trees and across the highway. Once there, they crept up the gentle incline where Ran had spotted the three separate tracks earlier in the day. His goal was to backtrack and use the bandits' tracks against them. He wished he could have had Ryu circling in the sky, but the falk was sound asleep back in the encampment. If nothing else, it would alert the merchants if Ran's mission failed and the bandits launched their attack as planned.

He couldn't think about that now. In the low light, he swept his eyes up and to the northwest, keeping his sight locked on the hill where Ryu had pinpointed the bandits earlier. As long as they made for the hill, they ought to be all right. Ran knelt and brushed his hand over the ground, feeling for any sign that his eyes couldn't pick out against the dark, rocky ground. He felt a small depression and used his fingers to feel for the edges. Satisfied he was still on their trail, Ran moved again, noting that everyone else had paused when he had. Good, he thought. If they could just keep that up, then there was a chance they'd accomplish this crazy venture.

The incline led them deeper into the hills. Scrub grass swished as they passed by, rustling against the material of their trousers. Ran's footsteps never made any noise as he picked his way ever upward. But behind him, Yasseh seemed to be having trouble with the gravel and small rocks that littered the ground. Ran frowned, but he knew there was little he could do about it. Yasseh hadn't been trained as a shadow warrior, and even if he claimed some knowledge of hard living, the fact was he was now far removed from that life. Luxury, Ran thought, had a way of grinding down a man's edge.

Kuva grunted once and nearly fell. Ran paused the line and moved back.

When he spoke, he cupped his hand over Kuva's ear. "You all right?"

Kuva nodded. "Slipped."

"We need to maintain absolute silence as much as possible. Sound will carry in the night, and they'll hear us coming if we aren't careful. Can you do that?"

Kuva nodded again, and Ran moved back to his position at the lead. He moved out, making a note of the areas around them that would offer up cover in case of unexpected attack. The ground sloped ever up and down, leading them through small wadis and then through concealed valleys that Ran thought could offer hiding places in case of discovery. They would climb, level out, or sink into a small depression and then reemerge only to climb even higher.

A stiff breeze whistled around them that Ran used to search for any unnatural sounds that might indicate that the bandits were coming toward them. He paused, controlling his breathing as he opened his throat to fully let the sounds of night wash over him, but he heard nothing. At the next high point, he checked their position and found that the hill Ryu had pinpointed was only a fraction closer. He glanced back and saw everyone breathing hard. That was to be expected, thought Ran. Traveling at night in near silence demanded a whole lot more effort than most ever realized.

When he motioned for everyone to take a break, the relief was palpable. Ran sighed and realized that if they kept up this pace, there was a chance they'd never make the hill before daybreak. Ran could do it, of course, but the people he traveled with were simply not conditioned to the duress. Ran waved Gunj over.

"Yes?"

Ran gestured to the others. "They're moving too slowly."

"I'm afraid we all are. Even for me, this is quite an effort." Gunj looked around the barren landscape. "I'd forgotten how much the mountains can rob a man of his strength."

Ran reflected on the statement. They were more like mountains than actual hills. From the highway, their appearance had been deceiving. Up here, however, the scope of their magnitude was apparent. And taxing. "If we can't increase the pace, we won't make it to our goal. It's that simple."

Gunj smiled. "You can't push them any harder than they're going now and maintain silence. Moving faster will undoubtedly make more noise. It will no doubt alert our foes that we are coming."

"I know," said Ran. "Which is why I want you to take over and lead them to the hill."

"Me? What are you going to do?"

"I'm going to go ahead and move much faster. I can make the distance easily on my own."

Gunj shook his head. "Is that wise? What if you get into trouble?"

"I've thought about it," said Ran. "But there's no other real option. If I can get to the hill first and see what things are like, then I can come back and we can either attack or formulate an ambush to take them down."

"You can move that fast?"

"I grew up in the mountains," said Ran. "Nehon has a huge range cutting through the country right in the middle. I grew up playing in areas just like this. I'm pretty comfortable moving along at my own pace."

Gunj glanced back down the line. "Yasseh will not like this change. He may feel that his opportunity to get revenge for the death of his son will be lost."

"It won't be," said Ran. "If anything, me leaving you all will only improve his quest for vengeance."

"Fair enough," said Gunj. "You go ahead, and I'll let the others know when you're already gone. That way, we can forestall any debate about it."

Ran put a hand on the smaller man's shoulder. "Keep to this route and head for the hill like we've been doing. If I get into any trouble, you'll know."

"How?" asked Gunj.

"You'll know," said Ran. Then he turned away and melted over the large boulder nearby, vanishing into the night.

Something moved up ahead of him.

It had been half an hour since he'd left the others behind. Ran had slid over the boulder and then down into the next valley before emerging on the other side at a higher elevation. The breeze blew even harder as it compressed between the two walls on either side of Ran.

But the breeze also brought a noise that was out of time with the landscape. And Ran could have sworn he heard the sound of metal on rock. Unnatural.

He slid into the narrow crevice between a rock and the wall of the mountain to his left and waited.

There.

A bit of loose gravel came down past him from the path above. Skittering rocks meant that someone was close.

A shape moved past him in the dark, and then Ran eased out and behind him, coming up quickly as he did so, snaking his arm around the man's neck and yanking him back and off of his feet. Ran used his body weight to take the man down, and, as he did so, he took all of the man's weight, controlling it as Ran sank on his knees and brought him into the ground.

Before the man could yell, Ran's dagger was at his throat. "How many?"

The man's eyes were wide open as he tried to process just what had happened to him. He shook his head, and Ran pressed the edge of the blade deeper against his neck. "I won't ask the question again. How many?"

"I'm a farmer," said the man with a gruffness to his voice.

Ran frowned. He supposed it was possible to work the land around here, but where was the man's farm? The area was dominated by peaks and valleys, and Ran had seen nothing that look like arable land. He pressed the blade again. "You're no farmer."

"I am, I swear it!"

Ran sighed. Had he made a mistake? He used his free hand to rummage through the man's clothing. He came up with a simple knife but little else. If he'd been a scout for the bandits, wasn't it likely he would be more heavily armed?

Unless he was ordered to move fast and then report back. Weapons, after all, weighed more. Ran eyed the knife. There was nothing remarkable about it, just a wooden handle around a full tang blade. The edge was sharp, however.

"Where is your farm?" Ran asked next.

The man pointed toward the same direction Ran was heading. "Just a mile over there."

"And you're out here late at night why?"

The man stayed silent. Ran nudged him again. "Answer me."

At that moment, Ran felt him move. In a flash, another blade appeared in the man's hands. Ran leaned back and away, narrowly avoiding the slashing cut aimed at his neck. As he leaned back, Ran used his legs to kick the man away from him.

Ran came to his feet even as the man launched a new attack. So much for him being a farmer, thought Ran. He backed away, aware that the narrow confines would restrict his movements. In the close quarters, his sword was worthless. Ran used his dagger to ward off the first attack and then cut back at the man. But the man ducked and stabbed in at Ran's groin. If the cut connected, it would be a fatal wound.

Ran leapt away and then lashed out with another kick. This time he caught the man's arm and heard a vague pop in the night. The man grunted and shifted the knife to his other hand. Ran hoped that would mean a less formidable opponent.

Unfortunately, his foe was gifted with using a knife in either hand. He came in fast again, slicing back and forth at Ran's midsection, searching for a killing stab that would end the fight. Ran backed up and then felt his back hit the rock wall behind him.

The man rushed in, sensing an opportunity.

Ran waited until he was fully committed and then pivoted as the knife shot past. As he did so, Ran buried his dagger in the armpit of the man and cut up and in, severing the underside of his arms. Blood seeped out, dark and viscous, and Ran knew he'd managed to mortally wound the man.

The man's knife clanked as it hit the ground and he sank to his knees. Ran moved next to him. "How many of you are there?"

But the man only stared up at him with vacant eyes and a smile. Ran nudged him once, and he toppled over into the dusty dirt. The scent of blood hung on the air, and Ran knew it would bring scavengers. He dragged the body behind a rock and did his best to cover it up. Then he resumed his trek northwest.

If the bandits had dispatched one scout, there was a good chance Ran wouldn't encounter anyone else on his journey. At least he hoped that would be the case.

At the next vantage point, he checked his bearings. The hill was perhaps only a mile away. Ran checked his gear to make sure nothing had become dislodged during the fight and then moved off again, using a cross-stepping pattern to ease through the narrow passes that seemed to be springing up around every bend. He shifted his long sword and then paused as another breeze whistled through him.

He heard nothing.

If the bandits had set the attack for just before daybreak, they would most likely be asleep right then. A sentry would rouse them at the prescribed time, and then they would proceed. Ran needed to get there, reconnoiter the camp, and see what sort of force they had. Hopefully, by that point, the other members of his team would arrive, and they could then coordinate together the best way to attack the bandits.

He glanced back, wondering where they might be. Ran had neutralized the only threat he'd seen so far on the trail, so they wouldn't have to worry about that. Speed was what they needed now. He just hoped they could pour it on and get there in time.

Ran tasted the air. He guessed a light drizzle would be falling by morning. That would make the ground potentially muddy and unstable for fighting. They would need to attack the bandit camp ahead of the rain; otherwise, it would be another thing working against them.

Skirting around more massive boulders, Ran worked his way ever closer to the camp. He sighted an outcropping that looked like it perched high enough to give him a view into the valley beyond, exactly where Ryu had told him the bandit camp lay. As he climbed toward it, he thought about where he would have stationed a sentry to watch over the camp. Not on the outcropping, Ran decided. That would have restricted the man's movements. Far more likely the sentry was positioned closer to the camp, where he could sound an alarm if anything threatened in the night.

But what was there out in this lonely landscape that would threaten an armed camp of bandits in the middle of the night?

Nothing, thought Ran. At least nothing they had thought about.

Sweat soaked his tunic as Ran finished his ascent and perched himself high overhead. With the cloud cover tonight, he didn't have to worry about the moon giving his presence away. He sat on the outcropping with his back to the mountain and stared into the valley below.

There.

He spotted the horses first, shifting and moving in the night as they fed and slept in a patch of scrub grass to the left of what looked to be the main bandit camp. Ran allowed his eyes to track right, but he avoided staring at the firelight. Even from his perch, it was substantial. No doubt the cold night air had forced them to create a fire big enough to keep everyone warm.

Ran spotted no tents, just bedrolls filled with people near the fire. He counted a dozen.

Ran smirked. Twelve people was much better than what he'd thought they might find. The numbers could have been easily three times that amount. But this was a good piece of news and very nearly manageable if Ran and his men timed their attack just right.

Where was the sentry, though?

His eyes tracked all over, but he couldn't see anyone up and moving around. That meant the guard had to be positioned somewhere else. Somewhere out of sight, perhaps. One thing was certain: Ran wouldn't find him sitting high above the camp.

He slid back down the outcropping and then made sure his tunic hadn't ridden too far up to expose his various weapons. Ran would need to get close to the camp to be sure of what they were facing.

Down the path he moved, always careful to make sure his feet didn't send any stones skittering away. He was just about to enter the camp when he sensed movement to his left.

And then felt the cold steel of a blade at his throat.

Chapter Thirteen

Ran's reaction was immediate and instinctive. As he felt the pressure of the blade pressing into his throat from the left side, he went with it, turned and dropped down underneath. Continuing to twist, he drew his own short blade and cut up at an angle, driving the edge deep into the sentry. The movement took no longer than the briefest of seconds to complete, and the sentry was caught completely off guard. His surprise was only evidenced by the startled gasp as he felt Ran's blade slicing into his gut and up into his heart even as Ran clamped his other hand over the man's mouth. The life dropped out of him and he sank into Ran's waiting arms, where the shadow warrior cushioned his fall even as blood streamed out of the corpse.

Ran carried the dead body away, aware that he was stained in the heavy scent of blood now. He dumped the sentry's body behind a large rock and then sorted himself out, trying his best to wipe the blood off of his hands and clothes. It wasn't going to work very well. The blood soaked into the tunic, and Ran wrinkled his nose at the scent of it mixing with his sweat. A hot bath was a long way away at the moment, but Ran permitted himself a moment to think about immersing himself in the scalding water. The soothing effects upon his tired muscles would be wondrous.

But he still had work to do.

Ran moved down the path and into the camp proper. Surveying the scene, Ran counted the bedrolls again to make sure he had the number right. Twelve. To one side of the camp, the horses whinnied softly and stomped their feet. Perhaps they could smell the blood on Ran and knew that he was an outsider. He hoped they would stay quiet long enough for him to make sure the ambush went off without a hitch.

Ran could have stayed in the camp and tried to kill a few of the bandits while they slept, but there was too much risk in it. If just one thug woke up, he'd quickly find himself outnumbered and facing some dangerous opponents. And given the proximity of the bandits to each other, the chances one of them would overhear the death throes of a companion were simply too likely to risk. Better, Ran decided, to make sure that his comrades found the camp and were ready to launch an immediate, overwhelming attack.

He moved back out of the camp via the path and headed in the direction he'd come, hoping that his comrades would soon arrive. It was critical that they attack before the bandits awakened and found the dead sentry's body. If that happened, any chance of a successful ambush was remote.

Ran waited another hour before he sensed something in the distance. A half mile from the camp, he knew that some sound could still reach the bandits, but he was far enough away that he could coordinate the attack when his friends got there. He heard a grunt far off and then the sound of pebbles clattering down the path. Ran almost grinned. He thought it likely that Kuva was the one who had grunted. Most likely the big guy had fallen.

He moved down the path and, using his ability to see better in the night, counted seven shapes heading toward him in the dark. One of them was farther out in front, moving like a ghost. Ran nodded. Gunj. The smaller man had apparently found his footing, after all, and was driving his followers to make better time than they had earlier.

Ran waited until they were nearly level with him before stepping out into the path. When he did so, Gunj nearly cried out. Ran waved him over, and they squatted beside the trail.

Gunj exhaled in a rush. "I didn't even see you."

Ran gestured down at his clothes. "You probably would have smelled me in another moment."

"What is that?"

Ran shrugged. "Blood. There was a sentry. I had to catch him as he fell or risk waking the entire camp."

"You're covered in it," said Gunj. "Stay in those clothes and you'll draw every animal in a ten-mile area to us."

"I'll get changed after we deal with this camp. They're all still asleep." Ran thumbed over his shoulder. "How did everyone else do?"

"Exhausted," said Gunj. "The distance was a great deal more than we estimated, wasn't it?"

"Yes," said Ran. "But it wasn't until we got into the mountains that we could tell that. From the highway, it looked much easier and closer."

Gunj took a water skin from his side and drank deeply. He wiped his mouth and then sighed. "Well, we're here now. We've got to give them some rest before we attack, though. Otherwise, they'll be facing a rested enemy."

"You look as though you could do with some rest yourself."

Gunj smiled. "I'm not as young as I used to be. Certainly I'm not gasping for air like Yasseh, but my joints are creaking from all the climbing we did tonight."

"And how is Yasseh?"

"I think his quest for vengeance has given him all the energy he needed to get here. But he'll still need rest and rations before we fight."

Ran nodded. "All right, we can take a rest. Let's get them fed and watered, and I'll sketch the layout of the camp while they refresh."

Gunj laid a hand on Ran's arm. "What about you? This can't have been all that easy on you?"

"I'm the youngest one here, I think. I'll be fine. I'll get some food and water into me as I brief you all. But I'll be fine."

Ran had no intention of eating, however. He had found that eating before combat made his stomach upset. If he knew he had to fight, Ran preferred doing so on an empty stomach. But he would take water.

As Gunj gathered the rest of the men around them, Ran found a stick and began sketching the outline of the camp. He looked up into the tired faces and smiled. "I'm relieved to see you all here, safe and sound."

Yasseh grunted. "You basically ran here, didn't you?"

"I had some distractions along the way," said Ran. He redirected their attention to the map he'd drawn in the dirt. "Now, let's get into this." He pointed at the small circle in the middle. "The main fire is here. All of them are clustered around it, sound asleep."

Kuva pointed. "What about guards?"

"Only one," said Ran. "I've already taken care of him."

"Which means we need to get this attack underway as soon as possible," said Gunj. "The risk of someone waking up to take a piss is greater. If they discover the sentry is dead, they'll raise the alarm and we'll be dead."

"Figure we hit them from varying angles," said Ran. "If we can hit them at the same time, then they won't be able to mount a counterattack."

"The way they're arrayed," said Yasseh, "we could kill them all and vanish before they even realized they were under attack."

Ran nodded. "It's pretty straightforward. Kill or injure as many as you can. If they somehow manage to regroup, be ready to retreat."

"So why are we sitting here jabbering away?" asked Kuva. "Let's get this done."

"We thought," said Gunj, "that you might like a rest."

"I would indeed," said Kuva. "But not when there's fighting to be done. I can rest later, on the way back to the caravan." He stood and checked his scabbard. "I'm ready now."

Gunj glanced at Ran and shrugged. "I guess we're ready."

"All right. I'll go first, and then each of you pick two bandits that you'll kill. When I give the nod, do the deed fast and hard. Make sure your shots are killing blows. If they only wound then we're going to have trouble."

Yasseh grinned, but there was no mirth in his smile. "They will all die. Twice, by my hand."

Ran had no intention of trying to calm Yasseh down. He couldn't imagine the grief Yasseh must have been feeling, even if Ran knew that Ejul was conspiring against his father. There might be value in Yasseh's rage. If anyone did wake up and they found themselves facing armed enemies, Yasseh would become even more formidable.

"Let's go," said Ran. He led them down the path back toward the bandit camp. They passed the boulder where Ran had hidden the sentry's body and then fanned out around the campfire. Ran slowly drew his short and long sword and watched as the others did the same. As they drew ever closer to the fire, Ran's heart ticked up a notch and he forced himself to breathe and calm it back down.

Ten feet from the bedrolls, Yasseh sneezed.

Ran grimaced as the thunderous explosion erupted from the portly merchant. But there was no time to waste. As soon as he heard it, several bandits woke up and started grabbing for their weapons. Ran shouted above the sudden chaos. "Now!"

He faced the bandit he'd seen in the tavern giving Ejul a hard time. Perhaps he was the new leader of the group. Maybe he'd even been the one to give the order to kill Ejul. Ran didn't know, and he didn't care. The bandit rushed him with a huge battle-axe, swinging it up and over his head to try to cleave Ran's head in two. Ran threw his short sword directly at the man's chest, causing him to lurch to one side to avoid the blade. As he did so, the weight of the battle-axe pulled his balance, and he stumbled. Ran charged in and cut down on the wrists, severing them before turning his long sword and cutting back up at the bandit's throat. Ran watched his blade cut into the thick neck muscles and then keep going. Even as the bandit's head lolled at a horrible angle to one side, he was already dead on his feet. Ran let the body fall away and turned to meet a new foe.

A smaller man wielding two slim daggers surged at him, slashing his knives across his body at crisscross angles. Ran kept his distance and waited for the man to commit his energy to a strike. But the bandit seemed content to stay back, trying to poke and slash at Ran only. The effect was a bothersome fury of would-be cuts that lacked any real commitment or strength behind them to turn them into mortal wounds. In his periphery, Ran could see melee breaking out all over the camp. He hoped his men would be all right, but in the meantime, he had to deal with the double knife wielder.

Ran edged his back toward the rock wall of the mountain, hoping his attacker would think he was retreating. He followed Ran, still waving his blades in front of him. Ran drew to within three feet of the wall and then stopped, using his sword to keep the attacker at bay. The attacker, thinking Ran had run out of places to flee to, now launched an aggressive attack. In the midst of it, one of the slashes became a stab aimed right at Ran's throat.

He'd been waiting for that. As he saw the blade plunge in, Ran sidestepped and dropped the point of his sword. Putting his weight behind the cut, Ran flipped the blade horizontally, and, as the attacker's weight came down, Ran stepped through, cutting with all his strength. The edge of the long sword sliced through the bandit's clothes and into his belly. Ran kept moving, severing the bandit's entrails and leaving behind a horrifying gaping wound. The bandit fell forward onto his feet, desperately trying to collect his guts and put them back into his belly. Before he could do anything, he fell over to his right side and lay forever still.

With two of the bandits killed, Ran glanced around. He saw more bodies scattered by the fire, and his men seemed to be making short work of their opponents. One of the other security guards had chosen a huge fellow to take on, but Kuva stepped in and calmly ran the big beast through. As he dropped, the security guard stabbed him the throat to seal the deal.

Yasseh, for his part, was calmly going around to all of the deceased bandits and plunging each of his family daggers into their hearts. Ran frowned. Overkill did little to excite him. It was unnecessary and a wasteful expenditure of energy better saved for a legitimate reason. But even while he himself would not do such a thing, he found he couldn't really be too judgmental about Yasseh's actions. The merchant had warned them, after all, that he would do exactly this.

Ran heard Kuva yell out and saw that the burly warrior had three men trying to cut him down. Ran dashed over and cut through one of the attacker's legs before the man even realized what was happening. Ran cut his legs off at the knees and then flashed his sword around to land a killing cut at the base of the man's neck.

Kuva roared and swung his massive broadsword around him like a tempest. His blade smacked the two other attackers away, and Ran helped him finish them off.

Sounds of battle tapered off and then died entirely, save for Yasseh's repeated dagger thrusts puncturing the air with the wet smack of steel meeting flesh. Ran looked around and saw that two of his men were nursing wounds, but neither seemed serious.

Kuva laid a hand on his shoulder then. "Thank you."

Ran smiled. "That didn't go exactly as well as I'd hoped it would go."

Kuva shrugged. "Definitely a bit more explosive and not as surprising, huh?"

"Something like that." Ran let out a sigh and only then realized how tired he was. He'd been going since the evening of the day before and here it was about to dawn over the surrounding area. He'd had nothing to eat and only a little to drink. He'd come miles across the land and finished by fighting off some formidable enemies.

"Now there's just the quick hike back," said Kuva. "At that point, we can all rest."

Yasseh had finished his grisly duties and sat on the muddy ground wiping his blades clean.

Ran called over to him. "When we get back, we could all do with a bit of a rest before we push on."

Yasseh smiled. "That sounds like a good idea."

"We can wait a day?"

Yasseh shrugged. "A day won't make any difference in the price of my goods. And since I've gotten vengeance on my son's killers, I see no reason why we can't take a day to give Ejul a proper burial and then rest up for the long trip ahead."

Ran could have fallen asleep right there. But he only smiled and said, "Good."

Chapter Fourteen

After a day of full rest, Yasseh ordered the caravan back on the road west. A convoy journeying back to Chulal passed them in the opposite direction, and the occasion was marked with a brief stop and exchange of news. Ran hung back, hoping to keep his face away from any prying eyes that might mention the presence of a Nehonian when they reached Chulal. The last thing he needed was Tanka learning about his presence on the caravan.

When the two convoys parted ways, Yasseh resumed his position at the lead while Gunj dropped back to ride with Ran for a while.

Ran set Ryu loose and watched as the falk soared skyward. "Any interesting news from the other convoy?"

Gunj frowned. "The usual, for the most part. Reports of bandits and thieves robbing along the trade route. It's nothing we haven't heard before, although they did also mention coming upon the wreckage of a small caravan about twenty miles from where we are right now."

"Wreckage?"

"The wagons were burned. But there were no bodies. It still smolders, apparently." Gunj sighed. "We'll probably see the smoke within the next few hours, I would expect."

"Do bandits around here routinely set fire to the wagons when they're done?"

Gunj shook his head. "No. It wouldn't make sense for them to do so since they'd need to be able to haul away whatever they stole. Burning things usually means something far worse than mere bandits."

"Like what?"

Gunj eyed him. "Slavers."

"They take the caravans as slaves? For what purpose?"

"Does it matter? They'll throw you in chains and march you anywhere they can sell you. Out here on the road, things aren't necessarily as civilized as they might be in the safe confines of a city. At the trading posts along the route, you can find just about anything you might want to purchase. That includes humans."

"I can't imagine it."

"Imagine what? Being a slave?" Gunj took a drink of water and then let the water skin fall back against his saddle. "Most people probably can't. I don't imagine very many picture themselves being a slave when they're young. But the nature of the world works in mysterious ways. The gods have their own plans. And so often they don't tell us what they are. It can happen to anyone, I'll tell you that."

Ran thought about his own life. When his parents were killed he had wandered for months before finding his way to the fog-enshrouded peaks of Gakur and the shinobujin school that became his home for the next nearly twenty years. Was he slave to the whims of the clan elders back in Nehon? Ran wasn't locked in chains and unable to move about, but there was a part of him forever indebted to the Nine Daggers clan for saving his life and giving him the skills he possessed now.

He sighed. And yet he'd already shirked that duty in favor of following the whims of his heart.

"My parents were slaves," said Gunj. "I was born into it."

"You?" Ran shook his head. "How can that be?"

"It just was. My father and mother were taken when their town was captured. They were sold into slavery. Fortunately, they worked for a wealthy family who treated them fairly well—at least as far as slaves go. And when my mother was pregnant, they took care of her. I grew up friends with the head of the family's son." Gunj paused. "We were close friends. And while I was not permitted to attend the training he received as a warrior, I always made it a point to steal inside and watch him going through his lessons. It got to the point where I started mimicking the movements until I could hold my own with a sword."

Ran sensed there was more to the story, but Gunj fell silent. Ran wondered whether it would be wise to press him for more information. But then Gunj cleared his throat and chuckled a bit.

"You all right?"

Gunj nodded. "Just remembering. There were some good memories in those times. Bad ones, too. Unfortunately."

"If you were a slave, how did you get free?"

"I ran away," said Gunj. "But it wasn't that I wanted to. I had to."

"Had to?"

Gunj sighed. "After a while, I got cocky. Young boys always do. I started lecturing the son about the proper way to hold a sword. He didn't like that I'd been watching his lessons and boasted that he could best me in a fight. I knew I could beat him, so I accepted the challenge. We got two practice swords and went at it. I never meant for it to happen. I just wanted to teach him a lesson. But as we fought he talked down to me. Called my family his pets. I lost control. On his next attack, I countered and struck him in the side. It was deep. Mortally so. I was sixteen at the time. And my friend was the same. He died on the end of my sword, staring into my eyes as all the life spilled from his body."

He grew quiet again, and Ran knew he shouldn't say a thing.

"I was a coward," said Gunj. "Worse, I was a well-trained fool. I let my pride get the better of me when I should have simply shut up and gone home, such as it was. But I couldn't do that. I was insulted, and I felt that I had to do something to save my family's honor. Not that we had any, mind you, but I always felt like we ought to be entitled to at least something."

"It must have been tough being friends with him when his father owned your family."

"Exactly. I must have been feeling like that for a while because when I snapped, I truly snapped. Of course, I was then faced with the reality of the situation. I ran. I would have been killed for what I did, and I knew it. So without even telling my mother and father, I ran off into the woods and never looked back. Not once. Not ever."

"But your family . . . ?"

Gunj shook his head. "I assume the worst. No doubt the master of the house would have been so overcome with grief and fury at what I had done that he would have extracted his vengeance upon my mother and father. I don't kid myself into thinking they somehow survived that. After all, look at what Yasseh did to the bandits in the camp."

"How did you find your way into his employ, anyway?"

Gunj nudged his horse. "I wandered for what seemed like weeks.

Living off the land, that sort of thing. Luckily, my father had taught me a lot about how to survive in the wild. Occasionally, I would come across a farm where I would bed down with the animals for a night. But I kept moving. Always moving. I knew that I would be hunted. Somehow I had to find a place to hide. I'd heard rumors about a temple in the south, so I headed there. No idea why. It wasn't like I knew what they did there, but it seemed as good a place as any. When you're panicking, anything can look like it makes sense."

"Did you make it?"

"A couple of close run-ins with the hunters who had been dispatched to find me, but yes, I managed to find it. From the outside, it looked like a terrible place. Just one tall tower built of dark rocks that seemed to pitch at an odd angle as it reached for the sky. They called it Han-dul-yo. I stood outside the wall that surrounded it and simply stared."

Ran smiled. "Did they let you in?"

Gunj cocked his head. "As I was standing there, the hunters finally caught up with me. I heard the sound of their horses and saw them galloping toward me. I ran for the wall and somehow—I still don't quite know to this day how I managed it—climbed over. The hunters demanded that the monks inside release me. The monks told them to leave. That whoever I was on the outside world no longer mattered. I had gotten inside and therefore they afforded me sanctuary."

"That must not have gone over very well." Ran thought about the similarities in their upbringing. Not quite the same, but not entirely different, either.

"It didn't. The hunters attempted to attack the monastery. No doubt they thought that a few old monks would prove to be no trouble for them. They were wrong."

"What happened?"

"It turns out the temple trained boys in an old fighting art called Han-dul. When the hunters attacked, they were met with an opposing force of men who easily killed every one of them. I'd never seen such skill before. They were masters of both unarmed and armed fighting. I knew then that I wanted to learn whatever they could teach me."

Ran nodded. He could understand wanting to have such power. It was what had made him excel in his own learning in Gakur. "How long did you stay with them?"

"Ten years," said Gunj. "They told me they had nothing left for me to learn and sent me back out into the world." He smirked. "I have to say that I thought for sure that I would be met outside the walls by the hunters. That they had waited for me somehow. Of course, that was ridiculous. And I had little to worry about. I was twenty-six years old and a far different person than when I had gone inside. The only thing that had remained the same was my small stature."

"And you found no one waiting for you."

Gunj smiled. "No. So I took to resuming my wandering. For some reason, I had no desire to go back and visit my former home. It was as if that part of my life was no longer accessible. Maybe I just didn't want to face the memories. I'd come to peace with the fact that I'd acted like a fool and a coward. But I didn't know how to deal with the guilt I might feel knowing my actions had caused my parents' death."

"You were young," said Ran.

"I was old enough," said Gunj. "But no matter. As I said, I resumed wandering the countryside. I walked everywhere, testing myself when the gods saw fit to put opponents in front of me who thought they could defeat me. I saw small towns and big cities and just kept moving. I don't know what I was searching for. Peace, maybe? Probably not. More likely I was looking for something I could call a home."

"You could have done anything," said Ran. "Why not travel the world?"

"I needed money," said Gunj. "And I wasn't going to start my new life by stealing. So I started looking for work. The trouble was, no one wanted to hire me. Because I'm smaller than most men, they never even gave me a chance. It was around that time I found my way to Chulal. I met Yasseh one day when he was arguing with another merchant who was trying to cheat him. I saw right away that Yasseh was being cheated. But this other merchant thought that since Yasseh was an outsider, it somehow gave him the right to rob him."

"You stepped in?"

Gunj smiled. "Let's just say I managed to convince the other merchant that cheating Yasseh was not the best thing to do. He agreed."

"And Yasseh hired you?"

"Not right away. While he was grateful, he wasn't completely convinced. So he set up a bit of a gauntlet for me. Ten men all offered a big bag of gold if they could best me. None of them were successful, and I took the bag of gold for myself."

"Yasseh must have loved that."

"I've been with him ever since. He treats me fairly, and I have no complaints. Until you arrived, I was pretty confident that there wasn't anyone better trained than me out there. You certainly put that theory to the test."

"My teachers were always fond of telling me that there is always someone out there who has been training longer, harder, and better than you. It's tough to remember that, but I've found it to be true. Humility can keep you alive."

"Confidence isn't always a bad thing," said Gunj. "Provided you know how best to use it."

"Indeed."

Kuva's voice rang out from the head of the caravan. "Smoke!"

Ryu's squawk overhead came a moment later.

Gunj frowned. "It seems we have arrived even earlier than I expected."

"Or the traders had their distances off," said Ran. He eased his horse forward until he was next to Kuva and Yasseh.

In the distance, Ran could see the smoldering husks of wagons. His right hand dropped to the hilt of his sword.

Gunj frowned. "Be on your guard. Kuva, put two riders out on our flanks. We don't want any nasty surprises coming up on us."

Kuva signaled for two men to branch out from the convoy. The rest of the caravan eased closer to the scene of devastation. As they rode closer, Ran spotted two bodies amid the burning wrecks, but their skin had been incinerated somehow. They were as black as the smoking wood that remained of the wagons.

"Not as small as what the traders led us to believe," said Yasseh. "It's possible this is another caravan?"

Gunj shrugged. "It's possible, but they would have been seen by the other convoy. More likely they got the distance wrong and we were closer than we thought."

Ran scanned the area. Something felt strange about this. As his eyes swept the ground, he caught something twinkling underneath a wagon husk. He slid from the saddle and walked over. As he did so,

Ryu swooped down and squawked once before settling on his shoulder. Ran looked at the falk. "You sense it, too, don't you?"

Ryu squawked and took flight again, leaving Ran with his thoughts as he drew closer to the gleaming object. It caught the sun's rays as it lay partially buried in the dirt.

"What is it?" asked Gunj.

Ran knelt in the soft earth and plucked it free. Bits of earth clung to it, but he brushed those aside.

And then felt his stomach lurch.

The ring was small. Too small for any of his fingers. It had been made for a smaller hand. Ran remembered seeing it as if it had happened only yesterday, when, in fact, it had been nearly two months ago in the forests back in Nehon.

"Ran?"

He glanced back at Gunj. "Yes?"

"Are you all right? You look as if you've seen the dead."

I hope she's not dead, thought Ran. He glanced at the ring he held and then squeezed it tight. It belonged to Princess Cassandra.

Chapter Fifteen

"What is it?"

Ran turned, aware that Gunj had seen his reaction. "A ring I think belonged to a friend of mine. But she should have been many leagues to the west by now." He paused. "At least, that's where I thought she'd be." He shook his head. "Something must have delayed her. And apparently she was with this caravan."

"Are you sure it's hers?" Gunj gestured around them. "There might be others like it. Someone could have stolen it from her even."

Ran smiled. "Not this woman. She would have fought a thousand men to keep it. She would have killed them all, too."

"That must be some woman," said Gunj. "In any event, just because you found the ring doesn't mean she's . . . dead."

"Where could she be then?"

Gunj pointed at an arrow jutting out of the burned framework of a wagon. "You see the fletching on that arrow?"

"I don't recognize the feathers they used," said Ran studying the end of the arrow.

"That's because they don't use feathers. They take their fletching from an animal called a laraxae. It's a bizarre creature with fanlike protrusions near its head. That's what they use for their arrows."

Ran eyed him. "Who?"

"Mung slavers. That's who attacked this column."

"You sure about that?"

"I'd stake my life on it," said Gunj. "I've seen enough of their handiwork over the years since I started working for Yasseh. This is definitely one of their attacks. It's their custom to burn everything they can't take with them to sell elsewhere."

Ran felt the ring in his hand and saw another image of Cassandra in his mind. "Where will they go? With the people who were in this caravan, I mean."

Gunj sat down on his haunches and rubbed his chin. "Could be any number of trading posts along the route. Or they could make their way farther north. There are outposts and towns along the mountain border that would no doubt pay handsomely for a fresh load of slaves." He sighed. "Mung slavers are quick and ruthless. They appear out of nowhere, strike, and then vanish before they can be tracked."

"No one's ever tried to stop them?" asked Ran.

"A few years back one of the merchants got tired of their attacks. He tried to put together a group. They rode out convinced that they were going to be victorious and come back as heroes."

Ran glanced around. "What ended up happening?"

"I don't know," said Gunj. "No one ever saw them again."

Ran looked back at Gunj. "I need to find them."

Gunj shook his head. "You don't find the Mung; they find you."

Ran ducked without thinking as his senses detected the sound of the arrow being fired. He felt the air break around his head. The arrow passed through where his skull had been a half second before. Ran's hand went to his sword, and he ripped it free of his scabbard in the next half second.

"Riders!"

The call came from Kuva. Ran glanced back at Gunj.

And nearly froze.

The arrow meant for Ran's head had embedded itself in Gunj's chest. The smaller man was rocked back on his seat, staring down at the thick shaft of the arrow jutting from his upper torso. Ran rushed to his side and knelt by it. The force of the impact had sent the arrow nearly all of the way through Gunj's body. Just a few inches of the shaft showed in the front. Dark red blood was already pooling at the entry point.

Ran glanced behind and saw the barbed tip jutting out of Gunj, just under his shoulder.

Gunj put a hand on Ran. "Don't worry about me. Get to them before they arrive. Strike first."

Ran didn't wait. He leaped back into the saddle and swung about. Kuva was right there with him.

"Plan?"

Ran shook his head. "Don't have one. Just kill the bastards."

Kuva grinned. "My kind of plan." He wheeled about and galloped toward the approaching band of riders. As Ran raced to join him, he could see the riders all clothed in black mail adorned with animal skins. They wore head caps of mail instead of helmets, and they appeared armed with short swords and compact bows. As one of the guards Kuva had sent out to the flank came racing back to join them, he was shot by one of the mounted archers. Another arrow appeared in the man's chest a moment later, sending him toppling from his saddle and into the ground. Two more arrows pierced him there as he tried to stand. He slumped back to the ground and lay still.

Ahead of Ran, three riders zeroed in on his position. Ran waited until he was close, then wheeled about to his left, using the farthest rider to his left as cover from the other two. As he swerved, he cut horizontally with his long sword and gutted the man on the horse. Fighting with his long sword on horseback wasn't the best use of the weapon, but as with every other skill he possessed, his elders back in Gakur had made sure he was able to fight regardless of the condition or environment. Ran gave silent thanks to them and whirled about to meet another attacker.

Kuva's roar sounded across the battlefield as he clashed with more riders. Kuva used his broadsword and cleaved two other attackers before they could punch their swords into him. He paused and then turned about to try to get closer to Ran.

Ran had little time to appreciate how well Kuva fought. Another rider came screaming at him, and Ran narrowly missed having his head sliced off by the slashing cut of the short sword. As he ducked, another arrow zipped past. The Mung slavers apparently didn't care about injuring their own in the process.

Ran brought his long sword overhead and cut down on the mounted attacker. The rider ducked right, but Ran adjusted his cut midway and sliced into the black mail. His blade only paused a moment before severing the mail links and biting deep into the clavicle of his attacker. Ran twisted his blade, and it sank deeper into the man's neck, spraying blood out into the air. He slid from his saddle as Ran yanked his sword free.

The sound of a horse behind him made Ran think he was about to get killed. He turned and saw Yasseh urging his horse on to faster speeds. The portly merchant raced into the fray hacking and cutting with his sword. The clang of steel on steel sounded over the grunts of men being killed. For a moment, it looked like the Mung slavers might fall back in the face of the stiff resistance they'd encountered.

But then they surged back ahead, fueled by reinforcements from somewhere to the rear. Ran saw more riders joining, and, on a hillside to the left, three archers were sending arrows screaming into the midst of them all. One of them found the other guard that Kuva had dispatched, punching into the man's eye socket and exiting the back of his skull. He dropped to the ground and disappeared under the hooves of the horses fighting nearby.

Ran winced and turned to meet another rider. The man cut furiously at Ran, who could barely block the assault. Using his long sword with one hand put him at a serious disadvantage. He let go of the reins and drew his short sword as well, using the two blades in tandem as if they were a windstorm. As his attacker's sword came down, Ran parried it with the short sword and chopped down with his long sword into the man's mail head-covering. Again, the superb Nehon blade made short work of the mail rings and cut into the skull. The attacker jerked spasmodically for a moment and then dropped to the ground when Ran's sword came free.

They were losing, however. Ran knew they simply didn't have the numbers to keep the Mung at bay. Worse, while the riders had kept Ran and the security team busy, other slavers had already begun assaulting the caravan itself. Screams of the dead or dying fell upon Ran's ears. If they kept this up, the Mung would kill everyone here and be content with taking what Yasseh's caravan carried.

Ran found himself near Yasseh. The merchant had an arrow jutting from his side and looked pale. Ran could see the shaft had gone deep; perhaps it had entered his lung. Yasseh's eyes were losing their brightness. Another arrow shot past but plunged into the ground.

Yasseh gripped Ran by the arm. "We are lost."

Ran shook his head. "We still have fight left in us."

Yasseh tried to smile, but a bit of blood came from his lips. "End this. Surrender now and those left will live."

What sort of life would it be? thought Ran. But Yasseh was right. If they didn't surrender, the Mung would simply kill them all. As his mind whirled, Yasseh pressed something into his hands.

"The last of my family daggers. Take it. Hide it on you. You may yet get a chance to use it."

Ran slid it down the front of his tunic.

Yasseh raised his right hand and called out then in a voice that was stronger than Ran expected. "Hear me! We surrender!"

A hush settled over the scene. Ran saw Kuva's face curl into a huge frown of disappointment. Even though he bled from several wounds, the big man showed no signs of wanting to stop and seemed perfectly content to continue fighting until he died. Yasseh was his boss, however. Even here and now. So Kuva drew himself up short and waited.

From somewhere behind the black mail raiders, Ran heard a voice. "Throw down your weapons."

Ran glanced at Yasseh, but the merchant had already ditched his sword. Ran looked at his swords. He might not have the same love of them that a Murai back in Nehon would, but the blades had served him well and he was loathe to let them go. He had no choice, however. With a grunt, Ran threw the blades off the left side of his horse. He saw Kuva do the same.

"Dismount," came the voice again.

Ran sighed and slid off his horse. The ground was slick with blood, and he held onto his horse to keep from slipping.

Yasseh dismounted awkwardly and fell to the ground, punching the arrow shaft deeper into his side. Another gasp of blood erupted from his lips, this time bright and pink. Ran knew he didn't have much time left.

The Mung raiders separated and another man rode forth. In contrast to the rest of the mailed riders, he wore only a cream-colored robe that draped over him like a large blanket. About his head, a turban of the same material hung low across his heavy brow. The texture of his skin reminded Ran of a brown snake, but his teeth were incredibly white, and he smiled as he approached Yasseh.

"My name is Iqban. Am I correct in thinking you are the leader of this caravan?"

Yasseh managed to get to his feet and gave a slight nod. "I am, indeed."

"No longer," said Iqban. "You have surrendered to me. I am sure you understand that you no longer have any control here."

Yasseh clutched at his side and mumbled a quick "Yes."

Iqban smiled again. "Are you hurt? I'm afraid I must apologize for the actions of my men. They sometimes get a bit too rowdy when it comes to securing for me the things that I sell."

"People," said Yasseh.

"Indeed," said Iqban. He looked down at Yasseh's side. Blood now ran freely out of the wound. "That looks terribly painful." He gestured to the wound. "May I inspect it a bit closer?"

Yasseh wobbled back and forth and seemed unstable on his feet. Iqban didn't wait for him to agree to the inspection. The slaver simply walked over and peered closer at it.

"Yes, I'm afraid that is rather a bad wound." He stood up and clucked his tongue once.

Ran heard the arrow release, and a moment later it impacted Yasseh in the middle of his skull. The tip of the arrow punched out the back side of Yasseh's skull. Incredibly, the merchant stood there with the arrow quivering in his head.

Iqban chuckled. "Amazing." Then he simply placed one hand on Yasseh's chest and sent him toppling backward. Yasseh landed on the bloody ground and lay still.

Ran frowned. "You didn't have to do that."

Iqban eyed him. "Actually, I did. He was nearly dead anyway. Isn't it better this way? I put him out of his suffering. If you think about it, I was being rather kind. A bit more kind, mind you, than I normally am."

Ran said nothing and waited for the slaver to finish surveying the scene. "Only four left alive?" He sighed. "That's not exactly what I would call a good haul on a day like this." He glanced at Ran. "What is your name?"

"Ran."

"And that other man over there, the big beast? What is he called?"

"Kuva."

Iqban nodded. "There now, you see? We're getting along fine. At this point, we'll be fast friends soon enough." He paused. "Well, perhaps not friends. But you'll certainly get to know me a bit better."

Lucky me, thought Ran. Could he make his escape? There were at least twenty heavily armed slavers around him. The chances of him being able to jump into the saddle and be away without taking a dozen arrows in his back were slim. Besides, if Iqban had taken Cassandra captive, then Ran needed to know where she might be so he could rescue her.

"Call your man over here."

Ran looked at Kuva and nodded. The big warrior walked over and stood next to Ran.

"Shouldn't have surrendered," he whispered.

"It was Yasseh's decision," said Ran. "We still worked for him at that point."

"No longer," said Iqban. "Now you are my property. If you do what you're told, I might treat you well. If you disobey any of my orders, then I will punish you. I can promise you this: my punishments are often far worse than what you might imagine."

"Where are we headed?" asked Ran.

"North," said Iqban. "But you needn't concern yourself with your destination. I'm grateful you and Kuva are able to walk at least. Strong men like you are exactly what my customer needs for his rather interesting project."

Ran sighed. After all of the trouble he'd gone through to journey west to try to find Cassandra, he was now heading north. Back to the place that his clan elders wanted him to investigate. It was almost as if the universe was telling him that he couldn't fight against his destiny.

Wherever it might lie.

Chapter Sixteen

As they walked north, the sky behind them was stained with a thick black smoke from where the Mung slavers had set the caravan afire. Whatever they couldn't take they set ablaze, including the bodies of the dead—both theirs and those from the caravan. Ran cast a glance over his shoulder at the dark skies and shook his head. Such a waste of life.

Kuva strode next to him, constantly inspecting his wounds for any signs of infection. "Never know what the bastards might have tipped their arrows with. No doubt this lot doesn't tend their weapons well, either. A man could get any sort of sickness from a touch of their blade."

"You're alive," said Ran. "That's something, at least."

"Aye," said Kuva. "But for what sort of life are we headed? You trust what this Iqban says?"

"I don't trust anyone," said Ran. "It's easier going through life thinking everyone around is beholden to some sort of treachery. That way, when you do come across someone who betrays you, it's not much of a surprise."

Kuva grunted. "There's a fair bit a wisdom in that, I suppose. Not sure how much I want to go around thinking everyone's out to get me, though. Not much room for having a good time with that line of thought, I fear."

"Granted. But neither is there room for surprise."

The wagons the slavers had taken from the caravan trundled along the thin trail they'd been following for the past six hours. Iqban had immediately ordered the prisoners off the highway and into the hills. A few miles away, they'd come across a small track that they now followed. For all intents and purposes, it looked like little more than a game trail, but Ran suspected the slavers had made it and used it to journey back and forth among their clients.

In addition to Ran and Kuva, the slavers had taken two of the merchants prisoner. Ran had no idea who they were, but the men were both older and heavyset. Ran doubted how long they'd last walking to their new position in life. He wondered if Iqban would simply kill them rather than have them slow down the caravan. It would probably come down to a matter of value: could Iqban get more money for them or did it make better financial sense to simply kill them?

Gunj had apparently died back at the scene of the attack. Ran had last seen him clutching at the arrow he'd been shot with before the chaos of battle had forced Ran to leave him behind. In the wake of the battle, Iqban's men had only pulled the two terrified merchants from the wreckage of the wagons.

Everything else was burned.

As they marched north, Ran kept his eyes glued to the sky. Ryu had to be out there somewhere. No doubt the falk would be wondering why Ran wasn't riding his horse any longer. Ran just hoped the bird had enough sense to stay away from the slavers. Still, he smiled at the thought that he had a friend out there.

"Still don't know why we surrendered," said Kuva. "We could have killed a few more of them, if you ask me."

"We could," said Ran. "And then we'd be dead right now as well."

"Better to die than live the life of a coward. It's a good thing none of my old friends were there to see it. I'd never live it down back in the halls of Suba." He shook his head. "I have to say I never figured you being one for such a thing as surrender."

Ran smiled. "There isn't always shame in throwing down your blade. You get a chance to see if the gods have other plans in store for you." Ran thought about how dishonorable the Murai of his homeland would find such an action, however.

"Are all warriors like that back where you're from?"

"Not all," said Ran. "The Murai who dominate Nehon would consider surrender a dishonorable act."

"I agree with them," said Kuva.

"Of course, they also think that ritual suicide is something that brings them honor."

"What did you say?"

Ran smiled. "Ritual suicide. First they make a horizontal incision in their lower belly using a long knife. Then a vertical cut up toward the heart. I imagine such a thing takes extraordinary control. But they do have to this, mind you, without uttering a single sound. To do so is also considered dishonorable. So they have a second—usually a close friend—stand behind them with their long sword at the ready. When the second judges the pain is about to become too great for the warrior to handle, he cuts the man's head off to save him from disgrace."

Kuva eyed Ran. "You're not funning with me, are you?"

"Not a chance."

"And this way of taking their own life . . . They think it's . . . honorable?"

"Oh, absolutely. The Murai are honor-bound to a code of ethics and morality. They're amazing warriors, but a bit too strict for my liking in how they live their lives."

Kuva stayed silent for a moment. "I guess maybe surrender isn't entirely a bad thing."

Ran nodded at the iron cuffs they wore, through which a thick chain had been threaded. "These present no real difficulty for me. But I have my own reasons for wanting to see where the slavers take us. There's a good bet it's going to lead me right where I need to be."

"Which is where?"

Ran eyed the horizon. A line of imposing jagged mountains topped with arctic peaks rose out of the hills like an enormous wall. "I'm not entirely sure yet. But I'll bet it has something to do with those mountains."

"Those mountains." Kuva sighed. "If we're headed for those, then it's a good bet we'll die there."

"What makes you say that?"

"I've heard stories. Some false, no doubt. But some true as well. And none of them has ever had a happy ending."

Ran clenched his jaw. Was Cassandra somewhere in those mountains? Would he ever see her again? He glanced at Kuva. "I don't intend to die anytime soon. Keep your wits about you, my friend, and there's a good enough chance that we'll both come through intact."

***

Ran didn't see Ryu for the next three days. With each successive hour of walking, the mountains ahead of them rose higher and higher until they started to block out the sky. A cold breeze swept over their frosted tips and blew headlong into the valley through which Iqban's convoy traveled. Kuva shivered as they walked, and Ran wondered if the big man had the tenacity to endure the lower temperatures. Each time the wind blew, Kuva would grunt and mutter. It earned him a quick lash of a whip from a guard at one point.

"This damnable cold doesn't bother you?"

Ran shrugged. "It's cold, yes. But so what? There's nothing that we can do about it right now. No fire to keep us warm. No real sunlight to warm our skin. So it's bad. I just have to find a way to accept it and keep moving. That's the only thing that's going to help: if we get to our destination faster and out of this weather."

Kuva shook his head. "I wish I had the same attitude that you do."

"You can. Just acknowledge the cold weather and then forget about it." In an instant, Ran was back in the mountains of Gakur. The wind howled and tore around him as he was led to the steep precipice. One of his instructors, Miyama, stood near the edge of the cliff, holding a thick rope. As Ran approached, he smiled.

"A beautiful day, wouldn't you say?"

Ran shivered in the ankle-deep snow. "It's freezing out here, teacher!"

Miyama had glanced at the sky. "Is it? I hadn't really noticed."

Ran shook some flakes out of his face. "Aren't we always told to be aware of our surroundings?"

"Indeed," said Miyama. "Unless that awareness intrudes on our inner peace."

"I don't understand," said Ran.

"You will," said Miyama. "Hold out your hands."

Ran did, and Miyama quickly bound them. He stepped back and motioned for Ran to join him by the edge.

"The problem with awareness is that while it is a vital tool you must use every day of your life, we must also be able to reduce our awareness to the point that we can, at times, defy reality." Miyama squatted down and tied a thick rope around Ran's feet before standing again.

Ran glanced at his feet. "What do you mean by that?"

"Our awareness informs us, but it can also imprison us by placing limits on what we view as possible, given the reality that we see around us. This weather is a perfect example. Your awareness tells you that it is extremely cold, and, as a result, you should feel that cold. You should be shivering and trying to get warm. While it is true that it is indeed cold, there will be times when you must be able to shut off that awareness and free yourself from any limitations in order to survive." Miyama nodded toward the edge of the cliff. "Now, if you would please . . . walk over the edge."

Ran looked down at the rope around his feet and swallowed. Another gust of wind tore at his exposed skin, and his teeth chattered harder. He moved to the edge and looked at Miyama. "You won't drop me?"

Miyama laughed. "Why would I do such a thing? The Nine Daggers have invested a great deal of time and effort in your training. We're not about to simply lob you off the mountain. The rope will hold, I assure you."

Ran sat down and then eased off into the empty space. As soon as he swung out, the rope caught at his feet and turned him upside down. Blood immediately rushed to his head, and the wind blew him perilously close to the jagged rocks on the side of the mountain.

Miyama's face appeared down by his feet, above him on the cliff. "You are now suspended upside down over a cliff in the middle of a winter storm. That is what your awareness will tell you. It will no doubt also tell you that you are freezing to death, that you will be smashed against the mountain and die a horrible death."

Ran's teeth chattered so much he could only nod.

Miyama smiled. "Your task on this fine day is to shut your awareness off. To close out the distractions of reality and instead focus inwardly on your true essence. Find your *hara*. Find your inner peace. When you do so, the limits of perceived reality will fall away, allowing you to do things that you have never even imagined."

Miyama's face disappeared.

Ran felt a flood of panic sweep over him. "Wait! Where are you going?"

Miyama's face reappeared, still wearing a big smile. "Where am I going? I'm going inside. It's freezing out here." His face vanished, leaving Ran dangling over the cliff.

A blast of wind buffeted him against the rocks, and Ran screamed for Miyama to come back. He didn't want this. He didn't want to deal with this task now. He wanted to be back inside, where it was warm and cozy. Ran wanted to be anywhere but where he was.

But that was his reality.

His eyes stung and his head pounded as more blood flowed into it from his feet. What was the point of hanging him upside down? Couldn't they have just as easily let him sit in the snow? He was shivering uncontrollably now, and each shiver seemed to send him closer to the side of the mountain when the wind blew.

What if Miyama was wrong? What if the rope broke? Ran risked a glance down and knew that from this peak to the valley floor was at least an eight hundred foot drop. He'd be smashed to bits on the rocks all the way down. More panic assailed him, and Ran felt his muscles tightening under the strain of thinking he was about to die.

Damn them all, thought Ran. Damn the Nine Daggers to hell for putting him through this: Anger made his heart beat faster. His face felt flushed, but not from the warmth of his inner self; from the rage he felt boiling in his veins. He'd do this damned task just to prove them wrong. They'd pull him up and see that he'd nearly frozen to death and still hadn't been able to find his *hara*. As soon as they did, Ran would lash out. He'd scream at them and tell them they were all crazy. Then he'd leave. Make his own way in the world. He didn't need them anymore.

Bastards.

Ran imagined what it would be like to be sitting in front of a blazing fire right then. Feeling the warmth of the flames licking at his face, making him sweat. He saw himself seated before a blazing hearth that throbbed as the flames danced in front of his eyes. With each new flame that sprouted up, Ran felt a throb in his lower belly. It was almost as if a pulsing energy resided there. Slowly, as he recognized the pulse, it spread through his body. Slowly at first and then more rapidly. From his stomach it spread up and down, eventually reaching his furthest extremities.

Ran forgot about the wind. He forgot about the snow. And he even forgot about the fact that he was dangling off the side of a mountain. He lost himself inside of his being.

Without giving it much thought, Ran reached up toward his feet for the rope that secured him. Getting his hands around the rope, he pulled himself up, back toward the cliff. The muscles in his arms strained. Sweat cascaded down his face as he pulled himself ever closer to the top of the cliff. Ran forgot about everything except for the goal of reaching the cliff. He pulled harder and harder until he at last scrambled over the lip and stood once more atop the cliff.

Ran untied his feet and then his hands. He stood there in the swirling blizzard and smiled.

Sweating.

Miyama stood there as well. Smiling.

"Ran!"

He blinked. The frozen mountaintop in Gakur vanished. Ran stood next to Kuva again.

"Where the hell did you go?" demanded Kuva. "It was like one moment you were here and the next you were off somewhere else. You just kept walking."

"Sorry," said Ran. "I was just remembering something."

"Must have been some memory," said Kuva. "You've been walking for hours like that."

"Hours?"

Kuva nodded up ahead. "Looks like we're almost there, doesn't it?"

Ran looked. The mountains that had been farther away only a short time ago now rose before them. Huge. Ominous.

They could swallow this entire valley, thought Ran. And us along with it.

Chapter Seventeen

"They don't expect us to climb that, do they?" Kuva nodded at one of the largest mountains ahead of the convoy. "There's no way we can get up that. I'm exhausted and starving. We'd die before we got even halfway up that damned thing."

One of the Mung guards strode toward Kuva brandishing a whip. "You keep your mouth shut. Slaves aren't permitted to speak."

Kuva growled at the guard. "You'd do well to stay clear of me, friend. I already don't like you. Chains or not, I'll smash your skull to bits and feast on what little brains the gods saw fit to gift you with."

A smile broke out on the guard's face, and he nodded. "Very well, have it your way." He reared back and prepared to unleash the whip on Kuva.

"Stop."

Ran heard Iqban's voice and turned. The leader of the Mung slavers trotted over. He glanced at the guard. "I don't need them showing up battered and abused. It lowers the price I can get for them if they look damaged."

"But sir—"

"But nothing. Put that away and resume your duties. If the big one gives you any trouble, simply attach a chain about his neck and fasten it to the back of a horse." He eyed Kuva. "Then startle the horse. I imagine his neck will break before it gallops a hundred yards."

Iqban kept his gaze fastened on Kuva. "Now, with that said, we're not going to have any more trouble from you, are we?"

Kuva frowned. "I only asked how you expected us to climb that mountain when we've hardly been fed and are exhausted from the forced march."

Iqban nodded. "Slaves aren't permitted to speak. Remember that. However, to answer your question: I don't expect you to climb that mountain at all."

"We're heading right for it," said Ran. "How else are we to get past it?"

"The mountain is our destination," said Iqban. "Now, before I grow weary of your questions, close your mouths and keep them that way. You have arrived at the place where you will be sold. The last thing I need are noisy and unruly slaves. I'd rather kill you than risk you harming my reputation." He turned his horse and trotted away, leaving Ran and Kuva behind.

"Well, that went well," said Kuva.

Ran smirked. "Are you deliberately trying to get into trouble?"

"I'm trying to find out information," said Kuva. "So when I make my escape, I'll have an idea of where we are."

"When *we* escape," said Ran. "You'll need some help getting out of these cuffs, unless you intend to smash them on the rocks or something."

"Can you pick the lock?"

Ran nodded. "Absolutely."

"Then why haven't we escaped already?"

"Because I think someone I know is trapped in this mountain. And I intend to rescue her before I escape." Ran shrugged. "Plus, if we try to escape right now, while we're under heavy guard, there's more chance that Iqban's guards will kill us. Once we're sold, I would think Iqban will be off to raid again. It might actually be easier to escape once we're inside."

Kuva frowned. "That's another assumption if ever I heard one, my friend."

"I'm learning that a lot of life is about assumptions," said Ran. "And hoping you're not making the wrong ones." He stared up at the mountain before them and wondered if he was putting himself and Kuva in even more danger. Then again, the clan had wanted him to come here in the first place. So even though Ran disliked the idea of deliberately placing himself in captivity inside of the mountain, it would enable him to possibly gather information. Was his new master in league with the forces beyond the mountains that Kan-Gul had said were planning to invade the south?

Ran watched as Iqban rode back and forth along the convoy. The two remaining merchants struggled to keep walking, and Iqban didn't hesitate to have the guards prod them along. The wagons clattered over rocks, their wheels taking a beating on the uneven terrain. But Iqban seemed unfazed by the effect on the wagons. "We need to reach the entrance before last light. Everyone move!"

Entrance? Ran frowned. Was there some hidden valley through which they would pass? Would it lead them to beyond the mountains? Snow began to fall as the questions plagued his mind. Kuva muttered something unpleasant as the first flakes struck his head. Ran knew the cold had dogged the big man's heels since they'd been on the journey north. Despite Ran trying to help him accept the weather, Kuva had suffered.

"We'll be warm soon," said Ran as Iqban rode past them. "Hang in there a little while more."

"I will," said Kuva. "If only to kill every last one of these bastards."

They walked another two miles, the snow piling up around their feet as they did so. Kuva started shivering uncontrollably, and Ran worried that the weather would bring the big man down for good. Surely Iqban didn't expect them to continue walking for much longer, did he?

In answer, Iqban drew up to a huge towering boulder that stood twice as tall as he did on his horse. He put his hand into the air and called a halt to their progression. Then he slid down from his saddle and walked toward the boulder. Placing his hand on a small indentation that Ran could scarcely see, he pressed inward and turned his hand.

The ground grumbled in response, bubbling up from somewhere beneath their feet.

"What madness is this?" said Kuva. "It sounds like the mountain intends to swallow us whole."

"You may be right," said Ran. "Look."

The boulder shuddered now, almost appearing to rattle against the side of the mountain. As it did so, cracks showed along its edges, and then the entire stone slowly moved to the side, giving the appearance of a mountain yawning. The opening seemed large enough for two horses to enter abreast of each other. Iqban smiled as the rock finished moving, and he glanced back toward the convoy.

"We will now proceed."

"Never thought I'd be so happy to hear those words," said Kuva. "No idea what lies inside that mountain, but it can't be any worse than staying out here in another blizzard."

"I hope you're right," said Ran. "I can think of many bad things far worse than being in a snowstorm. And this mountain doesn't look all that hospitable."

They moved forward, filing into the maw before them. Darkness surrounded them, and as soon as they were all inside, they heard the tremendous grumbling of the boulder sliding back into place. Slowly but surely the last vestiges of daylight vanished as the rock moved back into its closed position, sealing them all inside the mountain.

For a moment, nothing happened. Then, without warning, a series of torches sprang to life, emanating a weird blue flame that crackled as they burned. They illuminated the tunnel and seemed to stretch far off into the distance, gradually sloping downward as they proceeded.

"Blue fire?" asked Kuva. "Never heard of such a thing."

"Hopefully it's not some sort of magic," said Ran. "I've had enough of dealing with sorcery for a while. I could very much do without it for the rest of my life."

"Shut your mouths," growled a guard. "No one is permitted to speak from here on out."

Iqban led his horse and waved for the convoy to proceed.

Ran looked around, but could determine very little from his immediate surroundings. They saw no guards apart from those in Iqban's raiding party. The blue flames of the torches flickered and danced the same way real fire did. And the rock walls looked as though they'd been hewn by hand, no doubt by slave labor if Iqban had been supplying the man who owned this place with slaves as appeared to be the case.

They walked for half a mile before coming to rest before a large circular iron door set into the rock wall. Once again, the door was large enough to permit entry to men riding horses, and an intricate alphabet was etched across the iron. But Ran could read none of it. As far as he could tell, the script was something unique. He glanced at Kuva, prepared to ask him if he'd ever seen anything like it, but a warning look from the guard told him that would not be a wise idea.

Iqban rapped on the door three times, the knocks echoing back down the tunnel they'd just traversed. They waited for several minutes, and then Ran felt a rush of air blow across his face as the iron door swung inward, allowing them passage.

The air smelled of sulfur, and Ran wrinkled his nose at the scent. But it was at least warmer than it had been in the tunnel. Kuva grinned, and Ran suspected his friend was relieved to be out of the weather.

Iqban led them through, and, as soon as the convoy was inside, the door swung shut. More torches illuminated the area, and this time Ran saw guards. They were all equipped with spears, swords, and half shields that covered their lower arms. Their armor was uniformly plate, and the expressions on their faces looked fierce. One of them approached Iqban and clasped his hand.

"It is good to see you again."

Iqban smiled. "Mithrus. It is my pleasure to inform you that we have much to sell the king. Is he willing to see us now?"

The guard he spoke to, Mithrus, appeared to be in command. He nodded. "We've been expecting you." He looked down the line of the convoy. "Although I must admit I expected you to have far more slaves with you. Did you run into trouble?"

Iqban grunted. "The caravan we attacked had with them a better security company than I expected. They cost me a great deal of my men. Fortunately, I was able to take two of them alive."

"I count four," said Mithrus. "Who are the other two?"

"Merchants," spat Iqban. "Hardly worth the effort, I know. But they may yet serve some purpose that Zal can fathom."

Mithrus grinned. "In other words, you might be able to squeeze a few more pieces of gold out of him for your trouble."

Iqban shrugged. "I brought you a great many slaves the last time I was here. Not every outing can be as fruitful as that one was."

"Indeed," said Mithrus. "Only a fool expects to wake every day to sunshine." He nodded again. "Very well, let us get you situated, and then I will inform the king that he may come and peruse your offerings."

"Excellent," said Iqban. "The journey has been long this time, and I am famished. My men could do with a good meal as well, if that is possible."

"All things are possible for friends of Zal. In any event, I would not expect to leave for several days. The storms are raging now, and trying to leave would be foolish. Stay here and regather your strength. I am certain Zal will continue to have a great need for more slaves."

Iqban smiled. "That may not be a bad idea. But we will see what Zal says first, yes? It would be improper of me to presume to stay here without his offering it first."

Mithrus turned and led them deeper into the mountain. The mountain guards now surrounded the convoy as well as those of Iqban's raider force. The men seemed to know each other, and Ran caught snippets of conversation as they talked. From what he could gather, Iqban brought slaves to the mountain as much as twice a month. Over the course of the last year, he had sold the king—Zal, Ran assumed—nearly one thousand slaves. But for what purpose?

The passageway snaked around to the left and led them down at a deeper angle. As they walked, Ran noted that there were guard stations at intervals along the route, typically manned by two guards. He filed the information away and kept observing as much as he could while he walked next to Kuva.

For his part, the big man seemed relaxed and comfortable now. That's good, thought Ran. He would need Kuva to help him escape. Having a brute he could count on for sheer strength and intimidation would be valuable when confronting the number of guards that seemed to be stationed here.

The convoy drew to a stop as the passage leveled out in a grand cavern that stretched for two hundred feet in any direction. Mithrus motioned for his guards to fall back away from the convoy, and as they did, Iqban's men positioned the wagons and goods they had stolen from Yasseh's caravan for better viewing.

"You two," growled a guard. "Stand over there." He pointed toward a small wooden platform elevated above the ground by perhaps three feet. Ran and Kuva moved over, shuffling with the chains, and managed to get to the top.

The guards led the two merchants over to another platform directly opposite to where Ran and Kuva stood. When all was ready, Iqban looked at Mithrus.

"How does it look?"

Mithrus laughed. "You're asking my advice now?" He smiled. "I'm sure it will be fine." He gestured for one of his guards to come over. "Go inform his majesty that Iqban is here with another convoy."

The guard nodded once and then left down a passageway that branched off from the cavern.

"How goes progress?" asked Iqban.

Mithrus shrugged. "Fair. Not as fast as Zal would like, but then that's the price of digging, I suppose. With all of this rock surrounding us, we have to make exceptions for certain inconveniences. Still, the last lot of slaves you brought us seem to be performing well. Granted it's early yet and they haven't been worked to nothing the way the others have. We'll need many more replacements as those die off."

"Indeed," said Iqban. "And I shall be only too happy to supply them to you."

"Just make sure you keep the numbers up. I don't think Zal will be pleased with the few you have here. Possibly with the exception of those two. But he'll grumble that you didn't bring enough."

"I know," said Iqban. "I hope he likes the goods I brought him."

"We'll see soon enough," said Mithrus. He glanced back toward the passageway and nodded. "He's coming."

Ran looked over and saw torches coming toward them. The blue fire cast weird shadows along the passage wall, twisting shadows and bending them into strange shapes. Then the guard that Mithrus had dispatched reappeared. The guard stopped at the entrance to the passageway and clapped his hands twice.

"His Majesty, King Zal."

What Ran saw next surprised even him.

Chapter Eighteen

Zal was borne into the cavern on a sedan chair covered in gold and sapphires. The bright blue flames of the torches reflected in the cut jewels and cast a dizzying array of sparkles across the cavern, nearly making Ran wince at the sight of it. Zal himself looked to be a diminutive thickset older man with a flaccid body and a bloated demeanor framed by an unkempt gray beard that hung down to his chest. His eyes, however, looked black as obsidian, and he cast a discerning eye about the cavern as he was carried in.

Four slaves carried him toward Iqban and Mithrus and then gently lowered the platform until it touched the ground. The toll of the slaves' exertion was evident by the sweat that poured from their bodies.

"Iqban," said Zal by way of welcome.

Iqban bowed low. "Your Majesty."

"And what sorts of treasures have you brought me this time?"

Iqban smiled. "Your Grace, I have attacked a wealthy caravan traveling west laden with a variety of textiles, jewels, and expensive silks. I hope that you find it worthy of your possession."

"I need slaves, Iqban," said Zal. "Everything else is secondary."

Mithrus coughed, and Zal frowned. "Granted, I also need things I can use to pay my army. I'll have a look at the goods. But first, tell me that you've managed to secure more slaves."

"I have but four this time, Your Grace." Iqban took a breath. "While that number is far below what I brought you the last time, I think two of them at least may more than make up for the paltry numbers."

"Why so?" Zal glanced about the cavern. "Are they giants who can move tons of rock without any effort?"

"One nearly so, but the other is no slouch himself. They stand on the far platform awaiting your appraisal."

Zal stood on the platform and eyeballed Ran and Kuva. Kuva glared at him. Ran wanted to nudge him and tell the big man to rein his emotions in a bit. But Kuva seemed beyond caring.

"What is your name?" asked Zal.

"I am Kuva. From the house of Suba."

Zal waved his hand. "I do not care where you come from or which house claims you as their own. That no longer matters. If I decide to buy you, you will belong to me. To be used as I see fit. Your past is just that: the past. You can use those memories to comfort yourself at night, knowing that you will never again taste freedom."

Kuva glanced at Ran. "We surrendered for this?"

Zal eyed Ran. "You. What are you called?"

"Ran."

"And since the big man next to you felt a need to proclaim himself, where are you from?"

"Nehon."

Zal's eyes narrowed. "You're a long way from home, aren't you? What brings you to northern Igul?"

"I was hired to provide security for the caravan Iqban attacked."

Zal laughed. "It doesn't appear you did very much good, does it?"

"We killed a fair number of Iqban's men," said Ran. "Considering we numbered only four and they had ten times that number, I'd say we held our own as admirably as anyone could be expected to in similar circumstances."

Zal said nothing for a moment and then smiled. He turned to Iqban. "I like that one. He is clever with words and no doubt has a shrewd mind to match. I can use him."

Iqban pointed at Kuva. "And what of him?"

Zal sighed. "Useless in terms of smarts, but those muscles can be put to good use. I'll have him smashing stones along with the other slaves."

Iqban nodded. "I have two more. They're merchants, however, and no doubt unused to physical labor."

"Are those them?" Zal pointed at the opposite platform. "They look like the gods have used them as a chamber pot."

"The journey here was hard on them," said Iqban. "But I have little doubt you could find a use for them."

"Of course you think that," snapped Zal. "You're trying to make money. You'd sell me a dead man and claim he could still tunnel with the other slaves if you thought you could get another gold piece from me."

Iqban bowed low. "You honor me with such praise, Your Grace."

Zal laughed. "Only a rat like you would take that as a compliment." He sighed. "Very well, I'll take all four. I'm sure I can find something interesting to do with those fat ones. The other two can be put to work right away. How much will you take for the four?"

Iqban pointed at Kuva again. "He is worth a great deal for his sheer size alone. Two hundred for him."

"Two hundred?" Zal shook his head. "I'll give you one hundred fifty. Not one piece more."

"Two hundred and I'll throw in the two merchants."

Zal grumbled. "It will probably cost me that to keep those two fed." But he nodded. "Fair enough, two hundred for the three." He eyed Ran. "And what of the foreigner from Nehon? How much will you fleece from me for him?"

"One hundred fifty."

"Iqban," said Zal, "I'm starting to think you believe I have unlimited wealth. This little venture of mine is costing me a fortune as it is."

"A venture fueled by human blood," said Iqban. "You need what I sell and with all due respect, what I sell costs me a great deal of money in terms of paying the men who serve me and the variety of costs associated with my own operation."

Zal waved his hand. "Yes, yes, yes, I know all about your various costs. You run the same tired speech past me each time you come here. No doubt I do the same to you. So let's just get the deal done. I'll pay you an even four hundred gold pieces for everything you've brought here today. All the contents of the caravan, sight unseen. You'll be hard-pressed to find a better deal anywhere. And if you refuse the deal, I'll just have my men kill you."

If Iqban was troubled by the threat, he didn't show it. Instead, he smiled. "I would rather do business than war with my best customer. Four hundred is acceptable."

"Excellent," said Zal. He turned to Mithrus. "I want the wagons brought into the inner chambers, where I can figure out how to disperse their contents. Have your men see to that, please."

Mithrus bowed once. "My lord." He nodded at several guards, who immediately left their stations and took control of getting the wagons funneled down another passageway leading off of the cavern they were in.

Ran watched the wagons trundle away and wondered what would happen next. Zal seemed well-pleased with how negotiations had gone. The smile he wore was bright enough to shine across the room.

Iqban spoke first. "Your Grace, I wonder if it might be possible for my men and I to seek refuge here for a few days."

Zal swung his gaze over to him. "Why would you need to do that?"

"The weather on the way here grew steadily worse. Mithrus tells me that a blizzard is raging outside, and trying to make our way through that type of tempest would no doubt be too dangerous for us to consider. I would lose time and manpower to the storm. There is also the risk of avalanches throughout the route. It would be better for us to wait out the storm."

"Inside my kingdom?" Zal thought for a moment and then nodded. "Fair enough. You and your men are welcome to wait out the storm until it blows over. But as soon as it is clear, I need you to go out and find me more slaves. I need more manpower to make my plans come to fruition."

"I understand," said Iqban. "Thank you for your hospitality."

Zal waved his hand. "Think nothing of it. It will also give me time to count the payment to you, anyway. It works well for us both."

"We are content to set up a makeshift camp here in this place," said Iqban.

"Don't be ridiculous," said Zal. "I have plenty of room here. You will dine with me tonight. I will send several stewards to see to you and your men. Your men can dine with my soldiers. I take it they won't mind sharing a few meals with their brothers-in-arms?"

"I'm sure they'll be more than delighted. As I will be to sit and feast with you later."

Zal nodded. "Excellent. I have to see to a few things now, but will send for you later at your guest quarters."

"Thank you." Iqban pointed at Ran and Kuva. "And what of your new slaves, my lord? Shall I see to it that they are prepared for their tasks ahead?"

Zal shook his head. "I will have someone else see to that. Leave them where they are for the time being. My men won't let them get away." He sat down on the sedan chair again and clapped his hands. The four slaves who had carried him in resumed their stations and heaved the chair up.

Ran saw the grimaces of pain cross their faces. How much did Zal weigh, he wondered. Given that the slaves could hardly support him, it must have meant that Zal weighed more than it appeared. Either that or the sedan chair was heavy. Possibly, too, the slaves were undernourished and had little strength to carry the short king. Regardless, they bore the king out of the cavern, leaving Ran and Kuva alone with the two merchant slaves, Iqban, and his men.

"Well," said Iqban. "That went swimmingly." He clapped his hands and then walked over to Ran and Kuva. "I knew he would pay handsomely for you two. As long as you don't disappoint, then I should be in an even better position the next time I come through here with more slaves."

Ran decided to push his luck a bit. "What exactly is he doing here? Why does he need so many slaves?"

Iqban pursed his lips as if trying to decide whether he should respond or not. Then he merely grinned. "The most audacious plans in the world are often carried out using the best labor force of all: slaves."

"Slavery breeds resentment, though," said Ran. "How can you be sure that the slaves wouldn't make mistakes or deliberately sabotage a project in order to get revenge upon the person that owns them?"

"The threat of a painful death is usually enough to dissuade slaves from trying such things." His eyes narrowed. "And don't you get to thinking about trying something yourself. I'll come back here and personally stomp on your head until you die a terrible death if you do that. Understand?"

Ran only looked at him. There was no way Iqban could best him in combat. But Ran didn't say anything to upset the slaver. Instead, he only nodded.

Iqban appeared satisfied and then turned to Kuva. "As for you, you'd better mind your manners. Zal is notorious for his temper. You didn't see it here today, fortunately, but if you upset him, he will rain hellfire down upon you. You'll wish you hadn't done anything foolish, but it will be too late. For your sake, I hope you listen to me and do exactly what he says."

Kuva shrugged. "I haven't heard what he wants me to do yet. I can't really answer that question truthfully until I know what he wants."

"You'll be digging," said Iqban. "You and Ran both."

"Digging for what?" asked Ran.

Iqban's eyes lit up. "I'm not so sure I should tell you. After all, it's a big secret."

"We're not going anywhere," said Ran. Then he shrugged. "Of course, we'll find out soon enough, anyway, so if you don't feel like telling us . . ."

"Zal is digging down and into the mountain because he's convinced there's a civilization there that he wants to conquer." Iqban finished with a grin that told Ran he didn't much believe the story.

"You don't think there is?"

Iqban shrugged. "This is what I know: Zal needs more slaves. I bring him those slaves and I make money. That's about as far as I care to go in buying into his various plots. Zal burns through slaves because the conditions are horrible down in the mines, the work is grueling, and he feeds his slaves very little. Many of them die."

Ran frowned. If Cassandra was here, he would need to act sooner rather than later in order to free her. "Where are the mines?"

Iqban pointed at the floor. "The main mine shaft is below us on the bottom level. They've been excavating for nearly a year."

"That seems a short time. Zal only recently decided to do this?" Ran wasn't sure how much information he could get out of Iqban, but as long as the slaver felt like talking, Ran would keep asking questions.

"According to what *his grace* tells me,"—Iqban's tone betrayed his sarcasm,—"until recently, he was the king of the very same civilization he claims lies beneath us. He was apparently deposed, and a new ruler took over. Zal has been planning his triumphant return for some time, but it wasn't until after he secured the services of Mithrus and his men that he was able to focus on digging into their world."

"That would account for his appearance," said Ran. "Do all of the people look that way where he comes from?"

Iqban shrugged. "No idea. None of my business, really. Zal is hideous to look upon, but his gold is among the purest I have ever seen. And he has promised Mithrus and his men untold wealth if they help him take back his former kingdom."

"He's not paying them?" Kuva grumbled. "What mercenary would agree to fight for no pay?"

"They agreed to the promise of wealth," said Iqban. "Would you rather have a small salary now or possibly make tenfold if things work out?"

"Tenfold," said Kuva. "But if it didn't work out that way, I would stick my sword through the bastard who lied to me."

Iqban smiled. "And you can bet that Mithrus will do exactly that if Zal's claims aren't what he makes them out to be. Mithrus might find himself at the end of a spear if he can't deliver the money to his men."

"A risky position," said Ran.

"With great risk comes great reward," said Iqban. "Or spectacular death. In any case, my role is simple: find him more slaves. As long as Zal keeps paying me, that's all I care about. I don't work for gilded promises and cheap dreams. Gold buys my services, and gold alone. Zal understands this, and we have a relationship that works. You two will soon find out that Zal cares about very little except regaining his throne."

Chapter Nineteen

Ran and Kuva spent an uneventful night with Iqban and his men in the main cavern. Iqban threw them some scraps of meat and a pint of ale each.

"You'll need your strength for what lies ahead," he said with a laugh.

Kuva wanted to throw the food back at the slaver, but Ran stayed his hand. "He's right. Eat the food and drink the ale. We don't know if Zal even feeds his slaves. And if we want to escape from this hellhole, we're going to need some energy."

Kuva grumbled, but once he started eating, the food and drink vanished down his gullet soon enough. Ran ate his fill, aware of the old maxim his teachers had impressed upon him: if food was available, eat it. You never knew when you'd be able to eat again.

After eating, Kuva yawned and glanced at Ran. "You want first watch?"

Ran shook his head. "We'll both sleep. We need it."

"No guard duty?"

"What's the point? We're surrounded by Iqban's men, and we don't even know the layout of the tunnels here. And I don't think we're in any danger, per se. At least, not yet. We may as well take the opportunity to rest as much as we can. Sleep might be a precious commodity in the days ahead. Especially if we try to escape."

"Good point," said Kuva. He stretched back and lay on the ground. In seconds he was fast asleep.

Ran stayed awake a little bit longer, eyeing the surroundings. He could have easily picked the lock on the shackles and gone exploring, but he knew they'd get a chance to look at the caverns and tunnels soon enough. If he broke out now and got caught, he'd lose all surprise and they'd take more aggressive steps to contain him. And they might just have shackles that he couldn't escape from.

No, he decided, better to take the opportunity to rest and see what the new day would bring. He fell asleep hoping that the next morning would grant him a chance to see if Cassandra was here or not.

Ran awoke despite the lack of sunshine. His inner clock had nudged him, and he opened one eye. Iqban's men were already moving around, getting breakfast ready. Ran prodded Kuva, and the big man grumbled once before rolling over on a splinter that caused him to swear loudly.

He sat up. "I was dreaming we were drinking gallons of mead served by buxom barmaids." He looked around and frowned. "A far cry from the likes of this place, I'll tell you that."

Ran grinned. "When we get out of here, I'll buy the first round."

Kuva sighed. "Whatever they're cooking, it smells delicious. Think they'll offer us any?"

"I doubt it." Ran sensed commotion down the tunnel that led into the cavern. "I don't think we're going to be here long enough."

Kuva followed his gaze. Bright blue torch flames flickered along the tunnel walls and then Mithrus emerged, followed by a squad of guards. He headed directly for the platform where Ran and Kuva sat.

"Had a good night's rest?"

Ran shrugged. "As well as you can have lying on a wooden platform."

"It'll be sight better than your new accommodations, I'll tell you that." Mithrus nodded at one of the guards. "Unlock the shackles."

Iqban wandered over as the guard was fussing with Ran's cuffs. "Any word on the weather?"

Mithrus frowned. "Word from the gate outpost is that the blizzard still rages. Sorry, friend, but it looks like you'll be staying around here for a few days yet."

"This delay is costing me time and money," muttered Iqban. "If it doesn't subside soon, I might have to take my chances with the forces of nature. I'd rather battle my way through drifts than stay here and contend with boredom."

"You could help us with the slaves," said Mithrus. "There's some enjoyment in enhancing their suffering."

Iqban held up his hand. "My job is to procure them for Zal. Anything that happens to them after that is not my concern."

Ran watched the guard unshackle him and thought about trying to overpower him right then. But it would have been a foolish move, surrounded as they were.

"Don't even think about it," said Mithrus then.

Ran eyed him. Mithrus nodded and Ran turned his head. Twenty paces away, one of the guards had an arrow nocked on a bowstring. And it was aimed right at Ran. If he'd tried anything, the arrow would have killed him.

Ran turned back to Mithrus. "Zal wouldn't like one of his new possessions being killed."

Mithrus grinned. "You think Zal gives a damn about you? All he wants is your ability to mine rock. And we're about to find out just how talented you are at that job."

Iqban cleared his throat. "You're taking them now?"

"Unless you've got a better idea?" Mithrus nodded at the guards. "Surround them and make sure they don't try anything stupid. If they do, you are authorized to kill them."

Iqban stood in front of Ran and Kuva. "I wish you both luck. You were formidable enemies on the field of battle, and you have my respect. I fear this will be the last time we see each other, however. The catacombs below hold no solace for even mighty warriors like yourselves."

Ran smiled. "One never knows what the gods have in store for us. Who knows? We may yet see each other again."

"If we do, I will have little choice but to run you through with my sword," said Iqban.

"That is one possibility," said Ran. "The other is that I live while you die by my hand."

Iqban grinned. "I'm almost wishing I didn't sell you. Devising a prolonged painful death for you would be a very enjoyable activity for me."

"Keep thinking about it," said Ran. "You never know what the future holds for us."

"Enough," said Mithrus. "We'll see how cocky you are after a day's work down in the catacombs." He nodded at the guards. "Take them away."

Ran let himself be led away, with Kuva next to him. The squad of guards directed them down the tunnel where their flickering blue torches shone. Ran peered ahead and saw that the ground sloped downward at a steep angle. Set into the ground were wide steps. Torches higher up in braziers lit the way. Sounds reached his ears as well. Hammers and picks on stone, he reasoned as they descended lower into the depths. Each step he took, the air seemed to grow more stale and the scent of sulfur hung heavier. Next to him, Kuva coughed.

"This air is horrible."

"Get used to it," growled one of the guards. "You'll be breathing it until you finally die."

Kuva eyed him but said nothing.

The stairs curved around as they went deeper into the mountain. While the air stunk, it was at least cooler than Ran had expected. Noisier, too. With each passing step, the volume grew until when they at last stepped off the final stair, the din was enormous. Ran frowned and thought about covering his ears. But what good would it do? Eventually, he would have to get used to the noise. Better to do so immediately than suffer later.

Around them, the remnants of people toiled. Men and women both worked down here in the catacombs. Most of the men worked at hammering into the hard rock before them while the women lifted the heavy rocks and piled them in buckets on some sort of conveyor belt that led into a small tunnel climbing upward. Ran eyed the conveyor belt for a moment and wondered where the rocks were taken once they left the mines. Surely they had to be taken to the outside? Where else would Zal be able to store them? Eventually, he would run out of room.

Ran filed that away for the time being. Everything he observed was locked away so he could revisit it later when he was done working—whenever that might be.

The guards drew them to a stop, and Mithrus gestured around them. "This is your new home. You'll stay here and work. Once you're done for the day, the guards will return and escort you to your quarters with the rest of the slaves. If you've done a good amount of work, then you'll be rewarded with food. If not, then you won't. And you'll be expected to work twice as hard the next day. My advice, give it your all and don't think about escape. There is none."

There's always escape, thought Ran. But he said nothing.

Mithrus continued. "You'll be working together. One of you hammers while the other one gets rid of the rocks. Work fast. Zal wants to break through within the next week."

Ran eyed the wall of stone before them. How thick could it possibly be? What lay on the other side? If he'd heard correctly, there was some type of kingdom down here. But what sort of place could live inside of a mountain? How was that even possible?

"One more thing," said Mithrus. "While there aren't any guards here during the day, you do report to that guy." He pointed.

Ran and Kuva looked. Toward the far end of the catacombs was a towering figure that looked more like a beast than a man. He stood taller than anyone else, including Kuva. Dark, coarse hair covered his entire body and he held a long steel whip in his hands. A curved dagger hung on his belt.

"Who is that?" asked Ran.

"What is that, might be a better question," said Mithrus. "We call him Bagyo. No one knows where he comes from. Iqban brought him to us a while back, and we decided to use him after we saw what he can do to a man."

"What does that mean?" asked Kuva.

"It means that Bagyo doesn't like people who don't pull their own weight. Try to slack off and he'll punish you. Try to escape and he'll kill you. He might even eat you. There have been a few times when dead slave bodies went missing. We can't prove it, but we all think Bagyo ate them." Mithrus shook his head. "Pretty awful way to go, if you ask me."

Ran frowned. "Bagyo."

Mithrus nodded. "Don't do anything to upset him." He waved the beast over, and the giant came trundling toward them, his eyes cruel and unforgiving as he looked at them.

"New?" was the only word that came out of his mouth.

Mithrus nodded. "Yes. I've just been telling them all about you and the rules for living down here."

Bagyo chuckled. "Living. Ha."

Mithrus shrugged. "Call it what you want then, I don't much care.

But make sure they do their work. Zal has high hopes these two will be strong enough to ensure we meet the goal of breaking through within this next week."

Bagyo prodded Kuva with a stubby finger. "This one strong. He will work good."

Ran waited as Bagyo assessed him. The giant sighed. "This one smaller. No work so good."

"I'll work fine," said Ran. "Just let me get to it and don't worry about the fact that I'm not as large as Kuva there."

"You work. Hard," said Bagyo. "Otherwise, you get whip."

Mithrus laughed. "All right then, I'll leave you two in Bagyo's caring hands. Enjoy yourself. We'll return at the end of the work day."

"When is that?" asked Ran.

"When I say it over!" roared Bagyo. Instantly, the whip cracked, and Ran felt the steel tip bite into his shoulder, scoring a neat line down his arm that flashed red as bleeding broke out. Ran winced from the pain and stemmed the tidal surge of rage that swelled within him. He could have taken the whip and killed Bagyo with it, but what was the point? He was here to see if Cassandra was a prisoner. There would be time enough for dealing with Bagyo and Mithrus later.

Bagyo pointed at a section of rock. "There. You work. Now!"

Kuva put a hand on Ran's other shoulder. "You all right?"

Ran nodded. "I'll be fine. Whip hurts like hell, though. Does it look bad?"

Kuva shook his head. "Not really. Just broke the skin with it, is all. I'd get some water on it later, though. You don't want it to get infected. In a place like this, it will go bad real quick."

Ran sighed. "You want the pickax first or picking up the rocks?"

"Which one's better for you? You just got whipped, after all."

"I'll pick up the rocks first," said Ran. Doing so would give him an opportunity to move around a bit more than if he'd opted to hammer first.

"Fair enough," said Kuva. He picked up the pickax and started swinging it at the rock face. Bits of stone flew out from where the ax bit at them. Ran started collecting the rocks with a shovel and scooping them into the cart nearby. As it got fuller, he looked around, noting the route that the other slaves took to dump the cart contents into the carrying boxes on the conveyor belt.

His shoulder ached from where Bagyo had hit him with the whip, but Ran was determined not to let the pain keep him from doing his best work. Bagyo would almost certainly be looking out for him to slack off. And that would only earn him another whipping.

With his first full cart done, Ran got behind it and started using his legs to shove it forward. The small wheels underneath resisted moving along the uneven floor of the catacombs, but Ran put his shoulder into it and shoved it again. This time, the little cart shuddered forward.

Ran's breath was coming hard by the time he reached the conveyor-belt area. He unloaded the cart into the carrying boxes and watched as they drifted skyward on the conveyor belt. The more he looked at it, the more it looked like a viable means of escape. If the carrying boxes could hold the weight of all the rocks that were being dumped into them, then surely it could hold Ran's and Cassandra's body weight.

Kuva, too, he reminded himself. There was no way he could leave the big man behind.

Ran turned to bring the cart back. Bagyo stood close by, watching him intently through the thick black brows that covered his eyes. Ran nodded at him once then lowered his head and started pushing the cart back to where Kuva waited.

As he did so, he passed the entrance to another shaft. So Zal had two distinct points of entry being mined at the same time. Interesting.

Even more interesting was one of the women he saw working down at the end of the shaft. It was hard to make out any fine details, but Ran felt his heart bounce when he saw her.

Cassandra.

Chapter Twenty

Her clothes were tattered, and grime streaked her face, but Ran thought she still looked beautiful. She kept her head bowed as she worked, and Ran wished he could call to her. Even from this distance he could see that her once proud demeanor seemed nearly broken. Still, she couldn't have been here too long. And if she knew that Ran was here, it might help lift her spirits.

Ran took a chance and called to Bagyo. "This cart has a broken wheel."

At the sound of his voice, Cassandra looked up. Her eyes were momentarily dull until she spotted him. Then he saw a gleam come into them and just the hint of a grin.

Bagyo crashed into him from behind, sending him sprawling. "Get up!"

Ran turned and saw the beast standing over him. He pointed at the cart. "One of the wheels. I think it's broken."

Bagyo turned his attention to the cart and easily turned it over. He shook his head. "Nothing wrong with wheel."

Ran leaned forward and got slapped for doing so. He tasted a bit of blood and shook his head. "It wasn't moving properly. I only thought that I should tell you—"

"You work now," said Bagyo. "Interrupt me again and you get whip." He turned and thundered off.

Ran watched him go and then risked another look at Cassandra as he wiped the blood from his face. She smiled at him and then went back to working. She had seen him, though, and Ran felt better about the encounter as he returned to where Kuva still hammered.

Kuva frowned when he saw Ran. "You get yourself in trouble again with Bagyo?"

"It was worth it," said Ran. "The woman I was searching for is here."

Kuva put his pickax down. "She's here? In the catacombs with us?"

"Yes," said Ran. "Now it's time to formulate a plan to get us all out of here."

Kuva massaged his shoulder with his other hand. "That would be nice. I don't know how much of this work I'm going to be able to endure without a better meal than the one we had last night. Honestly, the work doesn't faze me much, but the lack of food certainly does."

Ran stopped pushing the cart and took up the pickax. "Let me have some time at it now. You've been working for a while."

"Fine with me," said Kuva. "Just be careful of your eyes. Tiny shards of rock fly off in all directions while you're swinging that thing."

"Understood." Ran hefted the pickax and swung at the stone wall before him. Rock broke off and tumbled to the ground at his feet. Ran settled into a rhythm of swinging the pickax, drawing back and breathing in, and then out as he swung down again. The rate he swung at was almost hypnotic after a few minutes. Ran stripped his shirt off as it soaked with sweat. He felt the muscles of his back and shoulders working well. After days of captivity, the release of swinging the ax actually felt pretty good.

Now that he had located Cassandra, Ran needed to figure out a way to escape from this place. He cared little for what Zal had planned; it didn't concern him. Nor did he expect the clan elders back at the Nine Daggers would think much of it. Ran's chief assignment was to scout the mountains in case the rumors of an invasion turned out to be true. Now that he had reconnected with Cassandra, Ran felt much better about carrying out that assignment. He and the princess could always head west after his mission was complete.

The question was: How were they going to escape?

An obvious option was the conveyor belt. It looked as though it ran right up to the surface and deposited all the rock out there somewhere. But without knowing more, it would be silly to try. What if the belt led them up to a guard station where Zal's men would simply kill them? Ran would need better information before he committed to that route.

The tougher option would be getting out the way they'd come in: through the tunnels. But escaping that way would leave them open to harassment from guards both from Iqban's team and Zal's. The less people they had to fight, the better. And if they could escape with no one being aware of it, so much the better.

Back in Gakur, Ran had been schooled on various methods of escape and evasion. His instructors had never taught him how to get out of a mountain, however. Jail cells and stockades, yes. But imprisoned as he was deep underground? Not an easy feat even for a shadow warrior. Still, Ran suspected the same principles ought to apply. He remembered one of the lessons he'd had back at the school.

Rinzo was a tall, thin, wiry skeleton of a teacher. He looked as though he weighed perhaps fifty pounds, but his thin frame belied an incredible strength. And Rinzo was famed in the clan for having successfully escaped a punishment of certain death in boiling oil. How he had managed to do was still a fiercely guarded secret that the elders kept from the aspirants until they had graduated the training.

"One of the keys to a successful escape is diversion," said Rinzo one warm morning in the late spring of Ran's tenth year in Gakur. "You need to make sure that the people looking for you are distracted or focused on something else. If they believe the real threat—you, for example—is elsewhere, then your path to freedom becomes that much more accessible. For that reason, you may be equipped with smoke bombs or devices for creating incendiary diversions. You may not always have these at your disposal, however, so you'll have to make do with what you have on scene."

"What if we don't have anything like that around us?" asked another student.

Rinzo smiled. "Then you have to create something out of thin air. Use your imagination, isn't that what we're always telling you? A creative mind is far superior to one locked within the confines of ego and fear. Shinobujin are taught to free themselves from those shackles so they can accomplish things that do not seem possible to normal people. In this way, you will also find the method to use if you are ever captured and imprisoned. It was the only thing that allowed me to escape a certain death when I was caught." He chuckled. "Of course, I had some pretty incredible motivation to do so. Being boiled alive in oil is not a very romantic way to die."

A soft breeze blew into the classroom, and Ran closed his eyes as it washed over him, driving away the heat of the day. When he opened his eyes again, Rinzo had vanished. The students with Ran glanced around, but their teacher was gone. Somehow, he had disappeared in mere seconds.

"Where did he go?" Ran heard himself ask. Surely Rinzo had to be somewhere. But the classroom held only one long table that the students sat at and a small circular table for any notes the teacher wished to present. Otherwise, the room was bare save for a small alcove holding a tapestry at the far end. The tapestry showed a mountain scene in winter with a fox making its way across the landscape.

As they watched, the tapestry shifted and Rinzo walked out from behind it. The class broke into shy laughter, but the expression on Rinzo's face was serious as he resumed his place at the front of the class. "You see my point now?"

The students glanced at each other. None of them knew what Rinzo might be referring to. Ran chewed his lip as he replayed the scene. He remembered the breeze. It was a delightful reprieve from the heat. And he had allowed it to distract him. His awareness had vanished in those few moments.

"You took advantage of the breeze," Ran said.

Rinzo swung his gaze around to Ran. "Go on."

"You waited to start teaching until we'd been here sitting in the heat for a while. You knew that there would eventually be a breeze. And when it came, we would all react the same way: by tuning you out to concentrate on the coolness."

Rinzo smiled. "Exactly. Which is why one of the best tools you have at your disposal—even when you have nothing else—is an understanding of how the human mind works. What it latches on to despite its best efforts at maintaining discipline. If you know these things, then you can use them to your advantage. The same way I used it to illustrate a point. Moving silently is no challenge for you now. You're all students that have been here for years. Now is the time to start developing your innate understanding of how people think. Where are the gaps in their awareness that you can exploit? What do they cling to as solid beliefs that you can manipulate to your advantage? Study this and study it well. It could save your life one day in the not-so-distant future."

Ran stopped swinging the pickax and looked around. The section of stone wall before him had been reduced greatly. Sweat soaked his entire body, and he felt warm and tired. But relaxed as well. He smirked. Remembering his lessons in Gakur usually helped him ponder on difficult challenges like the one he now faced.

"You've done some serious damage with that pickax."

Ran looked behind him. Kuva had just brought back the cart. "Guess I sort of got into the action of it."

Kuva chuckled. "I guess that's one way of looking at it. This is the tenth trip I've made to the conveyor belt. You've done more damage than I was able to do earlier. I think Bagyo is suspicious of how much progress we're making."

"Did he say something?"

Kuva shook his head. "No, but he's been looking at me like I'm some sort of toy for him to play with. I can tell you right now that I don't like that feeling at all. Are you serious about escaping from here?"

"Of course."

"Good," said Kuva. "Because the last thing I want to do is end up being some sort of plaything for that beast."

Ran set the pickax down and squatted on his heels, feeling the stretch in his thighs as he did so. "We just need to figure out a way to get out of here. I need to know if that conveyor belt goes all the way up to the surface or not."

"I tried looking up it the last few trips I made," said Kuva. "But I couldn't see daylight."

"That's not good," said Ran.

"Maybe it goes to another level and then turns? If it went straight up, then we'd be able to see daylight or snow or something, right?"

"Possibly," said Ran. "But we won't know for sure until we get a chance to talk to the other slaves. And even then we'll have to be careful. If anyone suspects we're trying to plan an escape, they might turn us in just to save themselves."

Kuva frowned. "Why on earth would they do that? They could get out of here, too."

"People are sometimes more intent on keeping things the way they are rather than attempt something new. There's a certain comfort in what they perceive as normalcy. Any challenge to that is viewed as a threat to them, and they'll sometimes do the craziest things to protect it—even if it means suffering still."

"If any of them rat us out, I will make sure they don't live to see the daylight again," said Kuva.

"Save your fighting for those we need to kill," said Ran. "Leave the others as they are. The hell they will have to endure is punishment enough."

Kuva grumbled and started shoveling more of the rocks into the cart. Ran watched him work and then started swinging his pickax again. He heard Kuva push the cart away and kept swinging the pickax.

"Ran."

The voice was soft, but he heard it and turned. Cassandra stood there smiling at him. Ran couldn't help himself and let a broad smile break across his face. He clamped it down after a second, however.

"You shouldn't be here."

She waved a dirty hand at him. "Bagyo is defecating in the channel the same way he does every day at this time. We have a few minutes."

Ran wanted nothing more than to sweep her up in his arms and kiss her, but he refrained. If the other slaves saw that and suspected something, they'd never escape. And he definitely wanted to get them both out of here.

"When did you arrive here?"

She sighed. "Four days ago. Iqban has more than one raiding party out at any time. We were taken so unexpectedly, we had little chance of fighting them off."

"Are you all right?"

"As well as can be expected," she said. "I wasn't sure how I was going to get out of here until I saw you. You do have a plan, right?"

Ran smirked. "I only just got here. I need some time to figure things out, but I'm sure we can get out of here. Hopefully before too much time has passed."

Cassandra nodded. "Don't take too long. The air down here is vile, and breathing it makes you weak. If you stay here too long, it will overcome you and you'll hardly be able to think straight. The sooner you get a plan together, the better."

"Will I see you later when we're done here?"

"It's possible, but it depends on where Bagyo puts you." She looked back and saw Kuva coming toward them. She pushed her own cart back. "We'll talk soon." She winked once. "I guess you're going to have to rescue me again, huh?"

"I guess." He smiled and watched her push the cart past Kuva. Kuva gave her a long glance and then turned the cart into their work area.

"Should I ask?"

"My old friend," said Ran.

"There's nothing old about that," said Kuva with a sly grin. "Even covered in dirt and grime, you can see she's a beauty."

"Well, the sooner we get out of here, the better chance I have of seeing her the way I remember her."

Kuva stopped pushing the cart and stood up, arching his back. "Good, because I'm already tired of pushing this damned cart. Give me that pickax again and let me hammer out some of my frustrations, will you?"

Ran handed the pickax over and glanced back down the tunnel.

But Cassandra had already vanished again.

Chapter Twenty-One

The work day ended as it had begun: with no real clue about what time it was inside the mountain. Ran found the lack of daylight unsettling and had to rely upon his internal clock to gauge how much time had passed. Bagyo stomped over and stood before the part of the stone wall they'd been working on.

"Work done. You go now."

Kuva set the pickax down and eyed Ran before looking at Bagyo. "Go where?"

"Back to your cells," said Mithrus as he appeared behind Bagyo. With him was a squad of guards, all of them heavily armed. "You'll get a meal and sleep. Work resumes tomorrow morning nice and early."

"I can't even tell what time it is now," said Kuva. "That meal had better be something I can use for energy and not some slop."

Bagyo started forward, raising the whip, but Mithrus put a hand on his arm. "No." He looked at Kuva. "Perhaps you'd rather discuss this with Zal? I'm sure he'd love to hear your complaints. The last slave that put up a fuss was drawn and quartered. Slowly. In fact, I think he was still conscious even after he lost his first arm and leg." Mithrus shook his head. "A mess, no doubt, but also rather effective at staying any complaints."

Kuva frowned. "Zal wants a breakthrough, isn't that right? He can't expect one if he doesn't feed us properly. Swinging a pickax all day long takes energy. Disgusting gruel isn't going to cut it. Slaves need to be fed properly or it's going to take us a lot longer to do the work."

"This needs to be complete by the end of the week."

Kuva laughed. "That's a nice dream. This wall is too thick. Even with both Ran and me working on it, we've barely scratched the surface. And we're in reasonably good shape. The other slaves you have here are in various stages of dying. They're so underfed, it's ridiculous. What Zal wants isn't going to matter if he doesn't feed us properly."

"He will kill you all if you don't break through that wall by the end of the week."

Kuva shrugged. "I don't fear death. And I'd go happily knowing that Zal didn't achieve what he set out to accomplish. You might think this is a complaint, but in reality, I'm speaking sense. If Zal wants his dream to come true, he's got to provide us with better food."

Mithrus frowned and muttered something to one of the guards. The guard vanished, and Ran was momentarily concerned that Kuva had pushed it too far. Perhaps Mithrus was sending for some sort of punishment for Kuva. And if Ran lost Kuva, his chances of staging a successful escape had just grown smaller.

But when the guard returned and whispered in Mithrus' ear, it was obvious Kuva wasn't being punished. Mithrus looked at him. "Very well. I will convey your sentiments to the king. In the meantime, you must return to your cells."

"Fair enough," said Kuva. He turned and walked right into Bagyo's fist. The big man crumpled immediately, and before Ran could do anything, several of the guards with Mithrus rushed in and dragged Kuva's body away. Bagyo held up a fist and aimed it at Ran.

"Stay."

Mithrus broke into a wide smile. "Your friend should have kept his mouth shut. At least you don't show any signs of being that stupid."

"What will you do to him?" asked Ran.

"What needs to be done," said Mithrus. "Bagyo will escort you to your cell. I'd advise you not to give him a hard time unless you're anxious to end up like your friend."

Ran waited until Mithrus had gone and Bagyo had backed out of the area before he walked out into the tunnel. Bagyo nudged him back the way they'd first entered the catacombs, but then steered Ran down a side tunnel he hadn't noticed before. Again, the tunnel was lit with the blue flame torches. Ran sniffed the air and winced. The scent of feces and urine clogged his nostrils. As they stepped into a new cavern, Ran immediately spotted the source of the smell: a pit the slaves must have used as a latrine was positioned across the way. There was no privacy, just a simple set of logs set up to permit several people to squat at the same time. Zal clearly cared little for the well-being of his slaves.

Around the cavern were holding pens for the slaves. Log timbers gave them some semblance of structure, but they were far from stable. Ran thought they looked like pigpens on a farm, but refrained from saying anything to Bagyo. For all Ran knew, Bagyo might have constructed them.

Bagyo shoved him toward one. "You go. There."

Ran nodded and made his way to the pen. He lifted the simple rope latch and then pulled the door open and walked inside. Hay littered the rock and dirt floor, but provided little cushion. Sleeping would be an exercise in futility for most of the other slaves, Ran decided. No wonder they all looked so haggard and exhausted. If they were being fed poorly and couldn't even get decent sleep at night, then they would be unproductive as they worked. Not that Zal would understand or even care about that.

He heard a scream then, a long plaintive wail that Ran recognized as belonging to Kuva. No doubt Mithrus and his band of goons were exacting some sort of horrible punishment on the big man for speaking up. Still, Ran respected Kuva for trying to make things better for the slaves. That took guts. His timing was terrible, Ran decided, but at least Kuva had tried. Ran just hoped that his friend wasn't being killed for his transgressions.

He squatted in the hay and looked around. There wasn't much happening, as most of the slaves had simply collapsed into their respective pens. Bagyo took up a post near the latrine and seemed unfazed by the horrid stench.

Escaping from the pen wouldn't be difficult, thought Ran. All he would have to do was simply unlatch and walk out. But escaping under the keen gaze of Bagyo would be more troublesome. He could do it, of course; he felt certain the beast had to rest at some point. But how long would Ran have before reinforcements were called in and every guard that Mithrus had under his control was dispatched to hunt them down? Certainly trying to get out through the tunnels they'd entered the mountain through would be nearly impossible. Although it might also be the last place they would look. Most escapees would opt for the easiest route, not the hardest.

Ran sighed. There were an awful lot of variables. If it were just him, he would have taken the risk. But he had Cassandra and Kuva with him, and that meant two times the risk.

The door to his pen opened and Cassandra rushed in, replacing the latch as she did so. "Shhh!" She looked through the logs at Bagyo, but the beast showed no sign of having seen her. Cassandra turned and slumped against the door. "Hi."

Ran smiled in spite of their surroundings. "Hi yourself. How did you do that?"

"Do what? This?" She plucked a strand of hay from the ground and started twisting it with her fingers. "Bagyo doesn't have very good eyesight. Mostly he just sees motion. If you're quick enough or move slow enough, you don't usually register, unless he's very close to you. Then he sees just fine."

Ran filed that away; it was good information. And it would make their eventual escape that much easier now. "How are you?"

She reached out and touched his face. "I've missed you."

"Me as well."

Cassandra sighed. "I look a state. My clothes are ridiculous. Even my hair."

"You're beautiful," said Ran. "Slave or not."

She smiled. "I'm not going to lie. When we were taken my first thought was that I'd never get to see you again. I threw my ring off in some sort of vain wish that you might find it."

"I did find it," said Ran. "But it didn't matter. Iqban's men overtook us shortly thereafter. I wasn't too upset. I knew you'd been taken and wanted to find you."

"You were coming west to see me?"

Ran nodded. "Yes. My clan wanted me to come to these accursed mountains, but I decided to go west."

"You defied your clan?"

Ran took the strand of hay from her and played with it. "In the end, not really. I still wound up here—exactly where they wanted me to go. So all is well, I guess. I took a rather bizarre route to get here, but they don't need to know those details. As long as I complete my assignment, I'll be fine."

"Can you complete it? Can you get us out of here?"

"No place is inescapable," said Ran. "I just need the right

opportunities, and we'll be on our way." He looked at her. "The people you were taken with, are any of them your friends?"

Cassandra frowned. "I wish I could say they were, but the lot of them are rude. They never liked me. Someone let it slip I was a princess, and they immediately treated me like I was scum. And that was before we were captured. So, no. They're not my friends."

"Because we'll have to leave them behind, most likely," said Ran. "I can't afford to take more than you and Kuva with me."

Cassandra glanced around. "Where is your friend?"

Another wail pierced the air. Ran winced and nodded. "He had some words for Mithrus. Mithrus apparently didn't like what he had to say, and they dragged him off."

"To the chamber," said Cassandra. "I've heard of it, but thankfully haven't seen it. One of the others taken with me was taken there and never returned. I hope for your friend's sake that he didn't say anything too bad. Mithrus is an evil man."

"He complained about the food," said Ran.

"Oh," said Cassandra. "That probably wasn't a good idea. Mithrus cares little for the welfare of slaves. Zal even less so."

"Do you know anything more about what we're doing here?" asked Ran. "They said we're tunneling down to break through to some sort of other place?"

"Zal is a deposed king. He comes from these mountains, but not on them—in them. Apparently his people live inside these walls and spend their entire lives mostly underground. Zal was exiled instead of killed, and forced to come here. This mountain range stretches for hundred of leagues, and his people occupy these mountains. But Zal resents his exile and hired Mithrus and his men to help him conquer his people when we break through the walls."

"Isn't there an easier way to reach his former kingdom? If they live in the mountains, they must have roads or something that they travel upon."

"I don't know," said Cassandra. "But Zal is clearly hoping to take them by surprise by tunneling into their realm. From the snippets of conversation I've overheard, there are other races that live deep within the mountains. And they're not as nice as the race Zal comes from."

Ran frowned. Subterranean people? It seemed too crazy to be real, but then again, he was inside a mountain, ostensibly a slave. Tomorrow he would go back to work swinging a pickax and pushing a cart. He took a breath and made a decision. "We'll need to escape soon. Zal wants the breakthrough to happen within this next week. If that happens, you can bet we will all become expendable. Mithrus and his men will most likely have fun slaughtering us."

"Mithrus makes me cringe," said Cassandra. "I've caught him looking at me, and there's little hidden in his gaze, if you get my meaning."

"I do," said Ran. "The sooner we're out of here, the better." He glanced around. "When do we eat?"

"Soon," said Cassandra. "Bagyo will make the rounds. It's not that good, but it does provide you some energy. I'd recommend getting some sleep after that. Tomorrow will be a better day for making plans." She moved closer and gave him a quick kiss. "I'd better go before the brute finds me here."

"He won't hurt you, will he?"

"I don't know. Bagyo is a weird creature. I've wondered if Zal captured him from one of the other races that live in the mountains. But I don't know for sure." She lifted the latch on Ran's pen and took a final look back at him. "See you in the morning."

Then she was gone.

Ran leaned back against the stone wall of his pen and sighed. If he was going to act, he would need to find out if the conveyor belt ran all the way to the surface or not. It would be a risky venture determining if it did, but he saw few other options for making their escape. As much as he would have preferred using the tunnels they had entered through, it simply didn't make sense to go that route with Cassandra and Kuva in tow.

He heard movement outside of his pen and moved closer to the logs to see what was going on. Bagyo had a big wooden pail in one hand and bowls in the other. At each pen, he would dip a bowl into the bucket and then pass it over to the slaves. Ran waited, and then Bagyo's face appeared at the door.

"Here. You eat." He thrust a bowl of gruel at Ran, who took it and started to slide back.

Bagyo dipped another bowl into the gruel and shoved that toward Ran as well.

Ran smiled. "I get double portions today?"

Bagyo shook his head. "That bowl not you. For other man."

"You mean Kuva."

"Kuva," said Bagyo. "That his." He moved on to the next pen, and Ran huddled over his bowl, slurping up the foul-tasting gruel. He swallowed it down as fast as he could, figuring the less time spent on his tongue, the less bad it would taste. The watery rice mixture had little bits of some type of meat in it, but Ran didn't feel like guessing what animal they were from. The sooner he got it down, the better.

He heard a rush of movement then and put the bowl down. As he did so, the door to his pen opened and two of Mithrus's guards dragged Kuva's body in, dumping him on the hay before leaving once again.

Ran rushed to his friend. "Kuva!"

Kuva groaned and rolled over. His eyes were nearly swollen shut, and bruises ran down the side of his neck. Ran shook his head. They had worked him over badly. He held the bowl of gruel to his friend's mouth. "Try to eat."

As Kuva lapped at the gruel, Ran's jaw tightened. They would escape.

But before they did, Ran would kill Mithrus.

Chapter Twenty-two

Bagyo eventually left after the slaves had eaten, leaving them free to roam about if they wished. But none of them seemed the least bit interested in doing so. Even Cassandra wanted to sleep.

"Don't get me wrong, Ran. I'm happy you're here. But until we can get out of here, I've still got to work or face Bagyo's wrath. To do that, I need to get some rest."

Kuva, meanwhile, had passed back out after eating the gruel. Ran watched him for a while to make sure he wasn't going to die, but Mithrus and his men had only roughed him up, and Ran guessed the injuries were mostly superficial—even if they'd left him horribly bruised.

For a few minutes, Ran sat in the pen, wondering about what his next move should be. Rinzo, his old instructor back in Gakur, had always been insistent when discussing escape techniques. Ran could still see the wiry elder standing in front of the class lecturing at length on how most prisons work.

"If you are captured, then escape must be your number-one priority—for one simple reason: the longer you stay in captivity, the more you risk being moved to a more secure facility."

"What if you're already in a secure facility?" one of Ran's fellow students asked.

Rinzo nodded. "The same principle applies. Perhaps even more. Your own spirit will also grow weaker the longer you remain in captivity. The time to escape is as soon as possible after capture. Look for any opportunities you can. Take the risks early, and you may find loopholes you can exploit. The security may not be as tight as it will be later. Take chances if you think you will be able to escape."

That was all well and good if you were alone, thought Ran. But what if you had two other people with you? And Kuva was injured. As much as Ran wanted to escape that night, he had to give Kuva time to rest. If he was well enough tomorrow, then they would make their attempt tomorrow night.

In order to do that, however, they had to first have an escape route. That meant Ran had to do some reconnaissance. He eyed the hay floor of the pen and noted that Kuva's breathing was now slow and steady. That was a good sign. The temptation for Ran to rest was strong. He wanted nothing more than to lay his head down after the full day of work and get some sleep. He had two people relying on him, however. Sleep would have to wait.

Ran lifted the latch to his pen and crept out into the cavern. Only one lone blue-flamed torch flickered on the wall, casting shadows. Ran eased out of the cavern and, at the entrance to it, checked slowly around the corner to see if there were any guards about. He saw none.

There had to be another part of the catacombs that housed Zal and his mercenaries. Ran hadn't seen it, however. He moved slowly down the tunnel back toward where the slaves dug during the daylight hours. There was a chance that Bagyo was still about, even at this late hour. Ran doubted Zal would permit the beast to live with the rest of them in the other part.

He found him soon enough. Bagyo snored loudly in one section of the work area. Ran approached with caution, but saw the slumbering beast huddled over a rock ledge. Ran had to move past him to reach the conveyor-belt area and made sure to watch his foot placement. Bits of loose rock were everywhere. Sending even one stone skittering across the cavern floor would risk waking Bagyo up. His training enabled him to move past Bagyo without a sound. Soon Ran eyed the entrance to the conveyor belt.

Nothing moved on the belt now. It had been shut off hours back when the slaves had finished working for the day. Ran noted a rudimentary lever on the wall that must have powered it somehow. The entrance before him was large enough to permit the slaves to dump loads of rocks through. It was just large enough for Ran to fit through, and he squeezed into the opening. Once on the leather belt, the space around him opened up a bit. He frowned. Kuva might find getting in here difficult. If was just as small at the top, the big man would be stuck inside the shaft.

Up above him, Ran saw the incline and had to brace his hands on the shaft walls in order to gain any purchase for his ascent. If he hadn't had to worry about Bagyo, Ran could have climbed the shaft much faster. But any sound he made risked alerting the beast below. So Ran made sure he maintained three points of contact at all times, while either his hand or foot scouted the next position. Ran gave thanks to his instructors back in Gakur who had developed his ability to see in the darkness. Inside the shaft, it was nearly impossible to see any details. The only illumination—if it could be called that—came from some ambient light up near the top of the shaft. That gave Ran hope that it might lead to the outside world.

It was cooler in the shaft as well, making Ran consider that there was air coming in from outside somewhere. The higher he climbed, the fresher the air tasted. He had to calm his excitement and force himself to keep from rushing the climb. His foot slipped twice on the leather conveyor belt from moisture of some sort. Farther ahead, Ran heard telltale dripping on the belt. Another good sign, he thought. Perhaps it was melting snow?

The belt leveled out without warning, and Ran bumped his head on the ceiling. His assumption that the belt only went up at an angle had been wrong, and he now had a bruise for failing to remain objective. Ran frowned and pushed the desire for this climb to end in a way out from his mind. He had to stay calm and detached. Whatever the climb eventually revealed, Ran would utilize it as best he could.

Hunger gnawed at his stomach now. The gruel had barely given him any strength, but Ran had just depleted his energy by engaging in reconnaissance tonight. He hadn't had any real choice in the matter, though. His training dictated he try to find a way out as soon as possible. Tomorrow would be a tough day, no doubt. Ran would simply have to gut through it.

The belt wound its way around a curve and then started back up again at a steeper angle. Climbing it now became even tougher. At this height, Ran was less concerned about noise filtering back down to Bagyo far below, but he still had to maintain some degree of awareness. As the belt climbed, the air grew fresher still, and Ran relished being able to breathe without wanting to vomit. If the climb produced nothing useful to his escape, it had been worth it to at least get some fresh air into his body.

Ran stopped climbing and sniffed the air. Smoke. And something else. He sniffed again, using a technique to rapidly breathe in and out with his mouth open slightly to help him distinguish what he smelled. After a moment of doing so, he felt his mouth water. He smelled food. Beef, most likely. Hunger swelled within him, and Ran felt his stomach grumble at the possibility of being able to get some real food into him.

Ran took several deep breaths and forced himself to stay calm again. The presence of food did not necessarily mean he would be able to pilfer some. Although if he had the chance, he would take it. The benefit gained from even a small portion of beef would be worth the risk, he decided. Especially if he had a full day of work ahead of him tomorrow.

Ran continued his ascent, and again the belt leveled off and then curved around. To Ran, it seemed almost as if the conveyor was coiling around on itself. He wondered how the belt kept moving in this fashion, since he would have thought a straight path would be most efficient. Then he decided he didn't much care. As long as the belt led him to a viable escape route, that was all he cared about.

The darkness inside the shaft lessened now as well. More ambient light seemed to be spilling into it from somewhere up ahead. Ran's muscles complained as he continued to climb, but he forced himself to forget the aches and pains. Ran focused on his breathing, as he so often did, to block out his mind. He knew his body would do what he demanded of it; it was his mind that would attempt to sabotage him. For that reason, Ran would breathe or use other techniques to distract his mind while his body worked. It was one of the most simple things he could do, and at the same time, it was also one of the hardest to master.

Noise.

Ran stopped mid-climb as the sounds registered. He couldn't pinpoint what they were, but they were definitely out of rhythm with the ambient sounds of the shaft interior. His awareness had detected them, and Ran now knew that he would have to be even quieter if he hoped to find out where the conveyor belt concluded.

He started moving again, this time even slower. His arms and legs were both stretched out, and the muscles along them shook from the exertion. Ran took a deeper breath and then pushed on. His eyes now saw flickers of blue light. Ran guessed there might be more of the strange blue torches up ahead of him.

The smells of something cooking also grew stronger with every small distance he traveled. Ran's mouth continued to water, and he had to continuously swallow to keep from drooling. He'd known hunger before, but not like this. Food fueled his body, after all, and Ran was demanding everything of himself at that moment. Anything edible would be welcome.

He sensed the opening before he actually saw it. As the conveyor belt lifted higher and higher, the flickering ambient light revealed a crude opening much like the one he'd first climbed into hundreds of yards below him in the bowels of the mountain. How far had he climbed, Ran wondered. He hoped the opening ahead of him would answer his questions.

More sounds reached his ears now. Metal. And voices. He frowned. So he wasn't alone. Did the conveyor belt empty out ahead? Had it reached its destination?

Ran crawled the last few feet and then laid his body on the belt itself. At least in this position he could sneak forward without worrying about the belt suddenly turning on. He moved incrementally. Inch-by-inch. The strain on his body was profound, but Ran kept his focus. The voices were louder now. He counted at least three of them. Other smells overpowered his nose now as well. In addition to some sort of beef, he could smell vegetables and even rice. Ran closed his eyes and imagined what sort of meal it would be. Perhaps a type of stew bubbling up in a cauldron over a fire. He shook the image from his head and crept forward the final few feet to the edge of the opening and looked beyond.

The belt leveled out suddenly and appeared to pass through a section of the shaft that was exposed in another cavern. In this cavern, Ran saw the making of some type of sentry outpost. Blue torches flickered on the walls while an actual fire blazed several feet away from the belt. Held aloft over the flames was a large iron pot. And around the fire sat three of Mithrus's men.

Ran turned his attention back to the belt. Perhaps four body lengths' distance were open here before the belt once again disappeared into a dark shaft on the other side of the cavern. That was a huge distance to attempt to cover without being seen by the guards. Granted, they wouldn't be expecting a slave to attempt the rigorous climb that Ran had just completed, but even if they didn't expect it, Ran's chance of making his way across undetected were slim.

One by one, the guards scooped out a huge serving of the beef stew from the pot and started noisily devouring it. Ran felt a wave of despair come over him. He had no idea what lay beyond, although he could feel a breeze of fresh air still blowing across his face. That was something. But it wasn't indisputable enough to risk three lives on. Worse, Ran had to wonder how easily Kuva and Cassandra could make the climb. In their weakened states—and after a full day of toiling in the catacombs—they would be exhausted. Ran was trained for this type of thing, but they weren't shadow warriors. The risk of them slipping during the climb and alerting the entire mountain was great.

Ran let his breath out slowly. He felt as though he had just expended far too much energy for a wasted trip. He had found out some important things, but it wasn't what he wanted to find out. His desire and his ego had deceived him with the thought that he might have found a viable escape route. Ran looked at the open expanse of belt before him and knew that he couldn't risk trying to cross the gap. If the belt was their only way out, then he had to save the element of surprise for when it actually counted. If he tried and now and was discovered, Zal and Mithrus both would know they had a problem. But if Cassandra and Kuva could make the climb tomorrow night, then Ran could use surprise to overwhelm the three guards and dispatch them quickly before they continued on their way.

He just hoped this was the only part that was exposed like this.

He took a breath and turned around. He would need to climb back down the shaft now and return to his pen. Ran figured he'd spent roughly two hours making the climb. Descending would be easier in some ways, but not in others. The risk of noise was always greater, he'd found, on the way down than on the way up. And with Bagyo slumbering far below, Ran would need to use extra caution as he returned. He just hoped the big beast slept all night long.

Because if he woke up and roamed around, or went to check on the slaves, Ran was going to have a very big problem on his hands.

Chapter Twenty-three

Ran was nearly all the way back down the conveyor belt when it started up.

Fortunately, Ran's hands were pressed into the sides of the shaft, and when he felt the belt move, he instinctively jerked his feet up off of the belt. Suspended there, he looked down at the belt and wondered why it had suddenly started up again. Had his disappearance been discovered? Had Bagyo gone to check on the slaves and seen Ran missing? Ran frowned and maneuvered so his feet could touch the walls on either side of the belt, giving his arms a break from holding himself up.

If Bagyo had discovered him missing, then the beast would have raised more of an alarm than simply switching the conveyor belt back on. There was no guarantee that Ran had used the belt to escape anyway. Ran shook his head in the darkness. No, perhaps Bagyo or someone else had simply switched it on to warm it up for the day ahead. Ran knew it was already after midnight. But he didn't know why the belt would need to be switched on right then.

There was a chance, he decided, that Bagyo had indeed concluded that Ran might have gone up the belt. Perhaps he was simply trying to cover his bases. If Ran had been caught on the belt, then the guards back above would certainly have spotted him when he came through the gap.

Ran worked his way down some more. The small comfort in the belt being on was that Ran didn't need to be as quiet as he had on the ascent. The leather conveyor belt made a ton of noise as it wound its way up the mountain. Still, Ran would need to make sure he didn't simply pop through the opening at the bottom and end up in Bagyo's arms.

He crept closer to the opening, now soaked with sweat as he did so. The fresh air he had enjoyed on the climb had been replaced with heat as the belt rumbled on below him. Ran paused to wipe his brow and then peered out of the opening.

He heard Bagyo before he saw him. The beast appeared to be whistling or humming some sort of song as he moved around the catacombs work area. Ran watched the hulking mass move past the opening twice and then disappear elsewhere. He sighed. This was going to be a huge problem. How was he going to climb out of the opening without Bagyo seeing him? Ran tried to crane his neck so he got a better view of the work area, but without knowing where exactly Bagyo was, escaping the hole was impossible.

I could bluff, he thought. If Bagyo saw him by the opening, Ran could simply tell him he'd heard the belt start up and assumed it was time to work. But would Bagyo believe him? As dumb as the beast seemed, Ran sensed he had more of an intellect than was apparent. Underestimating him could prove fatal.

The other option was to simply wait it out until the work shift started up. When Bagyo brought the slaves here, Ran could blend in with them and pretend he'd simply been overlooked. But as quickly as he considered it, Ran knew it wouldn't work. Mithrus had escorted the slaves to the work area. And Mithrus wasn't someone he could fool easily.

No, Ran had to get out of the opening and back to his pen as fast as he could. The safety of his friends and their escape plan depended on it.

But how?

Bagyo moved past the opening again, and this time, before Ran could think about it, he simply eased out of the opening, carefully landing on his feet between two rocks. Without pausing, Ran ducked around the corner and then out of the work area. All the while his heart hammered inside of his chest. But he didn't stop until he finally reached his pen. Sliding inside, he sat there breathing deeply to calm himself down. It had happened so quickly—almost as if his body had simply taken over and gotten him where he needed to be without any interference. Ran was grateful but simultaneously mystified by what had just happened.

Still, it had worked. No sense thinking about it too much, he finally concluded. Bagyo hadn't seen him, and that was a good thing indeed.

He glanced at Kuva. The big guy still slept soundly, his chest falling in time with his gentle snores.

Ran's clothes were soaked with sweat, and he shivered slightly as he lay on the hay. He figured he still had an hour or two before the new work day started up. He shut his eyes and breathed slowly, willing himself to fall asleep as fast as possible. In seconds, he was asleep.

He woke to the sound of Mithrus shouting for the slaves to gather themselves for the new workday. Ran groaned, rolled over, and sat up, wiping away the sleep from his eyes. By his own estimate, he'd had perhaps two hours of sleep. More than he'd expected, but far less than he needed.

Kuva grumbled as he woke up. "I'm not going to be very friendly to that scum today."

Ran shook his head. "Play the game for now, Kuva. You can kill him later."

Kuva touched one of the many bruises on his face and winced. "That bastard has ruined me for the ladies. If these don't heal, I'll give him a slow death the likes of which he's never dreamed of."

Ran smiled. "I'm glad you're okay. I wasn't too sure there for a while."

"Looked a sight, did I?"

"Indeed."

Kuva grunted as he stood up. "Takes more than what they threw at me to break one of my kind. Still, it wasn't very pleasant. I'll wager you heard my screams?"

"Yes. It didn't sound good."

"Pain never does," said Kuva. "Mark my words: when we get out of here, the wailing of Mithrus will wake the dead."

As the slaves filed out of the pens, Mithrus kept shouting for them to move faster. "Come on, you louts, Zal wants his tunnel to the other side completed this week. You've got a lot of work to do to make that happen. You don't want Zal to get angry, do you?"

Ran and Kuva moved out of their pens and into the line of other slaves. Ran saw Cassandra, but the princess wasn't awake yet or interested in looking at him. Ran still thought she looked beautiful, even dressed in tattered clothes.

"Ah, did you have a nice beauty sleep?" Mithrus swooped in front of them, blocking their way. With him were three guards. He clucked when he saw Kuva's face. "Oh my, did we get a little overzealous with our correctional action on you yesterday? That looks painful."

Ran could feel Kuva's temper wanting to explode, but knew if his friend did that, then Mithrus would simply hurt him all the more. So instead, Ran put one hand on Kuva's shoulder and looked directly at Mithrus. "Should we proceed to work?"

Mithrus switched his gaze from Kuva to Ran. "Don't test me, Nehonian. I could kill you without a moment's worth of work."

"I don't doubt it," said Ran. "But you did say that Zal would not be pleased if his tunnel wasn't finished. We would very much like to get on with our work."

"Oh, would you?" Mithrus chuckled and then swept his arm out to the side. "Then please . . . do carry on. Don't let us delay you any longer."

Ran eyed the gauntlet of Mithrus's guards but knew he had no choice but to walk through it. He nodded at Mithrus. "Thank you." Then he and Kuva walked past the guards.

As Kuva walked past Mithrus, the big man managed to keep his eyes staring directly in front of him. Ran marveled at his restraint, knowing that his friend would love nothing more than to rip Mithrus's throat out. As they moved down the tunnel to the work area, Ran nudged him.

"You did well back there."

"In my head, I just killed him twenty times." Kuva grinned. "I will take care of him for real one day very soon."

"Yes, you will," said Ran. "And then we'll be free."

"Free," said Kuva quietly. "That will be a good day, indeed." He glanced around and then back at Ran. "And when will that be, exactly?"

Ran held up his hand. "We shouldn't talk about that just now. Let me figure a few more things out and then we'll talk later. It's too dangerous to do so right now. Especially with Mithrus and his goons about."

They moved into the work area, and Kuva nodded at the pickax. "You want the first shift or should I?"

"You feel well enough to swing for a while?"

Kuva flexed his arms and then hefted the ax. "Yeah, feels pretty good, actually."

Ran felt a measure of relief. With such little sleep, the thought of hacking away at the stone was not a pleasant one. "I'll get the cart then. Let me know when you need a break, all right?"

Kuva nodded. "Good." He turned and started swinging at the stone. Around them, the sounds of other slaves doing the same echoed off the catacomb walls. Ran tried to look around for Cassandra but couldn't see her anywhere. He turned back and willed Kuva to swing harder. As soon as Ran could load up a cart, he could get out of their immediate area and make sure she was okay.

It took another five minutes before he was able to do so, but Ran pushed the cart toward the conveyor belt opening and then sighed when he saw Cassandra down at the far end of one of the other tunnels. He shook his head. The way Zal was trying to break through seemed entirely illogical to Ran. In his place, Ran would have concentrated all of the slaves in one key place. Progress would surely have been faster. Still, perhaps there was more to this way of doing things than Ran could fathom.

As he pushed the cart toward the opening, he saw Bagyo milling about. The beast was moving back and forth by the opening to the conveyor belt. Each time he did so, he stopped and sniffed the air. Ran nearly stopped right then and there, but doing so would have only provoked suspicion. Did Bagyo have a keen sense of smell? Had he scented Ran around the opening from earlier? Ran took a breath and continued to push the cart toward the opening.

Bagyo stopped as soon as he saw Ran. "You. Come."

Ran nodded and shoved the cart forward. As he did so, he collided with another slave pushing his cart and they went sprawling together across the floor. As they rolled, Ran mashed himself into the other man's body, trying his best to smear his clothes with the slave's. Given the horrid stench of the slave, Ran had to suppress his gag reflex.

Bagyo's hands plucked them apart and stood them back up. Ran looked at the other slave. "Sorry. I think my cart hit a rock."

Bagyo shoved the other slave away and pointed at Ran. "Come here."

He led Ran back to the opening and then stood by, again sniffing the air. Bagyo turned and eyed Ran. "You in belt last night?"

Ran stared him back in his eyes, knowing that doing so was an absolute must. "Last night? I was asleep. Exhausted after a day's work."

Bagyo leaned close to him, his mouth open and heaving as he sniffed Ran from top to bottom. Ran prayed he had enough of the other slave's stink on him to mask his own scent. Bagyo's breath hovered around Ran for a full two minutes. Ran kept his breathing steady and normal, just in case the beast could detect changes in body temperature, too.

Finally, Bagyo leaned back. Confusion creased his distorted face. "Guess not you." He pointed at the overturned cart. "Go. Get cart. Keep working."

Gladly, thought Ran. As he walked back to the cart, he breathed easier. Fortunately, the improvised plan had worked. But Ran would have to be careful to remember that Bagyo had an apparent number of traits he hadn't counted on having to deal with. Scent was a tough one to get past. There were ways, as Ran had just done. They were never palatable, however.

Ran collected his cart and then brought it over to the opening. As he fed rocks into the conveyor belt, he felt Bagyo watching him in his peripheral vision, still apparently suspicious. Ran made a great show of reaching all the way into the opening and brushing his sleeves against the opening itself. Each time he slid more rocks in, Ran reached a bit deeper, scraping his skin and clothes in the process. When he was done, he got the cart and started his return trip.

On the way back, he swerved down the tunnel where Cassandra was working. She looked up as he approached and nodded once to him.

"Are you okay?"

She nodded. "Just hate it here is all. I miss the outside world."

"I know," said Ran. He glanced around. Two slaves were busy hacking at the wall while another collected rocks only a short distance away from where Ran and Cassandra stood. Ran eyed him for a moment, but the slave never glanced his way. He was old and frail and clucked as he picked rocks up like he was tidying someone's messy house. Maybe he's already lost his mind, thought Ran. Easy enough to do in a place like this.

Ran lowered his voice. "It will be tonight. After everyone's asleep. I know a way. It's risky, but—"

Cassandra put a grimy finger over his lips. "*Shh.* Don't say any more. I trust you, you know that. You can tell us on the way there."

The touch of her finger had sent a jolt of energy through his body. Ran smiled and held her hand for a moment longer than he should have. "All right. Be careful today. You'll need all your strength for the journey ahead."

"Understood. Now get out of here before Bagyo starts looking for you again. The last thing you need is him on your case."

"You're right, of course." Ran turned and started pushing his cart back up the tunnel toward his own work station.

"Ran?"

He turned, and Cassandra stood there with a funny lopsided grin on her face.

"What is it?" he asked.

She grinned fully now and shook her head. "You really stink."

Chapter Twenty-Four

As the day dragged on, Ran started feeling the effects of little sleep. The pickax grew heavier with each swing. The cart became more and more unstable each time he had to push its contents to the conveyor belt. Even the air grew ever more humid and stifling. It was as if Ran were moving in slow motion, and there was little he could do to make himself feel better.

Sleep deprivation had been one of the things that the elders back at the Nine Daggers clan in Gakur had stressed could easily happen on assignments. Various environments and conditions would no doubt affect how a shadow warrior worked. As such, operatives had to be trained to deal with it.

Ran remembered the day he had walked into one of the classrooms high in a tower. He and four other students had been called there earlier than normal. When he arrived, Ran found the other students already there and one of the instructors, Eijiro, waiting for Ran.

"We've discussed before how you can never quite plan for every contingency that may arise in the course of a mission. Sometimes, things will happen and you may well wonder why they did. The universe, after all, plays a role in our lives and missions—whether we wish it did or not. As we are not yet able to bend the universe to our will, we must endeavor to be ready for anything that comes our way. That is the purpose behind today's lesson. You five are going to go through something that very few other people outside of the clan would ever think about willfully doing. But since we are not ordinary people, we hold ourselves to different standards. We do the things that others do not."

One of Ran's classmates raised his hand. "What is the lesson, Master Eijiro?"

Eijiro grinned as he walked around the students. "Did everyone have a good sleep last night?"

The students murmured and agreed they all had. Eijiro seemed pleased by this. "Excellent. Then you are starting this assignment off much better than you may find you will in the real world." He turned back to the student who had asked the question. "To answer you: today's lesson is learning how you function on a lack of sleep."

Ran frowned. "But it's morning. We just woke up a few hours ago. How will we know what a lack of sleep is like when we're already wide awake?"

Eijiro continued to smile and said nothing. Ran felt his stomach ache just a bit. He shook his head. "This exercise isn't just for today, is it?"

"Exactly," said Eijiro. "It starts today. It ends when you have all experienced the joy of being without sleep for a certain amount of time."

"How much time?" asked another student.

"It will vary depending on the student," said Eijiro. "Some of you will shows signs of sleep deprivation sooner than others. I will be watching all of you closely. Once I determine that prolonging the exercise will harm you, I will remove you from this room and put you to bed."

"So we just sit here?" asked Ran. "Do nothing?"

Eijiro shrugged. "You may do whatever you wish. The time is yours to move about. You cannot—must not—leave this room, however. To do so would place you in danger the longer the exercise runs. There are books in the back you can read. Food will be served four times each day. You should endeavor to exercise and keep your mind active during this time. You are not permitted to sleep. If you fail this exercise, you will be required to retest before you can successfully graduate. Is that understood?"

The students nodded. Ran felt a tightness in his stomach. Most times, the instructors told them about forthcoming tests. This was one of the few times they had sprung one on him. The tension in the room felt almost palpable as the students with Ran started realizing the gravity of the exercise and what it meant for their future careers. No one wanted to fail and have to go through this exercise again—especially now that they knew what it entailed.

"Boredom will be your constant enemy," said Eijiro. "The temptation for you to simply lay down will become overpowering at times. You must learn to resist it. We will not force you to do anything other than avoid sleep. If you can successfully battle boredom here, then in the real world, it will be somewhat easier to continue to fight even without rest."

"Somewhat easier," said another student. "But not entirely."

"Nothing ever is," said Eijiro. "But we endeavor to provide you with the most realistic exercises we can replicate within the safety of this school. This is one such exercise. Learn from it. Learn what happens to your body as it thirsts for more rest and you are unable to provide it."

Ran raised his hand. "Master Eijiro, what happens if we simply pass out?"

"If enough time has not passed, then you will be required to re-test at a later date." Eijiro grinned. "We know what the human body is capable of. We know how long we can go without food and water. We also know how long we can go without sleep. You students do not know that yet. In this exercise, you will learn." He looked at the timepiece on the wall and nodded. "It begins now."

Ran glanced at his classmates. There was a bit of nervous tension broken when they all realized there was nothing much to do but let time pass. Ran got to his feet and started doing some of the *taiso* body-stretching exercises that formed the foundation for the martial arts they studied here. He sank down and flexed his thighs and calves, twisting this way and that, enjoying the feeling of loosening up his muscles and ligaments. Two other students wandered to the shelves and chose a book to read. Another sat by the class window and stared outside as the day progressed. The last student immediately walked to Eijiro and told him he didn't feel ready for the test. Eijiro let him leave.

Four left.

The day dragged on. Ran worked his way through every unarmed technique he could recall. He performed them slowly, so as not to overly tax himself. But by the time the sun started heading toward the horizon, Ran felt the first twinges of exhaustion coming over him. Meals helped, but only for a short time. The spike from eating lasted perhaps an hour or two and then faded even faster. That first night saw Eijiro replaced by another instructor who watched over them with the eyes of a hawk. When one of the students dozed off, the instructor screamed at him. That helped wake Ran back up.

Eijiro returned the next morning. He looked refreshed and rested. Ran felt horrible. Each minute seemed to take days to pass. He sweated and at other times grew cold as his body struggled to figure out what was happening to him. Ran lost interest in the meals but ate anyway, knowing he had to keep his strength up despite the massive lethargy that had crept into his bones. On the second day, he did no physical exercises, judging he was too exhausted to try them. He tried reading a book instead and found the script kept melting all over the page as his eyes lost focus.

It would be one thing, Ran thought, if they kept us running all over the place. Then we wouldn't have time to think. But this is just monotonous.

"Feeling all right, Ran?"

He turned at the sound of Eijiro's voice. "Fine."

Eijiro grinned. "Good. Keep up the good work."

Ran frowned as the instructor turned away. Easy for him to say. He doesn't have to go through this.

At dinner on the second day, Eijiro left again and was replaced by yet another instructor. Ran knew of his reputation even though he had not yet had him for any course. The other students called him Weasel because of his thin, wiry appearance. Ran could have sworn the Weasel had whiskers growing out of his face, too. But he wasn't sure he was seeing anything accurately.

The Weasel seemed to love this exercise, though. When dinner was finished, he strode to the front of the class and clapped his hands. "So, two days in, are we?" He nodded at the four students. "Not bad, not bad at all. Not as good as when I went through this, mind you, but you lot don't look all that impressive."

As he said this, one of the students slipped from his bench and collapsed on the floor. The Weasel sighed and dragged the student out of the room, only to return moments later. "Three left now."

Ran eyed his classmates. There was no way, he decided, he was going to quit.

On the third morning, only Ran and one other student were left.

At some point during the night, the third student had been removed. Ran couldn't quite remember what had happened, his mind was truly one big foggy nightmare. Images swam in front of his eyes. He felt like he was drooling constantly. Each time he tried to walk around the room and do something physical to keep his mind from playing tricks on him, he would stumble.

The other student struggled to reach Ran. "I've seen you before. Are you in my class?"

Ran frowned. "I think so. I'm Ran."

"Akira," said the other student. "What happened to the others?"

Ran shook his head. "Gone. Just the two of us left."

Akira was an inch taller than Ran. He stood. "We've got to beat this thing. We can't let it get us. I don't want to ever go through this again."

"Agreed," said Ran. "But how? I can barely do anything right now as it is."

"We'll figure it out. We watch each other. Don't let either of us sleep." Akira grinned. "Did that make any sense?"

"I don't know," said Ran. "But it sounds good."

"I wish I could meditate with my eyes open," said Akira. "But I don't dare try it."

Ran smirked. "I think I could fall asleep with my eyes open at this point. Maybe we should nail our eyelids open or something."

Akira chuckled. Then Ran started laughing. Then they were rolling on the floor in hysterics. After several minutes of laughing, they sat up and Ran took a deep breath.

"That felt pretty good, actually."

"Yeah," said Akira. "You think it helped?"

"Don't know, but it didn't hurt."

They passed the next day by sparring in the room at slow speed. Ran found Akira very much his equal in most areas. Akira surpassed Ran in kicking, while Ran bested Akira with his throws. At the subsequent meals, they spent the time talking about favorite techniques and stuffing their faces. Ran felt a measure of invigoration. Maybe this exercise wasn't as bad as he thought it was.

The instructors came and went. Eijiro showed up a few times, only to be replaced by the Weasel and other faceless instructors. Time passed. Sometimes slowly and sometimes fast. But it passed, and that was all Ran and Akira cared about. If they could just hold on until the end, then they'd be all set.

On the evening of the fifth day, Akira went hysterical. He'd been fine, and then all of sudden he started screaming uncontrollably. He lashed out at Ran, and three instructors immediately rushed in and subdued him. Ran crowded them.

"What happened?"

"He's done," said Eijiro. "We're taking him out of here." The instructors carried Akira out and left Ran behind, alone in the room.

Despair fell upon him like a heavy yoke. Ran sat down and started crying. He was alone. Tired. Exhausted. Hungry. Cold. Hot. His body ached. His head throbbed. His friend had just been taken from him. When did this exercise end? Who had thought up this stupid thing? What did it prove? What was the point? Ran eyed the window. Maybe he should just jump out of it and save himself from this agony. Why was he even doing this?

He must have fallen backwards then and slammed his head into the stone floor. The room swam, melting into another picture of a face.

A face.

"Ran."

Eijiro hovered over him. Ran could barely process what was being said.

"You're finished."

"Wha—?"

"Done. Can you stand?"

Ran tried to move his legs. They didn't seem to work anymore. "I don't think so."

Eijiro smiled at him, his voice was warm and reassuring. "I'll get help. You can close your eyes now. You've passed the test."

"—Akira?"

"He passed, too. You did very well."

Everything fell away from him then. Blackness rushed in and enveloped him in a warm blanket of sweet slumber.

Ran slept for nearly two days. When he awoke, he was in his bed. Akira was perched on a bench nearby.

"How are you feeling?"

Ran had smiled. "Great."

"We passed," said Akira. "But only us. Out of the five. Congratulations."

Something exploded by the side of his head. Pain. A rock?

Ran blinked, and the images of Gakur vanished. He was back in the catacombs. Holding the pickax in his hands and swinging it hard. The last strike had sent a piece of rock zinging into his head. Ran put the pickax down for a moment and wiped the side of his head. His dirty hand came away slick with blood. Not too much, thought Ran. The injury wouldn't be bad. But he'd have to be careful. The lack of sleep last night was taking its toll on him. Still, he decided, it would never be as bad as what he had gone through with Akira.

He heard the rumbling of the cart as Kuva pushed it back toward their work area. Ran turned to look at his friend and then saw concern etched across his face.

"What's the matter?"

Kuva stopped pushing, clearly out of breath. He leaned on the cart and took a few breaths. "Tried to get back here as fast as possible." He heaved another breath. "I don't know what happened. I was down by the conveyor belt putting in the rocks."

"Yes?"

"It's Mithrus," said Kuva. "He came in and started talking to one of the other slaves. The slave pointed out Cassandra. Mithrus just grabbed her and took her away."

"Where? Where did he bring her?"

Kuva shook his head. "No idea. He just took her out of the catacombs."

Ran saw movement behind his friend.

Bagyo.

The beast looked at Ran. "You."

Ran hefted the pickax and thought about trying to battle Bagyo right then. But that wouldn't help Cassandra.

"What?" he said finally.

"You come. Mithrus want you."

Ran eyed Kuva. "If I don't come back, don't wait for me." He put the pickax down and followed Bagyo out.

Chapter Twenty-Five

Bagyo led Ran down a tunnel away from the catacombs and into another area of the mountain Ran hadn't seen before. As they walked, the ground sloped upward and the stone floor gradually morphed into some sort of tiled floor. The walls were also polished smooth. Ran glanced at his reflection several times, amazed at the amount of filth he'd managed to acquire in only a few short days.

Bagyo glanced back a few times and sniffed at Ran. That made Ran nervous. He wondered if the body odor of the other slave was starting to wear off. If Bagyo was able to smell through Ran's attempt at masking himself, then the beast might well know that Ran had indeed been inside the conveyor-belt shaft last night.

Ahead of them, Ran saw several of Mithrus's guards armed with short spears standing post beside a large stone door. On the doors themselves was some sort of regal seal. Probably something denoting the House of Zal, Ran decided.

As they drew closer, the guards sprang to attention, and one of them stepped forward to challenge Bagyo. "What business do you have here?"

Bagyo nudged Ran forward. "Mithrus tell me bring this one here."

The guard looked at Bagyo and then at Ran. Finally he nodded once. "Very well. We will escort him from here. Go back to the catacombs, beast."

Ran saw Bagyo frown and then turn away. As he did so, Ran thought he saw a glint of sadness in the beast's eyes. Bagyo took one final sniff at Ran and then plodded back down the corridor toward the work area in the catacombs.

The guard watched him walk away and then turned to Ran. "You come with us. If you try anything, we're under orders to kill you. Do you understand?"

Ran shrugged. "Sure." Rather than kill them both, Ran needed to know what had happened to Cassandra. There would be time enough later to settle scores.

The other guard pulled back on the door and waited until the massive portal swung open. Both guards then took up a position behind Ran, with their spears aimed right at the small of his back.

"Move."

Ran felt the tip of one spear bite into his back and started walking. The corridor was tiled like the one they'd just left, but the walls were covered with a variety of tapestries and paintings. All of them were of Zal. Ran managed to contain the smirk that desperately wanted to bloom across his face. Each tapestry or painting grew more grandiose than its predecessor, showing Zal in a variety of poses and heroic actions—none of which seemed to match the Zal that Ran had seen on his first day inside the mountain. It became obvious to Ran that Zal had a grossly inflated sense of self. But that was useful to Ran; he now knew one of Zal's weaknesses: his ego.

They turned left abruptly when the corridor stopped short. Farther down, a set of glass doors barred their way. As they approached, however, these swung open and permitted them access to a grand throne room. As they walked, Ran could see more guards, Mithrus, Iqban, and then on a throne three times his size, sat Zal.

He was dressed in several layers of gilded robes intricately woven with gold thread and studded with jewels. Those clothes must be worth more than this entire mountain, thought Ran. The guards brought him to within ten yards of the throne and then bade him stop.

Zal dismissed the guards with a wave of his hand. "Is this him?"

Mithrus, standing nearby, nodded. "Indeed, your grace."

Zal glanced at Iqban. "And this is the one you sold me, is that correct?"

"The one you said looked clever, yes, your grace."

Zal humphed. "Indeed. Well, apparently he's been quite clever already." His eyes came to rest on Ran. "Isn't that true?"

"I don't know what you're talking about," said Ran. "I've been working hard in the catacombs."

"And apparently trying to figure out how to escape as well," said Zal. He nodded to Mithrus. "Bring her in."

Mithrus, in turn, nodded to several of his guards. They left the throne room and returned a few moments later. Ran turned.

Cassandra.

She struggled against her captors as they dragged her into the throne room, but stopped when she saw Ran standing there. Her eyes asked him what he was doing there. Ran merely shrugged. What else could he say? He didn't yet know why they'd been brought here.

The guards dragged Cassandra over to stand next to Ran. When they were both in front of Zal, the small king leaned back in his throne and examined his fingernails. After a few moments, he sighed and looked at them both.

"So, Mithrus here tells me you two have been plotting to escape from my mountain."

Ran shook his head. "As I said earlier, I've been working hard in the catacombs. I can't see how anyone could escape from this place."

"So you've resigned yourself to the fact that this will be your home from now on?" asked Zal.

"Absolutely," said Ran. "I intend to do my best with whatever time I have left."

"Excellent," said Zal. "I'm thrilled to hear you say that." He looked at Cassandra. "And you, my dear? What sort of things have you been up to in the catacombs?"

Cassandra eyed him and then took a breath. "Swinging a pickax at a rock wall for hours upon hours until my hands bleed. Then I cart away everything I break from the wall and pour it into the conveyor belt." Her mouth twisted a bit. "It's truly rewarding work."

Zal nocked his head to one side, and the smile on his face continued to grow. "Marvelous. I'm so glad you're enjoying yourself. To hear Mithrus talk, I would have thought my hospitality was unwelcome. That perhaps you two were giving serious thought to escaping from my lovely home here."

Cassandra smiled, this time far more sweetly. "Why on earth would you think that?"

Zal nodded at Mithrus. "He told me one of his informants

whispered something about a plot to escape. Can you believe that? Granted, Mithrus is a suspicious type, anyway. And perhaps he doesn't think much of your suitor there—"

"He's not my suitor," said Cassandra. "He's just another slave I met in the catacombs."

Zal's smile deepened. "Really? And did you find him attractive? Perhaps you two have even been intimate back in the pens? Have you conjugated and lived out your torrid fantasies yet?"

Cassandra said nothing for a moment. Ran watched her struggle to control her temper. Eventually, she took a deep breath and kept looking right at Zal. "No."

"Which question were you answering?" asked Zal.

"All of them," said Cassandra without blinking. Even if he hadn't been standing near her, Ran could probably have felt the heat emanating from her body. Cassandra's features looked as though they were completely immobile, as if anything more than a feather would make her explode.

Ran marveled at her self-control. For a princess, it must have been nearly intolerable to be spoken to as Zal had done. Add to that the ignominy of being held captive as a slave and it was a wonder Cassandra hadn't simply tried to kill everyone in the mountain for forcing her to endure such pedestrian treatment.

Zal rubbed his nose for a moment and then sighed. "Well, it certainly seems as if everything is in order in the catacombs." He looked at Mithrus. "I told you there wasn't a problem. Sometimes it's just a matter of talking to people. Ask them the right questions and you find out the truth behind everything. Clearly, that's exactly what I needed to do here." He looked back at Ran and Cassandra. "Thank you for taking the time to come and answer my queries. I really appreciate that."

"We didn't exactly have a choice," said Ran. "You sent armed guards to collect us."

Zal shrugged. "Sometimes slaves can become somewhat . . . unruly. I learned that the hard way at the very start of this little venture I'm on. Give a slave too much freedom and they will no longer do what needs to be done. Give them too little freedom and they will resent you and quest for more. But give them just enough and they will work hard enough for your purposes while being too exhausted to do much else. It's a philosophy I've found works wonders with people."

Ran wasn't sure what to say to that so he stayed quiet. Cassandra still seemed too upset to utter a word.

Zal eyed Ran. "Not that I believe a single thing you've told me, of course."

Ran shook his head and started to protest, but Zal cut him off with a hand held up. "Don't bother. There's another thing I've learned in all my years: it's that people always lie when they think it will help their situation in life. You two are clearly planning something. I don't know exactly what it is yet, but I will find out."

Ran steeled himself. Most likely Zal would devise some sort of torture to extract the information. Ran wasn't too concerned. The elders at the Nine Daggers clan had put him through a very rigorous interrogation resistance course, designed to show Ran what the real world was like and how cruel it could be. The course had not been pleasant, but upon finishing it, Ran felt much better prepared for any eventualities that would involve torture.

Like what Zal was presumably planning.

Cassandra glanced at him, and Ran gave her a barely perceptible shrug. He needed to let her know that he would be fine. He wanted to say it to her, but then there was no telling how Zal would react to that. He might think Ran was boasting about his efforts to resist torture and intensify the process to try to break him faster. Ran felt confident he could hold out, at least for a few days. Hopefully by then he would devise a new plan for getting them all out of this horrible place.

The most important thing was giving them just enough information to let them think Ran was cooperating. If he could come up with a convincing story, then that would buy him time away from the pain. If there was one thing the elders had taught him above all others, it was that everyone breaks under torture. Because of that, the goal was to mitigate the amount of information disclosed. As far as Ran knew, Zal had no idea he was a shadow warrior. Perhaps he didn't even know what a shadow warrior was. At least right now, it appeared the only thing Zal wanted were the details of the escape plan. If Ran had some time to himself, he would be able to create a story that would both satisfy Zal and preserve the escape plan.

He hoped.

He wouldn't know until he got into the chamber and they started working on him. Some torturers were extremely skilled, he knew.

Others had no idea what they were doing, aside from producing massive amounts of pain in their captives. There was danger to both, but Ran preferred ending up in an experienced torturer's hands rather than an amateur's. An amateur would keep going until he killed the prisoner. An experienced torturer would know when to stop and when to go.

Ran took a breath. Whatever Zal had in mind, he hoped it would happen soon. If Zal waited too long, Ran would grow weaker in the catacombs, reducing his ability to resist torture even further. As it was, Ran was tired from last night's nocturnal foray. He wanted desperately to close his eyes and go to sleep.

He couldn't.

"You look tired," said Zal just then. "Perhaps you didn't sleep well last night?"

"I slept fine," said Ran. "But the pleasure of working for you is exhausting. There are only so many times a man can swing that pickax and not expect to be exhausted by it."

"But surely one such as yourself should be well-accustomed to this type of activity?"

Ran held his tongue. What was Zal implying? Did he know Ran was a shadow warrior after all?

"Being a warrior-for-hire and all," said Zal. "You don't get to do that sort of work unless you're in reasonably good condition, right?"

"I would argue that even being in shape is no match for the catacombs." Ran rubbed his right shoulder. "I'm feeling pain in places I've never felt it before." This was a lie, of course. As tired as he was, Ran wasn't too troubled with the physical labor aspect. He hoped that by rubbing his shoulder, it would give Zal an idea of where to start with the torture. If Ran reacted strongly to any prodding in that area, then they would think the effect was worse than it actually was. Deception was paramount, after all, if he hoped to eventually survive this and escape from the mountain.

He still had a reconnaissance mission to undertake at the behest of his clan.

Briefly, he thought about Ryu and whether the falk had flown back to Chulal or not. Perhaps even now Tanka was telling the clan that Ran had been lost. Would they ever send another shadow warrior out to look for him? No. That was the nature of his life. Accept the role and the risks that went along with it. Ran and others like him knew that if they got into trouble, no one was coming to save them. In some ways, he liked that autonomy. But now was one of the times he wished he had a friend to call upon.

Zal cleared his throat. "Well, I think this has gone on long enough. After all, I have a schedule to keep. Things to do and whatnot. I'm sure you understand. And whether you do or do not is irrelevant to me anyway. What will be, will be."

Ran nodded. "Let's get on with it then."

"Agreed," said Zal. "I admire the way you're handling this. Others in your position wouldn't be so keen to start."

"Sometimes you have to accept the inevitable," said Ran, still rubbing his shoulder. "I have."

Zal smiled. "Excellent." He turned to Mithrus. "You may take her away and do with her whatever you wish. Knowing you, that will involve some sort of tawdry action that will no doubt besmirch the young woman for the rest of her life."

Ran stepped forward. "She had nothing to do with this!"

Two guards appeared behind him and pinned his arms back, while two others grabbed Cassandra and dragged her away.

As Zal sat on his throne laughing, Mithrus walked over to Ran and stuck his face into Ran's. "I'm going to enjoy her in ways she's never even dared dream of." He chuckled. "Be sure to listen to her moans and screams while you await execution."

Chapter Twenty-six

Cassandra struggled as the guards hauled her away. Mithrus whistled as he exited the chamber, leaving Ran with the two men pinning his arms behind him. Zal was wiping his eyes and then stared at Ran without blinking. "Mithrus truly is a sick man. I imagine that poor woman is in for a rather rough time of it. A shame you won't be around to see what she looks like when he's done. I'm told his penchant for using his dagger on faces borders on the grotesquely artistic."

Ran eyed Zal. "She had nothing to do with this. Why don't you let her go?"

"Because there's no fun in that, frankly," said Zal. "And Mithrus needs a bit of a diversion, anyway. Life below ground like this is a tough adjustment for a warrior like him. It's been weeks since he's had anything to do with his excessive amount of energy. Your friend there will provide him with hours of entertainment . . . in more ways than one, mind you."

"I'll kill him for it."

Zal waved his hands. "Won't that be rather difficult to do when you're dead?"

"I'm not going to die," said Ran. "At least not yet."

Zal sighed. "Big talk considering my men have you in their custody. But do hold on to that bravado. It will be charming when you listen to the woman's pleas while you await your own grisly destiny." Zal looked at the guards. "Remove him from my sight. But put him in the cells closest to the chambers of Mithrus. I want him able to hear every sordid sound that comes from there."

Ran felt the guards shove him out of the chamber. He took one final glance back at Zal and set his jaw. There would be time for his death. For the moment, Ran had to coordinate his own escape and then find a means to rescue Cassandra before Mithrus was able to exact any sort of depravity upon her.

The guards led him down a side tunnel, and somewhere up ahead, Ran could hear Cassandra still struggling with her captors. He heard something that sounded like a kick and a guard doubled over in pain. Then he heard Mithrus's voice. "Enough."

There was a pause and then the sharp sound of a hand slapping flesh. Cassandra cried out once and then fell silent. The blow might have stunned her or even knocked her unconscious. Ran felt his blood boil at the thought that Mithrus had laid a hand on her. He forced himself to breathe and keep his rage in check. Anger was a useful tool; rage rarely so. And if he allowed himself the luxury of becoming emotionally unbalanced, his enemies would win.

Ran had no intention of letting them survive, let alone win.

The guard steered him into a holding cell and then closed the metal door behind them. Three quarters of the way toward the top, there was an opening that was just wide enough for Ran look through. His view was only of the tunnel walls outside his cell. But at least there didn't seem to be any guards around. No doubt they thought the cell impervious to escape.

Ran turned his attention to the interior of the cell, but a cursory examination revealed little in the way of exploitable weakness. The cell had been chiseled out of the hard earth and rock. It didn't connect to any other cells, and the metal door itself was thick enough that Ran wouldn't be able to force his way out. Even if he could, he had little room within the cell itself to maneuver. He leaned against the wall and closed his eyes, hoping to think of something that he could use to make his escape.

He still had the dagger that Yasseh had given him back at the scene of the caravan attack, but what good would it do inside the cell? He would need to launch an attack when Zal's guards came for him, presumably at the time of his execution. Ran would have but one chance to make his move, and it would need to be sudden and savage in order to succeed.

He stopped. If he waited, it would be too late to save Cassandra.

Mithrus would have already enjoyed his sordid fun at Cassandra's expense. For all Ran knew, Mithrus could be having his way with her at that very moment. The time to act wasn't when the guards would expect it; it was now, when they might not think he'd had enough time to formulate a plan.

Ran started banging on the door and coughing. He hacked for what felt like minutes before one of the guards appeared at the door.

"What is that racket?"

Ran gasped. "Water. Something in my throat." He retched and forced himself to throw up the little contents of his stomach. The guard backed away and shouted for some help. No doubt Zal wanted Ran alive until he could execute him, so if anything happened, the guards would be at fault.

As he continued to cough, Ran bent over double and used his right hand to draw out the dagger. As his hand closed over the hilt, he felt a surge of adrenaline flood his system. He primed himself by gasping deep breaths that would ensure he had enough air to fight with.

The lock on the door rattled once as the guard slotted a key into the lock and turned it. Ran was still doubled-over coughing as the two guards entered bearing a bowl of water.

"Here—" one of them started to say.

But even as the word left his mouth, Ran was already launching himself at the two men. Before they had time to react, Ran had punched a neat stab into the base of the throat of the man with the bowl of water. He jerked the blade free, spun and went low, slashing at the inside of the second guard's thigh before coming up with a single stab to the heart. Both men slumped to the ground. The bowl clattered against the wall of the cell before rolling to a stop in the pool of blood.

Ran regained his breathing and wiped the dagger's blade on one of the guards. The door to his cell stood open. He had scant minutes to find Cassandra, kill Mithrus, and then start their escape.

As he stole into the tunnel, he wondered if it would be enough time. It would have to be, he decided. And somehow, he still had to find Kuva and help his friend escape as well.

A single torch flickered high on the tunnel wall, illuminating a scant bit of the area around him. Ran used his peripheral vision to try and pick his way along. He was badly exposed right then, and he needed to reach wherever Mithrus had taken Cassandra without alarming the entire complex. Even for a shadow warrior, overwhelming odds were nothing to take lightly.

Ran kept the dagger tucked close to his body as he stole sideways down the tunnel. His lead hand stayed out in front of him, carefully guiding him away from rocky outcroppings and feeling along for anything else that might surprise him.

"Wake her up."

Mithrus's voice floated down the tunnel. Ran frowned. Cassandra had obviously been knocked out. Ran suppressed the rage burning within him again and forced himself to objectively assess the situation he would soon be in. He needed to know how many men Mithrus had with him. And then he needed to figure out how badly wounded Cassandra was. It was no use trying to escape with her if she was incapable of fending for herself.

He continued on. There was the sound of splashing water followed by coughs and sputters. Mithrus laughed then. "Welcome back, my dear. I trust you had a delightful little nap?"

"I hope the crows feast upon your withering carcass under a noon sun," spat Cassandra.

Mithrus laughed again. "That was very nearly poetic. But unfortunately, your skills are wasted upon me. I'm a simple man. I live by my blade and take what I achieve through force."

"Because no woman would ever give herself to you willingly." Cassandra laughed now. "Your manhood is questionable at best."

"You'll find out soon enough," said Mithrus.

Ran crept ever closer and saw the outline of the cavern where Mithrus must have taken Cassandra. Light flickered from within, and Ran watched several shadows reach out into the tunnel. He frowned. There might be as many as four men in there with Mithrus. Such odds weren't necessarily bad, provided Ran maintained the element of surprise. But if he was heard approaching, he'd walk right into a death trap.

"Undress her."

Ran's jaw clenched. The time for planning was over; action was all he had left now. He moved closer and took several deep breaths to flush himself full of air prior to combat. He heard the sound of fabric tearing. Cassandra gasped. Mithrus laughed. Several other voices laughed as well.

Ran gripped the dagger and moved to just outside of the cavern opening.

"Now, my dear—"

Ran slid into the cavern and immediately saw the targets before him. Two guards flanked Cassandra, who stood partially naked, with the glow of the fire behind her silhouetting her body. Mithrus stood with his back to Ran.

Ran didn't pause. He stepped forward and plunged the dagger into the base of Mithrus's skull, cutting to one side and then the other. Mithrus let out a quick gasp and then simply dropped, letting the blade slide free of his head as he did so.

The guards looked shocked at the sudden appearance of Ran, but their inaction proved to be their undoing. As Cassandra immediately grasped the implications, she elbowed one of the guards in the stomach even as Ran closed the distance between him and the other guard and feinted a high cut before diving low and stabbing up between the man's legs. The guard screeched and then fell forward clutching at his bloody groin. Ran stepped behind him and drove the dagger into the ear canal of the guard.

"Ran!"

He turned and saw Cassandra struggling with the other guard. He leapt across the fire and kicked the guard in the back of his leg, buckling the man's knee. Cassandra tore herself away from his grasp, and Ran moved in fast, driving the dagger into the man's neck. He gurgled and spewed blood across the cavern before slumping forward onto his face.

Ran watched as Cassandra gathered her clothes about herself. "Are you okay?"

The princess was fiercely proud. "I'm fine. Thank you for coming when you did."

"They locked me in a cell," said Ran. "I had to figure out a way to escape before I could find you."

Cassandra didn't seem to be paying attention. She was studying the corpse of Mithrus. She reached down and ripped his sword free from its scabbard. "This bastard meant to pollute my body." She raised the sword high overhead and brought it down on Mithrus's head, cracking his skull open with a single cleave. Ran watched bits of bone and gray matter ooze from the opening. Cassandra retched once and then turned away.

"Hang onto that sword," said Ran quietly. "Chances are we're going to need it."

He helped himself to the swords worn by the other guards. They were a bit unwieldy, but the more weapons he had, the better Ran felt. "We have only a little bit of time to get out of here before someone notices that Mithrus is absent and comes looking for him."

Cassandra grinned. "Something tells me that he's not some sort of all-night lover. We might even have less time than we think if any of his men know him well enough."

Ran smiled. "Good to see you still have your sense of humor."

"And my dignity," said Cassandra. "Thank you, Ran."

"Time for thanks later," said Ran, moving past her. As much as the thought of being with the princess attracted him, they had more pressing matters before them. "We need Kuva. If we have any hope of getting out of here alive, we'll need the big guy to help us out."

"So you know the way back to the tunnels?" asked Cassandra.

"I can probably find the way," said Ran. "But we're going to run the risk of seeing more guards."

"You can deal with them, though," said Cassandra. "Can't you?"

Ran frowned. "I'm tired. The truth is, you're going to have to help me. If we run into a squad of guards, you'll need to fight also."

"Fair enough," said Cassandra. "I'll hold my own. Just find Kuva and let's get the hell out of here."

Ran eased back out of the cavern and into the tunnel. He closed his eyes and tried to remember the direction they'd come from when Mithrus had dragged them before Zal. His gut was telling him left, so Ran headed that way, aware that Cassandra was right behind him. He glanced back. "Put a little space between us. If we get into trouble, that space will be crucial to us being able to fight properly."

"Sorry."

Ran smiled at her. "Don't worry about it. We'll get through this. I promise."

"I'll hold you to that," said Cassandra. "Which way?"

Ran pointed, and they kept moving. They came to a branch in the tunnel, and Ran felt that they should veer to the right. The ground sloped downward. Ran felt certain they were heading back toward the dig site. He just hoped that Bagyo wasn't anywhere about. The last thing he needed was to have to fight some giant beast.

A deep rumble sounded from somewhere far below them. To Ran's ears it sounded like an explosion. But what would be the cause of that?

"What in the world was that?"

Ran held up his hand. "I don't know. It came from below us, though."

"Should we wait?"

Ran heard voices to his left and pushed Cassandra back into the darkened recess of a wall nearby. A bunch of guards rushed down the tunnel a few feet from where they hid. They all had their weapons drawn. Ran frowned. What was going on?

He waited until after they'd gone before stepping back out into the tunnel. "I don't know what caused that explosion, but it certainly seems to have the place alarmed."

"Kuva's down there," said Cassandra. "He could be hurt."

Ran licked his lips. There was more risk heading down there now with all those guards in the area. But Kuva was his friend, and Ran detested the idea of leaving the big man behind to fend for himself. "I've got to risk it."

"We've got to risk it," corrected Cassandra. "If you're going, so am I."

"We might not make it out alive."

"Then we die together." Cassandra grabbed Ran's hand and led him toward the sound of danger.

Chapter Twenty-Seven

Cassandra led them down the tunnel. Before Ran could retake the lead position, they heard the sound of running feet. Cassandra raised her sword and cut down at an unseen target.

The blade came screaming down, but then ran right into the handle of a pickax.

"By Harbul's ghost, what are you doing with that thing? Trying to kill me already?"

Kuva's face emerged from the dark. He broke into toothy grin and eased Cassandra's sword blade from the shaft of the pickax. "Next time you take a swing at someone, try to make sure they're not a dear friend first, would you?"

Cassandra blanched. "Sorry."

"You very nearly cleaved my skull in two with that thing."

Ran came up and gave Kuva a quick hug. "Where did you come from?" He gave Kuva one of the blades he carried, and the big man grinned as he hefted it.

"Down below. We were working normally when all of a sudden all hell broke loose. One of the walls exploded, and then a whole bunch of armed warriors broke in from the other side."

"The other side?"

Kuva nodded. "Zal's been wanting to break through, hasn't he? Well, it seems someone on the other side decided to take the initiative and attack first. I was lucky to get out of there with my life, mind you. Zal's men are down there as we speak doing battle with them."

"Will they prevail?"

"I don't know," said Kuva. "When I left, there were literally hordes of troops pouring through."

Even as he said this, the sounds of battle seemed frighteningly close at hand. Ran eyed Cassandra. "We should get out of here now while we still can."

"You won't get an argument from me," said Cassandra. "The sooner we're free from this infernal place, the better."

Kuva hissed. "More guards coming. Let's get out of here."

Ran turned away from the tunnel leading down to the battle, and they rushed back toward where Mithrus had imprisoned Cassandra. Ahead of him, he could see more guards coming toward him. Ran led them into the chamber where Mithrus's body lay and waited as the guards stormed past. In the corridor outside they could hear Zal's voice clamoring for someone to find Mithrus.

"Uh-oh," said Kuva when he saw the corpse on the floor.

"Unavoidable," said Ran.

Kuva grinned. "Am I right in assuming that the cracked skull might be due to our overzealous female companion here?"

"You'd be right in assuming that," said Cassandra. "And I had good reason to do so, just remember that."

"Yes, ma'am," said Kuva. He looked at Ran. "We can't stay here. They're going to want their commander coordinating the defense."

Ran nodded. "All right. We're going right out of this cavern. Ahead there should be a branch, and the tunnel should slope upward. Let's follow that to the surface."

Kuva took the lead, and they exited the chamber.

And ran right into a squad of guards at the entrance.

"Stand fast!" shouted the guard leader.

Kuva had no intention of doing so and blundered into them, shoving them back into the tunnel and clearing the way for Ran and Cassandra to get out. As they did so, Kuva retreated so the guards were behind them.

The tunnel was wide enough for two men to stand abreast, so Ran joined Kuva at his side brandishing his own sword.

"Where is Mithrus?" shouted the guard leader.

"Dead," said Ran. "Your leader is dead. Let us go and we'll spare your lives."

The guard leader smirked. "We outnumber you ten to one."

"Numbers don't matter," said Ran. Somewhere behind the group of guards the sounds of battle grew louder. The clangs of steel-on-steel rang out and echoed along the tunnels. "And it sounds like your enemies are getting closer. You don't want to have to battle them behind you and us in front of you."

"We can handle them," said the guard leader. But then he turned as one of his men cried out. Ran saw a rush of figures pour into the corridor. They were smaller than the guards; much like Zal himself. And they were clothed only in some type of leather armor, brandishing shorter weapons better suited to fighting in the close confines of the tunnel networks they inhabited.

As soon as they saw the guards, they attacked. Screams and screeches broke out. Kuva stood his ground and cut down one of the guards who tried to flee.

Ran nudged him. "Let's get out of here."

They turned and ran down the corridor. At the branch, Ran paused and looked back. The sound of battle had died away, replaced by something far worse. As he watched, the smaller warriors that had just defeated Zal's guards had put down their weapons and started feasting on the bodies of the slain. Their fingers poked and tore at scraps of flesh, plunging chunks of muscle and fat into their mouths. The stench and sound of bloody flesh being devoured made Ran's stomach heave. He was momentarily thankful for the fact that his stomach had very little left in it.

"Ran!"

He blinked and turned, catching up with Kuva and Cassandra.

As they raced on, Cassandra caught up with him. "Why on earth did you stop?"

"Don't ask," said Ran. "Some things are too terrible to talk about."

The tunnel sloped upward, and Kuva led them. A few stray guards came at them, but more often they avoided any sort of combat. Already more of the underworld inhabitants were streaming up into Zal's domain, slaying anyone they found and feasting on their bodies. As they worked their way up toward the entrance to the catacombs, the sounds of horror grew louder. More of Zal's hired army fell victim to the invaders. But Zal had apparently gone missing. Ran felt certain he was around somewhere, but there wasn't time to settle up with him. The smaller invaders seemed ravenous and nearly unstoppable.

Certainly Ran did not have the resources to do so. His best option was to get out of the catacombs and back into the outside world.

As Kuva led them up the tunnels, Ran kept glancing back over his shoulder. Part of him expected that the invaders would overcome all resistance and then set their sights on the fleeing trio. But every time he looked back, Ran only heard the terrible sounds of the feasting invaders. They never seemed interested in giving chase.

At least Ran hoped they weren't interested.

But where was Zal?

Kuva's arm shot into the air, and they all stopped short. Kuva must have spotted something ahead of them. Ran worked his way up to his friend and whispered in his ear. "What is it? Why have we stopped?"

Kuva shook his head. "Something's not right. It's too still up ahead. It feels . . . unnatural."

"Unnatural."

Kuva nodded. "I don't like it."

Ran glanced around them. In the middle of the sloping tunnel, they were exposed again. And this time, the rock walls seemed much smoother than farther down. There would be no places to hide up here. Any interaction with Zal's men would no doubt result in combat. "We can't stay here."

Kuva's eyes narrowed, and he scanned from one side to the other. Finally, he sighed. "Maybe I was wrong."

"I doubt it," said Ran. "But if there's danger up ahead, it's almost certainly not as bad as what waits behind us."

Kuva eyed him. "What did you see back there?"

"The invaders," said Ran. "They ate the men they killed. It was as if they hadn't eaten in years, and they ate their fill in the most heinous of ways."

Kuva spat on the ground. "Curse them all. Let's move and get out of here." He stood back up and pressed on.

Cassandra looked at Ran as she passed. "Everything all right, Ran?"

"Not until we're out of this hellhole," said Ran. "Which hopefully will not be much longer."

"One would hope."

Ran looked back at the way they'd come. He could still hear the sounds of battle, although there seemed to be far less of it now. One side had to be winning, and Ran doubted it was Zal's mercenaries. The invaders had looked too powerful to thwart. He almost felt sorry for the men who were killed and eaten.

He ran to catch up with Kuva and Cassandra and was surprised when a sudden blow took him completely off his feet and sent him thundering into the wall of the tunnel. The air rushed out of his lungs, and he struggled to catch his breath. Numbly, he tried to bring his sword up, but that was batted out of his grasp.

"You bad man."

Ran's mind raced to fill in the blanks. Then the hairy paw lifted him up and slammed him back against the tunnel wall again. Ran struggled to keep from losing consciousness. "Bagyo?"

"You ruin everything, little man. Make Bagyo's home go away."

Ran shook his head, not only to deny the claim but to try to shake some sense back into himself. "Zal is the one you should blame. If he hadn't brought you here—"

"Zal give me job. Make me happy. Then you come and everything go bad."

Bagyo threw Ran again. Ran collapsed in a heap and wondered where Kuva and Cassandra were. He could certainly use some help in fending off Bagyo. The giant hairy beast loomed closer and plucked him off the floor of the tunnel before throwing him again. Ran tried to relax as he crashed into another wall. But he knew he was dangerously close to passing out. And if that happened, there was no guarantee he would ever wake up again.

Ran tried pawing about for his sword, but he had no clue where Bagyo had sent it flying. And before he could recover, Bagyo was back on him again, this time sending a thundering kick into Ran's midsection. He rolled with it, trying to go with the force of the impact, but Bagyo nailed him in the ribs, and Ran knew some of them must have broken.

He winced and came up on his feet. The only way he was going to get out of this alive was if he figured out how to fight Bagyo off. But he needed a sword to do that.

"Ran!"

Kuva's voice drew Bagyo's attention barely in time to avoid the downward stroke of Kuva's blade. Bagyo roared and batted him away. But Kuva was much bigger than Ran and Bagyo's strength was much more even with Kuva. Kuva drew back and prepared to cut at the beast again. As Bagyo rushed in, Kuva sidestepped and brought the sword up in a tight arc that cut into Bagyo's right arm.

Bagyo howled in pain and caught Kuva back across his face with a claw that drew streaks of blood and flesh from Kuva's cheek. But the warrior refused to give way and thrust his sword deep into Bagyo's side until the hilt was the only part still jutting out of him. Bagyo reared back, tearing the sword from Kuva's grasp, and uttered a massive bellow before collapsing on his face and lying still.

Ran heard his breath coming in spurts.

Kuva retrieved his sword and then touched the flaps of flesh dangling from his face. "This will no doubt send the maidens of Gallina fleeing at the sight of me."

"As opposed to that reeking breath of yours."

"You're one to talk. The stench of you carries through the tunnels like a plague."

Ran grinned. "Nice to see you again."

Kuva nodded. "Apologies, my friend. We ran into some more of Zal's men farther up the way there. Took us a moment to sort them out."

"Cassandra?"

"She's fine," said Kuva. "She was mopping up the last of them when I realized you weren't with us and came back down. Judging by what I saw, my timing was barely acceptable."

Ran got up, wincing as he held his side. "Could have used your presence a little sooner than when you came, I'll be honest. But better late than never." He scanned the floor. "He batted my sword away. I need to find it before we continue."

Kuva searched, and they found it within a few moments. Ran felt better having it in his hand, but the pain in his side from the broken ribs kept disturbing him. He had to find a way to shut the pain out or else it would interfere with his fighting ability.

"Stay behind me," said Kuva as they moved back up the tunnel. "You'll do neither of us any good if you have to fight. I've had broken ribs before. They're no joy. I imagine sleeping will be delightful for you for some time to come."

"I'd be happy just to put my head down upon a bed of hay," said Ran. "It feels like forever since I slept."

"You can sleep later," grumbled Kuva. "Something tells me we haven't seen the last of Zal yet."

"You think he's still around? Perhaps he was caught below and is being eaten even now."

"Doubtful," said Kuva. "Men like Zal are masters of opportunity. He probably had an escape route all mapped out just in case something happened. My guess is he's farther up by the entrance."

Ran frowned. The thought of more fighting pained him. But if that's what it took to get out of here, then he would have to do it.

Kuva stopped then, and Ran nearly bumped into him.

"What is it?"

Kuva glanced around. "Where is she?"

Ran felt a pang in his stomach. "Cassandra?"

Kuva nodded. "I left her here. She was fine."

Ran frowned. "She's not here anymore."

Kuva bent close to the ground and ran his fingers over the earth. After a moment, he stood back up. "She's been taken."

"By who?"

"I don't know," said Kuva. "But there was more than one of them. And my guess is they're heading the same way we are. Up and out of this place."

"Then lead on," said Ran. "The sooner we track them down and free Cassandra, the sooner we can get out of here."

Kuva shifted his belt and then set off up the tunnel. Ran looked around and then followed his friend.

Chapter Twenty-eight

It didn't take long for them to pick up the trail. Cassandra had very obviously dragged her feet as she was taken, and the tracks led them farther up the tunnel toward the catacombs' entrance. While torches still lit their way in spots, the area was filled with shadows, forcing Kuva and Ran to slow down or else risk blundering into an ambush. Ran assumed the lead from his friend, and they continued. When the tunnel grew too dark to see, Ran bent and let his hand kiss the top of the ground, searching for Cassandra's tracks. They stopped every ten meters to check and check again, but after several hundred meters, the tracks suddenly vanished.

"What's the problem?" asked Kuva.

"Gone," whispered Ran. "The tracks have vanished."

Kuva turned and looked back at the way they'd come. "Is there a chance there's a branching tunnel connected to this passage?"

"I didn't sense any," said Ran. "You?"

Kuva shook his head. "No, and I think we would have noticed a change in the air if there was."

"Agreed, which leaves us with only one possibility."

"That being?"

"They must have noticed what she was doing and picked her up."

Kuva grunted. "Someone is going to be moving slower than the rest of them, then. That means we have a chance to catch up."

Ran nodded. "We'll still have to be careful."

"If we're too careful, they'll get out of the catacombs and be gone before we can save her. I think, my friend, the time for being cautious is nearly at an end."

As much as he hated the risk of running into an attack, Kuva was right and Ran knew it. They'd so far managed to avoid detection, but what good was that if they risked losing Cassandra once her kidnappers got outside of the catacombs? The risk was real, and the danger to Cassandra was as well. Ran knew that he stood at the brink of either making the right decision or one that had the potential to haunt him for the rest of his life.

"Let's do it."

Kuva stood and sniffed the air around them. "They'll have a rear guard posted as they travel. If they're smart."

"We should assume they are."

Kuva nodded. "I'll take the lead. Once I engage with the rear guard, you get in there and grab the princess."

Ran frowned. "Who told you she was a princess?"

"I've known plenty of women in my time, my friend," laughed Kuva. "Cassandra is refined, even though she tries to hide it. Plus, judging by how she holds a blade, someone taught her some skills. And skills don't come cheap. She was either the daughter of a wealthy merchant or part of the aristocracy. I guessed right, though, apparently."

"If anyone finds out, she could be in danger."

"I won't tell a soul," said Kuva. "How are your ribs?"

"Feels like someone is standing on them. It's hard to breathe, but I'll get through it."

Kuva grunted again and then smiled in the dark. "I do so love the anticipation of battle. Where others get queasy, I enjoy the uncertainty of it. Life and death hover over you, waiting for the inevitable to happen. One outcome or another. At no other time is a man so acutely aware of his own power and frailty as he is just before he goes into battle."

"Underneath that burly disguise beats the heart of a poet." Ran clapped Kuva on the back. "Let's go get her."

Kuva dashed up the tunnel with Ran behind him. Their footfalls echoed as they raced on. The tunnel curved slightly and then widened out. The darkness dissipated, and Ran saw the huge door that had stood as entrance to the catacombs. At last they were back to where they'd started. Ran exhaled and then spotted six men. Two of them carried a struggling Cassandra. And one man led them all.

Iqban.

Kuva frowned. "I thought he'd left."

"The weather was too terrible for him to do so, remember?"

"It feels like we've been underground for weeks," said Kuva. "I don't even know what day it is."

"It doesn't matter," said Ran. "All that matters is getting her back and then getting out of here."

"Iqban!" roared Kuva.

The party of warriors stopped. Three men drew swords and rushed toward Kuva.

Kuva winked at Ran. "See you on the other side."

"Fight well."

And then Kuva stepped forward to meet the first attacker. The man rivaled Kuva's size, but his sword skills lacked. As he tried to bring an overhead cut straight down upon Kuva's head, the big man simply pivoted out of the way and backhanded a slash into the attacker's throat. The movement severed the attacker's head, which rolled into the feet of the second attacker, forcing him to leap over it as he charged forward. But Kuva was already going on the attack and stabbed the second man in the heart before yanking his blade free and meeting the side stroke of the third attacker with the flat of his blade.

Ran didn't have time to watch any more of the action. Instead, he dashed forward and met one of the men who had been carrying Cassandra. Before the man could draw his sword, Ran threw the dagger that Yasseh had given him. It punched into the base of the would-be attacker's throat, and he dropped.

Iqban gestured to the second man. "Get him! Quickly!"

The second man dropped Cassandra to the ground, and Iqban yanked her to her feet. Ran saw the second attacker rush toward him with his sword held up in front of him. Ran feinted to the left and then dropped to his right knee and cut up under the arc of the attacker's strike, slashing deep into the man's abdomen. Blood spilled forth, and Ran nearly gagged from the stench of entrails and the pain lancing out from his broken ribs. But he kept moving as the attacker sank to his knees.

Behind him, he was aware that Kuva had polished off the third attacker.

Iqban, however, wasn't done yet. As Ran and Kuva moved closer to him, Iqban drew a dagger and held it up next to Cassandra's throat.

"Don't move or else I will cut her throat."

Ran shook his head. "And what good will that do? We'll simply kill you then."

"Or we might not," said Kuva. "There are an awful lot of hungry cannibals streaming up from the depths of the earth behind us. Every one of Zal's men that they've killed have been eaten."

"You're talking nonsense," said Iqban.

"I wish we were," said Ran. "The sights and sounds that we left below are too terrible to wash from my mind."

"So, if you kill Cassandra, we'll simply wound you and then leave you here. Can you imagine being eaten while you're still alive? You'll feel every bite they rip out of your body. You'll beg for death. And you'll die . . . slowly."

Ran inched forward. Iqban's eyes showed his uncertainty. He might have suspected they were lying, but he also knew that if killed Cassandra, they'd be on him instantly.

The knife came away from Cassandra's throat. Iqban shoved her toward Ran and Kuva and then dashed down a side tunnel. Kuva started to run after him, but Ran called him back.

"Do you know where that tunnel goes?"

Kuva shook his head. "No."

"Then it's a safe bet that it might lead us deeper back into the catacombs. And we're so close to escaping now, there's no sense in chasing him. Iqban's time is limited. He'll either find a way out or else end up a meal for the invaders."

Ran removed the gag from Cassandra's mouth, and she breathed in a huge gulp of air. "Thank you. Again."

Kuva shrugged. "Just another day's work."

Cassandra looked at Ran. "We need to get out of here as fast as we can. I don't relish the thought of those invaders coming after us."

"Neither do I," said Ran. "I'm betting once we're outside, we'll be safer." He looked at the door barring the exit. "The only question is: how do we get out of here?"

"When we arrived, Iqban knocked three times," said Cassandra. "But they were clearly expected, and Mithrus must have stationed guards nearby to open the door."

"All the guards now are trying to deal with the invasion," said Ran. "Which leaves us to figure out how the opening mechanism functions."

"You two figure it out while I stand guard," said Kuva. "Such things as this are a bit beyond my ken."

Ran nodded. "All right, give us as much time as you can."

"Will do."

As Kuva moved to a position that allowed him to view both tunnels, Ran guided Cassandra over toward the iron door. "Would it make sense to try knocking?"

"May as well try," said Cassandra. "Who knows? It might even work."

Ran rapped on the door three times and waited. The knocks echoed painfully loud back into the tunnel. Ran grimaced at the thought of the sound carrying deep below and drawing the attention of the invaders. But it couldn't be helped. If there was any possibility of opening the door that way, they had to try it.

But after several minutes, nothing happened. The iron door remained as immovable as ever.

"So much for that," said Cassandra. "Let's try to figure out the mechanism for opening it." She looked at the hinges on the door and then backtracked toward the wall, running her hands over the rocks. "There's some sort of channel that runs along the wall. But it's been covered over with some type of plaster or baked earth."

"Where does it lead back to?"

Cassandra kept moving, and Ran saw she was getting close to the tunnel that Iqban had fled down. She stopped and looked back at Ran. "It leads in there."

Ran held up his hand and then came away from the door. If anyone was going into the tunnel, it would be him. With Iqban on the loose, there was no telling what might be hiding inside the tunnel. "Stay here with Kuva. And help yourself to a weapon from one of the dead guys there. If we run into trouble here or outside, you'll need something."

Cassandra nodded. Ran entered the tunnel and kept his free hand on the wall. The princess was correct. Ran could feel the channel beneath his hand, and he followed it deeper into the tunnel. He halfway expected Iqban to jump out at him at any moment and try to kill him, but he sensed nothing else moving with him in the tunnel. For the moment, it appeared as though they were safe.

The channel ended abruptly as Ran's hand grazed an outcropping of metal. He looked closer and saw that it was a knob of some sort. He tried turning it, but it didn't move. Peering closer, he saw a small keyhole at its base.

Locked.

He frowned and retreated back into the cavern. Cassandra looked up as he came back.

"Find anything?"

"Yes," said Ran. "It leads to a knob that you can turn to presumably open the door."

"So why didn't you open it?"

"Because it needs a key."

Kuva groaned. "Wonderful. I'm guessing there wasn't a key by the knob?"

"No," said Ran. "I'm assuming someone else has it. Perhaps Iqban. That would explain why he ran away. He still had a card to play, it appears."

Cassandra came closer to him. "What about your skill in picking locks? I've seen you do it several times now. Could you pick that lock by the knob?"

Ran took a breath. His ribs ached. "There's a chance I could, but it's going to require tools I don't really have." In truth, he'd never seen a keyhole that looked like the one by the knob. Even with his expertise, part of him wondered if he'd be able to pick the lock.

Kuva cleared his throat. "Ran, if you've got any sort of chance of getting through that lock, I suggest you explore it. And fast."

Ran looked up. Kuva was pointing back down the tunnel.

"More sounds of battle down there. But it's getting closer. A lot closer."

"How much time, do you think?"

"Depends on the people fighting, but I wouldn't think we have more than ten minutes. We need to get out of here."

Ran placed a hand on Cassandra's arm. "Stay with him. If I can get the door open, you two get out of here. Don't worry about me. I'll catch up."

Cassandra started to protest, but then stopped. Instead she smiled. "I won't insult you by insisting that I stay behind. I know you'd have Kuva carry me out of here by force if necessary."

"I care for you too much to let anything bad happen to you. You know that."

"I do." She leaned forward and gave him a quick kiss on the lips. "Do your best, Ran. But hurry up." She glanced over at Kuva and then back with a grin. "Kuva's not really my type."

The big man grunted. "I heard that."

Ran chuckled to himself and then headed back into the side tunnel. Once he was back at the knob, he drew out the slim lock picks he carried inside of his tunic waist band and set to work examining the lock. He slotted in one of the pieces of curved metal and then a straighter one, carefully raking them along what he judged to be the pins of the lock. He tested their springiness and then drew the picks back out before retrying it. This time he felt the pins move individually, and as he moved each into its respective place, he heard the clicks that told him he was on the right path.

Squatting down was making his ribs hurt like hell, though. Sweat poured down his face, and Ran had to use his arm to wipe it away from his eyes twice. He licked his lips and kept pushing the pins into place, hoping that his efforts would soon release the knob.

Two minutes later, Ran felt like he'd reached the last of the pins and slowly drew his tools out of the keyhole. He looked down at the knob and willed that it would move when he place his hand over it and turned.

Here goes nothing, he thought. He wrapped his hand around the knob and twisted.

It moved.

Almost instantly, he heard commotion from back in the chamber. A slow creaking told him that the door must have started to open.

"Ran!"

Cassandra's voice made his heart leap. "Coming!"

He started back up toward the chamber. They were so close to escape now, he could taste his freedom.

So fixated was he on getting back to Cassandra that he never saw the shadow come up behind him and knock him on the back of the head with the pommel of a sword.

Chapter Twenty-nine

Ran awoke to blackness and movement. The thudding pain in the back of his head and lurching motion made him retch. But he managed to keep control over his rolling stomach after the initial shock had worn off. The bouncing motion made his ribs hurt even more, however. They were in another tunnel. Ran's hands were bound behind him. and his ankles were also well-trussed. But who carried him? And who had knocked him out?

"Where am I?"

"Stay quiet or I'll slit your throat right now."

Ran closed his mouth. The voice was vaguely recognizable, but in the harsh whisper, Ran couldn't be quite sure who had spoken. Still, he suspected it was Iqban. As they continued to travel, the man grew tired, and his breathing became increasingly labored. Finally, he was forced to put Ran down against the wall of the tunnel. "You're heavier than you appear, especially for one as compact as you are."

"Muscle is heavy," said Ran. "And I make sure I don't grow fat."

"No doubt," said the voice, a little louder now. "I should have killed the woman when I had the chance."

Ran frowned. "Iqban? We thought you would have fled to places unknown by now."

"And risk running into those things that invaded Zal's lair? Not a chance. At least, I couldn't afford to do that when I was alone. But with you as my prisoner, I now have something of value to offer them."

"Why would they care about me?" asked Ran. "I'm nothing to them."

Iqban laughed. "There's more to you than meets the eye. That much is certain. I've traveled far and wide and have met many so-called wandering warriors. You are like them in some ways, but there is also something special about you. I watched you pick the lock on the knob. Such skills as that required are far beyond most warriors."

"My uncle was a thief, the scourge of his family," said Ran. "But he managed to teach me a few things when I used to visit him. Nothing special about that."

"Most thieves couldn't have picked that lock," said Iqban. "It was commissioned especially for the door to his kingdom, and Zal insisted it be as impervious to compromise as possible. And yet you had it open in under five minutes. It was most impressive."

"I got lucky," said Ran. He glanced around the tunnel and wondered how far they could have traveled in the time he'd been unconscious. He heard no other sounds. It was possible that Iqban knew other tunnels and had moved them far away from the main doorway. Kuva and Cassandra were hopefully long gone.

"Luck is for fools," said Iqban. "In this world, you either make your own luck or else you die working for someone else. No, my friend, you have skills that far exceed what most common warriors are capable of. And there is, I think, some terrific value in that fact."

"And you think those things—whatever invaded this place—are going to barter my life for yours?"

"Those things are the Mung. A race of underdwellers who are incredibly formidable in the close confines of the tunnels they inhabit. But they also have ambition. Grand ambition. And a desire to rule far more than just the paltry domain they have long existed in. Zal was the first to see the world above as a target worthy of conquering. But his plans for that very thing fell apart, and he was exiled by his people. Zal still dreams of conquest, of course, but he is nothing if he can't first get back control of the Mung kingdom."

"I still fail to see how they will grant you life in exchange for me. Why won't they simply kill you as well? After all, the prospect of being eaten by them back in the main cavern seemed to spook you enough into letting Cassandra go."

"Fear is a temporary thing bested by the logic of a rational mind, provided it has a chance to think things through. I was startled, yes, but only because I didn't know what was going on below. I thought it might have been that awful beast Bagyo rampaging."

"Bagyo is dead. I killed him."

Iqban smirked in the darkness, but Ran could see the whites of his teeth somewhat. "That is a relief. I hated that creature."

"It was unfortunate that I had to kill him," said Ran. "But he left me no choice, so I did it as quickly as possible."

"And seemingly without much effort," said Iqban. "Another indicator that you are something special."

"I'm not," said Ran. His side ached, and he shifted. "So what happens now? I don't imagine this is a good place to sit and wait for the Mung to come and find you. What's your plan?"

"I'm going to cut your legs free and then you're going to get up and walk. I'm not carrying you any longer. If you try to escape, I'll be forced to kill you."

Ran shrugged. "But if I don't try to escape and you hand me over to the Mung, I'll be as good as dead anyway. So what do I have to lose?"

"They may not kill you," said Iqban.

"Why not?"

"Because you're worth more alive. And if they decide to ransom you, they would stand to make many times your weight in gold."

Ran laughed in the darkness. "No one would pay for me. I'm worth nothing to anyone."

Iqban chuckled. "You may as well give up that line of talk. As I said, I have traveled many places. I'm aware of what the Murai warriors of Nehon are like. I'm also aware of another sect of warriors from that island nation. And they are nothing like their Murai counterparts."

Ran frowned. How could Iqban have known?

"I know there are plenty of lords across the world who would love to have an actual shadow warrior in their possession. You have long been sought by those you steal secrets from. No doubt one of them would pay handsomely for a chance at vengeance."

"What in the world is a shadow warrior?"

Iqban sniffed. In the dark, there was a flash of steel, and Ran felt his legs freed. "You can stand now and walk on your own. As I said, don't give me an excuse to kill you."

"If you did, your chance at bargaining with the Mung would also die."

“There are other ways to the surface than just through the main door,” said Iqban. “It might take me several days to reach the surface, but I could.”

“And your chances are slim with the Mung prowling about.” Ran got his legs under him and stood up, nearly wincing from the pain in his side. “But I won’t try anything.”

Iqban steered him away from the tunnel wall and then prodded him in the back. Ran grunted as he did so, but Iqban hadn’t noticed that his captive was in pain just yet. “Let’s get a move on. I want to put some space between us and your friends back at the main door.”

“They won’t leave me behind,” said Ran.

Iqban laughed. “Are you so sure? Once that big door is open, the temptation to simply flee will be a powerful one. How well do you know your friends?”

“Well enough to know that in spite of me telling them to leave, they won’t.” Ran glanced around as they walked, but none of the blue torches burned here. Iqban seemed to be steering them along based on memory alone or some other intuitive guide. But where were they headed?

“I should have recognized your abilities far sooner than this. I could have easily extracted more gold from Zal if I had done so.”

“Why would Zal care about what you think I supposedly am?” asked Ran.

“Zal is a fool,” said Iqban. “But he also appreciates a mighty warrior. We’ll see whether or not he survives long enough to care about what I do with you next.”

“I don’t think the Mung will want anything to do with me.”

Iqban chuckled. “You don’t know them very well.”

“And you do? I thought you worked for Zal.”

“I work,” said Iqban, “for whoever pays me the most. My motivations in life are simple and uncomplicated.”

Ran sighed. “I’m sure Zal would be most upset if he heard you say that. What about loyalty?”

“Allow me to give you some valuable advice. Loyalty is overrated. In fact, it’s far too expensive to ever consider buying in the first place. Money, however, keeps a man honest and law-abiding until such time as he can make more elsewhere. It simplifies life. Once you understand that people are motivated by their own greed alone and that any other allegiance is mere illusion, you will know how to make your way in this world far better than those supposed zealots who think their cause is just and honorable."

Ran shook his head. "I'm not entirely sure what you just spewed there, because all I heard were a few attempts to justify being a two-sided money-grubber."

"Why stop at two sides?" asked Iqban.

Ran sighed. "Indeed."

"Zal pays me well, but I've always had an eye out for other opportunities. When I learned what Zal was doing, I was the one who contacted the Mung directly."

"How did you do that? I thought they were sealed below ground?"

Iqban laughed again. "If that were true, then Zal would never have gotten to this place. I knew there had to be another route into the Mung kingdom. It took me some time, but I located it. The Mung were initially hostile, but eventually we reached an understanding."

"If you're so friendly with the Mung, then why did you flee earlier when I told you what we'd do if you killed Cassandra?"

"I had to give you an excuse to separate from your friends. I knew about the locking mechanism. I also knew that if my suspicions were correct, you would confirm them and then I'd have you."

Ran frowned. He'd written Iqban off as a scared fool, but the slaver had outwitted him. And now he had Ran right where he wanted him. Wherever that was.

"So what happens if Zal finds out about your treachery?"

"I'd imagine he wouldn't be too pleased," said Iqban. "Unfortunately for him, his hired army is in ruins, and even now the Mung will be closing in on him—if he's not dead already."

"And you're taking me where?"

"To the Mung."

"Wonderful," said Ran. Even as he said this, the tunnel started to slope downward at a steep angle. The air grew a lot warmer as well. So much so that sweat began dripping from his face as they walked. "Is it always this hot down here?"

"It will pass," said Iqban. "The conditions are much more temperate as we go."

Ran glanced over his shoulder, trying to figure out what direction they could have come from. If there was a chance that Kuva and

Cassandra were trying to find him, could he leave any sign behind that he'd come this way?

"Don't bother," said Iqban. "We're in another tunnel altogether. I highly doubt your friends will be able to locate the entrance, let alone follow it to its conclusion. And even if they did, they would be walking right into the heart of the Mung empire. Hardly the sort of thing I'd expect them to embark upon."

Ran frowned. He'd urged Kuva and Cassandra to flee the catacombs, but a part of him—a big part of him—wished desperately that they were searching for him. His chances of survival seemed to be dwindling by the minute the farther they got away from the main door of the catacombs and closer to the Mung kingdom. How would anyone find him? He could die down here, and no one—not one single member of his clan—would ever know what had happened to him.

The clan would think he had vanished. Or would they? Perhaps they might think he had deserted them. He might even be branded a traitor, and history itself might not look kindly upon his exploits. He was a new operative, but he had managed to defeat Kan-Gul. And even though he'd started this journey by disregarding clan orders, he was back in the very area they had wanted him to journey to.

He realized that his loyalty to the Nine Daggers was still firmly fixed in his heart, even though he longed to be with Cassandra. His clan had given him everything. It would be much harder than he had thought to turn his back on them.

"You're rather quiet," said Iqban.

"I'm just thinking about how many ways I could kill you," said Ran.

Iqban laughed. "You won't get the chance, I'm afraid. Once I'm rewarded by the Mung for my assistance in helping them initiate their attack on Zal, I'll sell you to them and take my leave. I'm thinking this part of the world might be a little too violent for my taste for some time to come. Perhaps a journey farther west is advisable."

"Why would you say that?"

"The Mung aren't the only people with designs of conquest. There are others far more powerful than the Mung who have long eyed the southern realms with envy and desire. I've heard rumors of a massive army to the north of these very mountains that is massing as we speak."

Ran's ears perked up. Was it true? "Rumors are just that. You don't know for certain, though, do you?"

"As a matter of fact," said Iqban, "I have it from several reliable sources that the army is on the move already. The weather is against them, however. They will need access to the Passage of Harangyo in order to make their way south. At this time of year, the snows and ice may block the passage and keep them from coming. But such delays are only temporary. When the spring thaws come, they will be ready to pour south and decimate any that would oppose them."

"Who rules this northern army?"

Iqban grunted. "A fair question, and one I do not know the answer to. If I thought they would be amenable to some type of arrangement whereby I sold them slaves, then perhaps I might go north myself and try to establish contact." He paused. "But from what I've heard about them through bits and pieces of information, they do not seem as welcoming as the Mung."

"Sorry you won't have a chance to do business with them," said Ran dryly.

"It doesn't matter," said Iqban. "I will be well paid by the Mung, doubly so when I sell you to them." He paused. "Now turn to the right and head down that tunnel. We are arriving."

Chapter Thirty

The entrance to the Mung kingdom looked nowhere near as grand as the iron door Zal had constructed for his own domain. The entrance was simply a rough-hewn opening manned by a trio of guards. Flickering torches of blue set into braziers nearby cast shadows over the guards and made them look, despite their small stature, more intimidating than they might otherwise appear. They wore bits of mail armor pieced together with leather straps and some sort of coarse tunic fabric underneath. Humanoid in appearance, their eyes were bigger and their mouths were full of teeth that were either naturally pointed or had been ground that way on purpose. Ran figured that they must look a sight when they smiled.

Iqban stopped a few meters short of the entrance when one of the guards challenged them in a guttural language Ran had never heard before. Iqban answered in kind, although it was obvious to Ran that the slaver had only recently learned the appropriate answer phrase, as he still struggled with pronouncing it. Regardless of his clumsy attempt, the guards seemed satisfied and allowed them to pass. As they did so, Ran felt their eyes roving over him and he wondered if they were trying to imagine what he tasted like. He shuddered at the thought, but then quickly pushed it out of his mind.

One of the guards assumed a position in front of Ran and led them down a narrow passageway that Ran and Iqban had to stoop a bit to get through. Farther on it opened up, but not until Ran realized they had just passed through a kill zone put there especially to force invaders into an uncomfortable position. He spotted ledges high above, no doubt there were archers who would be able to pick off invaders with ease as they struggled to get through the cramped confines of the tunnel leading inside.

"There aren't many of the Mung about right now," said Iqban. "I'm assuming most of them are helping with the invasion of Zal's domain."

"So we'll be forced to wait?" asked Ran. He felt at the knots that bound his wrists. Iqban had done an admirable job of tying them together, and reaching most of the knots themselves would prove difficult. Certainly he wouldn't be able to work himself free while Iqban was behind him. But if they got some time to rest somewhere, Ran would be able to work himself free. Even if the knots themselves were out of reach, he had other methods for freeing his limbs and regaining his freedom.

"I don't know," answered Iqban. "The king himself may be overseeing the invasion. Or he might have been inclined to let one of his generals lead the assault. Either way, it doesn't matter. Once the Mung have finished killing Zal's army, they'll come back here for a celebratory meal. We'll have an audience soon thereafter."

"And what sort of food gets served at this celebratory meal?" Ran still had images in his mind of the Mung devouring the unfortunate souls they had killed.

"About what you'd expect," said Iqban. "They are, after all, cannibals. I'd consider it a fair expectation that any prisoners they might have taken will be killed over the feasting fires and then served up to the Mung soldiers for their meal. They may also dine on live prisoners. I saw it happen once before."

"And yet you have no qualms about being here to do business with these creatures." Ran shook his head. "I can't believe that you're that much of a lover of money that you would do business with such a people."

"Just because they don't necessarily share my belief system doesn't mean they don't have the right to free trade." Iqban laughed. "I think you'll find that I am very pragmatic when it comes to the idea of making money."

"Pragmatic?"

"Surely. I don't care where my customers come from. I don't care what they might do in my absence. If their business is good, then we can have a relationship. It's that simple."

"It's rather nauseating," said Ran. "That a man such as yourself would care so little about the people he does business with. Don't you have any honor?"

Iqban nudged him in the back, and Ran felt his ribs ache again. "Honor is for fools. And I am no fool. I'm a businessman."

"Thankfully, the world is not run by businessmen," said Ran.

Iqban only laughed. "Of course it is. But the common people only see the what we want them to see. We give you your kings and queens and clerics and mages and other bastions of supposed power. But the real authority comes from those who control the flow of money. Without trade and commerce, even the strongest king will fall. Without the exchange of goods, no army can stand. Without the merchants, there is no life at all. We might bow and scrape before the figureheads we've installed in power, but we only do that to perpetrate the illusion of power. We control it all. We rule the world."

"Only until the illusion is shattered."

Iqban shrugged as they turned down a side tunnel to the left. "I doubt that will ever happen."

"It will," said Ran. "And your undoing will be your endless greed. The same greed that has brought you to this very point. If you lose sight of providing a service for others and only fixate on the end result—money—then you will certainly perish."

"You know little of the real world, Ran from Nehon. While I admire your tenacity and attempts to sway my thinking, they are for naught. Shortly, we will be presented to the Mung king, and then your fate will be sealed. It is out of my hands even now. As soon as we entered the Mung kingdom, your destiny was no longer mine to control. I've made my deals already. All that is left now is for the Mung to live up to their end of our bargain."

"And what if they don't? What if they double-cross you?"

"It's always a risk," said Iqban. "But the Mung are always steadfast in their bargaining."

"You'd better hope that's true," said Ran. "Otherwise you might end up on someone's dinner plate."

The Mung guard drew himself to a halt next to a room with an ornate door encrusted with jewels. He paused once, and then knocked. From inside, a guttural bark came in response. The Mung guard opened the door and then gestured that Iqban and Ran should enter. As they did, the guard waited and then closed the door behind them.

Inside the room, oil lamps blazed and illuminated the entire area. Iqban stepped forward and presented himself to the squat Mung seated on a simple carpet of lavish silken fabrics. With his legs crossed in front of him, and bedecked as he was in golden robes, it almost appeared that the little man was levitating. But the expression on his face was severe and anything but welcoming. Even when he saw Iqban, his demeanor did not change. Ran found himself wondering if the Mung had any intention of honoring their agreement. For the moment, he hoped they would, if only to give Ran more time to escape.

The Mung king, thought Ran, if this was even him, looked somewhat confused by Iqban's appearance. The leader's eyes rolled over Ran and did not stop. This didn't surprise Ran at all. He had been trained to be as unremarkable in his appearance as possible. Unlike the dramatic stature of other warriors, Shinobujin were trained to be the type of people you might pass on the street and then forget five seconds later. That was where their real invisibility came from, not some mystical magic.

"Iqban," said the Mung king.

Iqban lowered himself on one bent knee and bowed his head. "Zaqil."

"I was not expecting to see you again."

The Mung king did not appear to have trouble with the Common Tongue, although his speech was slower than Ran had expected. He wondered how a people that lived underground had come to learn it. Was Iqban their first contact with the upper world?

"I had reason to come back, Zaqil," said Iqban. He turned and gestured to Ran. "I thought you might find some use with this one here."

Zaqil's eyes once more roved over Ran, this time stopping and pausing every so often. Ran felt like a piece of food being appraised for its taste. "Why would I have any interest in him, aside from possibly eating him? Is there something special about him?"

"Indeed," said Iqban. "He is valuable to many of the lords that rule in the upper world. They would pay most handsomely for him."

Zaqil shrugged. "So you take him then. What purpose would I have in retaining such a man? We have no need for money. We mine the earth's deepest treasures and feast upon those who covet them. The ransoming of this man would hardly make us any wealthier or more powerful than we already are."

"This man is what is known as a shadow warrior. He is an expert at infiltration and the gathering of secrets. He is a formidable fighter in combat. I believe you would find him extremely useful even if you did not wish to ransom him."

Zaqil sighed. "Whose secrets do I need to steal?"

"Those of your enemies. As soon as you begin your conquest of the upper world, you are certain to run into many who would see you dead. A man like this could serve you well."

"Or a man like this could be served well," Zaqil laughed. "Frankly, Iqban, he looks far less impressive than you have described him thus far." Zaqil turned to Ran. "Is what this man says about you true? Are you really one of these shadow warriors?"

Zaqil had no attendants with him. There were no guards, either. Ran found this fact unsettling. But he also figured that if he lied, it might simply make Zaqil more inclined to kill him and serve him up as dinner. Ran glanced at Iqban. The slaver was already dead in Ran's mind. Zaqil, too, would not live to ever see the upper world or his dreams of conquest.

"I am known as a Shinobujin," said Ran. "What the outside world calls a shadow warrior." He took a breath. "I was captured during one of my missions and brought into the catacombs of the one known as Zal for the purposes of slave labor."

"Zal," spat Zaqil. "That damned fool. We still have yet to locate him. My forces have combed most of the tunnels and catacombs there and still he eludes us." He sighed and looked back at Iqban. "So what do you want to do, Iqban, sell me this man?"

"Ideally," said Iqban. "I also need safe passage back to the upper world. I do have other business to conduct up there."

Zaqil eyed Ran again. "I will need proof that this man is worth any sort of money at all. I'm not foolish enough to take a slaver's word, especially one who seems keenly concerned for his own wealth and welfare."

Iqban bowed low. "I would not be much of a merchant if I was not concerned with my safety first. How else would I be able to serve my loyal customers?"

Zaqil shook his head. "Save your silly talk for those who would believe such things. I am not one of them. If we are to come to a bargain for this man, I will do so only after I see an example of his prowess. You say he is good at fighting? Then let us see that for ourselves."

Ran frowned. With his ribs injured, his skills in combat would be a notch lower than normal. He placed one hand on his ribs and then winced. The injury was still tender. "I am injured. You may not be as impressed with me as you would be otherwise."

Zaqil regarded him. "Your ribs are broken?"

"I was thrown against the walls of a tunnel fighting a large creature. Yes, they are broken."

"I will have my doctors put a plaster on you that will lend some degree of support. And you will be given something for the pain. Otherwise, you will be expected to fight as normal. Do you have a preference for the type of weapons you will use?"

"No weapons," said Ran. "I will fight the Mung of your choosing, but we will do so unarmed. Is that agreeable to you?"

Zaqil leaned back almost in surprise. "That is most agreeable, actually. I have not seen a contest of unarmed fighting skill in many years. I think it will be wonderful." He turned to Iqban. "You will stay here until after the bout. If this man wins, then I will pay you for him." Zaqil clapped his hands, and the door opened instantly. He looked at Ran. "You will be taken to a cell where my doctors will examine you and give you treatment, as well as food. You may also rest there for a short period of time. The contest will commence in half a day."

Ran nodded. "Very well. Whom will I fight?"

Zaqil smiled. "You will fight me. As leader of the Mung, it is my responsibility. There are others among my troops who are mighty warriors, but as king, I surpass them all. You will meet me in the cavern of combat in twelve hours' time. Then we will see if Iqban here is telling me the truth about who you are."

"So, if I win, you buy me from him?"

"Yes," said Zaqil. "You will serve me unless I decide to sell you to some lord in the upper world."

"And what happens if I lose?"

Zaqil looked at Iqban and then back at Ran. "Then I will have no choice but to assume you are not who Iqban says you are. In which case, I will have you both trussed and cooked over a roaring fire while we feast upon your flesh." He smiled at Iqban. "For your sake, he'd better be as good as you claim."

Ran glanced at Iqban, but the slaver's face looked white as a sail.

Ran almost smiled.

Chapter Thirty-one

One of the Mung guards led Ran away from Zaqil's reception chamber and guided him down another tunnel for some distance. Ran tried counting his footsteps to get a vague measure of the distance, but his head was beginning to hurt from a lack of food. All day long he'd been getting energy from the spikes of adrenaline in his blood, but it was beginning to catch up with him. He felt waves of sleepiness wash over him and a gnawing in the pit of his stomach. Still, the promise of food and medical attention lifted his spirits. It would absolutely aid in his escape plans, and the thought of being able to sleep for a few hours buoyed his spirits immensely. While he was going to be fighting for his life, Ran wasn't too concerned about it just yet. As long as he bested Zaqil, he would live a little bit longer.

That was, if Ran even decided to go along with the bout.

There was an argument to be made for taking the medical attention and food and then making a break for it. With most of the Mung forces occupied with the invasion, Ran might encounter less resistance as he fought his way free. But the counter to that argument was that he desperately needed rest and recuperation time. He was barely able to keep from nodding off right now as it was, and the number of fights he'd had already had taxed his system to its limits. The opportunity for food, medicine, and rest meant that he would be in much better shape for his eventual escape.

Of course, he still had to take down Zaqil. The confidence with which the king had chosen to fight Ran was a little unsettling, and Ran had never fought someone of the king's stature before. But the same principles that had allowed him to survive as long as he had would no doubt prove useful in this contest as well.

The Mung guard drew to a halt in front of far less ornate door and bid Ran enter. As Ran ducked his head and entered the room, he saw that it was appointed with a large bed piled high with deep cushions. There were already two Mung attendants inside. One of them motioned for Ran to sit down in the chair nearby.

"I will tend to your injury," he said in halting common tongue. Then he slid the bindings off of Ran's hands.

Ran winced as he lifted the tunic and inspected his ribs, poking and prodding as he did so. But it wasn't overly rough and Ran appreciated the apparent care with which the doctor checked him over. He made a few comments in the Mung language and then looked at Ran. "Only one is broken. The others are bruised."

That was good news. One broken rib was a lot less serious than four. And while they would all hurt, Ran felt much better about his health than he had earlier.

The doctor ordered him to sit still as he applied a wet dressing of gauze and some sort of ointment over it. "This will harden and help ease some pain."

"Thank you," said Ran.

The doctor gestured for the other Mung in the room to hand Ran a draught of some type. "This potion will also eliminate any pain you are feeling. Be careful with your ribs and don't forget to try to keep them as immobile as possible."

Ran smiled. "I'm supposed to fight Zaqil in a few hours. I don't know how immobile I'm going to be able to keep them."

The doctor nodded. "The plaster will take some of the force from any strikes you might get. But be careful. Bruised ribs can easily become broken ribs."

Ran drank the potion and then noticed that there was a plate of food next to the bed. From the looks of it, there were several slices of meat and some green leafy vegetables he did not recognize. The bowl of rice was a friendly reminder of his home, however. The doctor noticed Ran inspecting the meat and smiled.

"It is beef. Zaqil knows you are not one who would follow our customs."

Ran breathed a sigh of relief. "I'm grateful for that. As hungry as

I am, I don't think I could stomach the flesh of another human being."

The doctor shrugged. "It is an acquired taste, I suppose. We are happy enough with it, but understand you would not be. This is one more example of the greatness of Zaqil. He is compassionate in that regard even as he prepares to fight you. Surely the mark of a great leader, no?"

Ran wasn't so sure about that, but he decided it was better not to insult his hosts. "I am extremely grateful for his generosity and compassion." Already the potion had reduced the throbbing pain in his side. Ran was thankful for being able to breathe without pain lancing his side as he did so.

The doctor felt around Ran's head for a moment and then nodded. "It has already started to work. That is good." He gathered his things in a pouch and smiled once again at Ran. "We will take our leave now. Eat the food and then sleep. The potion will work for perhaps a day. Certainly long enough to see you through your bout with the king."

"Very well," said Ran. "Thank you for your assistance."

"Good luck, Ran," said the doctor. "Zaqil is a formidable warrior in his own right. You will need lots of luck to defeat him."

"I'm sure he is," said Ran. "But if I don't do well then he said he's going to eat me. So I have much to fight for. I would rather not end up in his stomach."

The doctor laughed. "Good-bye." He and his assistant walked out of the cell. Ran heard the guard outside lock the door.

Ran turned his attention to the food and started devouring the plate of food and the rice. He needed all of it to get his strength back. There was a pitcher of water nearby, and Ran sucked it down as he ate. The beef was flavorful and tender. The vegetables, even though Ran did not recognize them, were nonetheless delicious. And the sticky rice melted in his mouth. After he had feasted, Ran leaned back in the bed among the pillows and promptly fell asleep.

Too soon, Ran heard the door being unlocked, and he sat right up in the bed. So much for the possibility of escape, he thought with a wry grin. But on the plus side, Ran felt wonderful. The food and rest, along with the medical attention he'd received, had reinvigorated him.

He felt like his old self, and the thought of doing battle with Zaqil actually excited him.

The Mung guard entered and motioned for Ran to follow him into the corridor. The guard didn't seem concerned that Ran wasn't in his hand ties any longer. Perhaps they felt safe here in their kingdom. After all, where would Ran run to if he tried to escape? That realization almost depressed Ran, but he pushed the notion out of his mind. He could recall how they'd entered the kingdom, and he felt certain he could find his way back and out if he needed to.

The big question at this point was, did it make sense to try? Something about the apparent nonchalance of the guard made Ran suspicious. Perhaps Zaqil was testing him. There might even be other guards stationed nearby as they walked to the arena. If Ran attempted anything, Zaqil might have given the guards orders to simply kill him.

Ran decided to go along as if everything was perfectly all right. If he saw an opportunity, then he would take it. But if an opportunity did not present itself, then he would fight Zaqil and win. Hopefully the king would be impressed enough that Ran would eventually get his freedom anyway. And if he didn't, then as long as he was out of immediate danger, Ran could formulate a better plan.

He thought of Kuva and Cassandra and hoped they'd managed to get themselves out of the catacombs. He wondered where they were at that very moment. Hopefully enjoying a good rest and some food, thought Ran. If anything, he felt a bit guilty that he'd been able to rest and eat. There were no guarantees they'd enjoyed anything remotely similar.

They might even be dead.

He frowned. No. Kuva would never let any harm come to Cassandra. And Cassandra was a worthy foe in her own right. If they'd escaped the catacombs, then they were probably trying to locate Ran. In spite of urging them to run away, Ran felt certain his friends would not abandon him.

He turned his attention back to the walk to the arena. As the guard led him through a variety of corridors, Ran saw more of the Mung people. Men, women, and children turned out to stare and point at him. Ran guessed he wasn't the first person from the upper world that they had seen, but he was obviously a novelty of some sort. He wondered whether it was because he was due to fight the king, or if they were wondering what his flesh tasted like. As he walked, he made a point to wave to the kids and smile at some of the women. If he could win over some of the crowd before they even arrived at the arena, then perhaps that would help him stay alive a little while longer.

They walked down a paved flagstone tunnel and then emerged into a huge cavern. A boisterous crowd of Mung greeted him as he entered. They were seated in rows of chairs that encircled the arena floor. Shouts and chants went up as Ran walked deeper into the arena. He stood and looked around. The guard remained with him and had to twice warn away a Mung spectator who insisted on coming to get a close look at Ran.

As Ran stood there, he wondered how many other fights had happened down in the arena. Certainly this wasn't thrown together in some haphazard fashion. The arena had been built specifically for combat, with the sides sloping inward at the top and outward at the bottom so fighters could not try to scale the walls and escape. The seats were also set high enough above the floor so that every spectator had an excellent view of the action happening far below.

No, he decided, the arena had been used and probably often. He wondered how many other fighters had come in just as he had, hoping for a chance at life. Had they won? Or had they ended up being served to the Mung aristocracy for dinner?

Ran spotted Iqban in one of the first rows. Seated all around him were a phalanx of Mung guards. Clearly, Zaqil wasn't taking any chances with Iqban. If Ran turned out to be a disappointment, Zaqil clearly intended to carry through with his threat. Ran realized he could easily choose to lose the match and ensure Iqban's demise. But that would only guarantee his own death as well.

And Ran had no intention of dying anytime soon.

A louder cheer erupted from the crowd. Ran turned to see Zaqil entering the arena, guarded by his own troop. They surrounded him as he entered and made his way over to Ran. Fans in the crowd cheered and threw strange purple flowers at him. Zaqil stopped every few meters and picked up a flower to smell it before throwing it away. The act made the crowd go wild. Ran had the distinct impression that the king was enjoying the adoration of the crowd and encouraged it as much as possible.

Zaqil stopped a few feet away from Ran and smiled. "You look well-rested."

"I am," said Ran. "And I have you to thank for that. I sincerely appreciate your generosity and kindness. Thank you."

Zaqil turned and addressed the crowd. He motioned at Ran a few times, and the crowd roared in appreciation. Zaqil turned and spoke to Ran. "I have told them what you just said. They appreciate, as do I, that you are grateful for that which I have given you."

"The food was marvelous," said Ran. "Your cooks are amazing."

Zaqil laughed and translated that as well. The entire arena started laughing. Zaqil eyed Ran. "They know exactly what will happen to you if you do not win this bout. I believe they see the irony in your complimenting our cooks, since they might actually be cooking you if you lose."

Ran smirked. "I get it. But I don't intend to lose."

"I'm sure the cow you feasted on had no intention of being served on your plate, either. But that is neither here nor there. Are you prepared to do battle with me in this arena?"

"I am," said Ran.

"And you see that I have no weapons about me?"

Ran pointed at the guards. "Plenty of weapons right there around you."

Zaqil nodded. "Indeed. But they will not remain in the arena once we begin. Some of my people tend to let their adoration of me get the better of them. I have entered this arena many times before and on several occasions have been mobbed by fans. While I do not mind such love and affection, my men tend to get a bit concerned for my well-being, as I'm sure you would understand."

"Certainly," said Ran. "Are there rules to this bout?"

"I will expect you to fight to the utmost of your ability. As will I. If, at any time, either one of us feels he can no longer continue, then three taps will signal compliance and surrender. Ordinarily, this would mean a draw, but in your case, if you surrender, it means you will be killed. Unless I think you have performed well enough to justify being pardoned."

"And if you surrender?"

Zaqil looked amazed. "I have never once surrendered in all my times fighting in this arena."

"There's always a first time for everything," said Ran. "What if you surrender first?"

Zaqil frowned. "If I surrender first, then you will have the option of leaving this place forever."

"I would be free to go? You wouldn't try to kill me as I left?"

"You have my word," said Zaqil.

"And what happens to Iqban?"

"What would you have me do with him?"

Ran looked at the slaver and shrugged. "You can serve him up to your people for all I care. He means nothing to me."

Zaqil nodded. "That would be acceptable. Are you ready?"

Ran smiled and looked at the crowds cheering them on. "I am."

"Then let us begin."

Chapter Thirty-two

Zaqil backed away, and Ran did the same. There was no use in attacking unexpectedly; Ran had no idea what the Mung king was capable of and to rush in might have ended the contest before it began if it turned out that Zaqil was actually a talented fighter.

Around them, the crowd went silent. Ran found the abrupt lack of noise unsettling. It was almost as if the spectators knew something he did not.

Zaqil, by comparison, calmly removed the cloak he'd been wearing and laid it on the ground some distance away. He walked back toward the center of the arena, calmly flexing his muscles, which Ran could see were well-developed, no doubt from years of other challengers. If Zaqil was a lead-from-the-front sort, he would have had a lot of experience. Ran appreciated that fact about the Mung leader, although he now pushed it from his mind and concentrated solely upon finding a weakness he could rapidly exploit. The sooner this contest was over, the better off he would be. Especially since Zaqil had given him his word that he could go free.

Ran circled around to his left. The Mung leader stood at least eighteen inches shorter than Ran, but Ran also knew that smaller foes could often be more dangerous. Ran would have the natural length advantage in his arms and legs, but if Zaqil could get inside that range, he could unleash a torrent of attacks Ran might have a hard time fending off.

In the end, it was Zaqil who made the first move.

As Ran continued circling, Zaqil suddenly rushed in and launched a barrage of kicks at Ran's midsection. Ran evaded most of them, but took a glancing blow off his hip that sent him staggering back. Zaqil's attack, although it had done little in the way of actual damage, produced a roar from the crowd, who were obviously well-used to seeing their king attack first. Ran realized that was why they'd gone silent; they were waiting to see how this contest would open up.

Zaqil was obviously also targeting the areas where Ran might be most vulnerable: his ribs.

Ran smiled and then readied himself for the next attack. This time, Zaqil leapt into the air and tried a flying side kick at Ran's head. As Ran pivoted out of the way, Zaqil dropped down to the arena floor and then rolled right underneath Ran's attempt at a counterpunch. As he stood, Zaqil delivered a thundering uppercut that caught Ran on the underside of his jaw and jarred his teeth. Ran went with the energy of the blow and let himself fall and roll backwards twice, trying to get more distance again. He needed Zaqil at a distance in order to take him out.

As he came up, Zaqil was already launching his next attack. Ran defended against the looping right punch aimed at the side of his head and then brought his elbow up into Zaqil's midsection. Zaqil's momentum meant that the king was unable to stop in time, and Ran's elbow strike punched him hard. His wind rushed from his lungs and the king stepped back, rubbing his chest thoughtfully.

The crowd went silent.

But Ran didn't stop. Even as Zaqil tried to recover his breathing, Ran was already rushing in with a lifting kick aimed at the Zaqil's groin. As he expected, the king started to pivot out of the way, and that was when he walked right into Ran's hook punch. The knuckles on Ran's hand landed flush with the king's jaw and snapped his head around. Ran brought the side of his left hand chopping down on the exposed side of Zaqil's neck, and as the king dropped under the blow, Ran brought his knee up into the same spot where he'd landed the elbow strike.

Zaqil dropped and rolled away, desperately trying to put some space between them.

The arena had gone deathly quiet, and Ran found himself wondering if they'd ever had a fighter who had managed to score hits on their king before. It seemed as though this was something entirely new for the Mung people. They did not seem used to seeing their king down on his knees.

Zaqil recovered and got to his feet. He smiled at Ran. "Very well done, Ran. Very well done, indeed."

Ran said nothing. Until Zaqil surrendered, the contest was still on and Ran didn't need any other motivation; the thought of being cooked alive was strong enough to make him want to make sure that Zaqil was well and truly defeated.

Ran rushed in this time, but Zaqil received his attack and then used Ran's momentum against him to flip the shadow warrior onto his back. Zaqil rolled with him, coming up astride Ran's chest and immediately headbutting him above his eyebrow. Ran saw stars and blinked rapidly, trying to regain his vision.

Zaqil rained down punches on Ran's midsection, and Ran felt the plaster covering his ribs start to break apart. Zaqil laughed now as he sensed Ran's desperation to unseat the smaller man. Zaqil had his legs somehow locked around Ran's midsection. Ran bucked hips, but the king stayed locked in place.

Ran launched his hip once more and then brought his buttocks down where he thought the king's ankles were. Zaqil grunted as the full weight of Ran's body came down on the vulnerable joints. It was enough, and Ran snaked his arm behind Zaqil's left and then jerked back against the outstretched elbow joint. He heard a pop, and then Zaqil cried out before rolling off of Ran.

Ran got to his feet, aware that his ribs were now aching again. He needed to end this as fast as possible or else he risked further injury to his side.

Zaqil rubbed the back of his left elbow. Clearly he was in some pain. But that didn't stop him from attacking again.

As he came forward, he stooped and scooped some of the earth from the arena floor and threw it at Ran's face. The crowd roared its approval, but Ran had used the same tactic before himself and saw it unfold, closing his eyes as he turned away. Most of the dirt flew past the area where he'd just been standing, and only a few of the particles hit him in the face.

Ran immediately went on the attack and threw a thunderous front kick at the king's exposed left thigh. His heel impacted, and Zaqil's legs flew out from under him, dropping the king face-first into the floor.

Again, the crowd went silent. Ran moved in with another kick at the king's back and drove it into the left shoulder blade. Zaqil cried out and rolled over, trying to launch an attack of his own, but on the ground, he was sorely disadvantaged. Ran leapt over his feeble attempt at a kick and came down, pinning the right ankle.

"Do you surrender?" asked Ran.

Zaqil eyed Ran. "Not even close." And then he threw another handful of dirt at Ran's face. This time, he scored a direct hit. Ran twisted his feet instinctively and cranked the lock he had on the ankle. But his vision had been compromised and his balance felt off. As he cranked the lock, he stumbled and then went with the fall, tucking himself into a roll that carried him away. He came up, furiously trying to clear his vision.

Too late. Zaqil had already managed to limp over and tackle him. They went down again, twisting and rolling on the floor of the arena. Since Zaqil didn't have to put any weight on his injured ankle, he was free to pummel Ran as they rolled. Ran brought his hands up, clawing at Zaqil's face. He ranked up and down, desperate to attack's the king's eyes so they were on somewhat equal footing. But every time he tried, Zaqil punished him by punching into Ran's ribs.

Finally, Ran managed to bring his hands up and around Zaqil's throat. He brought his fingers together and closed them in a vise around the Mung leader's airway.

Zaqil's immediate response was to bring his hands up and over Ran's in an attempt to break free. If Zaqil had been the same size or larger than Ran, the defense might have worked. But the smaller man simply didn't have the strength or maneuverability to break the choke hold. Ran tightened his grip even as Zaqil went back to work punching him in the midsection.

Ran blocked out the pain and kept squeezing, knowing that Zaqil would either have to tap three times or risk unconsciousness and death.

The punches kept coming. Ran kept his eyes closed and focused all of his strength on ending the fight. He squeezed Zaqil's throat shut and heard tiny sounds escaping from the king's mouth. He was close.

Then Ran noticed the punches were losing their power. The cheers from the crowd thundered in Ran's ears. They wanted Zaqil to do something—anything—to finish off Ran, but their king could not. Without air, he simply did not have the ability to fight.

And then three taps on his side.

Ran opened his eyes. Zaqil's face was nearly blue. Ran fixed him with a glare. "Are you sure you surrender?"

Zaqil nodded desperately.

"And you won't go back on your word?"

Zaqil shook his head. His eyes started to roll back. Ran released his hold and Zaqil rolled free of him, gasping and retching as he tried to get air back into his lungs. He was on his hands and knees with spit pouring out of his mouth as he heaved and sucked in air. Ran got to his feet.

The crowd went quiet.

Ran looked over at Zaqil and then went to help him up on his feet. He knew the ankle would be sore; he'd come close to breaking it. "Give me your hand."

Zaqil looked up at him and then smiled. "You are very talented, Ran from Nehon. It was an honor to fight you." He took Ran's hand and stood on shaky feet. Then he looked out at the crowd. "They are not used to seeing their king lose."

"I don't expect they are," said Ran. "I'm sorry they had to see that."

Zaqil shrugged. "It is good for them to know their king is not perfect. That I make mistakes like anyone else. Perhaps I should have trusted Iqban, after all."

Ran sniffed and wiped sweat from his face. "Iqban is not worthy of your trust. He would kill you in the blink of an eye if he thought it would earn him money. I was surprised to learn that you had even entertained doing business with him."

"It was not our first choice, but we needed things that he could provide. I would like to be free of him, however."

"Banish him, then," said Ran. "Or kill him. It makes little difference to me."

"Look at him up there," said Zaqil. "He is almost gleeful at your victory."

"Because he thinks you'll pay him for me now."

"He doesn't know of our arrangement," said Zaqil. "But that isn't a concern." He turned to the arena and spoke in a loud booming voice while holding Ran's hand high overhead. "You have seen the talent and ferocity of this man. He is truly an accomplished warrior worthy of honor and respect. Indeed, he has both from me."

The crowd went wild, and Ran smiled in spite of himself.

Zaqil turned to him. "I know I have promised you your freedom, but I would consider it an honor if you would feast with us tonight. Before you leave."

Ran debated. Part of him wanted to leave this place immediately. While Zaqil had shown him both grace and generosity, he also didn't trust the Mung leader entirely. The longer he stayed, the longer he felt like he was in danger. That said, if he refused, who was to say Zaqil wouldn't take it as an insult and then go back on his word? Ran sighed. "I do have friends looking for me, and I would like to return to them as soon as possible. But I would be honored to feast with you."

Zaqil clapped his hands, and his smile seemed genuine enough. "Wonderful. I shall make arrangements immediately." He winced as he put weight on his ankle. "Well, perhaps after the doctor has tended to my leg, that is. In the meantime, you are free to wander wherever you like in our kingdom. I can have a guard assigned to lead you around or you may go on your own. You are a free man, Ran, and you have bested me in combat. As such, you are my honored guest and no one will harm you while you are here."

"Thank you," said Ran. "I would like to return to my quarters and get some more rest, though, if that is all right with you."

"Absolutely," said Zaqil. "I think that's a rather good idea, actually. But when you awaken, if you feel like exploring, please do so. The feast will commence tonight, and I will send someone to your quarters with a change of clothes and a bath."

"What about Iqban?" asked Ran.

Zaqil shrugged. "I haven't decided what to do with him just yet. But we can talk about that later at the feast."

"Very well," said Ran. "I just have one final question."

"Which is?"

"What will be on the menu tonight?"

Zaqil smiled. "Have no fears, Ran. I know you are not going to become one of us and appreciate the taste of human flesh. I will spare you that as well. Tonight's feast will feature foods that you will enjoy as much as we will."

A wave of relief washed over Ran. "Thank you."

Chapter Thirty-three

Ran chewed another piece of the tender beef and then set his utensils down. Nearby, Zaqil sat drinking a tall mug of something the Mung called Haoji, which Ran figured was a fermented root drink. He tried it and found that it immediately started to affect his head, so he immediately asked for water instead. The last thing he needed was to have hits wits dulled by strong drink while he still considered himself something of a prisoner, despite Zaqil's assurances otherwise.

He had awoken from his nap and found a set of simple but comfortable clothes in a package outside of his door. The threads within the clothes seemed to shimmer at points when the blue torchlight hit them. Ran bathed quickly, reveling in the hot water they had somehow managed to tap. The clothes fit him perfectly, despite the fact that all the Mung were far shorter than Ran. And then he'd wandered around for a few minutes until a guard found him and asked Ran to follow him to the feast.

The feast room was nothing at all like the room where Zaqil had initially received Iqban and Ran. Instead of the simple design, this room was far more like a cavern, with a huge arching ceiling and many torches burning away overhead. There were scores of tables laid with all sorts of meats and vegetables. Ran saw a large fire in the center of the room, giving off a nice blanket of heat to the entire expanse. Servers rushed to and fro, waiting on what Ran assumed were the Mung aristocracy. Zaqil had waved him over to sit next to him in a position of honor. Ran had accepted and thanked the king for the opportunity to dine with him.

The food was as delicious as it had been when Ran first ate it back in his cell. The Mung cooks were certainly adept at preparing the food served here. As Ran ate, he watched the faces of the other Mung and wondered how they could be thinking about conquest when it seemed they had plenty of wealth and security underground. He voiced the question to Zaqil, who only smiled.

"It's true that we have much that we could ever want in our tunnels and caverns, but the source of our power is dwindling."

"What power?" asked Ran.

Zaqil gestured overhead. "Surely you've seen the blue torches. They burn, but not with a yellow flame. Haven't you wondered what it is?"

"I have."

"The fuel comes from a special rock we mine far below us. When touched with fire, it burns for weeks, giving us that blue flame. But we're running out of it. We have tunneled everywhere and found no other vein of it running in the earth. We get heat and light from the rock, and without it we would not be able to sustain ourselves for very long. The elders among the Mung have come together, and we have decided that the best option is to move aboveground." Zaqil sighed. "It will be difficult for many of us accustomed to being the only ones that live underground. It's a whole new world up there that we do not yet truly understand. That is another reason why we agreed to do business with Iqban."

Ran glanced around. Iqban was nowhere to be seen. "Where is he, by the way?"

Zaqil waved the question off. "We have the material means to purchase whatever we need to form a new empire aboveground, but what we lack is information."

"What sort of information?"

"Where we might be able to form a new kingdom, who might oppose us, what strengths they have. All manner of strategic questions that we would need answered prior to simply going aboveground. These mountains have given us shelter for eons, and leaving them presents a huge challenge for us."

Ran sensed he knew where this was going but said nothing until Zaqil turned to him.

"Is that why you invited me here tonight?"

Zaqil shrugged. "I would have invited you anyway. You bested me in combat, and as such you deserve the accolades. But I would be lying if I said I didn't also want a chance to discuss things with you. Specifically about how you might be able to help us in the coming years."

Ran allowed a small frown to cross his face. "How many know about me?"

"Everyone knows you beat me in combat. But not everyone knows about what you are or at least what Iqban claims you are."

Ran nodded. "It is imperative that no one know what I am. If we are have any sort of relationship at all, absolute trust and secrecy are the first orders of business."

Zaqil smiled. "I understand. Your identity will be known only to me."

"Iqban knows also."

"Worry not about him," said Zaqil. "I will deal with him when the time is right."

"As long as Iqban is alive, he is a threat to me," said Ran. "He would sell every one of my secrets for a gold coin if he thought he could profit from it."

"Indeed he would," said Zaqil. "But you need not worry."

Ran said nothing while he pondered their exchange. Shinobujin had routinely been employed to assist other kingdoms over the years. But such matters were ordinarily arranged by other Shinobujin, not field operatives like Ran. The novelty of this appealed to him. But there were certain things to consider. The Mung were a cannibalistic race. Ran wasn't sure how well that would transfer to the above world. Still, he knew that there were far-flung races and cultures that engaged in acts many would consider equally barbaric. And that hadn't stopped them from thriving.

"I would need to consult with my clan before I can formally agree to anything," said Ran. "You understand my allegiance must first be to them."

"I would think less of you if you said otherwise," said Zaqil. "There is much about you that I admire." He nodded. "That is perfectly agreeable to me. You should contact them and ask if the Mung empire may hire you to scout a location for us that you think would prove suitable for construction of a new fortress."

"There's a chance they might not agree to it."

Zaqil sighed. "I know. But I hope they would look at this as an opportunity to establish good relations with a race many people do not even realize has existed beneath them for thousands of years."

"They may well do that," said Ran. "I don't know how they decide which jobs to take or decline, but I will relay the information and then be back in touch with you."

Zaqil nodded. "When we escort you out, the guard will show you the entrance to use to return here at a later date. When you come back, you must recite four words which will keep you in good stead with whomever challenges you. They prove that you are a trusted ally of the Mung."

"What are the words?"

"*Bak chang huq yarol*."

Ran recited them, ensuring he got the pronunciation down right. After several moments of letting them sink in, he looked at Zaqil. "What do they mean?"

"The heart of life beats beneath." Zaqil grinned. "They are words every Mung child grows up learning. We swear an allegiance not to a king, but to the deep depths of the underground. Down deep below us is where all life comes from. A pulsing heart filled with warmth and fire. If that ever stops, we—not just the Mung, but all peoples—will cease to exist. Perhaps because we are closer to it and feel it everywhere in our domain, we appreciate it a bit more. But no Mung would ever turn you away when you say that to them. They will know the only way you would come by that knowledge is if you had been welcomed into our domain previously."

"I am humbled that you would trust me with this information," said Ran.

"Then we are even," said Zaqil. "You now know something about us that could potentially lead to our downfall. We each, as it were, have something over the other. I need you to realize that your secret is safe with me. To prove that, I have given you something of immense value to us."

"I appreciate that," said Ran. And he did. Zaqil's willingness to compromise their security so that Ran felt more comfortable meant a great deal to him. Try as he might, he found it hard to actually think of Zaqil as some sort of evil leader. If anything, it only reinforced his belief that the true enemy was Zal himself. Zaqil's men had made short work of Zal's hired army. But Zal had yet to be found.

"Will you be able to find Zal?"

Zaqil nodded. "He can run, but he cannot hide for long. My brother is as foolish as he is egotistical. Sooner or later, he will grow tired of hiding and come out to assume what he believes is his rightful place as king."

"Your brother?"

Zaqil smiled. "Yes. Although he was born to my father's concubine and not my mother. But that has never stopped him from trying to usurp power for himself."

"Iqban told me that he had been king and was forced into exile."

Zaqil had some more of his drink. "Yes, I would expect that to be the story he wove. It's one of the ways he functions. He concocts a good story and then tries to win people over to his side. He's been doing it for many years. When I uncovered his plot to overthrow my council, I gave him two options: death or exile. He chose the latter."

"But he didn't go far. He stayed right around here and then started building an army to take control by force. How does that make sense?"

"I knew all along where he was," said Zaqil. "I thought it better to keep him close and be able to keep an eye on him and his activities than to lose sight of him elsewhere. When it became clear what he was up to, I made my own plans and attacked before he was ready."

"Couldn't he just have attacked through the main gate?"

Zaqil shook his head. "He would know that it is too heavily guarded to get an army through. His only option was to tunnel in multiple places and try to a simultaneous attack. But we are incredible miners, and my people informed me when they became aware of the tunneling happening from the other side. We quickly surmised what he was doing and made arrangements to undercut him."

"You certainly succeeded," said Ran. "His troops were overwhelmed, and the results were . . ." Ran's voice trailed off.

"Yes, unpalatable to you. I understand," said Zaqil. "But when the Mung are aroused to their berserker state, their appetite increases tenfold. Anything within range is potential food. I daresay you were lucky not to have run into any of my men when you were over there."

"I count myself lucky as well," said Ran. "From what I saw, your troops are very formidable fighters, especially in the close confines of the tunnel networks down here."

"They know how to fight better than the mercenaries that Zal had hired for himself," said Zaqil. "They were no match in the tunnels, and my men took advantage of it to rout them utterly."

"A shame that Zal wasn't taken," said Ran.

"If you come across him in your travels, I would consider it a personal favor if you killed him," said Zaqil. "To say that I have had enough of his silliness would be an understatement. It's true we share the same bloodline, but there comes a point when even family is not above being called out on their stupidity. I would not tolerate such actions from my friends or even the men who serve me. Why should I tolerate it from family just because we share blood? It makes no sense."

"I lost my family at a young age," said Ran. "I was adopted by my clan, and they became my true family."

"You are fortunate to not have to have dealt with the pettiness of familial issues," said Zaqil. "It drains a man of his will to live his life by his own inner compass."

"How do you mean?"

Zaqil finished his drink and set it down. "Who we are is often the product of those around us. We grow according to what we perceive as the right way to do things. Our values are passed on to us by parents and relatives. At some point, though, we grow old enough to know who we truly are as individuals. How many people constrain themselves because their family wouldn't be accepting of their true nature? How many people truly enjoy the freedom to be who they are? Very few, I would wager."

"Put that way," said Ran. "I do feel fortunate. As long as my allegiance to my clan remains steadfast, I am free to do as I will."

"Indeed," said Zaqil. "You are blessed to be able to do what you wish. When Zal is finally eliminated, I will have that freedom as well."

"But you can already do as you wish."

Zaqil tapped his head and then his heart. "But here and here, it is still as if he is around me. All I hear is him berating me and insisting that I acquiesce to his demands because we are family. The number of times I wished my father could have kept his manhood locked up and not fathered such a beast are truly without end."

Ran laughed. "Here's to self-discipline and freedom, then."

Zaqil clanked glasses with him and then set it back down. "You must be ready to be on your way. I have kept you for too long already." Zaqil smiled. "I have enjoyed our time together. I hope you return with favorable news from your clan."

"Thank you," said Ran. "I will endeavor to return as soon as possible."

Zaqil clapped his hands and a guard materialized. "Escort our guest to the main gate and then back to where Zal built his main gate." He glanced at Ran. "I trust that will be okay? Your companions might even still be around."

Ran nodded. "That will be fine. Thank you again, Zaqil."

"Travel well, Ran." He stood and clasped Ran's hand.

Then Zaqil clapped again. From the left side of the room, several cooks pushed a large rack into the center of the room with a writhing form strapped to it. With arms and legs stretched akimbo, Iqban was then hoisted above the fire. Were it not for the fact that his mouth had been sewn shut, his screams would have echoed through the chamber.

Ran looked back at Zaqil, who only shrugged. "I told you I would take care of him. Now go, you have no wish to see this any further."

Ran turned and followed the guard out.

Behind him, Iqban's moans gradually faded away as he cooked over the fire.

Chapter Thirty-Four

It took them nearly twice the time to get back to Zal's fiefdom as it had when Iqban had brought him to the Mung kingdom, Ran decided as they walked. He wasn't sure if the guard was deliberately leading them around in circles to confuse Ran or not. Perhaps Zaqil had requested he do it, even though he'd pressed a small silken map into Ran's hands as they were parting. Ran knew the map would show him how to return if he was ever able to come back.

The tunnels were still a confusing maze, but Ran started to recognize several key features as they walked. His eyes had grown accustomed to the dim light, and he knew they were close when they took a sudden turn and ended up in the tunnel where he had picked the lock on the knob controlling the main gate. Cool air flowed into the tunnel, and Ran guessed that the door was open still. As he walked on, his Mung guide suddenly stopped and then handed Ran his sword.

"Thank you," said Ran, tucking the blade into his belt.

The Mung guide waved, then turned and headed back toward his home, leaving Ran alone in the tunnel.

For a moment, Ran watched him leave. The Mung turned and then melted into the shadows. Ran smirked. It reminded him of watching a fellow shadow warrior blend into the darkness.

Then he turned and walked down the tunnel to the main cavern.

The bodies of the guards that had helped Iqban kidnap Cassandra were still on the floor; their blood had dried to a sticky dark viscous liquid, and the smell was horrible. Ran scrunched up his nose and looked around for any signs that Kuva and Cassandra were still nearby. He found nothing.

The air inside the main cavern felt cooler than he would have expected. Judging by the gusts, there might even be a storm blowing outside, he concluded. He wondered how far Kuva and Cassandra might have gotten, but then knew the only way to find out was to follow them. Ran took a final look around the cavern and at the tunnels and then started his trek toward the outside world. He was relieved to have a weapon as he walked. Zal was still very much a threat, and if he stumbled across the miniature despot, he would gladly cut him down.

But his main focus was on finding Cassandra and Kuva. The tunnel sloped upward as he walked, and he found himself growing more excited with each step he took. Hope flooded him that he might soon be reconnected with his friends. Then perhaps they could find a place to rest and recover from their ordeal in the catacombs. A long rest would suit him well before he decided whether to continue with the clan's reconnaissance mission or escort Cassandra to the safety of her kingdom. Then there was the matter of Zaqil's request for help. Ran would definitely have to pass that along to the clan.A lot to do, he decided.

As he continued up the path, something disturbed him. It was hard to pinpoint what it was exactly, but as he walked, he felt pressure building up around him. In the air, nearby. Some sort of energy.

He dropped without thinking about it.

And the world around him exploded.

He awoke still by himself in the cave. His hand immediately went for his sword, and he was relieved to find it still there. Ran got up and shook himself off. The explosion had been a big one, but amid the debris that surrounded him, he could see no reason for it. Bits of rock lay scattered all over the place; some in big chunks, others in small. He picked one of them up and looked at it. It appeared to be exactly like the type of rock he'd spent his days mining for Zal's nefarious purposes.

But as he looked closer, Ran saw tinges of blue vein running through it. And as he held it in his hand, the blue vein started to glow and pulse, almost as if the rock itself were alive. Ran put it down on the ground and then continued walking up the slope. The way was harder going now, but it hadn't been blocked, fortunately.

Near the top of the slope, he saw movement. Hugging the rock wall, Ran eased himself forward. He hoped it was Kuva or Cassandra. But as he got closer, he could see that the movement came from about a score of Mithrus's guards.

Ran frowned. Zaqil had told him they'd mopped up all the pockets of resistance, but clearly they had not succeeded in killing everyone. Here were at least twenty heavily armed soldiers, clearly up to something.

He looked closer and saw a smaller figure directing them this way and that.

Zal.

The maniacal Mung despot was directing several slaves to put large boxes of something near the entrance of the cave that led to the catacombs. And behind Zal, Ran spotted two cages. What he saw next made his heart drop.

Zal had Cassandra and Kuva in one cage and roughly six Mung warriors in another. The Mung warriors clawed at the bars and hissed. Cassandra and Kuva sat dejectedly in their cage. Kuva clearly had some injuries, and dried blood caked his face and neck. Cassandra seemed to be tending to him, but it was clear they were being kept alive for some reason.

So close to the daylight, Ran marveled at how bright everything seemed. He'd grown used to being in the tunnels, but now he was back above it all. Judging by the amount of light, it must have been some time in the early evening. He was grateful he hadn't emerged at midday, when the light might have blinded him. As it was, the sky seemed gray and foreboding, with bloated clouds hugging the area.

He continued to watch the slaves placing boxes next to the entrance of the cave. What could they have contained, he wondered. He couldn't risk getting closer without exposing himself, so he would have to wait until darkness to inspect them. And then he had to work on freeing Kuva and Cassandra as well.

Looking behind him, Ran wondered if Zaqil knew that Zal was up here or still in the area. He'd asked Ran to kill him if he saw him. But against a force of twenty soldiers, Ran would need some help. He looked back at the cage of Mung warriors. If he could get close to them and use the secret phrase, they would know he was an ally and not their enemy. Freeing them would give the guards plenty to handle while Ran freed Cassandra and Kuva and then killed Zal.

It could work.

There was a lull in activity as one of the slaves collapsed. The soldiers moved in and started beating him, but the old man did not move.

Ran used the distraction to get closer to the entrance, tucking himself into a shallow depression in the cave wall that afforded him a good view of the area. As he watched, Zal ordered the unconscious slave brought over to the cage containing the Mung warriors. More of the soldiers used their swords to poke the Mung into one corner while a guard opened the door and dropped the slave inside. Ran watched this all, noting that the cage didn't require a key, but was more of a heavy latch lock. He hoped it was the same type of arrangement on the cage containing Cassandra and Kuva.

The guard slammed the door shut again, and the soldiers moved away from the cage. No longer restrained by the threat of swords, the Mung warriors set about eating the slave. Fortunately, Ran surmised he was already dead. And the Mung ate him quickly. Ran was far enough away that his ears did not pick up the sounds of the man being eaten. As it was, he had to turn away and try to quell the rolling in his stomach.

Zal seemed to revel in the bloodlust of the Mung warriors, however, and clapped his hands as they finished off the poor slave's body, leaving only the bones behind. Some of the Mung even gnawed on them as they finished. Ran watched the expression on Cassandra's face and saw pure terror there.

Ran stared at the sky and willed it to grow darker so that he could get his friends freed. But the light of the sky still showed far too much for Ran's comfort. He frowned. His heart pulsed faster, and he willed himself to slow it down. He remembered his teachers telling him not to be rash in his actions. Doing so would get him killed. And his friends. But in the real world, it was far tougher than back at the safety of his school. He could see the lives of his friends being measured in mere minutes if he chose not to act.

He turned away from the scene and stared back into the inky blackness of the cave. Somehow the darkness helped calm him. He'd been down in the depths of the catacombs for so long that it felt more comfortable to move in the shadows than in the daylight.

A clap of thunder boomed overhead. Ran turned back and saw that the clouds had opened up. A downpour fell on the entirety of Zal's party. But the rain quickly turned to snow, the white flakes coming down thick and fast. Ran grinned. He could use the weather to his advantage almost as well as the darkness. It wasn't perfect, of course, but given the circumstance, he couldn't have asked for better.

Zal's men ran about the entrance, moving boxes and supplies just inside. The remaining slaves were tied up near the cave mouth. The two cages of prisoners were brought to the innermost portion of the cave's entrance. They were now closer to Ran. He waited until the guards moved away after checking that the latches were still secured. Then he crept forward until he was behind the cage containing Cassandra and Kuva.

"Cassandra."

She turned, and her eyes widened. "Ran?"

He held up a finger to his lips. "Stay quiet. I'm going to get you out of here."

"Kuva's badly injured. He tried fighting all of Zal's men after they grabbed me."

"How did you get ambushed?"

Cassandra frowned. "It was my fault. I thought we were home free after we left the main entrance. Zal was waiting above and grabbed us as we came out."

"What about the Mung in the next cage?"

She shrugged. "I don't know. He already had them. He's repeatedly threatened to feed us to them. Did you see what they did to that other poor soul? Horrible!"

Ran held up his hand. "Don't be too hard on them. It's their culture."

"Eating people? No, thank you." She looked around to make sure no one was about and then turned back to Ran. "What happened to you? We looked in the tunnel, but you were gone."

"Iqban, the slaver. He knocked me out from behind and tried to sell me to the Mung king, who, it turns out, is Zal's half-brother. There's no love lost there. In any event, I won my freedom and came back straightaway only to find you both in this predicament. Is Kuva conscious?"

Kuva grunted. "Barely."

"How bad is it, friend?"

"Bad. I've lost a lot of blood."

"Can you hang on until I get things sorted?"

Kuva turned and grinned at Ran. "I'm not going anywhere."

Ran smiled. "You still have a sense of humor. That's good." He looked at Cassandra. "I'm going to free the Mung and let them handle the dirty work for me."

"They'll tear you apart!"

Ran shook his head. "I don't think they will. I know a few more things about them now that I visited with their king."

"Enough to make them your allies?"

Ran cocked an eyebrow. "I guess we'll find out." He moved to the rear of the cave again, sinking back into the shadows. Just in time, a guard made his rounds and checked on the cages. Ran watched him move over to the Mung cage. The Mung growled at the guard, who only laughed. Rand waited until he walked back toward the cave entrance and then moved over to the cage containing the Mung soldiers.

They must have heard him approach, because they glared at him with bared teeth.

I hope this works, thought Ran.

"*Bak chang huq yarol.*"

He whispered the words through the bars of the cage, and the Mung backed up in surprise. Their eyes wide, they spoke in whispers among themselves. Finally, one of them moved forward to the bars. Ran tried his best to not stare at the blood that caked his mouth. When he spoke, Ran could still see bits of flesh dangling from his teeth.

"How do you know our tongue?"

"Your king taught me those words himself. He said it would let any Mung know that I am a friend to your people."

The Mung soldier frowned and then appeared to translate what Ran had said to the others. He looked back at Ran. "You are friend?"

"I am. I'm going to free you. But you must promise not to harm me or my friends in the next cage there."

The Mung looked over at Cassandra and Kuva and then back at Ran. "If you free us, the men will kill us."

"No doubt they're going to kill you anyway," said Ran. "Wouldn't you rather die fighting than in some cage like an animal?"

The Mung didn't hesitate. "Of course."

"Then when I free you, you will have only a little time to overwhelm the guards before your advantage is lost. I will help you fight. But remember, do not attack me or my friends."

"And what of Zal?"

"Your king requested that I kill him if I saw him. But if one of you kills him, it will be a great honor for your people. It matters not to me."

"Very well. Free us."

Ran moved to the door of the cage and checked his surroundings again. The weather outside had intensified, and the snow fell thick and fast. Already icicles had formed at the mouth of the cave, giving the cave entrance the appearance of a mouth filled with sharp teeth. Ran smiled at the image and then turned back to the cage.

The latch came up easily enough. Ran held up his hand as he slowly opened the door, praying it wouldn't squeak and alert the guards. But it swung out smoothly.

In an instant, the Mung came forward out of the cage. They had no weapons, but as soon as they attacked, the guards they killed would provide them with arms.

"Ready?" asked Ran.

The Mung warrior nodded once. "For our king."

Chapter Thirty-Five

Ran moved quickly to the cage where Cassandra and Kuva were and motioned Cassandra over. "Can Kuva move?"

"No."

"Then move to the center of the cage. Otherwise someone might thrust a blade at you when the mayhem starts."

Cassandra watched the Mung warriors moving stealthily toward their foes. "Do they know . . . ?"

"They know you're not an enemy, yes." Ran saw the first of Zal's men disappear. "I need to go." He turned and drew his own sword before following the rest of the Mung toward the cave mouth. Bits of wet snowflakes twirled around them as the harsh winter wind blew them into the cave. Several cooking fires had been started, but that only served to illuminate the men the Mung were going to kill. As the light outside faded, the fires helped silhouette the soldiers.

Two more of Zal's men vanished. Then the Mung let out a war cry and rushed toward the men sitting around the fires. Zal's soldiers cried out and fell over from shock as the Mung swarmed over them, clawing and punching and kicking. As the men went down, the Mung grabbed up their swords and then used them against the soldiers who hadn't died in the initial assault. Zal's men managed to form a line and started fighting back.

Ran dashed ahead and took on the left flank. The soldier there glanced in Ran's direction but must have assumed that Ran was one of his mates, because he waved him on. Ran cut his head from his shoulders and then drove into the next man, swiping with his sword up and down, mowing down two more of the soldiers before they were able to ascertain what was going on.

The Mung never stopped moving ahead. Two of them died as Zal's men fought them back, but the remaining four pressed on, working as a team to attack two more soldiers.

But Zal's men had more than just swords with them, and four of them brought the spears out quickly. Together they formed an impenetrable wedge that skewered two more of the Mung, one through the heart and another in the throat. There were just two of the Mung left. With Ran.

"Enough!"

Zal's voice rang out, and something about his tone made Ran turn and see what he was up to. The Mung despot stood close to the cage where Cassandra and Kuva still resided. In his hand, he held a small box that pulsed blue. "Unless you want to see your friends destroyed, you will stop immediately."

Ran's arm hung in mid-stroke, but he allowed it to go limp. What did Zal have in his hand? But again, the conviction in his voice managed to sway him. "What are you up to, Zal?"

"I will detonate the boxes under their cage unless you surrender right this instant."

Ran looked and frowned. There were two boxes under the cage. Boxes like what he'd seen the slaves moving into the cave. What was so special about them? "So what?"

"Were you creeping about earlier when one of them exploded? You must have been to get into position to arrange this folly." Zal smiled. "Surely you've noticed the blue torches in the catacombs. The rock that powers them is a volatile substance that explodes when properly initiated."

Ran remembered the explosion. And the damage it had done. Two boxes of that stuff under his friends would blow them apart. If Kuva had been able to move, Ran would have let them out of the cage. But he couldn't do anything about that right now.

He dropped his sword. "Fine."

Zal's men took him by the shoulders and trussed his hands. The two Mung left alive were herded together and held at sword point by six of Zal's men.

In spite of the failure, they had managed to kill over half of Zal's men. Ran knew that Zal would settle for nothing less than brutal vengeance. But better to risk that than the deaths of his friends. Zal walked forward and opened another box nearby. From inside he took out two rocks about six inches across and brought them up to the captured Mung. He gave the rocks to the guards. "Attach the rocks to their backs."

Zal's guards roughly turned the Mung and strapped the rocks to their backs by wrapping rope around them. Zal addressed them in their language and then nodded to his soldiers. "Turn them loose at the mouth of the cave. Let them run outside."

The Mung were taken to the mouth and then prodded out into the blinding snowstorm. With their hands strapped to their sides, they floundered about, trying to help each other get free. Zal stood next to Ran and sighed. "They are fierce fighters, but not very intelligent. Watch." He aimed the small box in his hand and then depressed a small button on it.

Ran looked. The growing dark outside suddenly illuminated in a flash of brilliant blue energy. The two Mung were blasted apart, pieces of their bodies flying everywhere and staining the snow red.

Zal chuckled. "A good test, I would say. I mean aside from the one we tried earlier right before you showed up."

"Why would you kill them like that? They were your people."

Zal spat on the ground. "They were not my people. They stood against me and served my brother. Traitors to my cause, they deserved to die. As do you." He nodded, and the guards shoved Ran toward the cage where Cassandra and Kuva sat. "Put him inside and lock them in properly. I don't want any more surprises while we finish things up."

Ran climbed into the cage. "What are you up to, Zal?"

Zal turned and looked at him. "I'm going to detonate this entire mountain and bring it down around my brother's empire."

"What?"

Zal pointed at the boxes. "Small caches like this have been strategically placed at a number of places in the catacombs. When I detonate one of them, the others will all explode in a synchronized series of events that will utterly bury my brother and his people."

"I thought you wanted to conquer them?"

Zal laughed. "Oh, no. That was simply a ruse so no one would figure out my true intent of mining all the blue rock out of the ground so I could use it for my true purpose: the extinction of the Mung."

"They wouldn't be extinct if you're still alive."

Zal shrugged. "True, but I would be the only one of my people, and within a few generations my bloodline would be so diluted that none would ever know of the race that I was from."

"You want to kill them all that badly because you were exiled? Seems a bit extreme."

"You don't have the right to judge me," said Zal. "What do you know of my race? Who they are or what they've done to me?"

"*Bak chang huq yarol*," said Ran.

"Where did you learn those words?" Zal demanded. "Who told them to you?"

Ran smiled. "As a matter of fact, your brother did when I was his guest earlier today. He's a very proud man, proud of his people, and he seems to lead by example. He's concerned for their future and wants to insure they have one above ground."

"My brother." Zal shook his head. "Thieving bastard that he is. He would tell you all of those things, but he lies. My brother is a ruthless man hellbent on world domination."

Ran sighed. "I disagree. He was true to his word when we fought. He gave me my freedom."

"So you fought him? How did that happen?"

"Iqban dragged me there as his prisoner, intending to sell me to Zaqil for a price."

"Really, and why would he do that?"

Ran shrugged. "Because Iqban is crazy. Or at least he was. He's dead now."

"You killed him?"

"Your brother had him roasted alive."

"So you see how ruthless he can be." Zal held his arms out. "Do you even know what those words mean that he taught you? Do you?"

"The heart of life beats beneath," said Ran. "He explained their meaning and the importance of them to every Mung."

"You are a fool, Ran from Nehon," said Zal. "My brother is a master manipulator. He is an expert in telling people what they want to hear in order to get them to do something for him. Obviously he must have thought you were valuable enough to keep alive, which makes me wonder what he must have thought about you. Did he know something about you that I do not? What secrets did you tell him about yourself? My brother wouldn't simply let you walk out of his kingdom unless you could prove valuable later on."

"I don't know what it was," said Ran. "We fought, and he promised me my freedom if I won. I did win. He was true to his word. I actually respected him."

Zal walked over to the cage. "You would respect a man that kicked his own brother out of the kingdom?"

"Half-brother," said Ran.

"Family!" Zal wiped his forehead. "He should have respected me and my position enough to give me more than he ever did. But no, because I was the son of a whore instead of a queen, he used his position to trump me at every instance. While he ascended the steps of greatness, I was left behind like some pathetic little idiot. Told to sit in the corner and play quietly while the real royals attended to the serious affairs of running a kingdom. I was humiliated at every turn. And when I dared reach for something more than what I'd been given, I was stripped of it all and sent packing."

"Interesting perspective," said Ran. "I don't know which person I'd be more inclined to agree with: the guy who used me as slave labor or the brother who set me free. Tough choice."

"Impudent fool," said Zal again. "You might have a rosy version of my brother inside that dumb head of yours, but I can assure that he is nothing if not capable of letting people only see what they want to see. For you to see the real man he is, you would have needed to be there for years, not mere hours. You have been played and played well. I've never begrudged him his excellence in manipulating people."

"I don't think I was manipulated," said Ran. "And he could have killed me if he'd wanted to. I could have ended up as dinner for his people the way Iqban did."

"Iqban was a fool, too," said Zal. "Why on earth would he try to strike a bargain with my brother?"

"Greed," said Ran. "The same thing that led to your downfall, it would appear."

"This isn't about greed," said Zal. He stalked around the cage now, staring at Ran and his companions. "This is about righting the wrongs that have persisted for decades. This is about me demanding some respect and finally figuring out the way to ensure that I get some."

"So what happens, you tell your brother that you're going to blow him up and he suddenly decides to abdicate the throne? He already interrupted your invasion plans earlier. He'd decimate you."

Zal sniffed. "The invasion was a ruse. I told you that. My brother isn't the only one who can manipulate people. And I used him to my advantage. While his men were killing off my hired army, I was placing the explosive caches exactly where they needed to be in his kingdom. The only way I could have done that without being seen was if the majority of his forces were concentrating on killing my troops and defending against a perceived threat that simply never existed."

Ran shook his head. "You sacrificed those men to achieve your goals?"

"Oh, absolutely. Everything is to be sacrificed to make sure that this plan goes off."

"And you don't care that they died like that?"

Zal sighed. "Why would I care? They are hired soldiers. They assume all the risks of employment. If the prospect of death bothers them, then they clearly should not become soldiers. Only a fool would expect to walk into harm's way and not get harmed. They were tools for me to use as I saw fit. Mithrus had no problems with this. His men followed his orders to the letter."

"Mithrus is dead, too," said Ran.

"Just as well," said Zal. "He would have asked for more money. In any event, my brother used you just as I used the men who died for me."

"I disagree."

"Don't you wonder why he would set you free like that?"

Ran had no intention of telling Zal about their potential relationship. "It never occurred to me to ask."

"And he certainly wouldn't have let you wander around the tunnels of his kingdom as if you were a Mung citizen."

"He didn't," said Ran.

Zal leaned against the cage and pressed his face close to the bars. "Really? And pray tell me, how did you ever make your way back to here? You wouldn't have known which tunnels to take to get here."

"I didn't need to. Zaqil gave me a guide. A warrior who led me to the main entrance. From there I simply walked up and found you."

Zal leaned back. "He gave you a guide?"

"Of course."

Zal glanced around and then shouted for the soldiers. "Get them into the tunnel immediately."

The soldiers started shoving the cage deeper into the cave. Ran held the bars. "What's got you so spooked?"

"If my brother gave you a guide, then the soldier probably had orders to follow you here and report back what he saw. If my brother knows what I'm up to, he'll take steps to stop it." Zal backed away. "But don't worry. When I set the explosions off, you will be the first to die here. You and your friends alike."

Chapter Thirty-six

As Zal's men pushed the cage farther into the tunnel, Ran saw the slaves getting agitated. Several of them started poking at the shackles that held them to the mouth of the cave. If they could get free, thought Ran, then that would give him cover to work on the cage lock. He needed to get Cassandra and Kuva out of the cage as soon as possible. He had little doubt that Zal would detonate the blue rocks as soon as he thought they were ready to go or if he perceived any type of threat.

Had Zaqil used him? Ran didn't know. But in his position, Ran might have done the same thing. So he couldn't really fault the Mung king for having someone follow him, although Ran was a bit upset with himself that he hadn't noticed anyone following him. I must really need some rest, he thought.

Zal ran all around the cave on stubby legs, shouting orders to the remaining soldiers he had at his disposal. The pack horses that were in the small encampment were loaded up, although Ran suspected the horses thought it was crazy to even think about journeying out in a blizzard the likes of which was blowing now.

"Where are you going to go in this weather?" Ran called to Zal. "You wouldn't last a mile in that snowstorm. Your horses are terrified. You'll all freeze to death."

Zal eyed him as he directed more of his men to position more boxes filled with blue rocks around the area. "It's better than being blown up, I can assure you. And besides, I know of a shelter nearby."

"Will it still be there after you blow up the mountain?"

"Of course. It has stood for thousands of years."

Ran frowned. What sort of shelter could stand that long? "Who built it?"

"Settlers who have long since vanished from this region. It's a temple nestled in between the pass that leads to the northern lands." Zal frowned. "Now stop pestering me."

Ran grinned as Zal turned away from the cage. He immediately set about trying to jimmy the latch on the cage. It was a heavy bolt that snapped into place much like the one that Ran had opened on the Mung cage. The only difference was that Ran had been outside of the cage when he'd opened it, whereas now he was forced to use his hand in an awkward position. Fortunately, he'd been taught to be flexible and snaked his arm through just enough that he could barely reach it.

"Ran."

He looked back over his shoulder. Kuva motioned for him to come closer. Ran frowned. The big warrior looked pale. Ran knelt and patted him on the arm. "I'm here."

Kuva smiled at him. "I'm not going to make it. . . . I've lost too much blood."

"Don't say that, friend. We'll get you out of here."

Kuva shook his head. "Even if you're able to, what good will it do? You said yourself there's a terrible storm outside. I'll freeze to death before we can get anywhere safe." He swallowed and looked back at Ran. "When you get the cage open, take Cassandra and go."

"I'm not going to do that."

"You have to. There's no sense in three of us dying. I'm already dead anyway."

Ran said nothing, but gripped his friend's hand. "I can make this work." He thought about trying the healing action he'd used a month before. But even as he thought about it, he knew it wouldn't work. The extent of Kuva's wounds were simply too great and beyond what he could do.

"No, you can't. And I'm resigned to the fact that I'm not going to get out of here." His grip started to weaken. "But do me one small favor."

"Anything."

"When you get time to travel to Adosa, please tell my family I died in battle. Tell them . . . that I made sure our enemies knew the name of the house that brought them their end."

Ran took a breath and then swallowed against the lump in his throat. "I will sing your praises and make sure your family knows of your greatness."

Kuva smiled. "Thank you, my friend." He let his hand slip from Ran's and then shoved him away. "Now go. Your time is short. If Zal suspects anything, he will kill you and be done with it. You must get Cassandra out of here or my death will have been for naught."

"I won't ever forget you, Kuva."

Kuva's eyes closed. "Then that is treasure enough for my weary soul. It was . . . an honor to have fought beside you. May all your battles be joined by my spirit." Kuva muttered something in his native tongue and then slumped over to one side of the cell.

Ran glanced at Cassandra and saw that tears streamed down her face. His vision blurred then and he wiped his own eyes and took another deep breath.

"We have work to do."

Ran turned back to the latch on the cage and once more snaked his arm through. Zal was still orchestrating his men. The slaves were still fiddling with their shackles. And the horses neighed nervously as they stamped their feet on the cave floor. The energy in the air seemed to crackle, and Ran knew something was going to happen soon. Or perhaps it was just the passing of a mighty warrior.

Ran's fingers touched the latch, and he pushed it up and out of the bolt recess. Then he slid it back. The metal grated against metal, but the noise couldn't be heard over Zal's shouts. Ran glanced back at Cassandra. "I've got it."

She nodded and leaned closer to the door. Ran glanced around. Zal still had ten men, and Ran was unarmed. Somehow, they had to get out of the cage and either arm themselves or get past the cave mouth without anyone seeing them.

As he started to plot their route, however, the slaves finally succeeded in releasing themselves. They immediately attacked the guards nearby. One of the slaves threw himself at the guard. The guard stabbed him with the sword, but by then, the other slaves had already overwhelmed him. He went down, and his own sword was used to end his life.

Shouts and screams erupted from the other slaves as they ran to attack the guards. Zal dashed away from the mouth of the cave, back toward where the cage was. As he ran toward it, Ran slammed the door open, catching Zal right in the face. The little man went down hard.

"Now," said Ran.

He leapt out and helped Cassandra down from the cage. He glanced back inside at Kuva's body. "I can't leave him in there." He climbed back in and got his arms around the big man. Ran grunted under the weight but managed to get his friend out of the cage while Cassandra guided his feet down to the ground. They laid him next to Zal. Ran checked the Mung would-be ruler.

"Is he dead?" asked Cassandra.

"I don't think so," said Ran. "But that's easily remedied."

But Cassandra pulled him away. "Forget about that. The slaves will take care of disposing of him. We need to get out of here before any of his troops figure out we've escaped."

They ran toward the cave mouth. One of the soldiers saw the motion and moved to intercept them, but Ran was faster. As the soldier brought his sword down, Ran sidestepped and chopped down on the man's hand, breaking his wrist. The sword dropped and Ran backfisted the man in the face before moving behind him and breaking his neck. As he dropped, Ran grabbed his sword and they continued on.

The slaves, despite being outnumbered, had taken care of five of the remaining soldiers. They'd lost two of their own in the skirmish, however. One of the other soldiers fled on one of the pack horses. The whole impromptu camp had deteriorated into chaos.

The cold winds blew into the cave, and the snowflakes stung at Ran's face. He blinked, trying to clear his vision. When a particularly strong gust knocked him back, Ran turned his head to avoid it.

And someone slammed into his knees.

Ran's legs buckled. His sword was ripped from his grasp. As he fell, Ran tried to open his eyes. But then he took a fist smack on his nose, and his eyes welled up with tears. He shook his head trying to clear his vision, and another punch landed in his solar plexus. He sucked wind, but his lungs felt like they were on fire.

Ran rolled and came up on his feet.

"You won't get rid of me that easily."

Zal.

Ran shook his head. "You don't know when to quit, do you?"

"I don't ever quit," said Zal. "Not when I have a destiny left to fulfill."

"Your destiny is to die," said Ran. "And I am here to see it fulfilled."

Zal brought his hands up. "You might be interested to learn of the one thing I was always better at than my brother."

"And what might that be?"

"Fighting," said Zal. "It was the only area I surpassed him. Try as he might, and he did try, he could never best me. My brother is a good fighter, it's true. But I am far better than he is." He smiled. "So with that said, I invite you to try your luck against me. Without a sword."

Ran glanced at Cassandra. "Get going. If this goes bad, make a run for it. There's a temple somewhere around here that should offer you shelter." He pointed at his sword on the ground. "Take that."

She shook her head. "Why don't you just use it to kill him, and then we can leave together."

"He'll blow this place up if I don't agree to his terms."

Cassandra grabbed the sword and eyed Zal. "I hope he kills you very slowly."

Zal laughed. "You'd better hope he does, my dear. Because if I win, I'm coming looking for you out in those mountains. If I find you, I'm going to eat every bit of flesh from that delectable body of yours."

"Enough," said Ran. He glanced at Cassandra. "Get going."

He waited until Cassandra reached the cave mouth. She looked back and then stepped outside into the swirling blizzard.

"I should have killed you the moment Iqban brought you to me," said Zal. He circled around the cave, putting the Mung cage between him and Ran.

Ran scanned the ground nearby for anything he could use against Zal. There were weapons here and there, and a simple roll would bring them into Ran's grasp. But he had to make sure he did it subtly. If Zal suspected anything, he would detonate the blue rocks.

When the little man moved, Ran was surprised. Zal came screaming at him from around the corner of the cage and lashed out a high kick that nearly caught Ran in his side. He turned at the last moment and managed to avoid the blow. He dropped a fist at Zal's head, but the Mung simply dropped and rolled away.

As he came up, however, he threw a dagger right at Ran. Ran leapt to the side as the blade embedded itself in one of the boxes. "I thought we were doing this unarmed," said Ran.

Zal laughed. "You really are a fool, aren't you?"

"Apparently," said Ran. "You keep telling me that."

Zal came at him again, rushing in to tackle him around the waist. Ran dropped his feet back and drove his elbows down into Zal's back. The Mung grunted and then dropped, but not before he bit a chunk out of Ran's right calf muscle. Ran screamed as he felt Zal's teeth tear into his flesh. What crazy enemy was this that he would try to bite him while they fought? Then he remembered that Zal's true nature was one of cannibalism. Ran hadn't seen him eat anyone, but the realization startled him as he realized he should have expected it.

Zal's mouth was covered with Ran's blood, and Ran felt lightheaded. He swatted Zal away with his left hand, and the Mung staggered back, closer to Kuva's corpse. Ran followed him, limping heavily on his right leg. Zal kicked at Ran, trying to catch him in the groin, but Ran avoided it and punched Zal in his mouth. As he did so, Zal opened his mouth and let his razor-sharp teeth tear across Ran's fist. Ran felt like he'd just driven his hand into metallic teeth and glass. Blood streamed out of his hand.

Zal wrapped his arms around Ran and then lifted him off the ground. Ran felt his feet leave the cave floor, and then, as Zal dropped him back and down, Ran was forced to go with the energy of the throw to dissipate the force that came when he hit the cave floor. He exhaled hard and then tried to flush his lungs with more air.

Zal climbed on top of him and started punching him in the head. The Mung's fists felt like they were iron anvils. Ran blocked a lot of them, but the little man simply did not stop. More punches rained down on Ran, and his vision blurred as the area around his eyes began to swell up from repeated blows. Ran bucked his hips and sent Zal flying. Ran rolled and came up to his feet unsteadily. Zal came at him again, and this time Ran used the Mung's momentum to throw him farther back into the cave.

Zal landed and rolled to a stop close to Kuva.

Ran frowned. The last thing he wanted was to have to fight near the body of his deceased friend. He need to get Zal away from there.

Which is why he was so surprised when he saw Kuva's hand reach up and grab Zal around the ankle.

Zal screamed and looked down in time to see Kuva pulling himself up.

"No!"

Zal drove one of his fists down at Kuva's hands, but the bigger man was simply too strong and too heavy to shake loose. Zal stomped on Kuva's arm, but it did little good. Ran saw a fire burning in Kuva's eyes and knew that his friend would not let Zal go. Not now.

Not ever.

Zal must have seen that same fire, because the Mung's face changed. Instead of trying to free himself, he rammed his hand down into his tunic and pulled out the small box he'd used to detonate the blur rocks before.

Ran saw the action and then the gleeful look in Zal's eyes.

He heard Kuva's voice then shout loud and long. "Go, Ran! Go!"

Ran turned.

Dashed toward the mouth of the cave.

Threw himself out of the opening into the blinding snow and wind. The blizzard roared in his ears.

And then the world exploded all around him.

Chapter Thirty-seven

Ran awoke to someone turning him over in the deep snow. Flakes fell against his face and melted, streaking cold water down his skin. He opened his eyes and saw Cassandra leaning over him. "Are you all right?"

He sat up, aware that snow was melting through his tunic and making him wet. There was a whine in his ears, and he smelled something burning in the air, but otherwise, he felt okay. He glanced back at the cave entrance and frowned. It was gone.

"Where's the opening to the catacombs?"

Cassandra shook her head. "Gone. When Zal detonated the blue rocks, the entire mountain shook and rocks buried the entrance. I don't know what it's like inside, but I heard a series of explosions. They were muffled and gradually faded away, but it sure sounded like Zal's plan went off without a hitch. I don't know who could have possibly survived that."

Ran got to his feet with Cassandra's assistance. "He killed them. He killed them all."

"The Mung?"

Ran nodded. "I didn't think he was capable of it. They were his people, after all. But that didn't even seem to faze him. He was willing to do whatever it took to get vengeance on them for the injustices he suffered through. What drives someone to do something like that? Something so complete in its totality that there can never be a way back from it?"

"I don't know," said Cassandra. "But maybe somewhere, there's an answer."

Ran eyed her. "Something tells me that Zal won't find the peace he was looking for even in the afterlife."

"If there's such a thing," said the Princess. "I remain unconvinced, myself."

Ran shrugged and looked at the landscape. The blizzard continued to howl around them, and yet it was strangely peaceful. "I wouldn't have gotten out of there if it hadn't been for Kuva," he said quietly.

"Kuva?" Cassandra shook her head. "Kuva was dead before I left."

Ran stared at the mountain. "Then I was just helped by a ghost. He grabbed Zal and wouldn't let him go. When Zal decided to detonate the blue rocks, Kuva shouted for me to run. Something in his voice galvanized me to throw myself out of the cave a moment before it exploded. Any longer and I wouldn't have made it. I'd be buried under a million tons of rock."

Cassandra stayed quiet for a moment. "Maybe he wasn't quite dead."

"Maybe." But Ran knew what he thought. Kuva's spirit had been so strong that even death couldn't keep him from helping a friend. Another flake settled on Ran's eyelash and then melted down his face. Ran wiped his eyes. "Thank you, brother," he said quietly. And then he recited a mantra in his native tongue, his voice low and guttural, allowing the syllables of the powerful vocal trigger to be carried out into the wilds of the storm.

Neither he nor Cassandra spoke for some time after that. Finally Cassandra touched his arm. "We need to find shelter. We'll die in this storm otherwise."

Ran blinked and snapped back to reality. She was right, of course. The sooner they were out of the cold, the better. He glanced around. "Did you see if anyone else made it out?"

She nodded. "They did, but they all headed down into the valley where we originally came from. I don't know where they are. And frankly, they're not my concern. You mentioned something about a temple in the area. Are you sure it's here?"

"I only know what Zal spoke of. That the temple is built into the side of the mountain." He turned and studied the peaks before them. In the storm, it was difficult to see where one ended and the other began. Snow flew sideways, obscuring his vision, but as he scanned from left to right, he thought he saw something that looked vaguely unnatural on one of the mountains. He pointed it out to Cassandra. "I think that's where we ought to head for."

"That could be miles away," she said. "We might not make it."

"We definitely won't make it if we stay here arguing about it," said Ran. "And we don't really have any other choice except to try for it. With the cave effectively blocked, the best thing we could do is dig a snow cave, but that's no guarantee of survival. If we keep moving and can make it to the temple, then we can get out of the storm until it blows over."

"All right," said Cassandra. "Let's go then."

They huddled together and made their way across the snows to the foot of the mountains. Ran picked his way carefully, testing each step in case there was a crevasse he didn't know about. The storm had only started an hour ago or so, but the snows were already deep and the blizzard showed no signs of abatement. Ran shivered as they walked, and used his breathing to warm himself up. He did his best to assist Cassandra, but for her part, she seemed less affected than Ran was.

"Are you okay?"

She nodded. "Just let's keep moving. The sooner we reach it, the better."

As they walked, Ran stopped them every so often. Dangerous mounds of snow leaned precariously close overhead as they ascended the mountain. Any wrong movement might bring down an avalanche on top of them. Ran felt fortunate that he'd been brought up in the mountains of Nehon and was used to traveling in bad conditions like this. The Nine Daggers clan had situated itself deep in the mountains, where snows like this were common during the winter.

They traveled up and across a dangerous pass that gave them an overview of the valley far below. The thin lip of rock they stood upon stretched for half a mile. Ran felt certain he was staring at the Passage of Harangyo that Iqban had mentioned. And the slaver had been right: the valley floor below was a narrow stretch of land that would only permit perhaps twenty soldiers walking abreast access at a time. If there truly was an invading army coming this way from the north, this is how they would have to come through the mountains. Trying to cross the way Ran and Cassandra were at the moment would have been suicidal.

Ran pointed it out to Cassandra. “That’s the only way to get across these mountains in force.”

Cassandra nodded. “Wonderful. Can we keep moving?”

He grinned in spite of the conditions. Cassandra kept him focused on the priorities. They needed to find shelter. So if the Passage stretched below them, then it seemed appropriate to assume that the shelter Zal had mentioned must be around here somewhere. Perhaps it even overlooked the Passage itself.

Ran scanned once again, and there ahead of them the lip extended into nothingness and then reemerged just short of a perfectly flat outcropping. Ran moved forward and scouted the path before them on his hands and knees. The lip didn’t stop, but a bank of clouds had hidden it. He waved Cassandra forward, and she, too, got down on her hands and knees to make the final part of the journey.

As they crossed off of the lip and onto the wider outcropping of rock, Ran glanced back and felt a bit lightheaded when he saw how far they’d traveled and across what type of terrain. Only the necessity of survival could have motivated them to make that journey, he concluded. He stood and held his hand out to Cassandra. “You okay?”

She nodded and looked past him. “What is this place?”

Ran turned and regarded the flat stone edifice. Oblong rocks arranged in some sort of geometric pattern greeted him. From a distance, the face of the building appeared only slightly unnatural. But up close, he could see the workmanship that had gone into carving the stones. A three-sided effigy of some sort of creature stood in the center of the building. And beneath it, a gray rectangular slab stood in slight indentation to the rest of the wall that surrounded it.

Ran headed for it and was surprised to see that the gray slab acted as some sort of doorway. He waved Cassandra over, and when they stood under it the roar of the blizzard suddenly dissipated.

Cassandra looked around the slab. “Is this the way inside?”

Ran unsheathed his sword. While he didn’t think there was much chance of encountering an enemy this high up in the mountains, he wasn’t sure that someone else might not have made this place into a home of some sort. No one ever died being too careful, he recalled one of his instructors telling him.

Creeping inside, Ran surveyed the area before him. He had come into a small vestibule perhaps ten feet by ten feet. A single door directly in front of him barred any further progress. And for the moment, there was little else he saw of much interest. An old torch lay on the floor along with a rock. Ran used the edge of his blade to strike a spark with the rock, and the torch roared to life, illuminating the room. Shadows danced, and the light bounced off the intricately adorned walls.

Cassandra entered behind him. "Looks like some sort of temple."

"But to which deity?" asked Ran. He pointed at the symbols and scripts on the walls that surrounded them. "I've never seen this language before. If this is one of the tongues that people around here speak, then it's one that none of my teachers ever knew about."

Cassandra walked closer to the wall on the left. She ran her hand over the markings and brought it away. "The script has been carved into the walls so it won't fade away with time."

"It looks as fresh as if it were done yesterday," said Ran. "I guess whoever built this place wanted to be sure it stayed around for a very long time."

Cassandra turned back to the entryway. "I'm so glad to get out of that storm. I think if we were out there any longer, we might have frozen to death. As it is, my skin burns in some places."

Ran came over to her and examined her hands. They were bright red, but not gray or black. Ran breathed a sigh of relief. "You'd better let me see your toes, too."

Cassandra slid her shoes off, and Ran bent to look at her toes. But they were only slightly redder than her fingers. He stood back up. "You're right. If we'd had to stay out there any longer, things might be considerably worse than they are."

"But what now?" asked Cassandra. "We've got a torch, yes, but there's no wood here. We can't build a fire for much warmth. And there's no real way to sort ourselves out here. We're out of the blizzard, but if it keeps up? Sooner or later we're going to need food and better warmth than what we have here right now."

Ran turned and eyed the door. "That must be the proper entrance."

Cassandra stared at it with him. "Why do I feel like an imposter?"

"Trespasser, yes." Ran held the torch higher and studied the outline of the door. It was unremarkable. The hinges must have been on the other side, which meant it opened inward. There would be no way to simply pop the hinges and remove it if there was a complicated locking mechanism.

"There's a keyhole in the center of the door," said Cassandra. "Why do you suppose they put it there?"

Ran shook his head. "I don't know. But we've got a decision to make, I guess."

"Stay here or go deeper inside."

"Yes." Ran disliked the idea of trespassing in an ancient temple. But the reality of their situation was that they needed better shelter and a chance to build a fire for real warmth. Cassandra's fingers and toes could continue to suffer if they stayed here. And if the blizzard continued, they could actually get trapped.

Then there was the fact that Ran had finally arrived at the location the clan wanted him to survey. If he was to do his job properly, it would mean investigating the temple, whether or not he liked the idea.

"We don't really have a choice," he said finally.

"No," said Cassandra. "We don't."

Ran looked her over. "Still got your sword?"

"Yes."

"Good, because chances are we might need it."

Cassandra frowned. "In this old place? What sort of things are you expecting to find here?"

"I don't know," said Ran. "Anything is possible."

And with that, he went to inspect the keyhole before them.